DUNGEON BORN

Book One of
THE DIVINE DUNGEON Series
Written by DAKOTA KROUT

MOUNTAINDALE
PRESS

Table of Contents

ACKNOWLEDGMENTS

There are many people who have made this book possible. Chiefly among them is my *amazing* wife, who always encourages me to do the best at any task I set my mind to. I have a habit of getting excited about a new project and leaving the current one behind. For anyone who would like some advice, the best I can give you is this: I highly recommend marrying your best friend.

Finally, a great thank-you to all my friends and family who made their way through the awful early editions in order to give me advice and suggestions on storyline and descriptive writing. A special thanks to my friend Dylan S., who helped revise the first version of this book. Thanks to all your careful reading and comments; this book should actually be readable!

Prologue

They laughed when they murdered me. *Laughed!* Their squeals of delight were sickening as they reveled in the blood pouring from the jagged knife wounds spread across my chest. These disgusting people–I use the term *people* with trepidation–were obviously disdainful of all living beings. They killed me just for... for...? Odd. This was strange–I couldn't remember *why* they killed me. Who were 'they'? Matter of fact, *everything* was starting to become... hard to... remember...? I...

"Oh no, you don't!" The nasal, phlegmy voice of one of the assailants shattered the silence. He loomed over the broken, tortured body I was fleeing. "Dying won't let you off the hook! Hee hee hee! Stealing from me was the worst decision you ever made! Now you will *serve* me, *beg me*," he screamed, spittle flying; his mood shifted abruptly, as madmen's are prone to do, "to free you because of your own stupidity! Ha-ha-ha!" A smile was back on his face, though his eyes were manic and unfocused.

With his declaration and an arcane gesture, pain shattered my confused senses–pain more traumatizing than my recent death by repeated stabbing. I found myself being forcefully drawn toward a tiny gem in his hand. I screamed as only a tortured soul is able, albeit silently to the human ear. I imploded into the small gem, which gleamed brighter by the second. The agony became more intense, interrupting all rational thought until all I knew was torment. With a final gasp of pain, I became firmly embedded in the glowing gemstone.

"Welcome to your eternity, thief," the malicious voice spat at me. Then he coughed at me, spitting again.

W-wait. Spit wasn't red? With an unexpected spasm of his hand, I found myself slipping the surly bonds of earth. That is, I found myself flying.

Bizarrely, I could see everything around me, three hundred sixty degrees in perfect detail. We were in a mountain range with a beautiful and lush forest surrounding the base. The air had a stiff, crisp breeze flowing through it. The sun poured across the landscape with properties more befitting viscous honey.

One detail, in particular, stood out as I reached the apex of my flight. A group of people in armor which blazed with the reflection of the sun were walking toward black-clad bodies now sprawled in ignoble poses.

"Filthy Necromancers!" the largest, shiniest man roared, distaste evident in every motion he made. "Make sure to burn their rotten corpses and everything they have with them. It is sure to be tainted by the infernal." He glanced to where a—somehow familiar?—body lay broken and covered with blood and filth.

"Poor bastard, I'm sorry we weren't fast enough... to save you," he managed to say brokenly, keeping his voice low in an attempt to preserve morale in his followers. Mixed emotions skittered across his face before finally settling on anger. He then turned and began barking orders, the last I saw of his group before slipping over the edge of a crevasse, falling deep into the earth.

There was one final hole in the wall, where I got my last glance of the wide world for a long, long time. Gorgeous. It truly was too beautiful a day to die.

CHAPTER ONE

I fell for an extremely long time, rock blurring past me as my fall increased in speed. Dropping too long really, as I began to worry that I would shatter when I landed. This was a serious concern for me–momentarily. Then some shiny rock distracted me, light sparkling off it as I passed. Pretty! Was my mental state deteriorating? Ooh, that sparkle was red! The fall was probably only a few hundred feet, but since I was so tiny, it felt like miles, like hours to my distracted thoughts.

Bloop

I landed in a puddle! Rejoicing at the good fortune that had saved me from shattering when I landed, I realized that I couldn't remember why I was falling in the first place. I *had* fallen, right? I tried to think back, but hadn't I *always* been in this puddle, on this stone? Rocks don't move around, do we? Well, I was rather cozy here, nothing to worry about now at least. Filthy Necromancers.

Necromancers? I hated Necromancers! Where had that thought come from? I clung to it, trying to ensure that I would remember this. The thought wrapped around me, becoming one of my mental pillars, a foundation for my thoughts. Knowing I would remember my hatred for, um? Necromancers! Right. What the heck is a Necromancer? I don't really care, I suppose, but ohhh boy do I hate them! I finally looked around myself, trying to describe for my fleeting sanity how things looked.

I didn't really have words for things, but the names of them kept popping into my head. Rock. More rock. Water. Head? What? Where am I? What am I? Oh yeah! I'm a gem! A beautiful, shining gem.

Blue light appeared around me at the thought. Actually, it was coming *from* me! Am I a light stone? The water surrounding me began to absorb the light and, over time, became brighter. This took hours. Days? The natural light that managed to filter down to me came and went *many* times. Does that help? Does that mean anything?

Remembering is hard. I eventually gave up trying.

Time slipped by, and even the lingering remnants of memories faded, vanishing until I was near thoughtless as a babe. My mind became small and unconcerned with anything outside of my life from moment to moment. The water I was in froze and melted several times. When it froze it seemed like forever until it warmed up again! That was never fun.

One day, I noticed that the puddle I was in had slowly shrunk as temperature increased, but now water was coming down from above and refilling it! This made me really happy. That is a good thing, I think, having my puddle full. I like my puddle. But now it is getting too full? This had never happened before! My puddle was about to spill! Oh no, would that ruin it? **Drip** A final drop hit, and the puddle spilled over its stony boundary, pouring down the sides of what turned out to be a hollow stalagmite. Water must have taken the core of this rock and hollowed it out before I got here.

Something was happening, something... odd? Not bad, I don t think, but certainly odd. I was at the bottom of the small puddle in my rock, and whereas previously I could only see in a direct line of sight around me, I could now see everything where the water had overflowed to! Neat! More than see, actually! I could *sense* everything in that area perfectly—as if all of my senses were attuned to the space around me.

I tasted the salty stone, smelled the earthy fragrance, saw every flaw and nuance of the rock, and heard echoes of falling water. The perception only went as far as the water had drained, so it wasn't true sight or hearing or... but, really, it was better! More fulfilling and satisfying somehow. For some reason, I also *really* began to understand the rock I was on. After all, now I knew the word "stalagmite". I also knew it was made out of limestone, mostly calcium carbonate. Fun, new words! Even when the water that had spilled eventually dried up, my perception of the area remained.

What was that? There was a dark, earthy color moving through the rock, wriggling in set sequences like a worm moves through dirt. I reflexively reached out and touched it with my mind, and little sparkles of it pulled away from the stone and drifted toward me! What was this? How did it follow my mind? It kept coming closer, now of its own accord. In an act of defiance, when the dark color touched my crystalline surface, I grabbed at it and pulled it in, absorbing it. Shock rippled throughout my being.

It. Was. *Amazing*. The most delicious thing I had ever tasted in my life. To be fair, it was the only thing I had tasted in my life. I wanted more. I tried to reach out to that brown energy again, but it kept slipping away before I could "touch" it again. Was it mad at me? I kept trying, again and again, but I got *so* tired.

Refocusing on myself again and moving in disappointment, I looked at the energy I had absorbed. I "ate" what I could, savoring every bit while the light within slowly faded away until there was only a filthy, brackish-brown color remaining. Trying to "eat" this as well, I found it tasted horrendous, like roasted turds. Disgusted, I tried to "spit" it out, and surprisingly, it quickly streamed out of me and floated back to the rock around me, which drank it in like rainwater falling on desert sands. Wait a sec, what is a desert? Meh. What was I thinking about? I forget. There is food to be eaten. Hopefully I could get more!

Surprised at how quickly the brackish energy vanished, I watched as the brown energy in the rocks returned to a normal look, and the clean energy seemed to wave at me again. I tried to reach out, and success! I was able to make a few more sparkles flow toward me! A little more than last time too! Was that the secret? I just had to return the waste, then it would like me again? The energy I had already absorbed was pure white, slowly gaining color toward my normal blue.

Taking in the brown energy, I really focused on what I was doing this time, instead of just eating as quickly as I could. I was actually pulling the white energy from the brown, separating the two until only a dull brown color remained. "Spitting" out the filthy tasting remainder, I again pulled the earth colored light from the stone around me, continuing for a time I didn't know how to count.

Rain came infrequently; every time it did, the depth of my vision, my knowledge of the surrounding world, increased. Each stone the water washed over increased my knowledge. Soon, I could tell you the names of everything in "reach" and their properties. For instance, I knew just how much energy they contained, allowing me to calculate the sustenance I would be able to draw from them. I knew what they were made of, how tightly bonded they were, their density, and which of them would float–none of them. From this knowledge, I found more efficient ways of "eating". Pulling the brown stuff from sand released almost no energy, while more dense stones like quartz gave off larger amounts, so I made sure to focus on them.

During a powerful rainstorm, my knowledge of the world suddenly and drastically changed. The water had come again, and I was happy that I would be able to see farther soon. As my puddle finally overflowed, more rocks appeared to me, but the water also sloshed over *moss*. Moss... I suddenly knew everything there was to know about it. How you could grind it up and put it on shallow cuts to help wounds recover, how it grew with abundance when it had access to water and space, but most importantly, that it was *alive*. The life in it sang to me, tantalizing my senses with the knowledge that there was so much to learn and taste. In simple astonishment, I realized a new color was suddenly visible to me. *Green...* What a beautiful, vibrant color this tiny plant exuded. I stretched my mind over to caress this unknown, gorgeous, emerald light when it suddenly reached back. Shocked, I pulled away, and the light returned to the moss, seamlessly re-integrating with itself.

Tentatively and with great trepidation, I reached out again. So did the light! Connecting with it, the contained energy flowed toward me, similarly to the way the brown energy moved, though much faster and far more powerfully. I drank it in, then began to "eat" it. The crispest, flavorful salad in the world could not compare to the pure, delicious energy this small plant willingly gave to me.

I gorged myself, eating so fast I would have choked if I were able. Unlike the stone's energy, which only ever lasted a few bites, the green energy just kept coming, and I ate it until there was no more light coming in. Just as I thought it was over, a moss-ive burst of energy flew into me, so much that I nearly shattered! Terrified, I quickly absorbed the energy, simultaneously releasing the waste to return. When I finally had processed everything, I was full, something that had never happened as far as I had been alive. Also, I had made a pun, another first for me.

I looked back at the moss and was horrifically shocked at what I saw. It was no longer vibrant and living. It was crumbling before my eyes, turning to dust. I was disgusted with myself that I had killed it—not the death itself, which was just a natural part of life but the fact that I could no longer pull the yummy food to myself. Ruminating over the loss of this huge source of mouthwatering energy, I quickly brightened when I noticed that behind it there was a veritable carpet of the stuff, growing across the floor of this crevasse. I returned to the brown energy, slightly disappointed now by how hard it was to keep forcefully pulling it to myself. Hungrily, I waited for the rain to come again, so I could reach that tasty, tasty treat just out of my reach.

<Hello, little dungeon,> a measured, powerful voice reverberated in my mind.

< *What*?! Who... how?> I looked at everything I could see, but there was *nothing* around me.

<I am Kantor,> the voice continued.

<What is a Kantor?> I panicked a bit; a potential threat could find me, but I could not see it.

<Ha. So much to learn, and we have but moments. I wish I could explain all to you, but already, the wind moves me along. I must go as the wind takes me, and the air is turbulent in recent times. I digress. Youngling, do you know what you are?> The words Kantor gave me reverberated in my mind like a clarion call, so full of power I was afraid I would be killed by his speech, let alone whatever he could bring to bear against me.

<I... I'm a gem. I'm shiny.> I was unsure of how to answer; Kantor's words were confusing, intricate, and hard to understand.

<While... technically true, you are much more. You are a dungeon Core, a Beast Core that has gained the first level of its own sentience and has realized the consequences of life and death. This awareness is why you are able to hear me now, though I have whispered for weeks. Already I reach the furthest

range of my ability to communicate,> he spoke, sadness tinging his grand voice.

<Sentience?> I questioned, trying out the word.

<It means you are aware, young one. It means that you understand that things beyond yourself are alive. Also, it means that you *want.* Food, knowledge, power. To stay alive. You can now think of the future and make small plans, retaining memories of your own.>

I realized this was true. I did want things. I wanted to be alive. I remembered that I planned on eating the moss just out of reach.

<Good, you understand."> Kantor seemed satisfied. "<To allay your concerns, I am not right next to you, little one. We are communicating with 'mind speech'. This allows us to bypass the limitations of our bodies, in order to talk to those we wish. I have no *wish* to hurt you, but to help you become smarter and stronger. Although, before I explain too much further, you must satisfy my curiosity–what color are you?> Kantor probed me far too casually.

<Color? I'm> a word popped into my head from somewhere deep in my mind, as well as hundreds of subtle variations, <blue? Mind speech?>

<Blue? Good! Good. Yes, small one, mind speech. To talk to someone, all you need to do is intentionally send your thoughts to them. You can send words, pictures, ideas. Whatever thoughts you have, you can gift to another.> A tension I did not realize it had before seemed to vanish from Kantor's voice.

<I am going to help you, tiny one. I am moving along, and it will be a long time before you hear from another one of your own kind. I wish I could do more, but it would do more damage than good. If fates are kind, I will speak to you again someday.> He paused, thinking. I feared he had disappeared

when his voice sounded again, <To survive, you will need assistance. I am going to send you a helper. This is the absolute limit of what I can do for you currently. I... I wish it weren't so. Please don't absorb her. Her mother would be furious with me,> he... joked? I think? Kantor's voice was fading, becoming more strained as he worked to speak with me.

<I don't understand... but thank you, Kantor!> I cried out, desperate to continue hearing another voice in the darkness.

<Best of luck.> I could feel the satisfaction flowing from him.

CHAPTER TWO

I wondered what kind of help Kantor was sending me. This thought occupied my mind for a spare moment until my hungry gaze returned to the feast of moss waiting just out of reach.

<Soon, my scrumptious ones,> I thought to myself, chuckling with a slightly maniacal undertone.

"Wait, you're not evil, are you?" a voice questioned me.

<What is evil? Wait, what are you? Where are you?> I glanced around. Two voices on the same day?

"We'll talk about evil later. Much later. I'm above you, making sure you don't try to eat me," the voice called, echoing slightly, making it hard to pinpoint the exact position it came from.

<Why? Are you delicious?> I could go for a snack, I supposed.

"No! Nope, not even slightly tasty. I'm a Wisp. As in 'will-of-the'," the echoing voice assured me.

<What is will?> I was a bit disappointed. The voice *sounded* tasty.

"Oh boy." Now that just sounded condescending. "You really are a newborn, aren't you?"

<What is–>

I was cut off as I began speaking. "Yeah got it, you don't know too many words."

<...> Really, I had no idea what to say to that.

"Here is the deal. We are going to make a pact, a bond. This is more than an agreement; it is a sharing of power. You need help, knowledge, and a friend to keep you from going insane. That can be me if you will allow it."

<...> Now coy, the voice seemed to be trying to seduce me with gifts. I did like gifts I guess. Really, who doesn't? I was about to answer when it spoke again.

"You have to agree to give me protection and Essence. In return, I will do everything I can to make you strong and prosperous. If you die, so do I because nothing else can give me the Essence I need to survive." Seemingly frustrated, the voice was talking faster and faster.

<Please! Slow down! Can you just answer a quick question? It's just... Why do I need you?> I thought it was a fair question. I was doing fine on my own.

"I promise you that it will be worth it. Besides that, Kantor is too far away for me to return to, and no one else is coming to help or would even want to," she guaranteed.

<Well, when you put it like that... and Kantor sent you...> I trailed off. I *really* did not want to let down Kantor. <Sounds good! Teach me those big words, and it's a deal. Um, I don't know how to do all the things you want, but if you teach me I am... amenable.> I could already feel my intellect growing, just being in her presence. I was proud of that new word. Amenable meant that I was agreeable to the situation. I think. Yes. Whatever, the voice was talking again.

"Deal. Here I come." A bright ball of softly glowing, pink energy resolved itself from behind a stone outcropping that had been blocking my view. "Hello, tiny dungeon. I am Dani. Do you have a name yet?"

<Not that I know of. What does a name look like?> I knew that everything around me had a name, but I thought a name was just part of what a thing was. Wait! Was my name 'gem' then?! I was about to ask when Dani started speaking again.

"Well, then," she blatantly ignored my question, "since you are surrounded by calcium, I hereby name you 'Cal'."

<I like it!> I shone brighter for a moment to show my happiness. I had a name! A real name, not a description! I suddenly knew the difference! I felt like I was shaking in excitement. Actually, I was shaking? Vibrating really, the water around me moving enough to splash.

<What's happening?!> I was so startled that I even stopped eating the brown energy for a moment.

"Looks like I got here just in time. Quick, Cal, repeat after me! 'By the agreement we have made, I become your bonded partner'!" With that pronouncement and a resounding splash, Dani came down and entered my puddle. I followed her instructions, repeating her word for word. As I did, a beam of blue light shot out of me, and a beam of pink came from her.

As they touched, they fused into a beautiful light, which traveled along a shimmering path in the air that connected both of us. The fused pink-blue light entered her, filling her with light and energy. A blue blot formed in her body, surrounded by her natural pink coloration. Now the glow coming off of her was a light purple and far more intense, lighting up the air around her. The beam entered me as well, and I became a darker blue, nearly violet. I lost a *lot* of energy, the vibration subsiding as the link was formed.

<What was that?> I asked offhandedly, far less tense now. I was pretty hungry again. She had entered my pool, and just like when my water washed over the rocks, now I knew everything about pink will-of-the-wisps. I still didn't know the knowledge she contained, the experiences she had lived through. I hoped she would tell me stories. Hmm. Is it important that I only know about *pink* Wisps? Are there more colors? Do

they do different things? Oops, I hear Dani talking again. I guess I'll have to save my questions for another time.

"That was us joining, forming a bond. I can't believe you came so close to self-destructing! Have you never used your Essence before?" Dani's color darkened–which I understood meant that she was cross.

<Would you mind answering another question? What is Essence?> Seriously, she is just a deep well of knowledge, isn't she? So full of words and meanings!

"Really? Well, maybe that explains why I am purple now." She blew out a long sigh. "Essence is... complicated. The real name of it is 'Quintessence', but that is a mouthful, so it is usually shortened. It is the fundamental energy of the universe, the pure power of heavens and earth that is used by the basic elements to become... everything. Rocks turn it into earth Essence, water into water Essence, though both are impure forms.

Cultivating is the process of absorbing Essence from the Heaven and the Earth around you. It is a part of all things, and all things are a part of it. The purer you can refine it, the closer it becomes to the true form of Essence." She quieted for a moment, overcome by some far away memory. "Also, if the accumulated Essence you have is the purest possible, it is better for the both of us. It will make us stronger, healthier, and smarter. The Essence you are holding is really pure, so you must have cultivated all you could from that water before refining it until it became too dense for your Core. Good job so far!" She ended the topic on a cheerful note.

<From the water?> What the heck? There is Essence in my puddle?

"Yes, you are a blue Core, so you cultivate Essence from water," she explained *almost* condescendingly.

<I can do that? I've never pulled from water before.> I was inspecting the water for food but only saw my light.

"..." She appeared to be trying to speak.

<What?> Was she in pain? Did I do something to her?

"Then *where* did you pull Essence from?" She was really demanding. Was this bond really worth this scrutiny?

<Everything I've been able to touch so far, except you, since you told me you weren't tasty,> I reassured her. She seemed to be getting worked up.

"That shouldn't be possible... At this level, you can only cultivate from the element you are attuned to. Show me?" she forced herself to ask politely.

I *was* hungry. The joining had drained a lot of my energy, at least as much as the moss had given me. The moss! I was mentally drooling as I thought of the exquisite food, no, um, Essence that it contained.

<I'd be happy to, but... I can't reach the moss over there anymore.> I seemed pathetic I guess because she laughed and scooped up some of the water I was in. She didn't have limbs, so this impressed me an inordinate amount.

"The moss, huh? Sure." She flew over to the moss, and instead of pouring the water on to it, she blew it over ALL of the moss as a mist!

<AHH!> I exclaimed, my vision exploding outward. I had never before been able to see so much more at one time. With a gentle sprinkling, she had more than tripled the area I could see! The information gained from all of these new things was nearly overwhelming.

"What?!" she yelped, "Did I hurt you?"

<No... it's just, I can see so much more! It is so beautiful! I had wanted to have access to more area, after all. I didn't realize that it could be done so quickly. That was the only issue,

and it just startled me a bit.> My mind was distracted with sorting through all of the new things I had learned.

"Oh." She sighed softly. "You scared me there."

<You have already proven that I made a good deal bonding with you! Thank you.> I was really happy! It seemed that the more I learned, the faster I could learn *other* things. When I experienced something that coincided with another bit of esoteric understanding, I processed it even faster. For instance, since I already knew dirt and stone I was able to comprehend moss faster and more thoroughly because I knew where it got *its* food and energy–the dirt! It used dirt for all *sorts* of things. Hopefully, building the basics of my knowledge here would allow me to understand greater things in the future.

"That is what I'm here for, Cal." She gracefully accepted my compliment.

<Well,> I rumbled gruffly, somewhat embarrassed for an unknown reason, <I'm hungry, and you want to see me eat, sooo...>

"Go for it." She laughed, watching me closely.

I reached out for the veritable feast before me and started pulling in energy. Dani watched in amazement the entire time. Pulling from so many different groups of moss, I was again vibrating, much less than before, but still.

"Wow! But that corruption is really thick in you. Must be a side effect of pulling from an unattuned source." Dani gave a frustrated sigh. "Drat, you had such pure Essence when I got here."

<You mean the waste stuff? Yeah, I don't like it very much either,> I agreed, "spitting" the sickly energy back out to rejoin the plant.

"No. Freaking. Way!" She zoomed in for a closer look, making me feel a bit awkward. Why was she so giddy over me eating?

<What?> Without the waste, there was a little more room for food, and I was already eying an untouched patch of moss. Curiously, none of the moss had withered this time.

"You just got rid of your own corruption?! That's not..." she started accusingly.

<Possible,> I intentionally interrupted, <or you've just never seen it before?> I was getting a bit irritated over her telling me what I couldn't do when it was obviously happening right in front of her.

Trying and failing to come up with a good response to this, she conceded the point with a bit of ill grace. "Fair enough," she mumbled. "Are you already full again?"

<Well, I mean, I could eat,> I declared nonchalantly, licking my mental lips.

"Not what I mean, you glutton." She laughed. "I mean, we just joined. You should be low on power for weeks! If you are already full, that just means good things for the both of us in the future. You can pull power from multiple sources. We should really see what all is doable, but that comes later. First, let's get you an upgrade."

<More plants?!> Where was she hiding them?

"No, an upgrade for you, silly rock! Look, you are a dungeon Core. You grow your dungeon around your Core by releasing Essence in a way unique to dungeons, called influence," she explained, gaining my rapt attention.

There were things only dungeons could do?

She continued, basking in my undivided attention, "We need to spread your influence about as much as we can, and then when something is under your influence, you are able to fully understand it. When you fully understand something, you control it absolutely." She waited for a response.

<Go on...> I prodded her.

"Using the Essence, you collect you can directly alter the world that is under your influence. Doing so will drain you a bit, so you need to expand slowly, becoming a bigger and more important dungeon. Eventually, people will discover you and come in to explore you, looking for treasure and ways to make themselves stronger," she explained, shining brightly in her excitement.

"When people come, they bring things in like weapons, armor, magic, and even animals! Whatever is left in here you can study, absorbing it and gaining the knowledge of how to make it, use it, control it!" she enthused. "Even when people die, you can absorb them, make copies, and re-animate their bodies as zombies, like a Necromancer does!"

<What?!> My sudden shout nearly knocked her out of the air. <I HATE NECROMANCERS!> I was furious that she would compare me to those *animals.* I trembled in rage, losing control of the Essence in me as I did so. The stalagmite received the brunt of this released Essence, growing sharp quartz spikes, which quivered in time with the fury ignited in my Core.

"Cal! Cal! It is okay! I'm sorry, I didn't know!" Her voice calmed me down, the fear in her voice snapping me out of my fury in an indescribable manner. "How do you even know what a Necromancer is?"

<I... I'm sorry. I really don't know where that came from. I just hate them so much.> I was really confused and had no idea why her words made me so uncontrollably angry.

"It's okay, Cal," she shakily stated, still quivering slightly. "That actually may be for the best. There is a church that is quite powerful right now that tries very hard to destroy dungeons that have undead or demonic creatures in them. I was just trying to give you a comprehensive idea of what you could do."

<What? People try to kill dungeons? Are people going to try to kill *me*?> I was rather stuck on this point; it seemed somewhat important.

"Yes, but don't worry too much. Usually, they prefer to have dungeons stay alive as they are very beneficial to the world." She soothingly tried to appease me by telling stories of the world, "Flora and fauna alike prosper in areas with high Essence concentration. Plants can use it instead of good soil and sunlight, and animals become much stronger in the presence of Essence."

<Why do animals get stronger?> Dang it, she was able to distract me so easily!

"Animals gain Essence from the world mainly just by living their lives, and it makes them stronger over time. Other sentient creatures like Humans, Elves, Dwarves, or even Orcs are able to absorb Essence during meditation." She paused to let me fantasize about all the creatures I could eventually eat.

"Magical beasts have Beast Cores similar to your gem that grow inside them from birth. Every type of creature absorbs Essence but can only absorb the type they are suited to until they are *really* strong, which can take over a hundred years, roughly. This is why I think you are going to be *very* popular. The Essence you concentrate has no affinity that I can tell. It's just... pure Essence." She was still amazed by that fact. Pure Essence was unheard of; even the best cultivators had some taint.

<Is that good?> Did people try to kill popular things?

Dani snapped out of her reverie. "It means everything can thrive in your area of influence if you let it. Plants, animals, *Beasts*, and creatures of light and shadow."

<That *is* good though, right, and why are you emphasizing Beast when you say it?> It was tickling my thoughts oddly.

"Having really pure Essence with no affinity should be *very* good, I think. Heck, wars may be fought over the right to explore here! I am a lucky Wisp!" Dani gleefully exclaimed, flying in a spiral pattern. "Also, I am emphasizing it because Beasts are different from animals. They have gained awareness and can use Essence, becoming far stronger and much more intelligent than their original animalistic counterparts."

<This is all so interesting!> Much as I loved learning, I was far more enthusiastic about being able to *do* things. <So can we start? How do we start?>

Dani launched into *another* lecture, "Well, we start with an upgrade! Here are a few basics first, though. There are many different levels of Essence cultivation. Starting with the lowest, we have G, F, E, D, C, B, A, S, SS, SSS, Heavenly, and Godly. Each rank has ten levels within it, the lowest being zero and the highest at nine. When I got here, you were at G-zero, which is basic life with only the instinct to eat." She chuckled at that; I had progressed far in intelligence since then. "After making the deal with me, you moved to G-rank one, which opens the way for more complex actions and thought. You have enough power already to move to G-rank two, which lets you begin to grow your power and use your own influence *intentionally*."

<Intentionally?> I thought I already had been. Was she being condescending again?

"Remember those spikes poking out of you? Can you do that *without* being really mad?" Yup, definitely being condescending.

I tried but couldn't make anything happen.

<Nope. Where did those come from anyway? There was no quartz there earlier.> I looked at the reflective quartz poking out of the stone.

"You made it with your Essence. If you have absorbed it in the past, you can make it with your Essence. Another ability *unique* to dungeons." She showed off her knowledge once again.

<Wow! How do I make things, pretty lady?> I wheedled her.

"Upgrade first." She was firm on that point.

Well, poo. I thought flattery would do it. <So, how do I upgrade?>

She seemed appreciative of my work ethic. "Get as full of energy as you can. Then I'll guide you through the process."

Following her instructions, I cultivated and ate—no, I refined!—the plant's energy until I was shaking dangerously again.

<Dani... Help,> I began worriedly.

"It's okay, Cal. Focus on your crystal. Do you feel the flaws in the gem? There are a few perfect parts where your facets are smooth and sharp, without cracks or discoloration," Dani quickly and calmly coached me. "Feel those, find how it is that they bind perfectly whereas the other spots are rough or malformed. Now smooth those bad patches so that they are correctly formed. Try to make your Core as flawless as possible. Focus now, but don't rush it."

It was amazing. As she guided me, I could feel exactly what she meant and suddenly perfectly understood the body I was now in. Why had I never tried to understand myself before? I guess it was just not something a normal mind would do. The basic structure of my Core consisted of carbon but was reinforced by the Essence that I had refined to its most pure form. Only the center of my Core was truly perfect, and I could see that my mind resided within in that perfect structure. From this perfect facet, I got the blueprints of how my Core needed to be restructured and started applying pressure to the poorly formed outer carbon bonds.

"Careful now, not all at once or you may shatter yourself," Dani murmured, trying not to break my focus.

Click

A small patch of perfectly bonded carbon molecules formed.

Click* *Click

As I became used to the process, I was able to accomplish the task faster, letting me make more connections, faster and faster, until with a jolt I found there were no more poorly formed areas. A good thing too, as my light had dimmed enough to nearly extinguish. My mind, losing the single track intensity that had propelled me to this stage, nearly broke under the exhaustion I now felt.

"Cal! Are you awake yet? Cal!" Dani desperately begged, voice hoarse and weak.

<What's wrong?> I grouched sleepily. That was new. Could I sleep?

"You need to absorb... Essence. Please, hurry..." she pleaded, her light dimming as well.

Her words barely registered in my mind, my thoughts moving at a glacial speed. I was hungry. I reached for the moss, and as per usual, it eagerly flowed toward me as well. I started eating, and as I did, I only got hungrier, the input of Essence awakening my unquenchable gluttony. Greedily reaching for more moss, I pulled more and more energy from the entire patch of moss, until dying moss started to emit blasts of energy which shot into me. I stopped pulling Essence and looked nervously at where it came from.

As I suspected, a small patch of moss withered away, crumbling to dust as I watched. I finished refining what I had and realized that while this amount of energy would have killed me before I fixed my facets, now it was barely satiating my hunger. I turned my attention to Dani, who was beginning to glow again.

<What happened?> I prodded her. That was a bad idea. She woke up angry.

"You nearly killed us both is what happened!" Her glow was flashing to a deep crimson with fury. "You altered your basic structure until completion–without even stopping to recover! I had to close our connection just to stop from draining the last bits of Essence from you and nearly starved to death myself before you gained enough energy for me to safely take some! Do you have any idea how horrible of a death dying from lack of Essence is?!"

I tried to defend my actions, <But I was only doing what you told me to do?>

"I told you not to rush!" Her anger fading, her body slowly returned to her regular coloration. "Are you okay? Did you hurt yourself?"

<I'm fine,> I cautiously stated. <Hungry but fine,> I amended.

"Good." She blew out a breath. "Cal, you really need to have some self-preservation skills."

<I'll do better. I'm sorry.> I was ashamed.

"Don't be sorry, be smart! If you die, so do I! We need you to be the smartest dungeon that exists because we need each other!" she exploded, obviously still mad for some reason.

<I said I am sorry. I'll do better!> I promised her vigorously.

"Good. You'd better. Well, let's take a look at you." She flew closer to me, examining me for any flaw or defect. After a short time, she pronounced her assessment, "Cal, you are the most perfect diamond I have ever seen."

<I'm not a diamond. I'm a dungeon Core,> I reminded her. Was she still groggy from sleep?

"Well, you look like a flawless diamond. When you get full of energy, it'll be nearly impossible to break you, I bet." Her abrupt reversal of attitude threw me off, but her words were really nice. A pink glow joined my normal blue as I "blushed" from her praise. Interesting, it seemed my emotions could alter my coloration for a moment or two.

<You think I did a good job?> I tried for another compliment.

She granted my desire, "A very good job." Then my new favorite thing to hear, "Well, let's get some food, shall we?"

<I would love to, but I think I took everything I could from the moss over there. It started dying.> I felt a bit embarrassed about killing off my only good source of food.

She examined the withered moss and nodded. "True, but why didn't you finish the rest of it off?"

She never ceased to surprise me. <Then I wouldn't be able to get more from it when it recovered,> I explained carefully.

"Well! I thought you were just a glutton, but you keep throwing me for a loop!" She flew to me and tested the energy flows I was emitting. "I think I was wrong earlier. You must have been a G-rank three Core, just with so many flaws your energy came out scattered and weak. You have the cultivation base of a G-rank four now, and this allows you to have forethought. It's okay, Cal, try and finish off the moss there and take in its life energy. It is the remaining cultivation base of the moss, the densest concentration, so it will give slightly more energy than it does normally."

<But then the moss will be gone,> I forlornly reminded her.

"We will grow more. Just eat it already." Yikes! I didn't want to make her angry again.

<Okay then.> I waited a moment. <Be nicer,> I grumbled at Dani, and then I started pulling in the Essence, this time watching what happened to the moss. As I took more energy, it started wilting and becoming desiccated, like it had gone too long without water. I could tell the moment each strand died, as I was assaulted with a burst of condensed Essence each time it happened. As each strand died I grew more satiated, but when the last bit had crumbled, I was *still* not even a quarter full, and this was before I purified it and got rid of the waste, which was usually a sizable portion of the energy. When I finished cultivating and refining, removing the waste, I was about one-eighth full.

<I can't believe how much more energy I can take! This is amazing!> I felt incredible, strong, and powerful. That is not how I responded to her next question though.

"How do you feel?" She was testing the waters, looking at my cultivation.

I responded as honestly as possible, <Hungry.>

"Why am I not surprised, ya hog," she admonished flatly. "I think it is time for you to try and use your Essence. I want you to move the entire stalagmite you are on as far toward that cave as you can go. You are too exposed here; your Core should be *insanely* difficult to get to. Right now, anything could swoop in and grab you."

<How do I move?> I was excited, ready to learn a new skill.

"You reach into the area around you and tell it to move. Only you can really know what it will take, so if I can do anything for you, let me know." Well. That was rather unhelpful advice.

<I'll try.> I reached into the stone around me and eventually found what I needed in order to make it move. With horribly loud screeching, the entire stone area that was filled with my influence tore itself out of the ground and began jerkily moving toward the hole in the wall.

<Whoa!> I shouted, stopping my momentum.

"That's normal! If you left this area behind, you would lose a lot of your power. Everything filled with your Essence is, in reality, your body, and you are the heart, the soul. You can never willingly move your heart from your body, but you can reposition it. That is how dungeons grow and evolve," Dani explained courteously, then told me to hurry up.

Moving my form through the opening in the rock wall, I yanked my whole mass as far through the cave as I could; after *hours,* I finally reached a wall and could go no further. I settled to the floor with great relief.

"How is your Essence doing? Did you use too much?" queried Dani, fluttering about the cave and exploring its depths.

<Pretty good, that really didn't take too much Essence. How far did we go? A mile? Two?> I was *so* ready for a nap. Too bad I couldn't sleep.

"Close!" she sounded off brightly. "We got about forty feet or so before you hit a wall."

<What?! But my body– But that took hours!> I whined at her.

"I forgot that you can just barely see past your influence. How big do you think your body is?" She was leading the conversation somewhere.

<Thirty yards or so?> I pleaded to her, joking weakly.

She dashed my hopes immediately. "Your stalagmite is about two feet tall, and the ground you have at the base is about five feet in diameter. A bit lopsided where the moss was because I helped you grow there."

I was flabbergasted. <And... Me?>

"Well, you were a bit larger when you were a flawed gem," she paused, dangling the information just out of reach, "but now you are the size of a one-carat diamond. Soooo about six and a half millimeters."

<That's it?! Is that small? What unit of measurement is that?> I had so many questions!

"Yup, that's it. Stop being a narcissist! You can't worry about things you can't control. You have too much work to do if you want to become a big, strong dungeon, and you can start by spreading your influence." She was ignoring my questions again!

<I'm not a narcissist! I think. What's a narcissist? How do I spread influence?>

"Remember how I made all that Essence turn into a mist and spread it around?" she reminded me. "I need you to do the same thing but with your accumulated Essence. Concentrate hard on making the surroundings... you," Dani finished lamely.

Sure. Why not. <How much Essence should I use?>

"Keep going until I tell you to stop or until you reach those mushrooms," she directed, settling on to a grey stone outcropping to watch my progress.

Why was she being so unhelpful? <What's a mushroom?>

"You'll know it when you find it," she sing-sang in a know-it-all voice.

<Dani... Just... Fine.> I tried doing as she told me. Nothing happened at first, but after a bit of trial and error, a fine mist, more like water vapor, began emanating from my puddle.

The vapor went where I told it to, clinging to anything it touched unless some vapor had made it there previously. This vapor was true Essence, but I knew somehow that I could not reabsorb this. Is this what other people would come here to cultivate? Luckily for me, the amount of Essence I used to create the vapor, my influence, was minuscule.

<I'm doing it!> Soon I was at the edge of my territory and began forcing the vapor to expand outward, gaining vision and knowledge with every fraction of an inch.

"Hey! Go up and down too," Dani demanded, twitching up off her rock an inch to look at my apparently shoddy work.

<The floor and ceiling? Why?> There was so much to look at! I really did not want to waste time on empty space.

"Those need to be permeated with your Essence most of all!"

<Ugh...> Why couldn't she just tell me why? I sighed with frustration. She hadn't steered me wrong yet, I guess.

I reached as high as I could go and coated the ceiling and floor, then kept doing what I could to fill the chamber. Quickly, I found that I had tripled my range of influence and was just starting to get worried about the amount of Essence I had remaining when I found *mushrooms.* As I learned everything about this type of mushroom, I tasted it for the first time. It was made of a mixture of plant and earth Essence, and both types of Essence were more abundant than either the rocks or the moss had been able to contain or give me. While it was more difficult to take the Essence from the mushrooms than the moss had been, it was still far easier than the stone, and so I began to eat. Cultivate. Whatever.

The flavor was reminiscent of sweet salad leaves dipped in the rich chocolate that is the earth. I ate much slower than ever before, the complexities of this Essence eluding my slavering “tongue” until I discovered the trick of it, breaking the complex Essence down to its elemental form, separating it into its basic Essence, finally absorbing it in a sweet and fulfilling rush. The flavor was so wonderfully potent that I was nearly unable to hear Dani when she started to talk to me. “You made it! That is surprising. It only took you a few days!”

<That long? It felt like such a short time...?> I was still focused on the Essence I was acquiring, only listening to her with half an ‘ear’.

“Well, that isn’t surprising now, is it? Time doesn’t have the same effect on us as it does other living things,” Dani explained. “By the way, how do you feel now with your Essence?”

Turning my attention inward, it was obvious that the energy in me was less than it had been but not nearly the amount that I had feared it would be. The tiny amount of the mushrooms’ overall energy had replaced this much?! Surprised by this development, I told Dani.

“That is great! It means that although you are unique in many ways, my knowledge isn’t entirely useless!” she boasted with a ‘wink’ that consisted of her light dimming and shining in a strobe-like way. “As the range of your influence increases, the Essence of the world will passively flow to you, very slowly filling your Core to replace what you use. Obviously, it is *far* slower than actively pulling the energy to yourself, but as your range grows, so will the passive Essence influx. Eventually, you may not even need to pull Essence to increase in ranking.”

<This is great! By the way, have you ever had mushrooms before? Those white ones are safe for you to eat,> I promised her, feeling happy now that I was gaining sustenance again.

"I don't need to eat! The energy you provide me with directly fulfills those needs," she assured me. "How is that Essence by the way? You having any trouble with it?"

<Why would I be?> I retorted, slurping in a long stream of earth Essence.

"Well, that is a more complex Essence is all," she told me carefully. "It is intrinsically combined earth and water Essence, right? That is known as 'mud' Essence and is notoriously hard to cultivate from."

<Oh. Well, it didn't want to separate right away, but I got the hang of it!> I assured her, not stopping my gorging.

"You are going to be the most amazing dungeon ever. I just know it!" Dani then looked at the quickly wilting stalks of the mushrooms I was pulling Essence from. "Hey, you want to learn how to grow more of those?"

<Yes please.> More would be good. Much more.

She looked at me oddly. "I thought you would be more excited than this." Zipping over to me, she looked at my Essence. "G-rank five already?! This is wonderful! You are growing so well! And *so* fast," she murmured, *almost* with concern.

<I want to know how you can tell my ranking, but first those mushrooms?> The ones I was 'gnawing' on were going to die soon if I did nothing to spread out the drain on their resources.

Dani seemed to shake off her contemplative stupor. "Right, so, focus on the mushroom that you want to grow first—I'd suggest that reddish poisonous looking one. Got it? Okay, now focus on what it needs to survive. You should know all of that. Look at what it needs to grow and reproduce."

<I got it!> Growing and reproducing was almost its entire pattern, after all. A pattern was the intricate design that comes

together in a unique way to create everything in the universe. An inanimate object has a far less complex pattern that a living being, which explained why it was easier to absorb Essence from rocks than plants. Plants had really simple purposes in their life.

"Great, hold the pattern in your mind, exactly as it is. Got it? Good. Now pour a bit of Essence into the pattern, and try and integrate it into the flow that is moving through it. When it feels mature, make it produce and release spores into the room. When those land, you can do one of two things," she explained thoroughly, "either infuse the spores with Essence directly and grow those with your Essence, or slather that Essence-rich vapor on to the area they land, which will allow them to grow naturally but still *way* faster than they could otherwise. You can control how fast and where things grow by infusing different amounts of Essence into the area. Don't want something to grow? Don't give it any Essence! Really easy."

<Alright, I think I understand. First, focus on the pattern.> I concentrated, and the pure Essence inside me began to flow into the mushrooms pattern. The tiny stalk on the ground rippled and grew a little bit. <I did it!> Now to make it get large and reproduce. I fed it a trickle of Essence. Nothing seemed to happen, so I increased the flow to a steady stream.

"Stop, stop!" ordered Dani, dismayed. "It takes a moment to change into the Essence of its own... type. Oh my."

It was obvious that the mushroom absorbed the Essence because it began to grow at a rapid, mutated pace. I could see how much energy this took, nearly what it would produce in its own natural lifespan, and it still was not close to the amount I had given it. Continuing to grow, it suddenly shuddered and began to develop a crease in the stalk. As we watched, the crease grew, and the remaining Essence began to diffuse throughout the entire plant, focusing heavily for a bit on the crease. When the

Essence was stable, Dani flew closer to get a better look at the finished product.

"Ahhh!" she screamed as the plant lunged at her, the crease revealing itself as a mouth filled with sharp thorns instead of teeth. Zipping back to a safe distance, Dani stopped screaming. The mushroom exuded an air of disappointment until it settled back into its stationary state, looking just like a larger version of the others around it. "Too close! Ohmygosh that was scary!" Dani panted.

She came over to me, shivering, and continued in a brave voice, "Well, not what we were after, but congratulations! You made your first dungeon monster! There is an... issue though. It is a natural plant that gained cultivation ranks by absorbing Essence, not a monster you actually *created*. Because of this, it will not obey you completely, unless it swears loyalty to you. Since it can't make that deal, as a plant, you need to drain away its Essence."

<But I did just make it!> I looked at the plant. It was just a plant before; now it was a monster.

"You didn't, though. Do you understand it?" she prodded knowingly. "Could you make another one with the same pattern?"

I refocused on the monster–I'll call it a Shroomish–and tried to study it. I couldn't, for some reason. Looking at the Essence in it, I tried to grab it, then to coax it away but was met with severe resistance.

<It is not giving me the Essence.> How rude! Really, I was basically its creator.

Dani grunted, a very unladylike sound. "Oh right! As a monster, it won't just happily give you its life force. It needs to be defeated. Make a chunk of rock fall off the ceiling above it, squashing it and releasing its Essence, which will then be automatically pulled to you because it is in your influence," she verbosely directed.

<I'll give it a shot.> Concentrating on the roof of the cave, I carved a small rock away and let it fall. The Shroomish splattered with a keening sound, and the Essence shot into me, far more Essence than I had ever taken in one go before, as I had not drained it somewhat beforehand. The Essence was entirely different than I had been expecting, a much more complex blend of earth, plant, and a cool, refreshing feeling which revealed itself to be water Essence. It absorbed far easier than other Essence did but tasted rather bland to me. After the last bit had filled me, I turned my attention to the pattern of its body.

<It is so different!> I exclaimed in surprise. <It has an entirely different pattern! How did that happen? I don't know how to do that!> I was babbling, so I tried to stop talking.

"It is a natural evolution," Dani informed me. When all I gave in return for this information was confusion, she decided to explain herself.

"As you get stronger, you can make creatures evolve by supplying them with the energy to do so, or they can absorb items or different elements to change themselves naturally," Dani explained, looking at the splattered remains from a careful distance. "Usually, the Essence you supply would direct the changes, but since yours seems to be so pure, it must have allowed for it to become what it would have after decades of cultivating or a 'natural evolution'. You keep throwing me for a loop."

<I haven't touched you.> At least the cultivation stuff made sense.

"It is a figure of speech. Not a literal statement. Stay with me here; this opens up a slew of options for us that I hadn't considered." Dani was getting excited again. Should I be nervous? "We'll get to that, but first, try to recreate the Mob. And before you attack my verbiage, my choice of words that is, a 'Mob' is a short way to say 'dungeon monster'."

<Why not call it a 'Dum'? For '*du*ngeon *m*onster'.> Where was she getting that abbreviation?

"It just... It just isn't," Dani sputtered, seemingly exasperated.

I looked at where the Shroomish had originally been and was startled to see the body was melting directly into the floor; it was mostly goo at this point. Must be an effect of my influence. I tried to pay attention to what Dani was telling me to do, so I began listening carefully. Dani explained that to create a Mob, all I had to do was make a 'seed' of energy infused with the pattern of the creature I wanted to make. Apparently, this would even work if I wanted to make creatures that weren't normally made from actual seeds, all the way up to the largest beasts in existence, although those big creatures would obviously take longer to mature. Or lots of Essence.

I focused and made the needed pattern on an Essence 'seed' and watched as it absorbed the ambient energy in the room to quickly grow to full size. I would never know the difference between the original and the current one if it weren't for the fact that I could feel a link to the creature in my mind. I imprinted on it that it should not attack Dani, but anything else was fair game. I could feel its assent as it ate a smaller mushroom right next to it, then moved into a near hibernating state, waiting for any inattentive prey.

Finally done with the Mob creation, I returned to infusing an area with enough Essence to quickly grow plants and properly made the remaining regular mushrooms put spores out on to the Essence-rich stone. Following this, I resumed passively absorbing Essence and trying to increase my area of influence. After roughly ten days, I was able to fill the entire cave with a light coating of Essence and had reached the entrance of the cave.

CHAPTER THREE

"Good work!" congratulated a very bored Dani. The poor girl hadn't been able to order me around for days. I think it was wearing on her. "What you need to do now is work on concentrating the Essence as densely as possible in this room, and we will expand our work from there."

<What about the door? Won't it flow out?>

"If you focus hard there first, you can direct your will to cause the air to be too dense for less concentrated Essence to leak out, like a bubble," Dani distractedly stated.

I considered this for a moment. <I like bubbles. They make my puddle dance.>

"HA! What? That took me by surprise." She chuckled. "Try it out."

I worked on this for a few days as the Essence in the room became denser. The mushrooms and other flora I had discovered in the room flourished. Before I knew it, the room had filled with many varieties of moss, fungus, and other low-level plants. Grass tickled my senses. The regular mushrooms were the same size as the Shroomish, which had also multiplied as the original had put out spores. Because I had created the original Shroomish, I still had a connection to all of the others, known as 'dungeon born' creatures. The monsters were well hidden in the patches and growing stronger by the day.

Dani explained to me that being dungeon born means that I did not directly create the creature but that it was given life through me. This gives the creature the ability to function autonomously with the downside of not allowing me to take direct control of its mind. I can "ride along" in a dungeon born creature's mind from any distance and experience what it does; I also may be able to influence the creature if it remains of a lower cultivation rank than myself. When I am able to create creatures that are actually intelligent, I would use them as scouts outside of my dungeon. That way they can bring back things for me to study or attack other things away from me.

Eventually, I would need to have plenty of the dungeon born Mobs if I wanted to see beyond my boundaries. If I were to directly create every Mob, I would be able to control them much better, but the downside would be that they could not *ever* leave my depths without dying from lack of Essence. They simply could not survive in the wild without my help.

"I think that the Essence has been concentrated enough for us to start to expand. We need to have you make a tunnel, which we will build another room at the end of," Dani started babbling excitedly.

Another room to grow things in?! <Great! How do we start?>

"Build your Essence up on that wall, and convince the wall to open small holes and absorb your influence. Fill a tunnel about six feet tall by four feet wide. When you reach a point where you want to build another room, use your power to compact the stone to either side. The stone will be much stronger than the original and will serve to guide adventurers where you want them to go. It'll also likely glow with the accumulated Essence you put into it, which will look fairly spectacular if I say so myself," Dani directed, stopping only because she ran out of breath. Truly impressive as she did not have lungs.

I focused on the wall and made the stone become porous. Without a 'bubble' like the entrance had, the dense Essence in the cave poured into the wall like water through a sieve.

“Make sure to put curves or sharp turns in that are hard to see past,” Dani suggested.

<On it.> I already had the basic shape I wanted in mind, but sooner than I wanted, the air had become less dense. The concentrated Essence in the room had decreased through this forced osmosis until I had to push very hard to continue to move it forward. Finally, the Essence had reached an equilibrium that I could not continue bringing pressure to bear upon. Nearly drained, I stopped and began to sip on the power released by my lush garden. Since I had created them, even the Shroomish gladly put forth their energy for me to use. Feeling myself stabilize a bit more, I looked at the patch on the wall that glowed to my senses.

I hadn’t been able to move the stone, but nearly one hundred and fifty feet of rock was now under my influence, my direct control. My mind easily followed the path, and I found some very interesting things I had ignored in my haste. I found a material that revealed itself as polycrystalline tungsten. It was an intrinsically brittle and hard material and extraordinarily dense. Farther along, I found an iron ore vein and even anthracite! Anthracite is a rare form of coal that burns hotter and longer than normal coal and is a beautiful black color with a high sheen. I told Dani about these, and she got very excited about the possibility of having metal to tempt adventurers and miners with when they started showing up.

This was also when Dani told *how* I could create more than just monsters. With the same process as creating them, I could create seeds of other materials, like metals and stone. This way, I could inhibit mining to a small section of myself, so people didn’t poke around where I didn’t want them. Apparently, when people were mining it could really grate on my nerves. She suggested that when we made a place for mining, we stick to low-grade materials, especially at first.

"We don't want to bring in people that are too strong, too soon. Although dungeon Cores are supposed to be a well-kept secret, high ranked groups may know about you. You are a needed component in some of the highest powered spells, so if they find you, they will want to take you. If you leave the dungeon, your body, it will die. Even if *you* somehow escape, you will need to rebuild from scratch," Dani warned. "Which is also why you cannot cut yourself off from your body. You can't just burrow down and cover yourself in stone to hide unless you have no other option."

I reluctantly acknowledged her logic, <Makes sense, I guess.>

She seemed happy that I was listening to her. "Now, why didn't you move any of the stone? Was it really hard for you to let your Essence flow into the stone?"

I thought about my answer. <Not particularly. I just wanted to get the most influence possible, so I pushed it as far as I could, you see. I had to stop when I ran low on Essence because I don't like to worry you.>

"Oh." She flushed a bit. "Well, there was a lot of Essence in here. How far did you get?"

I tried to calculate the exact distance; I had just thought about it a moment ago. How long was it? <You know that I am terrible with distances. It felt like a really long way, though. More than a hundred feet for sure.>

"Well, considering it took you a few weeks to run low on Essence when you were pushing it, I'd be surprised if you didn't make it a really long way. I'm trying hard not to be surprised by you anymore." She glowed cheerfully.

<A few weeks? Wow, I really do lose track of time. Hope you weren't too bored.>

"You will get faster with practice," she responded flippantly. "I remember Kantor could change the entire layout of himself in a single night if he tried really hard. And he is a flying island so you know that has to be difficult."

<Wow! How did he learn how to fly?> I wanted to fly. That sounded amazing.

"Well, over time, a lot of really powerful dungeon divers died or lost gear that had strong enchantments, and he learned how to make them. He made huge Mana accumulator stones that he can fill, or they fill themselves maybe? Anyway, those stones power the enchantments, and he *flies* with that magic!" Dani elaborated, excited to have his full attention. "He also is always trying to help new dungeons grow so he can relax every once in a while. So long as you aren't a black or white stone, of course."

<Why those color stones? Is that why he helped me? So people would attack me and not him sometimes?> I started to get a bit heated. Was I just a way to divert attention? I don't want to be used like that!

"Remember how he asked you what color you were? If you were a black or white stone, he probably would have killed you. *Before* you ask, that means that they can only absorb energy from celestial or infernal energy. He doesn't dislike them, but they have no way to ever grow without horrible things being done around them." Dani stopped my attempted interruption, going into full lecturing mode.

"They both, celestial and infernal Cores that is, have ways to influence sentient beings. They should just use their minions to bring food, but what usually ends up happening is a war where demons are summoned and angels are counter-summoned to fight them. The stone can get really powerful with thousands of people dying around them, jumping from G-rank to A in just a few days if it is smart, but usually, crusades are declared to destroy them. It is really a lot of bother for everyone, so Kantor usually just kills them," she explained.

<That is nice of him, I guess,> I admitted reluctantly. Then I remembered the point of this conversation. <Will you teach me how to fly someday? It would be fun.>

"It's really just floating. He has to go where the wind takes him," she attempted to dissuade me, noticing my interest in the idea.

<Even still, I'd like to someday,> I demanded, to which she nodded and tried to distract me.

"That's a really long way away. Let's focus on building your body up, shall we? The dungeon that is. I am going to go look for plants outside that help to increase Essence or really any plants with a lot of different properties."

<Isn't that dangerous?> I nudged her nervously. <What if someone attacks you?>

"Well, it is almost noon, so I should be nearly invisible in the sunlight. Thank you for being concerned about me, cutie." Dani flirtatiously flew a few spirals around me. "Don't worry, I'll be right back." After ensuring I wouldn't be too nervous, she flew out and away.

CHAPTER FOUR

Alone for the first time in months, my cave was totally silent. Well, I could hear the plants slowly growing, but that was pretty quiet, if annoying. I figured that I may as well try and cultivate some Essence, so I gently connected to all of my plants and let their energy flow to me and connected to my newly energized tunnel and started pulling, then pushing hard. I quickly realized several things. Firstly, the tungsten and iron had much more Essence to give me than regular rocks, and secondly, anthracite had a colossal amount of Essence to give but crumbled as soon as it gave it away.

Receiving the pattern as I absorbed its Essence showed me why the anthracite fell apart–coal was made from decomposed organic matter! It was made from compressed plant Essence and didn't really have its own form. When I pulled the energy, there was nowhere for it to regain the lost Essence and it would fall apart. On the positive side, it was absolutely *stuffed* with Essence, and I was soon draining the anthracite exclusively. I had found what I assumed was a relatively small vein of the dark material, but by the time I finished off the last bit of it, I was ninety percent full, something that would have taken months to achieve with just my trivial garden.

Knowing that Dani had wanted me to make more rooms, I decided to surprise her when she got back and began compressing the stone in my influence to either side. With so much energy available to me, I was quickly able to open the passage. Now, I should say that this was not a quiet process. If you have ever ground two stones against each other, you will have a quiet and soothing version of what was transpiring at my location. Unbeknownst to me, this was usually a process that took many months at a time, in an attempt to remain hidden as long as possible. The vibrations caused by my expedited work caused problems around the mountain; landslides, rock falls, and a distant avalanche were triggered.

Just as I finished my fourth room, Dani zipped in at full speed. "Cal! Are you okay? There is an earthquake happening!"

<Surprise! I grew!> I paused, waiting for the glowing admiration to flow from her.

"Oh, Cal no," Dani whimpered. "We need to get ready. People are going to want to know what is going on."

<Did I do something wrong?> I was a bit sad that she wasn't happy with the new additions. <I was just trying to show you that I could do the things you wanted.>

"You didn't do anything wrong, Cal. Just a little... too fast for the moment. Usually, you would want to create an influence around the area you are going to move and force it to absorb the vibrations of the work you are doing. That way, you remain hidden. The next time you want to grow, make sure I am around, and I'll show you how to do it. For now, how about... you show me what you made?" Dani released a short sigh, trying to remain positive about the situation they were sure to find themselves in.

Flying through the new open space, she oohed and ahhed at the work I had done, the smooth tunnel walls and the new caves full of stalactites and stalagmites that I had included for visual effect.

"You made three more rooms? I didn't realize you reached all the way back here! I'm so impressed!" There was the praise I wanted. Aw yisss.

I pretended to be embarrassed, <Aww shucks, you are going to make me blush.>

"No, I am serious! You are growing so well! And your knowledge must be growing too. After all the work you put in, I'm seeing you as an F-rank zero dungeon! You are almost dangerous!" She half-praised, half-teased.

Hey! This was a moment of shining triumph! No teasing! <How strong do I have to be to be dangerous?>

"Well," she considered for a moment, "the average human toddler is about F-rank zero, but they don't have biting mushrooms sprouting from their feet. A human adult that has never done more than just normal farm work and has no weapons is usually around an F-rank four adventurer. At that level, they are derisively called 'fishies' by people that have spent time adventuring."

<What is a fish?> My unspoken thought 'does it taste good' nearly escaped me. I was more than just a glutton. Gotta keep telling myself that.

She nodded, noting my self-control. "A fish is an animal that lives in water, which people collect to feed themselves. Usually very weak, hence the nickname 'fishies' for new adventurers."

<I see.> I paused, considering. <Dani, how can I make myself more dangerous?>

If she had a mouth she would be grinning, I just knew it. "We can start by making more Shroomish, and you can try to evolve them or some of the others into stronger monsters. Next, we will make a few traps, like pitfalls, spike traps, or poison cloud spewers. Finally, we need to make a dungeon Boss."

<That all sounds great, but how do I make a dungeon Boss? And am I stuck with that forever?> I really have been enjoying changing things and didn't want to get slowed down due to a lack of imagination on my part.

"No, actually, when you get bigger, your dungeon Boss might actually become just an average Mob. It is just that you need to put a large amount of your power into your Boss so that it is stronger than the normal ones because it is going to be in your room to protect you and me. Also, you can't make a monster of your level or higher. So, since you are an F-rank zero, your best creature can only be of G-rank nine, and you only have the power to control one of them," Dani clarified.

She suddenly bounced in the air. "Oh! Oh! I forgot! Before we start with all of that, I have a present for you! When I was out looking for herbs, I had just found a really secluded grove at the bottom of a crevasse a few miles from here. The walls were really sheer, so it wasn't surprising that no one had been down there before. There, I found a tree in a clearing that was glowing brightly enough that it was noticeable even in the sunlight." Dani was quivering in excitement, flying in sporadic zig-zags.

Her excitement was exceedingly contagious. <What?! What was it?>

"Cal! I found a Silverwood tree!" she grandly announced.

<Wow!> How amazing! <What is that?>

"... Right." She seemed to deflate a bit.

<...What?>

"Sorry, I forgot that you are still very young," she apologized. "This tree has some of the most potent magic of any plant! It purifies the Essence of those around it."

<So? Purifying Essence isn't hard,> I scoffed.

Can a Wisp get headaches? Most likely no, but she seemed pained as she told me, "Cal, do you remember how shocked I was that you had removed the corruption you had pulled in while cultivating?"

<Yeah?>

"Well, most beings, which can only pull from their associated elemental Essence, gain corruption slowly but surely, no matter what they do. At the higher ranks, this corruption can block people from ascending to higher cultivation ranks."

That would be terrible! <Oh wow. I didn't know that. How will the Silverwood tree help?>

"Well, I took a seed. A single seed from a Silverwood tree takes years for the tree to make. Also, normally these will never grow outside of their groves, but I think that the Essence you provide might become a decent substitute for what it gets from the grove. If we can grow it, we can almost guarantee that people will come from all around to be here. It may even help to keep you safe if people come for this instead of focusing on trying to get your Core."

Another layer of protection would be nice. <You are the best, Dani! How can I grow it? Should I make a room for it?>

She coughed. "Well... that's the thing, if we want to give this its best shot, we will need to give it the most concentrated, pure Essence that you can give it. It will have to be in your Essence puddle with you. It might eventually take up a lot of room too."

<Will it hurt me? Is it dangerous?> Pertinent questions.

"Since it will be growing from your Essence, it should act like your creatures and listen to you, but you have to be careful not to absorb it. I really doubt that you could make a dungeon born version that would do the same as an original," she cautioned. "Also, I don't think that we can ever get another seed..."

I noticed her wince when she said this, as though she hadn't intended to mention it. <Why is that? Is it far away?>

"No... Well, for one thing, they really rarely make seeds. They are basically super concentrated Essence that accumulates into seeds, actually similarly to how you make your dungeon 'seeds'. The reason I don't think you can make them is that it takes S-ranked spiritual energy to duplicate the effects they offer. I don't know why; the trees are not S-ranked themselves. They have a very mysterious origin." She was circumventing her real reason; I could tell.

<What is the matter, Dani? What happened?>

She slowly answered, knowing she had my attention and I wouldn't be distracted, "It's... Right after I left there, the earthquake buried the whole area. The grove is gone."

Another thing I had done wrong. <Oh. Sorry again.>

She rushed to defend me, "It's okay. You didn't know. How could you? Should we try growing it?"

<Go for it. All this talk is meaningless if we can't even grow it right? Gimme.> I sent her an image of me growing hands and snapping my fingers at her.

Startling a laugh with that, she floated over to me and let go of a shining teardrop I hadn't noticed she had been holding in her body. It fell slower than I felt it should have, like gravity was a thing it deigned to obey only when it so chose and entered my puddle with only a small ripple. I tried to push Essence into it but could not get the energy to pass through the surface. With a disappointed sigh, I tried to collect the purest, most dense energy I had into an orb around the seed. Then turning back to the other matters at hand, I quizzed Dani on how to go about making a Boss monster.

She hesitated. "Let's move you to the last room. Then we will talk."

I remembered how hard it had been to move myself the first time and mentally winced. I focused on my pillar and tried to start the process. To my surprise, I moved smoothly and soundlessly.

<Why is this so easy?> I was having so much fun I started moving faster, zipping through the tunnels in an ecstatic blur. <This is so fun!>

"Ha-ha!" she laughed, flying along behind me. "It's due to you being in your body this time! Last time you were going along uninfluenced ground outside, and you were dragging yourself along. Now, in your influence, you control all of this!"

<Awesome!> Disappointedly reaching the final room, I slowed and put myself near the back, and with Dani directing me, I raised a small hill of stone around my pillar, leaving a hole in the exact center leading down to me and my puddle. With my Core better hidden and protected, I listened to Dani tell me how to make my Boss.

"Start by making the strongest monster you know how to," Dani directed. Quickly forming a poisonous Shroomish, I waited for further instructions. "Well, this process is pretty much the same as when you accidentally made your first monster. Basically, you just feed it more and more Essence until it reaches a point of evolution where it is as strong as you can make it. At your current rank, your Boss monster will become a G-rank nine if you give it everything it can take."

Her instructions seemed... lacking. <Got it. That's it? Just pump it full of Essence? Seems a bit anticlimactic.>

"I know, I know." She sighed at her lack of clear explanation, "Well, when you get stronger or learn more about magic or enchantments, even powerful creatures or plants, you will be able to direct the growth how you want it to go."

<Well, I'll look forward to that, then.> I started pushing Essence into the Shroomish and watched as it was greedily absorbed. Watching carefully as it started changing, I continued putting in energy until I suddenly felt like a wall had popped up between my power and what had previously been a simple

Shroomish. It began growing at an exponential rate, the power funneling into different areas of the plant in ways I would have never expected. The process slowed down, but spiky thorns began protruding from the stalk. They dripped with poison, and the gill-like ridges under the cap were holding spores that would be released in clouds when it was fighting.

"Okay, that looks cool. Can I name it?" Dani excitedly pleaded.

<Sure, I'm glad, actually. I was coming up with blanks. What do you have for me?> I cheerfully responded.

"How about 'Dire Shroom: Bane'?" Dani offered.

<Awesome! How will people know what it is named though? Does it matter?> Even if it were just for us, I still liked the name.

"Well, cultivators can use analysis magic to study things—similar to how we can—to check a Mob's information and what it can do. When they do so, it will show the name of the monster and any abilities that they know about. If they were to analyze it before it was dead, all they see is a name and its cultivation rank," explained Dani.

That was a handy tidbit to know! <You are just a fount of knowledge, aren't you! So I'm guessing that we just... leave him be?> I peered at the rustling form of Bane.

Dani puffed up with pride. "Yup, and he'll only get stronger the longer he is alive. Bane is strong enough to cultivate on his own. By the way, the title 'Dire' is applied to a really strong version of a creature. I didn't come up with that. Anyway. Let's move on to the other Mobs, and then the traps, shall we?"

<Great!> Moving as fast as we could, we evolved several new creatures. One of the mushrooms with healing benefits grew barbed spikes but on the inside. They didn't attack, but if stepped on, they would send the spike right through the top of

the plant, jamming into the foot. Once there, the healing properties would kick in, sealing the spike into healthy meat. If someone tried to pull it out or step away, it would tear their flesh, creating a much larger wound.

Even the moss turned into tiny grasping vines which would snag on to any objects moving by. The barbs on them would scratch and tear at whatever they connected to, hopefully dragging prey down. While not very dangerous by themselves, if someone were to fall into the other Mobs nearby, it could become very deadly. More of a support style Mob, I guess.

Switching to traps, we lined the tunnels with pitfalls—very thin stone that would crumble when stepped on. When fallen through, spikes at the bottom made from quartz would penetrate the flesh and shatter, dealing even more damage and causing wounds to become infected. I also put spikes in the wall, similar to the pitfalls. If someone leaned on the wall, they would fall through and into the spikes. Rock falls in the ceiling would be triggered when people stepped on certain areas that were pressure sensitive. On a whim, I made mushrooms grow around the base of the spikes in the pitfalls, hopefully adding a poison effect when people fell on to them.

Dani sounded tired when she finally called it a night for us, "Well, I think that will do for now. I don't think there are many more things for us to do except, well, how about you do some decorating. Let's add some inlay and embellish the entryway. We are still at the bottom of a crevasse, but I think that we should start to make ourselves look good before people find us." Dani looked around with a critical eye. "Eventually, we will make stairs down to where we are when we are really confident that you can protect yourself."

<Works for me. How do you want it to look?> Making things 'pretty' didn't matter to me so much. I'd help her decorate if she wanted though.

"However it is appealing you, maybe some geometric patterns, or loops or knots." She trailed off into silence for a moment. "Whatever you like."

We worked out a few basic ideas and, within an hour, had some basic patterns surrounding the entrance. It looked nice, and with the soft blue glow coming out the door, it would be hard to mistake the entryway for a regular cave.

Chapter Five

"Well, something had to cause it!" broadcasted an angry bearded man. "I lost half my flock. Maybe some meteoric iron is laying around? The whole damn mountain nearly fell over."

"Stop whining! We all lost part of our herd," a swarthy man walking beside the bearded one firmly demanded. "You know the dangers of living in the Phantom Mountains. Death is everywhere." This drew nods from the people around them.

A small group of sheepherders was walking along a sloping mountainside, sunshine streaming around them as they searched for the source of their sudden misfortune. The grass they were walking through was waist high, and while the day was beautiful and clear, the forest around the base of the mountain range visible from this lofty vantage, the mood was ruined by the incessant yammering of the bearded man named Tim.

A fresh-faced young man decided to input his thoughts, "Well, we are on a plain currently, right? Maybe when we get to higher ground, we will be able to see where it hit."

"Maybe you'll learn to keep your mouth shut when your betters are talking," Tim sniped nastily.

"Elder, maybe," murmured the swarthy man. "Better...?"

You got something to say?!" snarled Tim, turning aggressively on the man standing next to him.

"I think it is late, and we grow hungry," the swarthy man appeased the bulky form that was Tim. "Let's set up camp and return to our search in the morning. The sun will soon set as it is."

Fine," Tim grumbled. "Why not just give someone else the treasure while you are at it?" Throwing down his bag, he pulled out a bedroll and lay on the ground while the others set up camp.

The swarthy man eyed Tim. "Since you decided to rest while we worked, you can have the 'pleasure' of taking first shift this evening."

"Eat shit."

The swarthy man blew out some air in frustration, closing his eyes and taking a few deep breaths. "Tim, contribute, or we'll leave you to search on your own."

After staring at the other man for a few moments, Tim finally conceded with poor grace, "Whatever."

After dinner, the small camp wound down. The other men talked for a while, mainly about sheep, weather, and life in their semi-nomadic village. Slowly they fell into a light slumber with a still-angry Tim keeping guard.

Walking around the campsite to stay awake, Tim kept up a low, grumbling complaint until the light had faded to darkness in that peculiarly rapid way which seemed to happen on mountains. Shortly after twilight had faded to true darkness, Tim was making his way around camp for what 'must have been the hundredth time, those heartless bastards', when he saw a soft gathering of light emanating from the edge of the plain they were sleeping on. Moving to examine it, he found light flowing from a crevasse just past an unmarked grave that seemed to give off an unnatural chill.

"Well, would you. Look. At. That." His eyes were gleaming with the light of greed. "Looks like I found me some treasure." He set about searching for a way to the bottom, but the sides were simply too sheer for him to scale. With mounting disappointment and a realization that he was going to have to wake up the others and share his find, he returned to the group and roused them from their slumbers with kicks and curses.

Furiously, they started yelling at him but quickly calmed when he pointed out the glow. Anger turning to excitement, the group moved toward the hole in the ground and looked for a safe way down but, with frustration, decided they would need to wait till morning if they wanted to survive the descent.

Hours later, when the sun achieved its lofty placement on the horizon known as dawn, the men reeled out the rope ladders that highlanders always brought into new areas. Slipping the ladders down the side, they found that after only thirty feet or so, they reached the ground once more. Securing the ladders as best as they could, which was very well, they started their own descent. One by one, they got to the bottom, the first down trying hard to hold his enthusiasm in check as he waited for the rest. A total of five men stood before the cave entrance and deliberated about what to do.

"What is it?"

"You think it is a Beast lair?"

"Don't be foolish. They would never make that kind of art around the edges. It's some old city ruins!"

"Well," began the fresh-faced young man excitedly, "do you think it might be a dungeon?"

Turning to face him, Tim condescendingly talked down to him, "No, you moron, you think we would be the first to find a *dungeon*? The Adventurers' Guild pays a huge amount of money to scouts who find them. How could they miss this? It freaking *glows*. Keep your mouth shut when your *betters* are talking."

"Looks like the best way to find out what it is would be to enter it, don't you think?" the swarthy man supposed.

"Looks like." The group walked through the entryway, noting the abundance of mushrooms immediately.

"Are those redcaps? Those are good eating. Never seen 'em so big before."

"Careful not to mix 'em with those white ones. They are poisonous I think. I know the medicine man wanted some to make an antidote a few years back."

"Do you feel that?" prompted the young man.

Tim growled, rounding on him. "What now?"

"The air, it is so... clean. I feel healthier than I have in years."

"Me too. The ache in my bum knee is fading fast too."

"My shoulder feels nice."

"Hey, look. Even Tim doesn't look like such a sourpuss."

The men laughing at his expense, of course, had the sneer right back on his face, and Tim's glare shot daggers at the young man like it was the young man's fault the group was laughing at him. They decided to explore the cave a bit more, as it seemed well-lit and to collect some 'shrooms on the way out. By chance, they walked past each of the Mobs without rousing any of them and had gone through the tunnel far enough that the second room was visible before tragedy stuck.

"Ahh!" screamed one of the men as his foot went directly through the floor. He fell forward, his body vanishing for only a few moments before a wet crunch and a whimper floated up from below.

"Are you alright?"

"Can you hear us?"

"Where are you?!" The men clustered around the hole in the floor, trying to establish contact with their fallen comrade. They lit a torch and held it over the opening in time to see and smell their friend void his bowels in his death throes.

"Disgusting." Tim sneered.

Shocked looks were thrown his way as the remaining men discussed what to do. The words 'heartless asshole' were heard a few times as well. They had very little extra rope and no way to lift him from the crevasse. The decision was made that they would need to come back with rope the next day to lift him from his resting place, after informing any family he might have. They turned to leave when Tim's voice reminded them that they were here for a reason.

"You can all turn and run from a weak floor if you like, but I'm going nowhere empty-handed. If you leave, you forfeit any right to your share, I tell you *right* now," Tim announced firmly. These were practical men, and life was hard in the mountains. While they were shocked at the death, they knew Tim was right. Each of them hardening their hearts, they moved more carefully, unknowingly following Tim deeper into terrible danger. Death was everywhere in the Phantom Mountains.

Tim moved carefully, testing the floor with each step, hand against the wall for balance. Once, the floor crumbled, and the men laughed with nervous tension as Tim yelped and jumped back. Making their way into the second room, they saw it was similar to the first, filled with mushrooms and other plant life.

"Well, would you look at that?" the swarthy man breathed. He held up his torch, the light reflecting off something on the wall. "Well, men, I'd say we are going to become very rich. Unless I miss my guess, that is native iron. We're looking at the future site of an iron mine!"

With exclamations of joy, the other men whooped and shouted! This wasn't for nothing! Their livelihoods were saved, and they were going to become rich, influential men. Hearts much lighter, they followed Tim deeper in, almost throwing caution to the wind. This time, the swarthy man took the lead, testing the floor, keeping balance against the wall, and saved them twice when the floor gave way and when a large rock suddenly fell from the ceiling.

Entering the third room, they saw no metals, so went directly toward the adjacent tunnel. One of the men lost his boot when it got stuck in a clump of weeds and moss that must have hidden a hole. Testing their weight each step, they made it through the last tunnel without any major issues.

"What in the world is that?"

"What?"

"It's a big-ass mushroom! Look at the size of that thing! It must come up to my hip!"

"I don't see any more metal, but at least we're gonna eat well tonight." The fourth man laughingly walked toward the giant, red capped mushroom, intent on carving off a sizable chunk, when the young man gave an exclamation of horror.

"What?" Turning toward them, the man next to the mushroom never saw the mouth that closed around his torso, ripping him in half with a single bite.

Jumping back in terror saved the young man from the thorn that shot from the stalk of the mushroom, which instead embedded in the wall with a *twang*. Immediately shouting and vacating the room, they peeked back in to see if it were able to chase them. A glance at its stationary position convinced them that it wouldn't follow, and a thorn the size of a hand whistling past his ear convinced the swarthy man that it was time to leave. The room was also becoming very bright, which they took to mean bad things were about to happen.

The remaining three moved quickly down the tunnels, retracing their steps and were in the second tunnel when a puff of something was inhaled by the swarthy man, reducing him to a coughing mess. Blinded by the tears streaming from his eyes, something caught his foot as they were crossing the second room.

The young man looked back to check on the swarthy man just as his head fell on to a light yellow mushroom, and a spike suddenly protruded from the back of his head with an organic tearing sound. Knowing that the fallen group member was already dead, the young man sped up to get behind Tim, who was leaving him behind without a glance. They raced to the entrance to the first room and stopped, breathing heavily as they tried to make their minds stop spinning from the trauma they had witnessed.

"This... this is for *sure* a dungeon," Tim rasped, half laughing, half gasping. "I'm going to be so... *so* rich."

The young man's head snapped up at Tim's comment. "What? What about me?"

Shaking his head, Tim angrily turned away from the lad and viewed the room. "Boy, do I have to tell you again to shut your mouth when your betters is talkin'? Do you even understand how much this is going to change my life? What would you be going to do with the money anyway? Better to let me take care of this, you stupid–"

With fire in his eyes, the young man watched the mushrooms devour the man he had just shoved into them. "You were never my *better*, just older than me. Much older. Also, my name is Dale, you jerk." He left the cave and started home quickly, preparing to become a very, very rich man.

Chapter Six

I watched with great excitement as the first explorers walked into my depths. I watched them stop and was horrified for a moment when I thought they were about to turn back. Then they turned and walked right into the garden! Each step was almost close enough for an attack, but they somehow didn't ever *quite* move within reach. A man stepping quickly never even saw a Shroomish miss its bite at an ankle. My disappointment kept ramping up as each trap was just... walked around! Not one plant got an attack off, no traps were working... until suddenly one did. A man shrieked and fell on to the spikes! The others exploded into motion, trying to see what had happened to him. They lit a torch and somehow missed seeing the reflective spikes in their haste to find a way to save the man.

Suddenly, though, their concerns didn't matter to me anymore.

The dead man's Essence blasted into me, more varied and elaborate than any I had ever had the pleasure of enjoying before. The power was so vast that it was simply impossible for me to contain it. Fire, water, air, earth, celestial, and infernal–all the basic Essences–were pouring into me and processing themselves. He released raw, unstable, pure Essence into my Core and into the world around me as it overflowed.

Dani tried to help, "Cal! Try and collect it in a shell around you! Make a larger body for yourself!"

Through the pain of my vibrating body, I listened to her words, forming perfect facets of pure energy around me. Nearly doubling in size, my new body had barely solidified into a perfect, comparatively empty gem when I felt the second man die. His life force flamed into me, filling my newly improved

Core to the brim with energy. I was able to look out into my dungeon and see Bane chewing on something when the third rush filled my Core. I tried to solidify the outpouring energy into a larger crystalline system, but it wasn't working!

<Dani, what do I do?!> I screamed, the pain making my vision strobe.

"Push it out! Release the Essence out into your body, the dungeon!" Dani shouted back.

Nearly smacking myself for not thinking of it, I sprayed the condensed Essence out of me, allowing it to accumulate in the air as my vaporous, Essence-rich influence.

"They made it to the entrance, you should be okay, Cal," Dani stated with obvious relief. I felt the fourth man die at that moment, and as the Essence ripped through me, I focused on pushing the overflow out as hard as possible. The thick energy already pouring out of me condensed further, forming a beam that shot directly upward and out of me. The beam continued for several seconds until returning to a more mist-like form as I stopped having energies dumped into me.

<Ow,> I complained, an understatement if I had ever spoken one.

"Well, congratulations, my F-rank eight Cal. You survived your first dungeon dive," Dani tiredly informed me. "See how lots of people dying around you can affect your rank?"

<I jumped in rank that much? Wow. Humans have a lot of Essence in them.> I was carefully monitoring the Essence I had gained.

"Yeah, they do. Good work. Um. How do you feel right now?" Dani inquired, oddly nervous for some reason.

<What do you mean? I feel good. Pretty full, I guess,> I offered questioningly.

Dani looked at me then did her version of a shrug, bobbing up and down a bit. "Well, I was just worried. People did just die in here, and I thought that you might be scared, horrified, or just plain upset."

I considered this for a moment. <Well, this is what I need to do to get stronger, right? I don't think that I have the same morals or values as flesh and blood creatures. It isn't so much that I am happy they died, I am happy that I lived. I'm glad that I got stronger. The cost of it is just... the way it happens.>

Dani agreed. "It is what you are. You're right. Always remember, the people that come here are risking their lives to get stronger and to get rich. It is a risk that many will not survive, but it is their own choices–and greed–that will drive them here."

<I'll remember, Dani.> I promised myself that I would try not to put my life on the line for greed.

"Good," she stated firmly, "and by the way..."

<Yeah?> I prodded her to continue.

"The Silverwood tree sprouted!" she shouted, unable to contain herself any more.

<Wow, look at that!> The tiny seed had fragmented away from the plant, like an egg releasing a creature, only for the roots to absorb the solid Essence the shell had been composed of. The tiny roots glowed and started moving hungrily. Growing at a pace I was surprised at, the roots expanded outward, drinking the Essence that filled my puddle.

<Aww, my puddle,> I pouted sadly, trying not to let on how much I was actually worried.

"I'll bring you more water, you whiner," Dani grumbled at me. The roots quickly reached to bottom and were waving around looking for something. "Cal! Make dirt and open holes in the rock that the roots can go through! Hurry!"

I did as she asked, making strong, healthy, black soil under the rock of the small hill surrounding me and little holes that the roots shot toward like intelligent beings. I could always make the holes larger, so I decided not to let dirt get in and muddy up what was left of my poor puddle. The roots sank into the rich dirt and quickly burrowed in, seemingly finding their new home to their liking.

I was impressed by how many roots had grown. There had to be hundreds of tendrils extending from the tiny plant. If I were not in the midst of the root jungle, I would have mistakenly believed that the sapling above me was a regular plant, and no one looking at it from an angle would ever be able to see the advanced root system it had created in just a few minutes. Finally slowing, the minuscule sprout stood proudly, a full three inches tall. The roots must have been a few feet long each. Therefore, this was very misleading.

<What an odd plant.>

Dani chuckled at my understatement. “You aren’t kidding! Are you getting any information from it?”

<No, > I grumbled, <it must be beyond my understanding at this point.>

“Don’t worry about it too much, you have a lot of growing to do, after all. Things have been going really easily for you thus far. It is not overly surprising that you will be plateauing as you get older,” she explained cautiously. “Also, we need to talk about what happened during that fight!”

<Agreed. Why wasn’t I able to expand my Core when I was full of energy? That was really dangerous for me.>

“Well, not what I wanted to start with, but increasing in rank is not always just a matter of raw power. It requires forethought and insight into the world around you. As you grow in power, what you do can reshape the world. To achieve these insights, you need to fully understand what you are changing, *how* it will affect the world around you, and *if* you should do it."

<Well, that is very profound,> I teased.

"True, though. When Mages use Essence to warp the universe, they are saying the true name of what they want and infusing it with their power. This is called an incantation and is the way they cast spells without objects. Now, words without power mean nothing, and power without knowledge is dangerous. All you knew to do was make your own body larger. You don't know how to make power automatically direct itself or how to refine Essence further," Dani wisely stated.

<Refine it further?> Wasn't my Essence really pure, though?

"Yeah, Essence is only the most basic form of energy provided by the heavens and the earth. To break into the 'B' rank, you will need to learn to further refine Essence into Mana, to get into the S-rank you will need to learn about spiritual energy, and when we finally escape the SSS-rank and move into 'Heavenly', you will need to find a 'fundamental' energy," Dani started a lecture as I silently groaned.

"To progress into the E-rank, you have to start the process that will activate your refinement. What is your energy doing right now, for instance?" she prompted leadingly.

<What do you mean? It is doing what it always does. Glowing while waiting for me to release it.> Even as I uttered the words, I knew it was the wrong answer but still the one she wanted to hear.

"Bwa-ha-ha!" she mockingly laughed. "This is why I, your Dungeon Wisp, am here for you, young one!"

<Oh wise leader,> I dryly replied, <please, share your hard-earned knowledge with this poor being.>

She chuckled evilly as she began, "Oh, you are gonna learn today. Start by releasing about half the energy you collected back into the air. You need to start less full than you are or it won't work." Apparently, what I needed to do next was to focus on my exact center–easy for me since I was *perfectly* symmetrical, thank you very much–and start spinning my Essence along the outer edge of my Core. After a few hours, I was able to get it swirling to Dani's liking.

Next, I had to pull the absolute smallest thread I possibly could from the large swirl and pull it to my "center". According to Dani, the center of a being was actually the center of their soul, where Essence would feed into their life-force. Therefore, the better the quality of the Essence, the stronger the life-force and the more robust the soul. Needless to say, I had to work for quite a while before Dani reluctantly allowed me to use the thread I had stretched. Everything before that quality was quickly rejected by her.

Connecting the incredibly fine strip of Essence to my center, I began to spin it in the opposite direction from the large swirl. As these competing swirls continued to spin, the fine inner center started to accumulate. Apparently, this process was called a "Chi spiral"–pronounced "Key spiral", Dani told me haughtily.

The Chi spiral had several functions that helped to further process Essence. An individual's Chi spiral was a vast amount of intricately knotted Essence; the more complex and complete the pattern woven into it, the more Essence it can hold and the finer the Essence would be refined. Dani compared this to packing clothes in a bag by stuffing them in versus neatly folding them and carefully placing for maximum storage capacity. The downside was that it took a long time for the Essence to be refined, but I was assured that as I became more practiced, it would become faster. On a positive note, the swirling light was absolutely *gorgeous.* The light moved and played along my facets, sending shimmering fluorescence across the ceiling above me. While beautiful, I hoped the tree above me would grow fast enough to soon hide the emanating light.

It took a lot of focus to keep swirling the Essence incongruently, but I was again assured that it would eventually become automatic to me. While my goal was to create a very complex Chi spiral, at this level, it was exhausting just to keep it moving at all. The important process started, we had some free time to discuss what had happened during the incursion by humans.

"The monsters in here need to be stronger, ranged, or able to move around. That group made it into the Boss room without having to fight a single time!"

<I know, but how can we make that happen? I'm not sure how to do that. I can't direct their evolution.> I was a bit distracted by my need to keep my Essence swirling properly.

"I have a thought." Dani gleefully chuckled. "You jumped all the way to the eighth rank in 'F', while your Boss stayed down at G-rank nine. I'm betting that you will be able to absorb him and make him a common monster at this point, though much smaller if you want several. Then we can start on a new Boss!"

I slowly acquiesced, 'nodding', <That's a great idea! By the way, what should I do about the bodies of those humans?>

"Oh nasty, I had forgotten the smell." She sneezed and shuddered.

<I don't have a nose.>

"Lucky you. Just study them. As soon as you know how their bodies work, they will automatically dissolve into your influence. Easy-peasy cleanup. Oh! Let's see if they had any gear with them!"

Now armed with the knowledge of how to make humans, I could easily have made skeletons or zombies to fight for me, but I just could not get over how upset a constant reminder of Necromancers would make me. Looking at the items they had with them, I learned how to make several new things: poor quality wool shirt, wool pants, rope, bone dagger, wool boots, wool belt, waterskin, and a leather bag.

There were also a few copper coins in the bag, which is when Dani explained how currency worked and had me make copper coins with the exact same imprint these had on them. I made them out of pure copper, though, not the low grade, shoddy copper alloy these were made of. I needed to have pride in my work, after all.

Dani went quiet for a moment, like she always did before having something interesting to say. "Let's talk about loot."

<Loot. Got it. What's that?> I wanted to know, and she would always drag these conversations out to keep my full attention.

Surprising me, she jumped right in, "Loot is a payment system for defeating monsters. It helps distract adventures from taking everything they see and will guarantee that people will come back if they survive. Escalating the reward to more elaborate items for coming deeper in the dungeon increases the odds that you will have more opportunities to kill them off and become stronger."

How would that work? <So I just litter the ground with trinkets?>

"No, and this is kinda cool. You know how you grow creatures with a 'seed and pattern'?" She was amused by something. I nodded my assent, and she continued, "Well, the concept is the same, but you attach the 'loot' seed to the monster, and when it dies it triggers the 'seed' to grow. It is really funny to see because if you don't know how it works, it makes no sense! Imagine someone accidentally squishing a patch of moss, and out pops a helmet! I bet they would scream! Haha!"

That sounded hilarious, and I could not wait to get started. She cautioned me not to make it too obvious to start, though and to try to make things properly. No dagger handles that had a boot instead of a blade for instance and to eventually try to make enchantments on items that made things worth the effort to obtain. Don't put a dancing enchantment on a wand, put it on shoes, for example.

The smaller mushrooms could be used in potion-making and for food already, so I only attached coin loot seeds to them. Really, even my Bane could be mostly used as potion material—if they knew what they were doing—so I just gave him a larger coin value, and sometimes, he would drop sets of clothes or a dagger. I made the dagger better than what I had found, substituting iron for the bone blade. It was heavy and brittle but far more effective.

Next, it was time to absorb Bane and make more of him. Resisting a bit at first, he eventually gave up his energy, and I was able to study his pattern. Easily able to replicate it, I made several Dire Shroomish: Bane monsters in each room but the last. They were smaller and would only come up to the knee of the last group but were now the ranged attackers of my dungeon.

Now, it was time to make a new Boss. Since my last was at G-rank nine, and I could create one up to F-rank seven, this room was about to get significantly more dangerous. On Dani's recommendation, I tried to combine the pattern of Bane with the patterns of other things I knew how to make. Each attempt at combining Bane with other mushrooms failed for some reason. Casting about for a way to understand this, no easy answer came to mind. Almost ready to scream with frustration, I was just about to pour energy into it in an attempt to *force* a natural evolution when my mind skittered over a Mob I didn't know. Looking closer, I saw that a patch of the moss had upgraded itself when it had tripped a person and eaten part of his foot.

The new monster, Bloodmoss, could still do everything it had been able to–grasping, holding, and scratching–but had a new passive ability: Vampirism, Taste for Blood! Dani was characteristically excited that my monsters were getting stronger and told me that if they fought and won, the longer they stayed alive, the more powerful they would grow. Each eradication would flood me with energy, but a part of it would also go directly into the monster who helped with the kill. Since it wasn't energy purified by me first, the Essence taken would alter the path of its growth. I decided to plant a few Bane Mobs on the ceiling, so they had less chance of dying during a fight.

"Vampirism, huh?" That is a really good ability, but you should be careful not to give it to too many creatures. Technically, it is an infernal alignment ability, and if you have too many demonic traits, the church may become... nervous and call for your destruction," Dani warned me in a tone that brooked no argument.

<Yikes, yeah, how about we avoid that. Do you know what it does?> I requested.

"At this level, if it gets blood on it, the damage will heal a little, automatically repairing its pattern which will fix the Mob's wound. If not damaged, it becomes a little stronger and harder to hurt. The higher levels have different effects, but you will need to reach them to know what they do. I'm not an expert on the infernal," Dani recounted, thinking hard.

<Good to know. I'm gonna try something real quick.> Since grafting mushrooms on to Bane hadn't worked, I tried with

the moss. The pattern glowed in my mind, successfully building a new monster. Analyzing this pattern, I was surprised to see letters and numbers on it.

When I mentioned the numbers, Dani zipped over to congratulate me again. “Oh! You can use your viewing ability on abstract concepts now! Great, now you will know when you progress in rank and can view the cultivation base—or rank—of other creatures. The word you see on that pattern is how strong the monster will be once created. If it is one level below you, you can create it but not upgrade it.” She paused for breath. “If it is lower, you can attempt to use your Essence to make it stronger, though it may not always work.”

I made an educated guess, <Well, this guy is one rank below me. Can I make him into my Boss monster?>

“Okay, but remember that if it is one rank below you, it will be really hard to absorb it back if you don’t like how it turns out,” she unnecessarily warned me.

<Yes, dear.>

“I don’t nag you. I explain,” she huffed with a glare.

I focused hard on the pattern, for the first time infusing it with the refined version of Essence from my Chi spiral. This had an interesting effect, as the fine energy went exactly where I wanted it to instead of filling the entire template with diffuse energy. It took about eighty-five percent of the power I thought it would, and Dani told me this was because I was being more efficient. I planted the ‘Seed’ on to the ground and watched as it sprouted into a scary mushroom.

It reached its full height around chest level for the men that died here and was very similar to the Bane except for a few minor details. A carpet of moss spread out from its base, and I saw it flexing into ropey groups that would be able to grab prey and pull it into an effective attack range. It also had the

Vampirism effect, so attacking would greatly benefit the monster. Its name? Dire Shroomish: Bloody Bane. I could hardly wait to see it fight.

Chapter Seven

Dale had returned home with the sad news of the deaths of his comrades, citing a landslide which buried all of them. The recent events and his guileless, lightly bearded face meant he had no issues convincing the townsfolk of his sincerity. He shed tears from soulful, brown eyes for the lost men... while at the same time selling everything he owned. With the money gained, he purchased the empty parcel of land containing the dungeon—claiming it would be good grazing for the sheep he was planning to buy. His claim to the land secure, he sent a letter to the Adventurers' Guild, announcing that he had found a new dungeon and was willing to allow adventurers to come into it for a percentage of the yearly profit it brought in. Since this was the standard agreement, he had no trouble enticing a small party to travel from the Guild and appraise its value.

Within a few weeks, a group of four travel-worn individuals had arrived in the small village. Quite an event to have any travelers at all, this far into the mountains, people were shocked to see not only armored knights, but an *Elf* in the group! Every courtesy was extended, but they only accepted a bath and a hot meal. After meeting with the elders, the group found Dale and got the mostly unedited version of events that had transpired from him, without the murder coming up for some reason.

Without even bothering to stay the night in the cramped village, Dale and the group started off immediately into the mountain, hurrying to the entrance but failing to make it by nightfall. Camping a few miles from the entrance, the men explained that sleeping in the vicinity of a dungeon with only a small group was tantamount to suicide, as monsters tended to be drawn to the energy emitted from even weak places of power.

"So what are you guys actually going to do when you get there?" Dale quizzed them.

"Well," pronounced the large man with plate armor, looking uncomfortably at the men around him, "when we first came, it was to assess the value, but after hearing that a brand-new area has already been able to kill four men, we decided to destroy it. If it is this strong and was not here when the scout came through only a decade or so ago, it is likely that it has some kind of infernal origin. The reports of our scouts killing a coven of Necromancers in the area about that time give credit to this."

"But this was supposed to be my new source of income! I sold everything I own to make sure this land was ready for you!" Dale pronounced, face draining of color. "I'm ruined." He sank to the ground, head in his hands.

"Ach," an easy-going Guild member tisked at Dale. "Lad, take it easy. The Guild will pay you ten gold for your trouble and five each year after that for the rest of your life. That is what it is worth to us to stop Demon wars."

"Ten gold...?" Dale breathed. In the mountain, that was enough to live like a lord for a solid decade. For two gold and a small bribe, he could likely buy the whole mountain since there was so little worth to the land. It was harsh and nearly impassable, especially in winter.

"Ten gold... up front, before we go into the lair. If we decide that the dungeon does not need to be destroyed, we'll be wanting that back, but we will leave you half as a down payment."

"O-of course! Not that I think a small place such as this would be able to hurt any of you, certainly," Dale stammered.

Laughing, the other men agreed with him and started a watch rotation, settling in for the night. When dawn broke, they continued on their way to the crevasse.

"Oh yeah, look at this. Some old mountain lion tracks here, bear there, and even a few goats, lots of rabbit tracks too. Look a bit old, though. We may have been alright sleeping here," guild man number three–as Dale thought of him–informed them, pointing out the tracks as he called them out.

"Should I know your names?" blurted Dale suddenly. By the furtive glances and shaken heads, he assumed the answer was no.

"I'm guessing we are close to the entrance? I am feeling an uptick in ambient Essence." The smooth voice of the Elf broke the awkward silence.

"Very close, it is right over here. I left the rope ladders to help us and brought an extra just in case–" Stopping mid-sentence, his eyes nearly burst from his head as he saw that the crevasse was no longer a hole in the ground with sheer walls but a solid looking, spiral, stone staircase leading to the depths.

"Well, that makes it easy." The Elf stepped forward, and after a brief look of concentration, pronounced the stairs safe to use.

"It's like an invitation!" Dale declared nervously.

"That is exactly what it is," the large man replied ominously. "Stay here, Dale. Keep all this money safe for us, okay?" He poured a small sack of clinking coins into Dale's hand. "We will be right back." The group started their incursion into the dungeon, weapons coming out and slowly beginning to shine with accumulated Essence.

Coming into the garden room, the group waited in formation, studying everything in their path.

The cold, logical voice of the Elf began cataloging his surroundings as soon as they entered, "Mushrooms and moss, some good for making antidotes, one a needed ingredient in weak health restoration potions, a few monsters with unknown yet weak abilities. But that, men, is why we are here." The Elf pointed at a reddish patch of moss growing innocently in the garden.

"What is it?"

"Bloodmoss," the Elf grimly alerted them. "It is a known component in infernal potions and enchantments. If purified, it makes some of the most high-grade, non-magical bandages that can be produced. The issue is, it needs concentrated infernal Essence to gain the vampirism-style ability it almost certainly has."

All sense of relaxation gone, the men set about systematically destroying every living thing in the room. Within just a few minutes, only a few charred scraps remained. A few copper coins suddenly rained to the ground.

"Bribery will not save you from your despicable ways," a taciturn man with a glowing holy symbol on his chest announced in a ringing tone. "Onward!"

Quickly moving on, they expertly destroyed or evaded every trap in the tunnel and gave the same treatment to the next rooms and tunnels until they were in the Boss room. As they stepped in, with the large man holding a tower shield in front of them for cover, the over-zealous cleric boldly stepped forward, proud of their easy travel to this point and ready to finish the mission. The smile left his face as he was pulled to the floor, a vine dragging him quickly to the center of the room.

"What? This is a G-ranked dungeon. How did it sneak up on me?" he shrieked, fighting to secure a handhold on the too-smooth floor. The others sprang into motion, moving to his rescue as a large thorn pinged off the shield. Despite the sneak attack and the subsequent battle, the strength of the Boss was nowhere near enough to even dent their armor.

With only a few slashes of a sword and a quick flash of fire, the Boss crumbled to the ground and was mostly reabsorbed, all but a few coins and useful parts of the mushroom. Studying the body before it vanished, the Elf grimly noted the vampirism ability it had before noticing its cultivation rank in shock.

"This was an F-rank seven Boss! Where did that come from? Did anyone else see monsters above G-rank nine?" A round of negatives followed his question as he kept an eye on the shroom. The large man maintained that he had found where the Core was hidden but that there was a plant in the way. "Carefully get it out of your way, then–" Looking up, the Elf saw the plant in question as a sword was drawn back to cut it out of the way.

As the sword came down, a blast of wind knocked the burly man away.

"Oh-ho! Looks like it had another trick up its sleeve!" the big man said, brushing off dirt and springing upright.

"That was me." The Elf was walking over unnervingly calmly and quickly inspected the small tree. "Whew. Just in time! If I had let you cut that tree, I would have had to declare war on your Kingdom on behalf of my race."

"You whaaa?"

"Look carefully. That is a Silverwood sapling," the Elf stated, calm in a way that terrified the human men. This was the sort of calm shown only to enemies directly before their annihilation.

"Y-you don't say..." The large man nervously chuckled. "Forgive me, I have never seen one before. I will dig it up so that we can move it to a suitable location."

"If you are able to find a way to do that, you will have to show me," the oddly flat voice resounded from the Elf, "because untold generations of Elves have been unable to find a way to do it. Which is why we build cities where we find them, not the other way around. I think it is safe to say this is *not* an infernal dungeon. That kind of Essence would stunt its growth severely, and this one, though young, is vibrantly healthy. I'd say our mission is complete, though I need to put protections in place for this tree. After all," his face jerked upward, staring hard at a point near the ceiling, "if anything were to happen to the tree, I am sure the Elven-kind would destroy everything nearby in an attempt to find what had happened," he blandly stated to apparently no-one.

The others looked at each other in worry and confusion but did nothing that may upset the powerful Mage. As per his instructions, they moved while he cast powerful protective magic on the tree and handed over a gold coin, a silver coin, and a small, high quality, honed steel dagger. The large man was grumbling at this until he was smacked in the head and pointedly glared at by the final member of their party. These items were placed on the floor in the room, and the Elf moved to usher them out.

The cleric made a pointed, haughty noise in his throat. "I cannot, in good faith, leave this place until I have ascertained for myself that this is not a place of darkness." He pulled his glowing holy symbol off his neck and held it by the chain. "I *will* be placing this near that dungeon Core. If it is evil, god's might will smite it. I will not allow even the specter of war stop me from doing this."

A smirk appeared on the Elven face. "Go for it. Heh."

Eying the Elf, the cleric slipped the pendant down into the hole, skillfully maneuvering around the many roots just visible. At the furthest effective range he could manage, he chanted a prayer and waited a moment. When nothing apparently happened to the gem, he apprehensively began to speak, "Well, it seems that you were correct my frie–" In horror, he looked at the small amount of chain remaining in his hand that he had pulled out of the hole. "My pendant!" Furiously whirling on the Elf, he said, "You knew that would happen!"

With an innocent look on his face, the Elf defended himself, "Well, I thought my manner was sufficient warning, but, well..."

Three of the men started laughing loudly at the protestations of the cleric–until they stepped into the first room where a small mushroom was innocently awaiting them.

The large man spoke quietly, "I thought we had cleared this room."

"We did," grunted the cleric, the first non-complaint in several minutes.

An arrow *thunked* into the mushroom, rendering it into pulp in an instant.

* *Clink** * *Clink** * *Clatter** * *Thud**

Announcing the fall of a gold coin, a silver coin, a steel dagger, and a shining pendant on a chain, the noises were the only ones heard for several seconds.

"How the...?" a confused voice.

"My pendant!" a joyful voice.

"My money!" a greedy voice.

"Oh, dear. It is a *fast* learner," a soft voice.

CHAPTER EIGHT

I was terrified when these people destroyed my first room in a blaze of fire. I should never have made it so easy to get down. I just really had a thing for the spiral staircase ever since Dani had suggested it. It was such a cool idea, and it would allow animals to get down here. Obviously, I needed to start upgrading my monsters; these people were spooky.

<Dani... I think they are going to kill me,> I uttered slowly when the strange looking man talked about my Bloodmoss.

“It’ll be okay, Cal. Can you tell what rank they are?” Dani replied soothingly.

<No, I just visualize an ‘X’ when I try to analyze them. I can’t analyze their gear either... What is going on?> I demanded, voice low and scared. I liked to understand things.

“The gear makes sense; their aura would protect it unless it got too far away from them. Oh! I never told you about auras! You see, when an aura is present, you can’t affect things in the same way. Their Essence flows in such a manner that it interrupts your control in the area. That’s why you need monsters and traps, else you could just eat them directly. Every living creature has an aura–just so you know. Even you! Your aura is the size of your dungeon but is disparate in any given area. Hence why theirs will block your control,” She paused a moment, “but you can’t read their aura at all? Nothing? No information whatsoever? I’ll go look.” She zipped away, her light fading to invisibility.

I was suitably impressed. “Wow, where did you learn that?”

"I get stronger when you doooo," her sing-song voice echoed back to me. A few minutes later, she appeared in front of yours truly, obviously upset. "Cal, the humans are C-ranked, and the Elf is B-ranked. We might be in real trouble."

<What can we do?> I was determined to make it through this trial.

Her voice was lowered to an almost-whisper, "Hope they get bored and go home?"

I growled at her, <Not super useful, thanks.>

"I... *wish* I were joking. They could kill us without any effort *at all.* Stay quiet, and maybe they will not look for you?" She pretended to be hopeful, though she was obviously overly optimistic.

They were just about to enter my final room, so I directed the Boss to attempt a sneak attack. It worked! Then... it didn't. I heard them talking but couldn't focus past my terror. A face appeared in the hole over me! AHH! The man raised a sword... and fell over with an 'oomph'! Finally, able to hear their conversation properly, I was amazed that the tree offered me so much protection. When the Elf looked directly at Dani, though she was invisible, I knew his veiled threat was actually for me.

"If anything were to happen to the tree, I am sure the Elven-kind would destroy everything nearby in an attempt to find what had happened."

Shuddering, I watched as they cast magic and left a few offerings. One of them even fed me a symbol with celestial Essence infused in it! I filed the enchantment on it away for future reference. As they left, Dani spoke up.

"I *cannot* believe that just happened. All of that to give you *tribute*?" She started laughing, the previous feeling of impending death moving away.

I shushed her, my concentration too honed to be polite. <Hold on, I'm trying to finish these.>

Obviously affronted at my lack of happiness, she demanded, "What are you doing? Celebrate with me!"

<Attach it to a Shroomish...> I mumbled. <Done. Whew. I wasn't able to activate the thing, but he seemed really sad that I ate his necklace. I gave them all a copy of what they gave me in tribute.> I felt really weak right now. Their auras had made it difficult for me to put the mushroom back in the room, especially when they were getting so close to it.

"... You never cease to amaze me, Cal," Dani declared. "For a dungeon, you are surprisingly giving. That Elf was right; you are a really fast learner. Also, for being a low level, you are really adept at making monsters perform better than their rank should allow. Concepts come easy, and you are able to absorb every type of Essence..." She started mumbling too quietly for me to hear.

<What? I'm just trying to do the correct thing for us. Starting a feud with the church sounded like a terrible idea.> She had told me that the church was powerful, after all. Did she mean a different church?

"Politics too, now. Cal... do you have any memories that are...? *Before* you became a dungeon?" she prodded, looking hopeful yet still worried.

A flash of a knife, pain, filthy Necromancers...

<Just little flashes,> I admitted. <Is that out of the norm?>

"There is *no* way," she muttered, "Cal, were you a... human?"

I considered. The Elf had seemed too foreign so...<Yeah. I think so at least.>

"Oh wow. Oh boy, oh boy." Swooping around the room, Dani was trying to process this new development. "Cal, how did this never come up? This explains so much."

<It does?! Great! Um, I guess it didn't come up because I don't really remember anything and it didn't seem important?> I voiced weakly, knowing this answer wouldn't work for her.

Dani stopped flying and looked right at me. "This is very, *very* important. Let me explain. Unlike beasts, animals, and plants, humans and other close relations like Elves or Dwarves have the ability to use *all* kinds of Essence. While they may have a greater affinity for one or the other, they are *made* of all of them, so can use them all to some extent if they have the training."

Well, that cleared up a few things. <So, that is how my Bloodmoss got infernal energy?>

She bobbed vigorously. "Yes, and it also explains why you can absorb all of them without ill effects! I still don't know how you can get rid of the corruption, but we will... figure it out." Enlightenment touched her. "Cal! That is why it is so easy for you to learn some things! Words and concepts especially! It is because you are *re-learning them*!"

I was watching her insane flying and weaving with a bit of concern for her mental well-being. <Dani, you need to tell me why this is such a big deal.>

"You are *unique*! That's why! Remember how I told you dungeon Cores were usually naturally occurring? The gem *always* forms first, and usually, a Beast who dies nearby, or maybe a strong animal, gets pulled in entirely by accident."

<But Kantor could talk. He wasn't a human?> He had certainly sounded human or at least more intelligent than a simple animal.

She moved around in a pattern I had associated with a negative. “Nope, he was actually an Alpha Dire Wolf when he died. It took him something like fifty years to learn how to ‘talk’ in a way that humans and other sentients could understand.”

I wanted to know more about Kantor, but I *needed* to know about myself. <Okay, I get it, but why is this such a shock to you?> My single process mind finally broke through her babbling.

She was almost too riled up to answer me directly. “Humans never get pulled into Beast Cores! *It doesn’t happen*! It never has, Cal!”

<I… don’t think I was pulled into a Beast Core. Do the words ‘soul gem’ mean anything to you? I think I was trapped in one by those disgusting Necromancers.>

She squealed a bit. “That makes perfect sense! Oh. My. Gosh, Cal! We have so much to learn! Imagine, *ME* being the first Wisp to be bonded with a cunning, human-soul dungeon! We are going to get *SO* famous.”

Well, when she puts it like that… I ‘grinned’. <You know it.>

Chapter Nine

We decided we probably had some time before people delved into my depths again. I was particularly nervous that another group would come in soon, due to every living thing in my dungeon except me, Dani, and the Silverwood tree being dead and reduced to ash when the jerks–I mean the scouting group–had come through. It was not too hard to make new Mobs and plants, but each one took some energy to produce. Without a source of ready Essence to replenish me, I had to go really slowly.

<This sucks.> I definitely did not whine.

Dani had heard this, or a variant thereof, rather frequently in recent times. "You are just grumpy because you are hungry. Why don't you eat some granite? Mm-mm, tasty earth Essence!"

<It takes too long.> I huffed. <I'm not grumpy.>

"We used to call it 'hangry'. It means angry because of hunger. How is the first room going?" She tried to divert my attention to happy thoughts.

It didn't work. <It's going. The stupid plants are too small for me to eat without killing them, and I can't eat the Mobs because they need all their stupid Essence if some stupid person comes in here.>

She rolled in the air, her equivalent of an eye roll. "Definitely not grumpy. I'm surprised all of your grumbling didn't start another earthquake."

Not dignifying her comment with a response, I focused all my waning power on increasing the number of Mobs in the first room. I had made 'biting' Shroomish more populous, remembering how people were just walking through without having to fight at all and included a few of the ranged Bane types where the biters were especially thick. I felt good about the strength contained in the first room but thus far had been unable to even grow moss in the remaining rooms.

<Instead of making fun of me, how about you go find me some new plants? The last time you did it, it really paid off by me not dying, after all.> I did *not* grump at her.

"Fair enough. I could use a break from Mr. Grumpy-face." She zipped away, her retreating form shouting, "Take a nap!"

<You know I can't nap, rude little firefly,> I rumbled after her. She was way too far away to hear me, but I swear I heard her chuckle. Brat. I switched to absorbing energy from the rocks and metals in my influence, but I swore I was getting less than I had ever before. Keeping my Chi spiral going was starting to get easier but still took a bit more concentration than I liked. Pulling hard on the energy sources, I was able to regain a trifling amount of Essence. I was sitting far below what I felt comfortable with, but this process simply took a lot of time. Twilight was falling outside when Dani returned.

"Nothing too special this time, Cal, sorry," Dani started, "I did get some flower seeds and a few more herbs that smell really good. Let's see, I got basil, parsley, and some... mint I think? Not really scary, I know, but you are starting to smell a bit." She tested my mood jokingly.

<Sounds good, Dani. Sorry I was so grumpy. I guess you were right,> I apologized sheepishly. <The last few hours of eating helped a lot.>

"Aww, thank you." Dani flew over and dropped the seeds and herbs in front of me to make it easier for me to study them. Within a few minutes, I had made copies and planted them along the tunnels. That would freak a few people out. I chuckled at the thought. 'Oh no, basil! Look out, it's mint!' Maybe I would get lucky, and someone would be allergic to them and die from a bad reaction.

<Heh,> I chuckled, projecting accidentally.

Dani glanced over. "Hmm?"

<Oh nothing, just thinking. These are going to look really good Dani. Thank you for getting them. They are going to be really colorful, by the way. I figured out how to mix a few attributes of the seeds together.>

"I knew you would like them!" She beamed, then whispered, "Narcissist."

I gasped at the unexpected attack. <I am *not*!>

"Well, you do spend all day every day looking at yourself soooo..." she teased me.

I played along, <It is as far as I can see, rude-oh!>

The friendly banter continued for a bit until Dani got sleepy and flew over to the ledge she tended to rest on. As a living creature, she still had to sleep occasionally. For the rest of the night, I focused on growing plants. Mint grew like a literal weed, covering anything I gave it access to very quickly. The basil grew a bit slower but had much thicker leaves and was quite a bit hardier. The flowers blossomed, adding splashes of color around my otherwise somewhat monochromatic dwelling. And each of these plants gave off a heady aroma, which is what eventually awoke Dani.

"Mmmm something smells good. You making me breakfast?" She yawned.

I smiled at the thought of me trying to cook. <No, but go fly around and tell me what you think! I grew all those seeds you gave me.>

She took off, and I could soon hear multiple sounds of appreciation. Coming back rapidly, she pronounced, "You know, if you wanted to be really boring, you could feed an entire city for decades."

I responded tartly, <I am not a farm, thank you very much. I just don't want to have bad body odor.>

"Dead body odor," she quipped, looking over for a reaction.

<Well, yeah, what did you think I meant?> I questioned confusedly.

Dani acted like I was intentionally not understanding her pun. "Never mind. Today, lets–"

An odd sensation alerted me to an uninvited guest. <Shh! Wait! There is something on the stairs!>

She went still for the first time since waking up. "What! Dungeon divers again this soon?! We aren't ready!"

<No, it doesn't feel like that.> While I had made the stairs, my influence was not yet dense enough to see what was on them. I made a note to focus on that when I had some Essence stored up. <It is coming to the entrance. I should be able to see it any second now.>

<...>

"What is it?!"

<I don't know! I've never seen anything like it before.>

"Should I be worried?"

<No, it is just coming in. It doesn't seem to be doing muc– *It's attacking my herbs!*> I howled, desperately searching for a way to fight back.

Dani was aghast. "*All of them?!*"

<No, just the one for now. It isn't in range of the Bane Shroomish yet. Now it is just waiting, staring at my mushrooms!> I really didn't have the energy to make more plants. As it was, my Chi spiral had no excess swirling Essence to pull from, and I

was exhausted. I asked Dani to take a look, as she could connect with me with a bit of effort. Her reaction shocked me.

"*Bwahahahah!* Cal, oh sweet, naive C-cal," she laughed, choking on the words. "That is the scourge of the mountains, the destroyer of herbs, a *mountain bunny!*" I could get nothing else from her for a few minutes, as she was laughing too hard to catch her breath.

Grumbling, <It's still eating my plants! What's a bunny? Is it poisonous. Does it have sharp teeth?>

"No," she gasped a bit still in an attempt to contain her mirth, "they are plant eaters! Usually prey for the larger animals and Beasts, they survive by being really prolific."

Prolific? <Meaning?>

"That they have babies really fast, and a lot of them," she explained offhandedly, used to me asking questions about new words.

An idea came to life in my mind. <... Dani. *Idea,* Dani. Do you think I could spawn these as Mobs?>

Catching on instantly, she replied, "I think so. These are low F-ranked animals."

I had been able to study humans, but the complexity involved in the pattern made them too far beyond my knowledge or power to produce. A mindless husk? Sure, though the mushrooms were more useful. If I were able to produce an ambulatory, semi-intelligent creature, no matter how weak, it would be a huge stride forward for me. For us, really.

<Dani, get ready! It's moving closer!> I took aim.

It came in range of the Bane, and when a speeding thorn penetrated its skull, my mind exploded with information.

Chapter Ten

It had taken a few weeks of hard travel, but the group of mostly C-ranked adventurers had finally reached a city large enough to have a Guild office, an Elven embassy, and a church with a B-ranked priest. Going to the embassy first, as the Elf in their midst had seniority, they made their report to the incredulous Elven ambassadors, inciting a near riot as they rushed to make memory stones to hold the news.

Memory stones were Beast Cores that had been further refined by Essence to be able to hold copies of memories, skills, or other pertinent information. When someone used a memory stone, they would gain all of the information in the stone as their own ideas and memories, allowing them to gain knowledge quickly and easily. This helped with learning skills, cultivation techniques, and even fighting styles. Depending on the quality, more people could use them before their power was exhausted, at which point they would crumble and become useless. Higher grade stones could be refined with Mana and were able to hold items in a sub-dimensional space, nicknamed a 'Bag of Holding' as these high-grade stones were usually attached to bags in order to hide their identity, being very expensive to purchase.

A few Elven delegates were selected for their endurance, rare amongst Elves, given supplies and a memory stone each, and told to make for the Elven nation, allowing nothing to stop them. Their horses were spelled, allowing them to run the entire distance without discomfort, and the Elves were given potions that would mimic the effects of a good night of rest. Riding within the hour, the Elven nation would soon prepare to move part of its population to this newfound Silverwood location.

Their Elven leader's mission complete, the party split to make their individual reports. Most went to the Guild, but the priest went directly to the Church. After a short prayer near the altar, he went in search of the Bishop. Although he needed to wait a short while, he was admitted when they heard the seriousness of his business.

"Good afternoon, my child," the sonorous voice of the bishop spoke. "Tell me of your travels."

"Thank you for seeing me, your grace." The cleric gave a short bow. "With the rumor of a dungeon being discovered in the mountains, we were dispatched to check the rumors validity. As per regulation, we gathered a Mage, B-ranked, several Guild warriors, and myself to determine if the dungeon were an infernal cesspool. Upon arrival to the village, we were guided to the entrance of what was indeed a dungeon and quickly and easily dispatched the creatures inside. While we did find plants with a vampiric effect, there was no evidence beyond that to suggest infernal designs."

Taking a breath, he continued, "To ensure this, I lowered my blessed pendant to the dungeon Core. Far from being destroyed or even slightly damaged, my pendant was absorbed."

"Is it a celestial dungeon, then?" the Bishop interrupted, nearly as concerned about this possibility as he was at the thought of an infernal dungeon.

The cleric shook his head. "I was unable to discern that fact, but as we were leaving, a small mushroom appeared in the first room. We killed it, but as loot, it dropped... this." He pulled out his restored pendant, handing it to his spiritual leader with a flourish.

Brow furrowed, the bishop inspected the pendant and the Essence contained within. "This is odd. It has no affinity that I can sense, but it certainly is a Runed item. The Inscription to turn aside infernal creatures is correct but cannot be activated without being filled with celestial energy. Therefore, I am sorry to say, this is useless."

Crestfallen, the cleric sat down. "I had hoped you would be able to find what affinity it had. I just assumed my knowledge was insufficient to ascertain its origins."

"We can always try prayer." The bishop held the pendant in his hand and began to pray. The celestial Essence which was his greatest strength extended to and entered the Inscription on the pendant's face. Dropping the necklace after an instant, the bishop looked at it in shock.

"Your grace?"

"W-we need to build a church in that area forthwith." The Bishop looked down at the pendant which was now nearly humming with celestial energy. "As my prayer touched it, all of the Essence it contained gained a celestial affinity. This pendant alone represents six months of Inscription work, purification, and prayer. If that dungeon drops more, we will have a potent weapon against the darkness in the world. I think... I think I know the perfect person. Go and find Father Richard for me."

The cleric blanched at this order.

FRANK

The group that went into the Guild was finally able to relax as they returned to their erstwhile home. Grabbing some beer from the counter, they dropped an expense report with the secretary and moved to make their accounting. Explaining that there was indeed a new dungeon, no the mountains had not finally driven the sheepherders insane, the local Guild leader was about to dismiss this as a beginner training area of no importance when he was told of the Elven nation's mobilization.

The Guild Master twitched, and he just knew he would be getting a headache soon. "What? Why? No! Come on! It is a low F-ranked at best, suitable for giving our fishies some combat experience, and you told us it dropped only copper on the Mob death. The loot isn't even good enough for us to justify setting up a *training camp* there. It is too far out of the way!" He was concerned by this direction of events. When the Silverwood tree was explained, he closed his eyes and grit his teeth.

"Oh, you boys just love dropping a shit-storm of politics on my head don't you?" At their confused glances, he growled, "That land is already contested by the human Kingdoms of the Phoenix and the Lion; now the Elves are going to be making a claim. We need to get there first." The Guild Master groaned softly, sitting back against his chair.

He created and sent out orders for craftsmen, hunters, and fighters to prepare to march to the mountain. He also sent a message to the Mages' Guild, a high level of the Adventurers' Guild that only B-ranked cultivators or higher were allowed entry to. Asking for inscribers and enchanters for an emergency mission, he specifically asked for members who specialized in dimensional magic, as he had a feeling that a portal to this disgustingly remote location would be exceedingly beneficial.

A chill passing over him, he turned to the patiently waiting, slightly tipsy group. "What was the affinity of the dungeon?"

"Far as we could tell, it didn't seem to have one, Frank." The large man from the scouting party belched.

"Is that so? Hey! It is *Guild Master* Frank to you, bub." A distant look passed through Frank's eyes, and he amended his message to the Mage Guild. No affinity and a Silverwood tree?

That was a combination that promised fast advancement through the cultivation ranks. That could offer power and great influence to whoever established themselves in the area. Frank now intended to lead the first group of settlers and to stake a claim. This sort of thing didn't come along every day, after all.

Chapter Eleven

The bunny's death provided me with intimate knowledge of its pattern, and I expected the energy to slam into me as usual, so I braced myself for impact. Instead, the Chi spiral showed its usefulness for the first time ever! Where the energy had before stuffed my core full of the newly-gained Essence instantly, it now surrounded me and was held in a slowly swirling pattern in the outer spiral, awaiting cultivation.

<Wow! Look at that!> I was thrilled by this new development, and I really wanted Dani to be excited too.

"Yeah, that looks neat. I am glad you are holding that spiral so well. I kind of expected you to get lazy when you weren't getting much Essence! Don't be too surprised now. That *is* what is supposed to happen." Dani was a master at making a compliment into an advertisement for a better work ethic.

<It finally makes sense why I have to hold this pattern for cultivation! Now I can refine the Essence into Chi threads on my schedule rather than having to get rid of the excess! It's all coming together.> I knew I should never doubt Dani, but until now, the intricate pattern I had been forcing myself to hold seemed to have no purpose while taking a lot of effort and concentration to maintain.

Waiting till I had fully processed all of the Essence, which took an hour or so even with all my attention being bent to the task, I made two young rabbits. Instead of feeding them Essence until fully grown like I could have done, I tried to conserve the energy I had remaining. They would grow quickly in the Essence-rich air of my dungeon anyway and should be able to mate soon; especially since the pattern I had focused on while creating them gave extra strength to their fecundity.

<How long until they can reproduce naturally?> I offhandedly interrogated Dani, my attention focused on watching my new creatures bound around the room playfully.

"Well," she snorted, a very unladylike sound, "seeing as you have two male rabbits, it may be a long time."

That shouldn't be too much of a problem. <What time frame are we looking at here? Like three, four days?>

She released an explosion of air, a cross between a snort and a chuckle, remembering that I had only been aware of life for a few months. "More like never, Cal."

<Uhm.>

"You need a female in order for them to... copulate, Cal." She seemed frustrated, knowing I didn't understand her laughter or odd embarrassment. She started floating toward the entrance. "I'll go try and lure one down here."

<You can do that?> That could be handy in the future. Why hadn't she done that before?

She laughed in a haughty tone, as if to highlight my ignorance. "I am a will-o-the wisp! I am the preeminent expert at luring all manner of creatures to their doom."

<If you say so. Hurry home!> Never know when someone is going to attack, after all.

She stopped in midair, hovering malevolently. "Who said I'm going right now? Maybe I want a nap!"

I hadn't thought of that! We had been rather busy, after all. <Oh sorry, you normally only sleep once every few days so I–>

"Cal, I'm being intentionally difficult. Ugh. I'll be back shortly. We need to work on your understanding of sarcasm."

She did indeed return shortly. Apparently, there was a rabbit warren nearby, but until the stairs were put in place, there was no way for them to reach me. The rabbit that followed Dani down in a hypnotized state was larger than the first bunny had been. Dani later explained that this was because it was an animal. Usually females tended to be larger than the male, an interesting concept as only male creatures besides Dani had entered my dungeon to this point. In the time it took for a spike from a shroom to find the skull of the female rabbit, I had a slightly altered pattern of the rabbit ready to be used. I made a few young versions and waited impatiently for them to reach adulthood.

DALE

Guild Master Frank looked at the staircase leading to the depths below. A gust of wind blew a spicy mixture of scents upward, and he could feel a hint of raw Essence.

"This is the place, huh?" Frank turned toward the owner of the land, Dale.

"Indeed, milord," a nervous Dale spoke. Although now the richest man in his village, he knew the Guild Master could likely crush him with the weight of his wallet, using his strength or influence to kill every person Dale knew without facing any repercussions.

"Not much to look at are ya?" Frank glanced at the now uncomfortable Dale.

"E-excuse me?"

Frank shook his head and started again, "Look, Dave–"

"Dale. Common mistake, sir." Dale paled with the realization he had interrupted this powerful figure.

Frank grunted at the correction. "Whatever. Listen, you are about to become more wealthy than most small towns. The standard Guild agreement is five percent of all profit from the dungeon will go to you, the finder and owner of the land."

Dale coughed as he interrupted again, "Sir, I plan on giving a portion of that to the families of the men who found it with me and died trying to escape." Luckily for him, the jerk he had murdered had no family. "Will that, uhm, be an issue?"

"Huh. Good on you, lad. Might actually be worth me remembering your name. Your money, I don't care what you do with it," Frank disinterestedly offered, though Dale brightened significantly at the words. "I have a different idea for our agreement. The standard is all well and good, but think on this. For the first five years, you get *three* percent. That should still be an income of several gold per *week* as it matures, a bit less before then."

"During those years, the other two percent comes to me, and I will use it to outfit you with a team, basic equipment, food, lodging, and teachers who will help you fix that... mess... of a cultivation base you have." Frank gestured at Dale when he said this, making him flush with embarrassment, though he didn't understand the insult.

Frank gave a short explanation of cultivation to Dale when he saw the obvious confusion on his face. He informed Dale that everything passively absorbed Essence as long as it lived. Even plants that lived long enough could even become somewhat powerful as their cultivation slowly and naturally allowed them to become stronger. There was a certain disadvantage to this, though because even when people did not actively cultivate their Essence, they still absorbed some from their strongest affinities through passive accumulation.

Since they had no Chi spiral and therefore didn't reduce the amount of corruption they obtained, their cultivation base became full of tainted Essence, which spread through their bodies, eventually killing them as 'old age' set in. Dale was obviously suited to the earthen element, showing surprisingly strong affinity by pulling in large amounts of the tainted Essence. The issue here was that he reeked of corruption to the trained senses of the Guild Master. With low Essence and high corruption in his cultivation base, Dale would never be able to move into the higher ranks of cultivation. Heck, if he kept pulling earthen corruption at this rate, Dale would die of a heart attack in ten years, tops.

"Thank you for explaining a bit about cultivation, sir, but as to giving up all of that profit... Why would I do that? How would that help me? That is a *lot* of money, sir." The confused young man worried that Frank was trying to swindle him. Just because he was from a poor village didn't mean he was stupid!

Frank nodded and calmly began listing his thoughts on the matter, "There are a lot of reasons someone would kill you. For now, just the income you are going to receive will be enough for some. You will also soon gain political enemies, as you will receive a vote on any matters pertaining to the growth or destruction of this dungeon. If you stay at the fishy rank, they may kill you out of hand just to get you out of the way." Dale had paled as he realized the accuracy of each implied threat, so Frank paused to let him think and absorb the information for a moment.

"If you accept my terms, I will also admit you into the Guild directly, which will give you good people to turn to for advice or help. You will have a perfect dungeon to train in without having to fear traitors in your party; with us beside you, you will have a unified front against people who try to take advantage of you."

Dale didn't know what to say, and his mouth opened and closed a few times.

"Of course," Frank nonchalantly continued, "you will have to obey our laws, but they are very straightforward. Oh, and after the first five years, you will return to five percent income, beyond what you personally make of course. This continues until your death, at which point any heirs you produce will split the income."

Still, no words were passing Dale's lips.

Frank decided to roll out the heavy hitter, as casually as possible. "One more thing, if you reach the Mage rank of cultivation, B-rank that is, your natural lifespan tends to jump into the *hundreds* of years. Unless killed, you won't die for a *very* long time. At the Saint rank–or S-rank–we have been unable to determine the natural lifespan. It is just too long for anyone but another Saint to measure," Frank finished, letting the temptation flow.

Dale finally found his voice, "I... Wow! Of course, I accept! Yes, and thank you, sir!"

Frank grinned at Dale's newfound exuberance. "Excellent! And no more calling me sir. I work for a living. It is 'Frank' when we are alone with our Guild or 'Guild Master' around strangers. We will get you outfitted tomorrow and start your training right away. Report to me at first light."

CAL

It had been about two months since the group had last left my area when Dani told me people were gathering above. I had made few improvements since then, mostly cosmetic, no new rooms. The Mobs, at least, were more interesting than they had been.

The rabbits' population had exploded, the best part being that they were all under my control. Since I had created their parents, even these new creatures were dungeon born, meaning they were given life through my power as a dungeon. Their living in me generated plenty of Essence, which I constantly gathered a significant amount passively. Enough Essence, in fact, that my plants were near obsolete as an energy source but still grown to feed the rabbits.

That reminded me, a minor yet entertaining war had occurred as the rabbits ate the plants and the shrooms tried to rescue them. Due to this civil war, I had imprinted on both subsets that they were not to fight each other, and the rabbits would need to eat from certain areas. They started getting along far better, albeit uneasily, when I forced the arrangement. The different groups moved to be on friendly terms when the mushrooms found that rabbit feces were excellent fertilizer.

I had, of course, evolved the rabbits. Their natural pattern put them in F-rank two, and I was able to increase the average Mob to F-rank five. I was still stuck in F-rank eight myself but was hoping for a breakthrough soon. With so much varied life, the Essence in the rooms became denser, as the amount produced was more than I was able to consume and cultivate on a daily basis. Not only was this good for the creatures living in me, as it helped them grow, but Dani assured me that dungeoneers would be ecstatic as well.

Evolving the rabbits had greatly benefitted them; they now had far stronger muscles in their bodies and a stronger skeletal frame to match. When their bones ossified to accommodate their new system, a smooth nub of bone had also grown on their skulls. I had originally assumed this was the start of a horn, but it never seemed to develop past a nub. The reason for this growth soon became apparent. No longer timid creatures, they competed for food and mates by sprinting at their adversary, jumping and head-butting them with their bone nubs. When they jumped, their bodies grew rigid as they braced for impact, and their bone nubs cracked into their opponent. The first to fall unconscious lost the right to the mate or feeding ground they were after. I had named them Bashers, and I thought they were adorable.

I hadn't been able to develop a new Boss, and I was now out of spare Essence to experiment without becoming dangerously low on power for a few weeks. Being that my current Boss was at the maximum ranking I could create, it was not that I could make a stronger one, though I was hoping that I could make a mobile one. Directing a few of the Bashers into the Boss room to help him during the fights, I settled in to wait for some easy prey. I was as prepared as I could be.

Dale

Dale slept poorly that night, as the excitement the next day would hold plagued his dreams. He awoke before dawn and broke his fast with some leftover foodstuff. When the rest of the small tent city began to rouse, he went to the main Guild tent to await the Guild Master, still gnawing on some tough yet filling jerky.

"Oh good, you're punctual. I was going to have my boys douse you with a bucket of water if you were still sleeping!" Frank laughed jovially.

"Ha...?" Dale chuckled, petering off as he saw the serious looks and slowly shaking heads from the working staff that were being directed at him warningly.

"Well, let's get started. I have a tutor for you to help catch you up on the basics. Did you bring any money with you?" Frank looked at him questioningly. When Dale shook his head, silently cursing his stupidity, Frank continued, "No matter, we'll put it on your credit. I know you will be good for it after all! Our agreement was only for standard equipment, but I'd prefer to give you armor that you will be able to use for a longer time. If we do that, though, you will need to pay the difference. Is that reasonable?" Frank waited for Dale to nod, almost imperceptible as his eyes wandered over all of the treasures displayed just in the tent they were standing in. "Great! I will cover the cost of repairs for you when you need them. You'll pay us for the equipment over time then, but the tutor is on me, as per our agreement."

They moved into a storeroom and started looking at the available equipment. The prices attached to them made Dale choke a bit, but Frank efficiently moved along the rows, pointing at armor for the staff on duty to bring them. A full set of plate armor was eventually gathered by the leader before they moved into an armory to find a good weapon to use.

"Every swung a sword before?" At the expected negative, Frank grunted and moved on, "Axe?" No trees on the mountain, only around the base. "Bow?" Wouldn't be able to use it in plate armor. "War mace it is. Maybe a morningstar," he mused, tossing a few ideas around. "I'd start you with a spear, but in a confined space like a dungeon, that is more of a–shall we say–liability."

Deciding on a morningstar, Frank turned on Dale and demandingly grilled him, "You know how to use one of these?" It was essentially a stick with a spiked metal ball at the top.

Dale tried to inject some humor, "Spikey ball goes into the enemy?"

"Correct! I think we found the armament for you." Frank grinned and handed the weapon over.

They moved into a tent with the purchased equipment, and the staff helped him put on all of his new, shining armor. It was a matching set, so Dale thought he looked rather dashing. The layers kept coming on, first the padding, then the chainmail, and finally the plate armor. It was so heavy that Dale could barely move; if he hadn't been fairly used to hard work, he wouldn't have been able to stand. Finally, Frank came over with a shield, presenting it as a short term gift.

"This is an enchanted training buckler. It is the smallest shield type, but I really don't think you should carry too much more weight." Frank looked frankly at his already straining and sweating initiate. "It is called a 'training' type armor because it helps you to learn to block correctly." He demonstrated by swinging his fist, and the shield pulled Dale's arm into position to stop it. "You are going to want to learn how to use a shield correctly as fast as possible. It'll save lives–especially yours."

"Wow! Why is it short term? This is great!" Dale enthused, happy that this shield could block attacks for him.

"Allow me to demonstrate." Tossing a rock to the side of Dale, Frank moved in and slapped him in the face as the shield swung to knock the rock away. "It tries to block the first threat, and it'll take more muscle than you have to put it somewhere else."

Dale felt his teeth to make sure none had loosened. "Well. Point taken."

"I'm just glad we waited before putting on your helmet," Frank mentioned. Dale groaned internally at the thought of more armor.

Frank did not take kindly to the whining. "Until sundown, you are going to wear that armor, each day until I tell you otherwise. You are far enough behind your group that you will need to train constantly to catch up. Your muscles will hate you now, but you'll thank me later. Eventually, you might move to a different fighting style and wear less armor, but for now, we do things my way."

A staff member walked over and handed Dale his bill. "Here you are, Sir Knight. We have applied the Guild discount, of course."

Dale's eyes nearly left his skull as he saw the total. One platinum, thirty gold, forty silver, and six copper. That was more money than everyone on this mountain combined had ever seen before. Would he ever be able to pay this off?

"You are going to need to work hard, but I think you have what it takes to succeed. I sense serious ambition in you lad," Frank spoke kindly. Dale's mind flashed to murdering Tim, and he nodded. Dale had ambition in spades. "I'm going to send you to your tutor now. Pay attention to what he says because that armor will mean nothing if you fail to improve yourself."

They walked over to a group of men preparing their armor and weapons. Unlike Dale who had shining armor, those in the group who wore it had scratched, dented, well worn, and patchwork armor. Walking directly to a man wearing only wrapped cloth, no discernable armor at all, Frank introduced him as Craig, a monk and Essence specialist. A monk was not a religious man like a cleric but someone who focused on their chosen martial arts to the exclusion of all other knowledge. As an Essence specialist, he would have focused all of his life on cultivation and Essence management, making him an unmatched expert and teacher in his area of study.

"Craig will be your supervisor and tutor. He also has an affinity for earthen Essence, so he will be able to give you the very best guidance." Frank handed a memory stone to Dale, telling him that it would allow him to skip a few steps in learning how to control his Essence. "Craig, if you would be so kind as to teach him how to properly cultivate, I would appreciate it. It'll be better if he knows now before we strip him. Last time didn't work out well." With this ominous foreshadowing, he handed Craig a small item, wished Dale good luck, and set off to start working for the rest of his busy day.

"Nice to meet you all. My name is Dale," Dale stated. "So... how do we start?"

"You the guy who found this shithole?" one of the men grunted, polishing a massive shield.

"Um. Yeah," Dale stammered. The other man coughed, hawked up some mucus and spit to the side.

"Great."

Craig spoke then, ignoring pleasantries and launching directly into lecture mode, "Dale, you are what we call a 'fishy'. This means you are an F-ranked newbie, thrashing around and trying to figure out what is going on. You are going to be useless in there today and even more so tomorrow. Let me be very clear about what we want you to do. Your job in the dungeon is to *not die.* No heroics, you do only what we tell you to. That is *it.* You follow?"

"Yes. Sorry," Dale apologized, not even sure why he was doing so.

"Don't be sorry. Just pay attention. We were all there once, but for us, it was many years ago. I'm going to give you a cultivation technique, and since it'll be going through a memory stone, you'll be able to use it without years of practice. That'll let you catch up quick, once we fix this," he waved his hand at Dale's entire body, "cesspool of a center you have going on here." He reached out and motioned for the stone Frank had given Dale. Dale dropped it in his hand as he wondered what could possibly be so bad about him that everyone kept mentioning that he was filthy on the inside.

Craig took the memory stone and placed it against his head. Focusing intently for a few moments, a silvery light streamed into it. Handing it back to Dale, he told him to press it against his forehead and try not to fall over. He enunciated 'try' a bit too much for Dale to be happy about.

"That's it?" Dale inquired, looking at the glittering stone in his hand. The light inside of it seemed to whisper to his senses.

"That's it," Craig promised.

Pressing the stone against his head, knowledge of how to consciously pull in Essence from the earth and earthen sources flooded his mind. Dale saw how to control the Essence, allowing it to flow through into his body to his center without damaging himself or gaining too much corruption and how to begin a Chi spiral so he didn't waste the Essence he gained. Most importantly to Dale, he could finally see what his own center looked like.

The clearer the energy, the better, as it showed high refinement and low corruption. When Essence was poorly processed, it retained some of the features of its source. While Craig's memory of his center, which came along from the memory stone, looked quite clear with only a tinge of coloration showing his affinity, Dale's looked like a mixture of mud and feces. Cesspool of a Core indeed.

"Oh my." Dale nearly gagged. He tried to start a Chi spiral like he was supposed to, but the thick Essence in his center only bubbled and moved like mucus, refusing to do more than ooze in a circle. "What actually *is* this corruption?"

Craig was watching him and nodded when he saw him try to move the corrupted Essence. "Good question. Listen up, I'll only explain this now, and never again. Corruption is a side effect of the energy of the heavens and the earth being turned into the universal basic elements. Everything begins as purest energy, but the world creates things out of it, yes?"

Dale nodded. "So, rocks and stuff?"

"Pretty much. To do this, the item is formed, but then its 'identity' seeps into the pure Essence, corrupting it. A rock, which at its basic form is this stored energy, adds its 'identity' to the energy, which then becomes earthen Essence. Essence joins together in complex ways to form combinations which form what we call higher Essences. Fire and water to form steam, water and earth to plant, and so forth. Those lucky enough to gain affinities in multiple elements can become higher level cultivators very quickly if they have access to all of the elements they need. For instance, fire, water, and earth form a soot affinity. The combinations are endless, allowing for any kind of material or even life," Craig lectured briefly. "Essence is endless, and the more of each type of basic Essence in an area, the more Essence is generated. If you somehow got all of them to coexist together, you would have a very powerful Essence generator."

"Your job now is to try to purify all the Essence you can accumulate back to its cleanest state within your center. Now you understand? Any more questions? No? Good. We're going to take care of the mess you have right now, don't worry. After that, it is up to you and your hard work," Craig finished, ignoring the fact that Dale actually was trying to ask more questions.

They began their descent into the darkness below.

CHAPTER TWELVE

<People are on the stairs, Dani. Get ready for an incursion! This is gonna be *awe-some*,> I nearly sang, enthusiasm dancing in my mental voice.

The group approached my entrance, moved into formation and started their workday. Now that I had semi-intelligent creatures under my influence, I could move into my Mobs' minds and directly control their movement. I was only good enough at this to do it one at a time but was assured—by Dani of course—that with practice, I could control a squad of monsters at the same time. The rabbits were hidden in the thick vegetation, so the room had no significant difference from the original mushroom-Mob appearance. This would be fun!

The men walked in and began slashing at the Shroomishes, quickly targeting the ranged Banes. When their attention was focused on a particularly thick grouping of mushrooms, I sent <Attack!> into the minds of the hidden rabbits. Taking direct control of the largest, I launched my new body at the back of someone's knee. A direct hit in the tender pressure point and the man fell. The attacks on the other humans had varying degrees of success with a few landing decent hits against legs, some bouncing off armor, and one even being knocked away by a shield that moved when the guy wasn't even looking! He must be really aware of his surroundings.

The dozens of rabbits were almost entirely silent, but when they hit armor, it sounded like metal being beaten or, as Dani told me, a 'gong' or hail falling on tin. The man who had fallen was being pummeled, but his thick armor allowed him to quickly regain his footing. One man stepped on a spike-filled Shroomish, which had to hurt as he twisted his ankle, but even the underside of his boot was armored enough to stop the spike from entering his flesh.

The men had been taken by surprise but were an efficient team and quickly turned the tides against me. A sword dropped down, slaying some Bashers, but most of my creatures were nimble enough to avoid it. A few of the fighters used weapons that required less skill, such as a staff, while another struck with his fists, and these quickly decimated my ranks. Sounding a retreat, I directed the Bashers into a bolt hole which made it impossible to attack them without magic.

"Did they just run away? I've never seen Mobs run away before." One of the men sounded suspicious of my motives. Good.

An answering grunt came in reply, then resolved into words, "Ugh. Just keep an eye out. We don't want to be ambushed again. These aren't magical Beasts, right? Just weird looking, mutated rabbits?"

"Looks that way." A few answering grunts showed the others' agreement.

They moved further in, ignoring the other plants. Entering my first tunnel, I really wanted to hit them from behind, but they were too wary. I didn't want to lose more creatures, though I captured the energy they released upon death, which was enough for me to bring a new one back to roughly the same stage of life. If I made them young instead and let them grow unaided at an accelerated rate, I gained much more Essence than I had invested in their progenitors; it was actually a nice way to gain Essence quickly.

Skillfully avoiding traps, the group rested just before entering my second room. When they had finished catching their breath and with looks of determination, they moved to attack the denizens of the second room. A similar situation developed, and by the time they had killed half of the prolific Bashers, their legs had to be in great pain. Take that! Minor inconveniences! Even with the armor, each hit was as strong as a decent mace blow landing and must have been doing some damage. The only one I couldn't seem to hit was wearing almost no armor whatsoever, just some kind of cloth, and I was nervous that he would be casting spells soon.

Sounding the retreat once more, I watched as they inspected the loot I dropped for each death–usually just a couple copper, but if they managed to take out the one I was inhabiting, I gave them a bit extra. Nothing major, usually extra coins or a boot if I felt I could get away with it. So far they had found three *left* boots. Maybe I am evil.

I really was getting frustrated. Why did I have such high-level groups? I studied them as they entered the next tunnel and could see that most of them were C-ranked, but the one with the shield was F-ranked! I decided to focus on him as my most likely meal.

When they entered the third room, I waited until they had cleared about half the room before the Bashers attacked, and I had most of them charge at the shielded one. Right before they jumped, a Bane hiding on the ceiling fired a thorn directly at his head, and he *blocked* it! This did open him up for attack from the Bashers, and sensing victory, they pounced as hard as they could, pummeling his shiny armor from multiple sides.

He dropped to the ground! Redoubling their efforts, they slammed against him, trying to crack his metal shell. He weakly counterattacked, but the Bashers easily dodged. They continued throwing themselves at him. Then I realized I was down to only two in the room. I had gotten too focused and forgot to retreat, dang it. The group finished the remaining two off and tried to gather their collective breaths.

"What the abyss?" gasped the one I had been beating on.

"They must have decided you were the weak link and gone for the kill. They seemed to frenzy a bit there. None of em ran this time," the unarmored one verbalized. "You okay to continue?"

"Yeah," Dale spit out a bit of blood, weakly finishing with, "try not to let 'em hit your chest, guys."

"Duly noted."

"And why are there so many boots down here?!" That got a chuckle from his team and from me.

They limped toward the final room, preparing to meet the Boss. Peeking at him from around the corner, they decided on their battle plan. Too bad for them, I could hear every word, of course. I adjusted my plan accordingly and got ready for their charge. None of them had ranged weapons, an obvious lack, which would put them in the best range of the Bloody Bane. Since he had no real intelligence, I could not directly control him, but the hidden Bashers were ready for my hostile takeover. I watched the group countdown to zero on their fingers, then silently charge the Boss.

<Terrible idea, really,> I thought maliciously.

The F-ranked man had stayed near the entrance, so when the Bloody Bane released a cloud of poisonous spores, he was outside of it. These men were so strong that the poison was really only enough to deal a little damage, make them cough, and whatnot. The poison would have been far more effective on the weak one in the now-not-so-shiny armor. Ah well, such is life. Time to go with plan B. The carpet of moss constricted, grabbing the weak one's foot. A Basher hitting him from behind convinced the youngster to fall flat on his face into the moss as it dragged him as fast as possible to the Bane. The other members were finishing off the Boss when the lightly armored one noticed his predicament and came to his aid.

Drat, I had nearly maneuvered around that armor! I let a holy symbol drop as a token of my appreciation for the good fight and would make sure to talk to Dani later about ways to improve my tactics. They got very excited by the holy symbol for some reason, probably the etched Inscription that came pre-made on it, so I decided to make that more... rare, in the future.

DALE

"You guys okay? Dale uttered around a swelling lip.

"My legs feel tenderized, but I'm fine otherwise," grouched the burly man carrying the massive shield near the front.

"Pretty good for such a low ranked place," commented a man who was wielding daggers. "Did you see that necklace? I wonder if it is legitimately inscribed..."

"Let's bring it to a cleric when we are done here—could be worth something. We need to move on to the next stage, though." Craig abruptly cut off the conversation.

"What would that be?" Dale's voice wavered apprehensively, as the other men turned to look at him with varying degrees of either pity or excitement.

Craig exhaled through his nose and turned toward Dale. "Remember how we said we were going to get rid of that corruption?"

"Well, yeah. That was the whole point of this right? That's why we had to be near that Silverwood tree... right?" Dale looked at the men nervously while pointing at the small sapling.

The men had surrounded him now, and Craig continued in an eerily calm voice, "Not quite. For one thing, that tree is too immature still but mainly that is a higher level technique. It helps people break into the B-ranks and convert their Essence to Mana. No, we are going to actually remove all the Essence from your center... by force."

Dale started looking around a bit wildly. "Um."

"It isn't like we are going to beat you, kid. Relax," the dagger-wielding man tried to calm him down. "Still, it isn't exactly a fun process. Here, start drinking." He handed Dale a water skin. "Drink until you think you are going to hurl, then drink more."

"Okay..." Removing his helmet with hidden relief, Dale took the water and drank. Every time he stopped or slowed, the other men told him to keep going. When he was looking queasy and obviously holding back his bile, Craig motioned for him to stop.

"This next part is dangerous for you. You are going to swallow this." He handed Dale the small package the Guild Master had given him. "It is a Beast Core. What happens when a Beast Core is swallowed is very, hmm, interesting. If done willingly, all of the Essence in your Core will flow into the gem, taking the corruption with it."

"Then it will continue pulling Essence from your body until there is nothing in you but your personal life force, which it will also take if possible. Unwillingly ingesting one leads to a different fate, but we'll not have that issue, *right*?" Craig eyed Dale with a threat lingering in his voice.

Ensuring Dale was paying attention, Craig looked him in the eyes and enunciated, "When I tell you to–and *not* before–you need to begin cultivating as fast as you can. You now know how to; that technique is a permanent part of your memories.

Draw the Essence in this cavern into yourself as fast and cleanly as you can with your new technique. We'll start your Chi spiral before we leave. Make sure you follow my directions exactly. The timing of this can be tricky. If you start too early, you are going to leave corruption in you. Too late, and you die. Get it? Listen to me through the pain."

"The pain?!" Dale challenged, his head swimming.

"Forceful removal of what allows you to *live* tends to hurt a bit. The job of your fine squad members is to get that Core out of you when it is time, hence drinking all that water. You're going to get punched in the stomach a bit. Which reminds me, armor off the top half," Craig directed as if he had not just told Dale he was going to be attacked by the shield holding mans' ham-sized fists.

Dale complied, forcing himself to stay calm, though the whites of his eyes were showing and he was starting to breathe heavily. After reducing the weight on himself, he grabbed the water skin drank more. He was nearly sick, but he told himself that anything to reduce the following stomach blows would help in the long run. Bracing himself, Dale waited for Craig to give the signal to start. It didn't take long.

"Go."

A bit more water helped the small gem slither down his throat, and Dale focused his mind on the filthy energy within him. There seemed to be no effect, and he wondered if this were just an excuse to terrify him or beat him up. Then he 'saw' a tendril of light leave the gem and reach for his center, twisting and turning through channels that Dale couldn't understand. The light connected; Dale then saw a gentle brown light pull away from his center back to the Core. It was a nice, tingly feeling until the murky brown Essence touched the surface of the Core.

The energy ripped at his Core suddenly, taking in the Essence like a starving man eating cake. The pain came then, feeling like acid washing through his blood, destroying the tissue and knitting it together by grasping his flayed flesh and nailing it back down with salt covered spikes. Darker Essence flowed like blood from a ruptured artery into the Core, which was also growing muddy. Dale was gasping, on his knees as he watched this unfold inside himself. Eyes wild, he saw the last few Wisps of Essence leave his center, emptying it completely. For a moment the pain subsided, Dale thinking it was over somehow.

The pain erupted again–in new and torturous ways. Like a hollow needle had entered his veins, sharp pain penetrated dozens of points on his body and pulled with a strong vacuuming force. Every bit of the corruption inside of him was being pulled to the Core, which was *not* being gentle. Dale's nose began to bleed as his head shook violently, looking for any escape from the pain.

Craig grabbed his head to help control the seizure. "Almost time now, Dale. Focus! If you don't cultivate and we get the Core out of you, your life energy will attempt to fill the void, which will assuredly kill you. Feel the energy around you, and get ready to pull! Let nothing else matter!"

Dale's mind shook. The world was wavy around him, his head spinning. He opened his eyes, revealing burst blood vessels and reached out for the energy of the heavens and the earth, preparing to pull it in as soon as Craig said...

"Now! Do it now!" Craig shouted. For a brief, shining moment, the pain abated again as the gem looked for a new source of Essence to fill itself. Dale knew this relief was a lie and began cultivating. Having never done it intentionally before but knowing how, the energy stalled a bit at first, then started to flow into him steadily. The Core, which had almost latched on to its host's life energy, found a new and easily accessible meal. Returning the pull back to Dale's center where the Essence was beginning to accumulate, it was nearly drinking this fresh source when Dale's body began to shudder from well-placed blows.

"Bleaeghght!" The huge amount of water ingested previously happily made a reappearance, cheerfully splattering across anyone who didn't move fast enough. Some well-digested jerky found a new home, and after a few waves, finally, a small gem appeared.

To those present, it was obvious that energy was trying to reach back into Dale from the gem, trying to re-establish the connection it had momentarily lost. Using the steel-shod end of a staff, one of the men crushed the gem, releasing a flash of brown light. Turning to look at Dale, the group waited as he scrambled to absorb Essence properly. Craig watched him carefully, nodding at the tiny spiral that was forming. He corrected Dale gently a few times, allowing the energy to be as pure as Dale could make it.

"This is as easy as it is going to get, Dale," Craig promised him. "For some reason, the Essence in here has no affinity. You can pull the Essence from all around you, and it is nearly free of any taint. Personally, I love it here, Mobs and all." The other men nodded agreement, all settling in to cultivate. "We can only stay so long, though. Eventually, the Essence in the air will lessen, and we will need to leave in order for it to replenish. Once out of here, your spiral will be pure, but you will need to continue to cultivate. Make the threads as small as possible, and remember to purify it as much as possible before you absorb it."

Dale was still pale, bruises showing and his body shaking. Never before had he been this tired, and he wanted to collapse. As he pulled more Essence into himself, he remembered how foul his center had been before and vowed to have the purest Essence of any of his fellows.

Time passed as it always did, and the room's ambient Essence began to wane. Dale still pulled in more until Craig gently made him stand and don his armor. "Remember to keep that spiral going. Soon, it'll continue even in your sleep and become natural to you. Grab your weapon. We don't know how many Mobs we are going to have to fight to get out of here."

CHAPTER THIRTEEN

I was stunned by the actions of these men. Was this a normal occurrence? When they crushed the Beast Core, it released all of the man's accumulated Essence into me. I greedily took the gift, shunting the corruption into the stone around the room, making it stronger. Though the young man—who I now recognized as the one who had first escaped me—had taken off his armor, it never moved far enough away from the group to allow me to absorb it. Too bad, but what can you do? I made plans to get his armor when he made a mistake in the future.

The real shock came when the group sat and began to cultivate. I was carefully watching for any chance to attack them when their auras allowed me to pass through for the first time ever! While they refined their Essence, I was able to direct some of it to myself. Not having to refine it on my own allowed me to add it directly to my own spiral. I was still considering the implications when the group stood and made their way to the entrance. In the last few hours, my spiral had significantly increased in size, which allowed it to spin much faster. When it spun faster, the fine threads also attached to my Chi spiral more rapidly. The stronger I became, the easier it was to gain Essence more quickly.

Also, as an added bonus, there was a small pool of acid that I was able to study. It seemed like very strong acid, and as I absorbed it, it became apparent that the sulphuric acid could become a potent weapon if used properly. I also studied the broken Beast Core and realized that it had a similar makeup to my own gem.

<Dani, am I a Beast Core?> I seemed to catch her off guard, and she scrambled for an answer.

“Mm, kind of. Sorry, I thought we went over this earlier. You were originally a soul gem, which is a Beast Core that has undergone strong refinement. It is pretty rare because it takes at a minimum a Mage with infernal capabilities to produce, and I’ve never heard of them using it for human souls before you,” Dani expressed thoughtfully. “Most infernal users have to go into hiding if they want to get stronger, as most places frown upon demon summoning and Necromancy.”

<Can’t imagine why,> I dryly stated. <I think I can replicate the Beast Core; would that be at all useful?>

She perked up at this statement, “Seriously? Yeah, that could really come in handy. You could use them to store excess Essence in, like really weak Mana accumulators, which could help you if you are getting too much at once to absorb.”

She gleefully continued, “Also, you could try and attach them to your Mobs. A Beast Core in a creature allows them to jump to the first level of sentience when they accumulate enough Essence and have a Chi spiral. Then your Mobs could become stronger than you while you retain control of them. Since you gave it life, even if the Mob died, you would be able to re-absorb the energy contained in the Core and re-make the Beast with the exact same ranking and spiral!”

<That sounds amazing! I’m going to see if I can make this work with their patterns!> I started trying to attach the pattern of the Core to my creatures. Sadly, no matter how much I tried, I couldn’t merge them. Disappointed, I told Dani the news.

“Well, we will just need to make stronger monsters then, won’t we?” she pronounced, full of determination.

<I think we need to revamp the entire structure soon. The traps aren’t working, and I don’t have enough chances to attack. I’m thinking of adding more tunnels that go to dead ends—hopefully literally—and a couple rooms that have no monsters in

them to make people nervous and slow down.> I was becoming better at subtle puns.

"That's a great idea! How are you doing on energy right now?" Dani queried. I was fairly certain she didn't catch the 'dead end' pun, or I was sure she would be laughing right then.

<I'm about half full, but with the Chi spiral, that is a *lot* more Essence than I've had at one time before. Oh, and something odd happened earlier. When those guys started cultivating, I was able to take a bit of the loose energy for myself. Is that normal?> I wanted her to say 'no, you are super amazing and special' but...

"I... think so? That is one of the reasons you let the air get dense with the extra unrefined Essence instead of focusing it all on a task, I believe. We are approaching the end of my knowledge of dungeon habits, though. It should have taken you near fifty years to get to this point!" she stated almost accusingly.

<You're welcome,> I replied haughtily. <What, you wanted to be saddled with a moron for fifty years? I think not!>

"Ha! He called my bluff," Dani chortled ruefully. "What do you want to do first? Make the Beast Cores—or should I say Essence accumulators, or would you like to rearrange first?"

<What do you think? The moving and building is going to take a lot of energy. Should I try to make the accumulators first?>

"Hm. When you put it like that, it does seem like the obvious choice," she mused. "I think that may be a good idea."

I decided with her where to put them. Luckily, they were small enough that it didn't take a lot of space. I made three to start with, equidistant from me and each other, in a triangle around me but below the stone of the hill I had made. I didn't want people getting greedy, after all—that was my job. I settled in for the quickly approaching night, respawning my Mobs and increasing my influence. I decided that I would not make the changes incrementally; I would do them in one quick event when I was ready. Soon, people would get complacent with my setup, and I hoped the transition would deliver some much needed power to me.

Dale

Dale took off his armor, carefully placing each piece down in reverse order so he could figure out how to put it back on in the morning. The men had been far more genial toward him since they left the dungeon; he'd noticed fighting together tended to form bonds. He continued to spiral his Chi as he had been taught, and when he was finished undressing, he looked at his battered body. Covered in welts and bruises, his poor body had hardly any skin on it that was the normal coloration. He began to shake, the trauma of the day finally finding a hold in his mind. Focusing on his Chi spiral to take his mind off the terror, he noticed that it was far harder to pull Essence from the earth than it was from the air in the dungeon. Working hard to keep the Essence as pure and fine as possible, he quickly fell asleep.

Splash!

"*What the abyss?!*" Dale shouted, flailing his arms as he tried to fight off his unknown assailant.

"Good morning, sunshine!" A grinning menace, Hans was the group member who had been wielding daggers the day before. He loomed above Dale, holding an empty bucket.

Dale wanted to fight back, but his body suddenly reminded him of the torture it had just gone through, and instead, he groaned piteously. Hans pulled him to his feet and made him put on his armor.

"Keepin' that spiral goin'?" Hans's grin got wider the more Dale grunted. "You're a lucky one, aren't ya?"

"How so?" Dale muttered, pulling his chainmail over his head.

"You get to start that spiral pretty young. What are ye', twenty-one?" Hans inquired.

"So? You're in your thirties. Is ten years that big of a difference?" he grumbled, annoyed at the now damp armor he had to put on.

"Hmm." Hans chuckled. "Well, yes, it is. Also, to join the Guild, you have to go through the process you just had or come in with a fairly pure spiral already goin'. Plus, this here be the first non-attribute dungeon I've ever heard-a. Usually, you gotta travel a lot to get to one that has your element type or risk stripping your center in the open with no ready Essence, if you are desperate."

His grin somehow widened. "And I'm glad I look so young! Well, I am the youngest in the group, just my mid-sixties, after all."

Dale looked up in shock, failing in an attempt to make a witty remark. "What? You are kidding me."

"Frank told you that the lifespan of a Mage is calculated in hundreds of years, yea? Well, the life of a cultivator ain't too shabby." Hans danced around a bit, light on his feet. "We age slowly enough that we have the effective lifespan of three or four people. If we break into the Mage rank before we die, our body heals up the ravages of time even more."

He stopped and looked at Dale. "Meeting Frank was the best thing that ever happened to you, and don't you ever forget it, boy-oh. People kill to get into the Guild if we ask them to.

You'll notice pretty quick that you are about to become a whole helluva lot stronger and harder to hurt. That'll be your Essence toughening you up. There's a whole slew-a benefits. Including that enchanted armor you're wearing."

Dale looked at the gear he was putting on, surprised. He hadn't known anything but the shield was enchanted.

"Heh, about what I figured. You think it was hundreds of gold for poor equipment? That discount dropped it to about twenty percent of its market value." Dale was nearly vomiting from this revelation. The full price would have been over five hundred gold?!

"Yeah, Frank musta figured you'd be able to pay it off pretty quick, or he'd have given ya only decent gear. That stuff will become light as a feather and let ya be as mobile as Craig in his blasted cloth when ya learn how to cycle Essence through it, o'course. Right now, it's a good muscle builder I bet."

"I hurt everywhere, if that's what you mean."

"Yup, that's what I mean," Hans retorted flippantly. "Time for us to get some food. Don't want what kills you in the dungeon to be hunger."

They walked to the mess hall tent and got in the line. Early enough that they got through fairly quickly, they were just starting to eat when a chef walked over to them.

"WELL, HELLO THERE!" boomed the Chef, "Going into the dungeon are you?" He had stopped blasting his voice when he saw them wince. "Sorry, used to train soldiers, poor bastards. Listen, I hear there are pretty decent herbs down there. No one complains right now, but it's hard to eat food that tastes of dirt."

Handing a few sacks over, he continued, "Fill these up, and I'll make it worth your while. Different plant, different bag. Got it? Great!" He turned away, paused, then finished menacingly, "Don't fill 'em up, and I'll make sure you get your... just desserts?"

Hans looked at the chef warily and responded in a voice that was almost bereft of his previous accent, "Hmm. Dale, I'm gonna let you in on a secret to a long life. Never piss off your chef, your boss, or your wife. I even rhymed it for you. That'll help ya remember. Also, when you get famous, never let someone make a song about you. Never ends well," he advised sagely.

"Did someone make a song about you, Hans?" Dale looked at Hans, trying to figure out if his alternating accent was just for fun or if he had taken a blow to the head.

Cough, "Well, I'm full! Don't forget to bring your bags. It's your first quest, after all." Hans hurried away... *blushing*?!

Dale followed him at the greatest speed he could manage, his armor creaking and groaning almost as much as Dale was, and they found the rest of their group waiting. Craig looked over at Dale and examined his Chi spiral. Pleased by his continued work and the high quality of it, Craig gained a bit of respect for the young man. Stronger men than Dale had been broken by the destruction of their center.

"Good to see you up and about. I'm impressed you found the time to bathe," Craig stated blandly, making the others laugh and Dale get a bit pink around the ears. "Today, you are going to take a more active role. I want you near the front of the group killing Mobs. The best way to get good at fighting is to practice, after all. Gotta build that muscle." Dale nodded seriously, and they walked toward the entrance.

The goal today was to mimic what had been done yesterday–fight the Mobs and cultivate. They would also be stopping for all loot so that the Guild could determine what they valued most. As they neared the center of the first room warily, they readied their weapons for the expected ambush attempt. Easily slaying the mushroom type Mobs, including a ranged type that Dale was able to practice blocking with, they were a bit confused when none of the rabbit types appeared.

"What is going on? Where are the Mobs?" Dale asked mistrustfully.

"How about instead of worrying, you just collect your herbs?" Hans countered. While Dale did so, the others exchanged dark looks and collected the dropped loot and mushrooms. They made their way to the next room and, again, only found mushrooms. This continued until they finally came to the Boss room. The Bloody Bane was awaiting their arrival, and they were glad to accept the challenge. A short fight ensued, the humans being the victors after only a brief struggle.

No holy symbol this time, but a fistful of copper coins and two right boots clattered to the ground, which were collected by the other members as Dale sat and began to strongly cultivate. While not as dense as the previous night, the Essence in the air was allowing him to cultivate far more than he would be able to in a week topside. The others joined him and, within an hour, were moving back toward the entrance, done for the day.

CAL

"Tell me again why you aren't attacking them?" Dani seemed frustrated that I was holding back my Mobs.

<Sure! You were in their camp yesterday, right? Well there were other groups getting ready to come down if I am not mistaken, yes?> I was asking a leading question, so she stayed quiet.

When she nodded, I continued, <Here is my thought. We give off a sense of weakness to the really strong groups like this one, and they eventually become overconfident. When a weak group comes down, we catch them entirely off guard and make sure none return to warn the others. The strong group thinks the weak ones were killed accidentally because they know how easy the fights are.> I really hoped she would like this plan.

"That is... actually brilliant," she stated, eying me as though I had been replaced by someone else.

I pretended to be hurt. <Why do you sound so surprised?>

She brutally ignored my pain. "Aaaanyway, why do you think this will work?"

<Well, it looks like that strong group is going to be the first to show up every day, trying to soften me up for the others. You said they called this a 'training ground', correct?>

"Yeah. I see. That makes sense. So most of the groups should be rather weak. I propose that we give regular fights to most of them and only wipe out a party once a week or so. Enough people are showing up out there that I think that could be attributed to poor group decisions," Dani amended my plan prototypically, making it a better one.

<That is... brilliant,> I mocked her.

"Hey!"

<Ha! No, it really is a good idea. We don't want too much attention, or they'll send high ranked people with the lower groups all the time.> I allowed my admiration for her to seep into my 'voice'.

"I agree." She brightened considerably. "How is the place looking?"

<I think I have it all reset. I added a few more Bane types to the second room. I felt that the number of ranged Mobs in there was a bit low.>

She agreed with my estimation, "Sounds good. Did you have any ideas for the acid yet?"

<Yeah, and I discovered a really interesting thing about it. I tried combining it with monsters, and it didn't do anything, so I tried combining it with some of the different materials I had gathered. One combination seems promising. When I added hydrogen and oxygen to the mix, it vastly increased the potency of the acid. I tested a small amount of it, and it dissolved a rabbit within about ten seconds!> I tried to keep the volume of my voice down, but this scientific breakthrough needed to be known!

She dimmed and turned a bit green in a way I had taken to mean disgust. "Wow. That is horrible. Also, I don't know what you are talking about, Cal. I think that you forget that when you absorb things, you learn their name and what that name means. When you say those words to me, they have *no* meaning, and I can't remember them... Just tell me what you are going to call it."

<Oh. I didn't realize that. Sorry. I'm thinking of calling it 'etching solution' because it eats into everything it touches. Seriously, this stuff is dangerous.> I hoped she would heed my warning; that Basher had seemed like it was really in pain.

She looked at me questioningly. "When did you make this stuff?"

<Well, you went to sleep, and I got bored–> I began sheepishly.

"And when Cal gets bored he creates deadly stuff for entertainment," she interrupted dryly.

<Kinda.> I was a little embarrassed but also glad she was starting to have a high opinion of me, even if it was a little dark. <It's good for us in the long run, though. Speaking of the long run, in your opinion, what is it going to take to get me to F-rank nine?>

She started considering something and spoke slowly after several seconds of intense thought, "Well, I think you have enough understanding of how things work, so now it is a matter of raw power. When your Chi spiral fills two-thirds of your Core, you should break into F-rank nine. At the rate you are going, it should be only a few weeks, faster if you get large influxes soon."

I did some quick calculations in my head, judging how much Essence I was gaining recently. <Well, I am about half full of Essence in my spiral, but haven't been getting many large inputs recently. If people start dropping, I might make it in a few days.>

"No rush, Cal. Slow and steady makes for a strong power base. I was actually thinking you should try and compress that Chi spiral down. I don't want to sound mean, but I think you've been getting complacent and layering it on without using all the available space. It's a bad habit," Dani admonished, directing my attention to all of the space I was wasting in my Core.

She was right, and under her watchful eye, I worked on compressing it down as much as I could. There was a *lot* of empty space that I was not using, it turned out. By the time I was finished working to improve myself, I had a significantly smaller but far denser spiral spinning at greater speeds.

"Good work! Remember that the faster it spins, the more well-refined it will be, and faster spinning makes for faster Essence gathering as well." She sounded very pleased with my effort.

I knew she was right, and my laziness may have really been costing me, especially now that I saw how fast the spiral was spinning. <Sorry, my mind had been on other things recently. I'll try to remember that real power is not in what something looks like but in the quality of the effort that it takes to get there.>

She beamed at me. "I'm proud of you, Cal! You don't shy away from your faults and work hard to improve yourself when you find them. Ooh! By the way, I think a new group is coming in!"

She was, of course, correct. I decided to follow her plan and give them a regular fight. When they came into the first room, I ambushed them at the center and watched as my Bashers got in several nice shin-shots before they finally took my minions down. Retreating at about half losses as usual, I watched as they paused in the room for a bit to recover and gather the loot. While they did so, I scanned their auras, double checking and pleased upon finding that this was a D-ranked group, none past the fifth ranking.

They continued onward, pushing through the pain as the promise of treasure stirred them from inaction. Already a few coppers richer, apparently the equivalent of a week's pay in the area, they were determined to make it big. The second room was harder for them, as I attacked with the rabbits before they killed off the Shroomish, making them work harder to block the poisonous thorns while their legs took a beating. By the time half the swarm of Bashers was defeated, inspiring a retreat, the men looked exhausted and filthy. Covered in blood from my rabbits and bruises of their own, they certainly looked ready to call it a day. Most of them at least. One of the men, trying to convince them to keep going, pulled off his helmet and started arguing energetically that the group should continue.

He began stalking toward the next tunnel, very inspirationally shouting, "To money!" I saw my chance. The Bane on the ceiling by the tunnel took a clean shot, impaling the man with a hand-sized thorn directly through his temple, piercing the skull in one blow! Even if the initial attack hadn't been enough to kill him—it was—the poison, though weak, was administered directly to the man's brain. He fell, and as soon as his aura winked out, I was able to work on directly dissolving his armor with my influence, the process essentially aging them until they fell apart as tattered, useless chunks while I took the pattern I needed to recreate it. The suddenly rusted remnants of his armor clanging to the floor startled his team greatly, their eyes showing white as their faces drained of blood in shock.

From their perspective, it had been over in an instant. The fallen man's teammates saw a thorn impact their friend, then saw him drop and hit the floor, for some reason almost naked. I left his wool clothes on his corpse as I already had a few sets of those to work with, but I got all of his armor and his well-made sword. Neat. Apparently, he had been fairly rich; the sword was *really* well made! They tried to pick the remains of the fallen gear back up, but I had bound it all to the floor by growing a layer of stone around it while I worked to break each piece down and study it, making it impossible for the frustrated humans to take. Furious, they grabbed their fallen comrade's corpse and departed, faces grim, when the dead man's Essence finally made its way to me.

<Oh, yeah...> I moaned in pleasure. The D-ranked man had far more pure and abundant Essence than any I had ever had the pleasure of absorbing. Carefully adding it to my spiral as densely as possible, I watched as my energy re-grew to nearly half, this time much stronger than before I had compressed it.

<That's the stuff. Dani, you wanna try any of this?> I groaned in ecstasy.

She looked on, hungry but unable to touch the Essence until it made its way to her through our bond. "Brute, you know I can't take that directly, and what happened to taking out groups slowly?"

I thought quickly; we had made a plan, after all. Finally, I mentally shrugged. <Well, there is no way anyone will blame anything but that man's overconfidence. Removing your armor when in a hostile area? Tsk, tsk. Not a smart move.>

"To be fair, he only removed his helmet. *You* removed his armor. You dirty dungeon!" She chuckled at her own joke. "But you make a good point. Congrats on the Essence! I'm glad to see that that worked out so well. Also, how good is that armor?"

<Eh, it is okay I suppose. No enchantments or anything fun on the armor, but I got a full set of plate mail and the chainmail it goes over. I'll adjust the size for medium and larger guys and put them out as loot, most likely. The sword is more interesting, though.> I left off tantalizingly, knowing her rabid curiosity would make her ask.

"How so?" She was rather impatient today, wasn't she? I smiled to myself.

<Well, it had a temporary enchantment on it. I think it is an augmentation that sharpens and cleans the blade. I think I can alter it a bit to add it to the spikes the Bane shoots, but that isn't what I am interested in.>

"Oh?"

<Correct me if I'm wrong, but the enchantment like this is temporary because it was cast on the sword. It looks like tightly woven Essence, not something else like Mana, and it is always active. Permanent enchantments are formed by cutting

Inscriptions like on that pendant, then putting your own Essence into the Inscriptions right? That allows you to turn it on or off at will.> She was keeping up with me so far. I could tell.

"Sounds correct so far. Just so you know, cutting those in is called 'inscribing', and when done properly, it is called a 'Rune'," she took a quick second to boost my knowledge.

I acknowledged her input and continued, <Well, I am wondering if I can use the Beast Cores to power enchantments. Since they can store Essence, it should be possible to draw the energy from them and not yourself right?>

Dani went quiet for a moment. "Well, in theory. It *is* possible to use specially refined Beast Cores as Mana accumulators, but the cost is usually so high for even a normal Core that no one—that I have heard of anyway—has tried it for just *Essence*."

<Okay, good. Next, I am wondering if I could use the corruption in a stone for anything.> From her reaction, I think the answer I was about to get was 'no'.

"What? Corrupted stones are useless. No one can manipulate it so..." She went silent, realizing that I had been able to move the taint around rather easily.

She walked right into my trap! <Right! I can, and when I put it back in items that naturally have the stuff, like rocks and metal, they become stronger and sturdier, closer to their pure elemental form! I'm wondering what would happen if I used the corruption instead of purified Essence to fill a Beast Core, then used that stone to create an enchantment!>

"I don't know." Dani slowly thought through the implications. "It is an interesting idea, though. Go for it, I mean, you can always make more Cores, right? Remember, though, you haven't encountered all of the different Essence types that exist, so make extras."

I set up a few more Cores next to the ones I was planning on using for Essence overflow, then increased the amount of them to six each. One each for fire, water, air, earth, infernal, and celestial Essence. Since my main prey was humans, I figured I could eventually fill them all up. Next, I looked at the sharpening augmentation on the sword. An enchantment was just a specific pattern of Essence placed on to an item, and if it was inscribed without mistakes, it could become a Rune, which was a permanent enchantment powered by Essence only when you wanted to pass energy through it.

The reason permanent enchantments, or Runes, were rarer was due to the pattern needing to be *perfect.* If there was a flaw, the Essence would flow out of the Rune, and the pattern would be useless, at best. At worst, it would activate and have an unintended effect. Conversely, when done properly, it was difficult to remove an enchantment because the Essence that flowed through it would eventually strengthen the pattern, again known as a Rune or Inscription, placed on the item, to the point where if it were made on wood, you could burn the log away and the Rune would still be stable. Not that they were indestructible, far from it, really. It would just take a lot of strength–or applied knowledge of where to strike–to destroy a well-used Rune, but it could be done.

The downside to using a Runed versus an enchanted item was obviously that *you* needed to provide Essence to it in order for it to function. This is where the Beast Cores would potentially come into play. With Mana being a far more potent source of energy that would last far longer, I could see why people would wait to get Mana accumulators set before going to the expense of creating really good Runed items, as correctly and permanently inscribed items were properly named.

I had some time before the next party would come to fight, so after resetting the place–not hard as the last group barely made progress–I tried to apply the enchantment to the daggers I could make. I was quickly frustrated, as I could not directly integrate the Rune into the pattern. I could splice creatures together for goodness sake! Did I not have enough knowledge to cut a pattern into a chunk of metal?! Oh. Wait.

A flash of inspiration struck, and I 'grew' a dagger in the Boss room. Then with infinite patience and precision, I formed the most accurate lines possible by creating acid molecule by molecule on to the blade. A new group had entered the dungeon and cleared the first room by the time I was finished with my newest creation. Now, to test it! I extended a few lines of Essence into the Rune, and... it flared to life!

Under my watchful gaze, the edge of the blade constricted at the molecular level, forming tighter bonds along each edge. Along the entire blade, tiny imperfections fixed themselves, leaving no space for blood or gore to find a foothold. It had worked! Now it would never need to be sharpened, and a quick flick of the blade would cast off all viscera that it accumulated.

Now for the dangerous part, as I might have lost all of my effort. I absorbed the dagger and looked at the pattern that appeared in my mind. Yes! I could now directly create this dagger with a Rune attached! I called it a 'Honed Steel Dagger', and I was very proud of my work. Turning my attention to the fighting happening in–oh my, the third room already? I quickly and gleefully took control of a large Basher and made a concentrated attack on the group attacking me. Bashing into the legs of the least armored human–as the creature's namesake suggested–the archer stumbled, and I was able to do some considerable damage to him before his pals finished off my remaining defenders.

I watched the man cry in pain. <I think I broke his tibia and fibula,> I casually informed Dani.

"Mmm. That sounds *dirty*! What do you mean?" Dani lecherously inquired.

I breathed a snort at her odd sexual humor. <I broke his leg below the knee. There are two bones there, and in a human they are called tibia and fibula. I don't know if that would be the same for a different race.>

"Ah. Got it." She seemed less interested now that she realized I wasn't playing along and making a sexual reference.

I watched the man sob on my floor as he writhed around. <Think that will be enough for them to leave?> I questioned distractedly, mind back on my new dagger.

She looked at them through her connection to me. "I doubt it. Plus, they're already healing him."

<They can do that?> Enraged, I turned my attention back to the group and watched as another lightly armored man directed wood-type Essence–specialized earth and water that is–into the man's leg, which I assume knitted the bone back together as he was soon able to stand up. Then walking with a limp, he and the party moved into the tunnel toward the next room.

<That's not fair!> I gasped in fury.

"Your Boss Mob can heal by hurting people, so why is this a surprise?" Dani did not seem to understand my indignation.

<It... It's just... Fine! Be right, again!> I huffed, unable to form a proper response.

"I will, thank *you*," she replied primly.

They attacked my Boss, the Bloody Bane, with everything they could muster. I directed a few Bashers into the fray at critical times, knocking them off balance long enough for a spike to land in an arm or a vine to whip someone across the helm. The fight lasted much longer this time around since the group was already tired and in pain.

Finally, the Boss collapsed. I had failed to take them out but had still gained some important knowledge, so I dropped a silver coin for each of them as well as the coveted holy symbol pendant thingy. Though lightly poisoned, the men still were wildly excited. The archer whose leg I had broken nearly wept, and kept repeating, "I just *knew* it would be worth it!" I was confused by this. Why were they so happy? I demanded the information from Dani. She informed me that the currency system was such that one hundred copper coins was worth a silver coin, one hundred silver coins were worth a gold coin, and one hundred gold coins were worth a platinum coin, whatever that was.

Apparently, I had *drastically* overpaid these guys. Silver and copper were easy to make, so I wasn't worried about it until Dani informed me of what the consequences may be, "If everyone thinks you are going to be worth a month's pay for an hour of fighting, they will come in and kill absolutely everything over and over, just looking for a way to avoid working elsewhere. Humans can be rather... enthusiastic in their greed."

I winced at this. <Yikes. I'm not ready for that.>

"I agree and am glad you realize it." Dani watched the men who were wandering around the room.

Each of the men who had taken a thorn and become poisoned pulled out a vial and drank something. Then the man with the plant affinity worked for a while to get his team healed up enough to stop their bleeding as they relaxed and cultivated for a while.

<What was that? They drank something,> I muttered suspiciously.

"Probably an antidote for the poison," Dani whispered since the men were so close and her voice was audible if humans paid attention.

I tried to keep my curiosity under control but couldn't manage it. <Oh. Thanks. Also, can only plant affinity users heal?>

Dani couldn't refuse an opportunity to educate me. She glanced at the humans focused on their Chi spirals, then moved into a furiously whispered lecture, "No, actually all of them can heal. There is a solid reason they don't all do it, though. Apparently, the problem is that they *feel* the element used, so being healed by a fire cultivator is not that pleasant, as it tends to feel like your body is being cauterized. Earth grinds really badly, as if your bones were being crushed. Cool and soothing water cultivators are sought after, and apparently, plant or wood feels like roots or worms squirming through you. Since he is a wood cultivator, he is not the ideal healer for a group this size, but most likely, he was the only trained healer they could find."

<What about celestial and infernal?> She had said 'every type', after all.

"Celestial healers are called clerics and are usually a part of the church. They are actually the most effective healers, but traveling with them comes with strings attached. Infernal users... I doubt they would heal anyone but themselves, but I think their version of 'healing' hurts worse than getting the wound originally would."

<I wonder if I can make something useful out of that information... Thanks for letting me know, Dani.> We watched

the men cultivate for a while before eventually getting up, stretching, and leaving. They were the last group of the night, allowing me to focus hard on cultivation and the concepts I had acquired over the last few days.

That was the night when I broke into F-rank nine.

Chapter Fourteen

Dale woke up quickly, feeling something amiss. Something was wrong; there was a threat to him in the area. For several weeks, his team had been going into the dungeon at first light, and Dale was becoming stronger, his battle-trained senses more aware to impending danger. Slipping from his bed, he moved stealthily to the tent flap. It began to slide open, and the grinning head of Hans slowly peeked into the room. Stepping into the room fully, a bucket of ice-cold water became visible.

Dale shuddered internally; he had only been woken up a few times with that water, but each time it was worse. Last week, the water had ice in it somehow! It was mid-summer! Ice! Dale's eyes narrowed as he prepared his counterattack. He carefully reached down and flipped the water back on to the startled Hans.

"Gotcha, you bastard!" Dale yelled, following up by attempting a brutal slapping combination attack on Hans.

"I'll get you, ya brat! You got lucky today, but you can't stay awake forever!" A drenched Hans scampered off yelling threats, leaving a cheerful Dale to get reacquainted with his armor. The full group met again at breakfast, the team having decided to eat together each day. Unexpectedly, the chef decided to swing by again as they were finishing their meal.

"MORNING, lads!" His voice faltered and dropped a few decibel levels at their wince, "Did it again, sorry. Listen, I'm gonna be makin' the herbs that are available in there a daily request. They tasted so darn good on my foods that I had them examined by that there apothecary that showed up and has been making those fancy potions. Turns out they are jam-packed full-a

Essence and help with all sorts of minor health issues that I've been seeing recently. So I'm gonna be cooking with 'em a lot."

Looking Dale in the eyes, he added, "Since y'all are the first to go in every day, I figured you'd be able to grab the best bunches. Get 'em for me, and everyone around here'll eat better, and I'll be sure to tell 'em yer ta thank. Or the food'll get worse—maybe I'll 'accidentally' burn yours every day, and I'll still tell the other men yer ta... thank." With that, the oddly well-muscled chef walked away, whistling off key.

"Sure is a fan of the carrot and the stick," Dale murmured. "Shall we make sure to bring back those herbs?"

"Yup."

"For sure."

"Agreed."

They moved to make their way into the dungeon, Dale in the lead. With the good tutors, clean Essence, and constant work, Dale had progressed to the F-rank six rather quickly, as well as put on some solid muscle. Now not only was he able to keep up in his heavy plate armor, he had a good handle on the skills and abilities he needed to decidedly defeat the deadly denizens of the dark dungeon.

Within an hour of hard work, they had cleared the dungeon and were finishing off the Boss. As they did daily, each sat and cultivated, but an oddity in the behavior of his friends made Dale look up, noticing the men staring at the Silverwood tree.

"What's going on, guys?" he inquired dreamily, almost in a trance as he worked to gather the loose Essence into his center.

"The tree has been growing a lot recently. We are wondering if that is normal," Craig let him know, frowning at an internal thought.

"We're also trying to figure out how this tree will help us move into the B-ranks," Hans stated. "It isn't exactly a common thing to have access to, after all.

"Sadly, we won't know until the Elves start making an appearance." Craig derailed the conversation with a hand wave. "Well, let's head on out, nothing more to do here. Dale, you should work on integrating what you have absorbed into your Chi spiral. Don't fill up too much or it will be harder to process."

Carefully making their way back to the surface, they were startled to see that the place was bustling with movement, people running around and shouting orders to each other. They noticed that Guild Master Frank was in the largest, loudest group, shouting at another, somewhat taller, man.

"No, you *can't* have that space! We've had it roped off and claimed for the Portal Mage's to build on for weeks now!" Frank was red in the face, spittle flying from his lips.

"You are going to deny the *Holy Church* an area that will be able to best serve the people? This will be the center of the goings-on in the area, and who better to guide people than the church?!" the taller man angrily intoned, his voice ringing out clearly in a manner trained to catch attention.

"The PORTAL MAGES!" Frank roared, throwing his hands into the air. "That is their *exact job*! They guide and send people where they want to go!"

"Well, the church sends them where they *need* to go!" the tall man boomed back, unimpressed.

Frank saw Dale's group walking over and visibly worked to calm himself. "It's a moot point. The man who owns all this land is here; he'll make the decision," Frank declared smugly, knowing that Dale was a friend.

"Excellent, where is he?" the taller man demanded. Frank pointed at the group, and he walked over. Going directly to

Hans, whose face he could see was grinning, the man introduced himself, “I am Father Richard. A humble cleric,” Frank snorted at that pronouncement, “who has been promoted to run a church in this area, as it is obviously *sorely* needing guidance. That man,” he jabbed his finger at Frank, “has been trying to place *travel* and *leisure* over divine teaching, and I *demand* that you tell him that this is the perfect location for a church!” he finished in a ringing tone that reached every ear.

Hans looked from Father Richard to Frank. “Well then. Frank, it *is* the perfect location for a church,” Hans told his Guild Master and nearly burst into laughter at the look of triumph on Richard’s face and the wry look on Frank’s.

“And. There. You. Have. It!” Richard crowed, throwing his hands in the air and beaming.

“Excuse me, Father but–” Dale began. Unfortunately, he wasn’t able to match Father Richards pealing voice.

“The Lord provides, and we will have a beautiful place of worship and–”

“Hey!” Frank barked, thrusting his finger at Hans. “*He* isn’t the landowner.”

“He–” Richard whirled on the now maniacally laughing Hans and fixed him with a glare.

“Father, it *is* the perfect place!” Hans laughed so hard he fell over. “I... ha-hah... I told him, just like you asked!”

Everyone was chuckling except the crestfallen priest, so Dale decided to speak up. Lifting his visor, he said, “I own the land here, Father Richard.”

“Oh. You? Well. Right, lad, listen,” Richard quietly muttered, “I need this, I think my promotion to this place was a punishment. My branch of the church displeased the bishop, and when I was finally up for promotion to a location-based diocese instead of being a wandering minister, I was told to come here and build a worthy house of worship. I can't be put to the side, I just..." He sighed sadly, looking at the chunk of land he wanted. "I need to make something *memorable* here."

"Does it need to be that exact spot?" Dale looked around and saw nothing really special about the area.

"It looks like all the other flat land around here is claimed. All these tents, I'm sure people have plans to build. How much of this land do you own? A few acres around the dungeon entrance?" Richard searched.

"Not exactly. I–" Dale began with a smile, only to be cut off again.

Richard interrupted with a frustrated growl, "Not even that? Rats, the land price here must have skyrocketed when this was found. I'll never be able to afford to build a church near here–"

"Father!" Re-gaining his attention, Dale grinned. "I own this mountain."

"What?!"

"When I discovered the dungeon, I originally did buy only the land directly containing the dungeon. It took everything I had. When the scouting team showed up, they left me with enough gold to buy this entire mountain, since there had never been anything useful found on it. And, well, since it is a contested mountain range, the price was right," Dale revealed with a grin, adding on accomplishments to drive the price of renting land up subconsciously in Richard's mind. "I bought the land from both the Lion and the Phoenix Kingdom, just in case. It helped that my intelligence as a sheepherder was somewhat underestimated. Both Kingdoms assumed I wanted uninterrupted grazing pastures, not a valuable resource like a dungeon."

"Brilliant!" Frank whispered. He hadn't realized the forethought Dale had put into his good fortune. When land was purchased, any deeds were signed with Mana-infused ink that was impossible to fake or forge. The contracts had to be honored by both Kingdoms, when before, the contested nature of the mountain would allow one of the Kingdoms to attempt a hostile takeover if he had only bought from the other. In fact, the contract for the land would also be enforced magically. Frank wondered if Dale knew about this aspect of his purchase.

"Listen," Dale tried to placate the priest, "I think you should move further away from here. What if beasts are drawn to this place and attack your church? What if something breaks out of the dungeon? Will you stand in the way and fight when creatures are attacking your followers? Will–"

"Yes," Richard told him seriously.

"See–" Dale sputtered to a stop, train of thought derailed. "Wait, what?"

"Yes, I will," Richard calmly promised. "I will protect them."

Dale tried again, rubbing at his temples as a headache threatened, "Look, Father, praying at a problem won't make it go away. It–"

"Yes, it will." Father Richard chuckled darkly.

Dale tried again with a sheepish chuckle, seeing why Frank had gotten so angry. "Father, you aren't understanding me."

"No, you aren't understanding *me*." Father Richard grinned and bowed his head. Murmuring a short prayer, he gestured at the empty lot that he had been after. For a moment, nothing seemed to happen as the sun rose higher in the sky. A word came out of Father Richard's mouth that shook the air and made no sense to Dale, followed by a beam of light that tore from the heavens and settled into a perfect square on the entire lot for several glorious seconds. The sound created was amazing, a cross between a choir singing... and rock exploding. When the light faded several moments later, the ground had been fused into perfectly clear glass, three feet straight down. The heat coming off of the molten land was enough to singe Dale's eyebrows, even from this distance.

The Father turned back towards Dale. "You see, young man, I am a rank-A priest. If someone were threatening my flock, I would be more than willing, nay, I would *cheerfully* send them to the creator."

Dale watched the clear liquid of the ground steam, all impurities apparently burned away. "Well. The spot, ah, is yours it... seems. Let's make a lease, shall we? What are you willing to offer as payment?" Dale tried not to be stunned by the casual display of apocalyptic destructive capabilities.

Father Richard snorted at Dale's attempt to seem nonchalant. "Many things. Firstly, I will build my own building. I will provide healing to people as needed, for a small offering. With this many people, families are bound to arrive. It won't always be the simple military camp it is now. A church in the area will alleviate many concerns families may have. I will teach and train youngsters for no charge and accept any into my order who are gifted with an affinity for celestial Essence."

"I will be able to provide them a means to gain this Essence in the proper ways. Often, children with celestial affinity are small or weak because they cannot gain any Essence. I will teach them how to properly cultivate through their prayers."

"Finally, I will provide a bank to the community that will not be corrupt as a non-morally guided bank would be. We will only take a small amount in fees that will provide the bulk of our income and our rent to you, which will be determined by a percentage of the gross amount we earn."

Dale was impressed by this man's knowledge of the world but realized that as an A-ranked person, he could be several hundred years old. "Father, you seem very knowledgeable and wise. I do agree to these terms, though I must ask, why did it take so long for you to be given a church? You obviously have the power and wisdom to stand alone."

"We, my sect of the church that is, have fallen out of favor with the Bishop due to our favored style and practice of worship," Father Richard disclosed brightly, happy that the land was his.

"Why? What do you do that he doesn't like?" Dale was genuinely curious.

"We do the Lord's work as our penance, our service to the world. We hunt demons and the undead. Pardon me, I have work to do!" Father Richard jauntily stated, moving toward the small market area to find craftsmen.

CAL

Dani had been correct; wiping out a party every week or so caused no undue attention, as the number of dungeon divers increased. Apparently, the promise of long life and vast riches caused people to ignore the danger inherent in this occupational choice. Go figure. Only a month and some change since they arrived, now a sea of adventurers waited on a line for the Guild to grant them permission to enter; only the first group of the day showed up on a regular basis. They seemed to have some kind of precedence, maybe? That didn't really bother me, though. Thanks to the constant Essence gains I was making, I had gained enough power fast enough that six of the Beast Cores around me held their own Chi spiral. They weren't sentient stones, of course; I spiraled their Essence manually. Thanks to keeping these Cores charged, I was able to fill the rooms with Mobs nearly as soon as the humans vacated them, allowing multiple groups to enter in staggered time frames. I would eventually use or absorb the Essence accumulated in the Beast Cores, but I would have choked on the amount of energy I was gaining; I could not just take it all in. Similarly, the corruption stones were also becoming full, but try as I might, I could not make them spiral. They just sat there, glowing with their corruption's respective color.

Thanks to the massive group of people moving through me and the large amounts of deaths that occurred seemingly by their own stupidity, just a few short weeks after entering the ninth rank of the F series, Dani was coaching me on how to move into the D-rankings.

"Let me explain to you what needs to happen, Cal. The reason it is called 'breaking' into a new rank is that you need enough knowledge and power to further 'break' your Essence and the mental barriers to advancement. I need to warn you–it hurts. A lot," she started seriously. "To get into the D-ranks, your Chi and Essence spiral needs to shatter into a 'fractal'. This means that each part of the pattern has the same statistical character as the whole." She took a breath as I attempted to understand her meaning.

"In other words," she clarified," your Chi spiral needs to become a spiral *made* of spirals which are *further* made of spirals. The Essence swirl that it draws from needs to become a swirl *made of* swirling Essence. This will, when you manage it, allow you to astronomically increase the Essence you can hold and absorb at any given time, at least a hundred times more at any given point."

I kept pace with her lecture, making affirmative noises as she spoke. <That sounds really difficult.>

"It is, and it will take a lot of your Essence to break down the other Essence. The payoff is absolutely worth it, though. I've been making you practice splitting your focus, which is why we waited until you had those Beast Cores swirling with energy. Spinning multiple spirals is really good practice for this. Also, it is a benefit that humans will never get to use." She made sure I was paying attention and told me something rather unexpected, "Now, achieving a breakthrough may take a few days to do, and will require all of your focus, so I suggest that tonight when everyone is out and going to bed, you grow a wall of stone to block them and keep them out while you do this."

<What?! Why?> This was very unlike her. She usually was encouraging more fighting and got after me sometimes when I didn't take an opportunity to finish off an opponent.

It turned out that she had a very good reason though. "People may get–hmm, upset? When they are unable to find monsters to kill and loot, that is. Since your attention will be focused inward, Mobs won't respawn if killed. Adventurers may look for... other ways... to get money or find a new source of energy to cultivate from."

Waiting for evening was torture when I was this excited, but I was able to gain more energy from cultivators by pulling refined Chi from them as well as when a lucky shot from a thorn staggered a man and a Basher crushed his skull. When the sun disappeared behind the mountain range, a soft grinding of stone could be heard if one was close and paying attention.

Before attempting my breakthrough, I etched in the enchantment for protection and durability I had gained from a shield after a lucky kill some time ago. At the activation portion of the Rune–where I would normally deposit Essence into–I placed the corrupted Core instead, which was full of earth and created a shunt that sent its energy into the Rune. The energy oozed into the pattern, slowly filling it to completion until, with a dull flash and an awkward flatulence-esk noise, it successfully activated the Rune!

<Dani, it worked! Look! I made corruption useful!> I loved being the first to discover something; it made me feel smart and pretty.

"Great! Hopefully, it'll hold until you are ready for people to come back in," she congratulated me while reminding me that the clock was ticking.

Door now in place, I got down to the serious business of breaking into the D rank. I tried starting the process where the Essence was churning on the outer rim of my gem, but it interrupted the flow of Essence entering from outside. If I tried at the end, where it was being pulled and processed by the Chi spiral, it blocked the flow.

I broke through my pride and finally asked for assistance, <Huh. Dani, where do I start?>

Obviously, she had been waiting for me to ask. "You need to find the smallest part which doesn't affect the rest and begin there. It should pull Essence from the rest of the Chi spiral as a thread that is the same comparative size as the thread coming from the Essence into the Chi spiral."

Mentally moving deeper into my Chi spiral, I reached the exact center where the Essence was no longer processing, only spinning. Holding that minuscule amount of energy with my mind, more of an idea than an energy source, I began rotating it in the reverse direction of the remainder of the accumulated Chi. My mind almost broke in pain as my very being was twisted counter to the rest of my soul. Somehow, I was able to stabilize the first position in its new rotation before forcing myself to continue. I should note, all the Chi I contained was a single thread from the center to the outer edge, and if I stopped working, I would need to begin again with this first bit. Spinning it in the opposite direction did not break this thread but, instead, stretched it further, making it even thinner and well refined.

From that point in time, I needed to do two sequential areas along the thread simultaneously. Obviously harder and more painful than just one point, it was required in order for the energy flow to properly continue. This continued one spot along the thread, then two. One, then two. Each distinct position along the line was slightly larger than the one previous, and I needed to take frequent breaks to ensure all the preceding spirals were turning at the same rate. I had no idea how a flesh and blood body would be able to survive this process; I was in intense pain, and my body did not actually have nerves. Maybe the pain of the soul was the same no matter what type of being you were?

In a constant state of breaking down the Essence, I held each pattern time and again until I was certain I would be able to do so naturally with minimal concentration before I moved to the next. Eventually, I came to the end of the Chi. I was very excited at the prospect of completion until Dani sent me a sleepy reminder that I would need to do this with my Essence spiral as well, the outer edge that stored and drew in loose Essence.

Forcing the changes on to the swirl was easier now that I had figured out how to properly mold it, requiring less concentration to achieve the result I wanted. Still focusing intently on not making mistakes, I reached out, and along the spinning Essence, I made tiny vortexes that hungrily pulled power from the one previous until, finally, I came to the start of the spiral. The start of the spiral pulled loose Essence from the world around me. Luckily for my sanity, the pain of this process was far less than working on the Chi spiral had been, being so far from the center of my soul.

Until I was able to subconsciously hold this pattern at all times, allowing it to become a natural process for me, I would need to manually spin every single vortex at the same rate along the whole thread. Holding the pattern in shape was using an exorbitant amount of Essence, allowing me to see why this particular breakthrough was so difficult. When I asked Dani how I was doing time-wise, she let me know that I had been focusing for four days, still faster than she expected.

<My brain hurts,> I complained, projecting an image of a brain turning into ooze.

"You don't have a brain," she reminded me somewhat insensitively.

<Sure, rub it in. How are things going out here?> I quickly scanned my area to see if there were any obvious problems.

"Good, people tried breaking in a few times, but I think they are now just waiting." She seemed smug about our door being unbreachable.

I checked my Essence levels, which, though depleted, I found that I still had plenty to work with. <Well, they can wait a bit longer. If you think we are ready for it, in my opinion, it is time to change things up in here.>

"Excellent! By the way, congratulations on your new D-ranking!" she cheered me enthusiastically.

If I could blush... <Thank you! I know it is just D-rank zero at this point, but the first five ranks are all about direct Essence accumulation, right?>

"Pretty much. D-rank six and above require greater knowledge, but at this rate, I think you will get there soon." Dani glowed warmly, showing her approval.

<Wonderful! Let's start... now.> Reaching out to the Essence contained in the Cores around me, I slowly and carefully pulled it in, rejoicing at the greater amount of Essence that I was able to take into myself. Still being careful as I did not want to disrupt the new energy pattern I had spent days creating, I collected every single drop of Essence they contained. One by one, the dancing lights in them went dark, their accumulated Essence flowing into me. I quickly felt bloated; each of the Cores had held nearly half the amount of energy I had been able to contain while I was in the F-ranks.

When they were empty, I still had not increased in rank but was now energized enough to move a large portion of the area I held influence over. Daily, I had slowly extended downward but had never taken the time needed to move the stone in the area, simply extending myself. The area I could now open up would–slightly–more than double my size horizontally and allow me to have another *entire* floor added vertically.

Now ready to begin, I followed Dani's instructions and began 'correctly' moving the stone while absorbing the vibrations, so as to not cause deadly destruction I would not be able to capitalize on. Luckily, the process was not quite as slow as I had originally worried about–creating a buffer zone was simply a matter of willpower–so within a day or two, I was able to add three more rooms on the first floor and a total of eight on the new second floor.

I increased the number of tunnels as well. Obviously, the old layout was not working at the best efficiency for slowing adventurers. Instead of just one tunnel connecting all the rooms, I now had many tunnels that connected to either each other, nothing but traps, or a room that didn't allow for access deeper into the dungeon. You would never know if a room connected without first exploring it because each of the tunnels connected at opposite ends of the room, having a sharp turn that you could not see around. Some of those turns did indeed allow people to venture deeper in, but the majority were eventually dead ends.

I left the rooms and traps on the first floor mainly alone, not bothering to alter them too much. One major change on the first floor was a vain attempt to alleviate the annoyance created by people poking at my walls by moving the iron vein into the entry room. This wasn't so much an attempt to help prospectors as a way to provide raw materials so people could mine the ores and turn it into new items for me to study.

Moving on to the lower floor, I placed traps with highly pressurized acid pockets that would blast into the air at high speed if the thin stone covering them were disrupted. I had found that even if an item were destroyed by means other than me breaking it down with influence, as long as the destruction happened in my dungeon, I could obtain the pattern. Therefore, I was unconcerned if armor and weapons were damaged or destroyed by my etching solution. At a few of the dead end tunnels, I placed large slabs of stone that could be dropped, trapping the occupants in a room containing light drippings of acid, which would turn into a downpour when people were trapped or could possibly explode if exposed to open flame.

Everything I made was, of course, an attempt to gain as much Essence as possible, but I liked to reward intelligence and ingenuity, so I *always* added ways for these traps to be deactivated. I wanted people to continue coming down here, after all, and with a reputation as a place where the smartest and strongest could almost always prevail, people would always assume they were among the ranks of the 'certain survivors'.

Finally done with the cosmetic and trap changes, it was time for me to try and upgrade my Mobs, then make a Boss monster for the lower floor. I kept the Bloody Bane as the floor Boss of the first level as I didn't really care to make him a common Mob. To be frank, he seemed a bit... lackluster. After all, the entire time he had existed, he had never managed a kill!

I looked into what I had available for Mobs. I could try to upgrade my Bashers, but what would they grow into? I was uncertain if pouring Essence into them was the correct way to go about things here. Maybe I should just use what I had, fill up the dungeon with a large number of Mobs and wait for inspiration after opening the door. Hang on a second... the door? The door! Of course! When the Bloodmoss had absorbed Essence and infernal energy, it had naturally evolved and gained vampirism-style abilities. With my ability to move corruption, could I build Mobs in the style I wished?

Nothing to do but try! But where to start? First, I created a few of my Bashers and made them hold still so I could... experiment on them. Which kinda feels creepy to think, but it had to be done! They were all at the second rank of the F series, so I had some room to grow them. I decided to start by attempting to increase one's ranking by infusing it with air corruption and Essence. I poured a bit of each into the Basher, and it started to noticeably grow. I added more, feeling confident with this plan, when the poor thing gave a startled squeak and exploded into a bloody mist, which slowly settled on the walls and floor, scraps of fur and bone plopping wetly on to the other Bashers in the room.

<What the *abyss*?!> The other Bashers were now fidgeting, desperately trying to fight the compulsion I had placed on them in order to run away.

"Well, that was dramatic. What, ah, what just happened?" Dani seemed far too calm for the literal bloodbath that had just occurred.

<I was trying to rank it up, and it just... popped!> I exclaimed wildly. Did my voice sound shrill there?

"That's odd. If you are just giving it Essence, it should have easily and naturally assimilated it." Dani was now concerned.

<Well, I mean, I was trying to add a tiny little bit of taint to it to give it new abilities,> I confessed innocently.

"Oh, that makes sense. It seems like a sound plan at least... Hmm. What did you use?" Dani inquired in a calm tone.

<I went with air corruption. It looked like it was working but obviously not.> I walked her through the process I had attempted, followed by the obvious end result of the test.

She considered what I had done, then offered an explanation, "Your Bashers don't normally have much air Essence in their makeup, do they? Maybe that one's body rejected it, or maybe you just added too much taint too quickly. Try again, but add less taint at a time," Dani declared, settling in to watch.

<You want me to try with air again?>

"Why not?"

<Because the last one exploded.>

"It's a figure of... Yes, try air again, Cal." She slowly exhaled.

Selecting another one of the Bashers cowering on the floor amongst the gore of its brother, I again started adding corruption; slowly this time. As before, this one started growing rapidly.

"Stop!" Dani ordered. I did, waiting for an explanation. "Look, the amount of corruption almost overtook the Essence it can hold! That is probably what happened with the first one. Are you adding corruption and Essence at the same rate?"

<Yeah, about half of what I was adding was air-type corruption.>

"Try a smaller amount, maybe... one part tainted to four parts pure Essence?" she directed. We continued on the same rabbit, and it started growing again, albeit slower. When it had gained enough to get to F-rank six, I stopped adding Essence and waited for a result to become apparent. As I had hoped, it gained an elemental ability!

<Yes! It worked!> I exulted in our success.

Dani was a bit more impatient. "What does it do?"

I looked at what the bunny could now do. <It's called Cleave. What does that mean?>

"Ooh, cool! That means when it attacks, it'll hit an area in an arc in front of it. Since it is air based, it'll likely create an intense gust of wind with each hit that will form the arc. Even if it misses, the air may extend and successfully land an attack!" Dani told me triumphantly.

<Wow! That *is* cool! What should we try next?> I was excited to continue my experimentation.

Water corruption had yielded no effect, and I was loath to try infernal. We moved on to earth, where our effort rewarded us by granting a new ability.

<It *grew* armor!> I breathed, awed by the form of the new Basher. Nearly double the size of its fellows, the thick muscles and tough bones were now also hidden under plates of what appeared to be stone. This could be considered a tanking unit, the member of a group able to take the most damage.

A tank type unit was fairly common. For instance, the knights in the groups that came into the dungeon with their thick armor and big ol' shields were a good example of a tank. By having one of these as a Mob, I could have my other Mobs focus on attacking and hope that *this* creature would remain the main target of adventurers because of its size and formidable appearance.

Next, we tried adding the Essence of fire to the pattern of a basher, but each time, the Basher would scream and spasm on the floor until it died. A few tests of this determined that no matter how diluted I made the combination of fire taint and Essence, I could not make a successful prototype. With some trepidation, we decided to move on to infernal taint, as we were running low on options and infernal *was* the most plentiful in my arsenal, after earth corruption, of course. This we were more careful with, going *very* slowly so we didn't accidentally create an uncontrollable demonic animal.

Again stopping at F-rank six, we watched as the animal started panting heavily; it began shuddering, almost having a seizure. I watched its bones grow longer and denser, becoming harder than even the earth-type Basher. The nub of bone on its head grew, expanding longer and tapering into a sharp point. Its growth slowed, but it had gained a dark, solid horn. The muscles on its back legs strengthened; though fully grown, its size was roughly equivalent to the air-tainted basher.

I was a bit let down. The last creation felt so anti-climactic! <Well, it got a horn but no ability.>

"No, it did! Look at the *horn*!" Dani shouted.

I looked and examining it, saw 'Hardened: Armor piercing'. <How is that an infernal ability? Wait, how is that on its bones? I've seen something similar but only on a few weapons.>

Dani toyed with a few ideas, finally conceding, "No idea. Maybe it combined with its own natural Essence to produce it?"

I had already turned my mind to the next attempt I was going to make. <I guess. Well, shall we try celestial, too?> Not waiting for her response, I turned my attention to the next Basher and began the process. I tried to regulate the celestial taint moving through it, but unlike the forceful joining that had been obvious with the other types of taint, this basher absorbed celestial taint like a sponge. Instead of a one to five ratio like the others, this type ended up gaining closer to one part celestial, three parts Essence–significantly more than the others.

Cutting the flow of Essence off at the F-rank six, I watched as the Basher twitched, absorbing the Essence flowing into it. Unlike the obvious pain the others had gone through, this one almost seemed to be writhing in pleasure. The fur along its body turned blond, nearly golden. Its body actually *shrank* a bit, unlike the others who had more than doubled in size. Its muscles reconfigured, gaining fast-twitch muscle–good for sprinting and fast reactions–whereas the others had gained tough, slow-twitch muscle for endurance and strength. The nub of bone on its head turned pure white with golden threads moving through it, looking like a vein of gold in a slab of marble.

"Well, it looks *adorable*," Dani cooed.

I whooped, <It has an ability! 'Mend'. Does that heal?> We obviously had different priorities.

"I think so. It may actually be a stronger version of the healing ability we've seen. It'll likely take a lot of energy to heal, so I don't think it'll be able to do it very often. I mean, look how *tiny* and *cute* you are!" She was talking to the bunny now, who rubbed at his face with his front paws.

<Cute and resource intensive. It took a lot of celestial corruption to make. Way too much to be a common Mob, and I doubt it will be a great fighter...> Of all the taint we had accumulated, the smallest amount we had was by far celestial.

<Well, I may not be able to make these common Mobs, but let's see what they can do.>

I lined all of my new Bashers up in the room and made them race to the end of the room and back in a test of speed. The earthen, armor covered one was obviously the slowest; he also could not turn very well at speed, as shown when he rammed into the wall and shattered a large chunk of granite before turning around with no apparent damage.

"Damn!" Dani whistled.

The air and infernal types were near matches for speed; the infernal won simply by the length of its horn. In terms of top speed, none of them were able to match the celestial type. It took off, bounding to the end, jumped off the far wall to conserve momentum, and returned to its spot before the others had made it to the first wall. When it stopped, it sank to the floor, exhausted and panting heavily. This little guy was a sprinter, not a marathon runner.

It was almost time to reopen the dungeon, so while I wanted to run some more experiments, we needed to finish up. <What do you think, Dani? I'm leaning toward boosting a version of the armored one to F-rank nine, making him my new Boss. The others I can make mostly common Mobs, especially earth-type, small, armored ones.>

"Sounds good, and how about we place warrens in the Boss room for the healing ones to hide? Then when the Boss gets hurt too bad, they do a sprint-by healing, returning to hiding to avoid dying. Then you won't need to spend more Essence to make new ones, and we can surprise groups who thought the fight was over."

<Perfect! Oh, Dani, what would I do without you?> I wildly overacted, pretending she was even more helpful than she really was.

She was ready for my snarky-ness today, unfortunately. "You'd likely still be gazing lovingly at moss."

<Ouch! Fair enough, cruel overlord!>

We got ready to create the new and enhanced Boss, marshaling our thoughts and readying my Essence while we discussed the best way to proceed. After absorbing all of the new Bashers and carefully studying each pattern, I was prepared to begin. Applying the ideas of the last few hours, I made a new armored Basher and began to flood him with Essence and corruption, literally the energy of the heavens and the earth.

He began to grow again, and I applied more earth taint than I had originally planned. Slowly, he began to grow and eventually passed the F-rank eight. At F-rank nine, his armor fell off, and new plates began to form. Collecting from the nearby granite, particles flew to join into the new, thick plating. The grinding rock segmented, allowing for greater mobility, while the multitude of plates themselves formed piecemeal as hexagonal chunks, which would make sharpened weapons skitter off without finding purchase.

In the end, this monster was near the size of what Dani called a 'black bear'. Over waist height on a human, the creature weighed in at close to three hundred pounds. Due to the amount of time and Essence I had devoted to it, I decided that I would need to wait until someone killed it before absorbing the pattern. I saw that it had a new ability, but its aura was strong enough that without absorbing the Boss, I could not tell what it did.

Placing hidey-holes around the Boss room, I directed a few golden rabbits to them, making sure they could help or escape from any part of the room. Then to fill out the second floor, I made roving squads of the improved Bashers and named them. The small earth-types I named Smashers, the air-types Oppressors, and the infernal Impalers. The Boss got an actual name, Armored Basher: Raile, while the golden ones had a slightly different flavor to their moniker, Glitterflit. That one was Dani's suggestion.

I made squads of two Bashers, two Oppressors, and one Impaler each. I placed a few thorn-shooting Banes along the tunnel ceiling to make people look up instead of looking for traps. Then interspersing the rooms with several squads each and a few Banes for ranged attacks, I was as ready to re-open as I could be. Confirming with Dani, I drew the Runed door into the ceiling for later use, then settled in to wait for the next group foolish enough to attack us.

CHAPTER FIFTEEN

After a normal morning routine of breakfast and boasting, the first group of divers adjourned to the dungeon as per usual. To their great shock, the entrance was gone. A slab of stone that was obviously not a natural part of the surrounding landscape blocked the opening.

"What is this?" Dale murmured, poking at the obstacle.

"I'm unsure, but there is an energy moving in it that I am... unfamiliar with." Craig sounded exceedingly confused. "Nothing for it, men. Let's alert the Guild Master."

They climbed up the stairs, quickly moving toward the large tent housing the upper echelon of the Guild. They had to walk past the area which had been converted to glass, the rays of sunshine bursting from the glorious dawn glimmered off the reflective surface with awe-inspiring intensity. They arrived at the tent, quickly being granted an audience with a harried-looking Guild Master.

"What? What's the matter? Why aren't you in the dungeon?" Frank growled at a clerk as she dropped a stack of paperwork on his desk.

"That's what we're here about, Frank. Dungeon's closed. There is a big ol' slab of rock in the entryway, and it has some kinda energy moving in it I can't decipher," Craig dropped into an unfamiliar cant of dialogue as he talked to Frank.

This got Frank's attention, as Craig was a well-known expert of all things Essence. He was widely thought to be the next man that would be moving into the Mage rank, a great interest to the Guild as the Mage rank was something that was attained usually twice a decade or so. If Craig didn't understand whatever the issue was, it could be very serious.

"Humph. Alright, I'll send you a Spotter. Go check it out when he gets here, then have him report back to me. Actually, one of you come tell me what it is. They would stop to write a report for me to read. As if I didn't have enough to do..." He scribbled out a note and sent a runner to find the specialist. A Spotter was a Mage-ranked person who specialized in determining the hidden properties of an unknown item. They could read Inscriptions, energy flows, and had a deep understanding of history and the lore of most abilities that had been seen before. They were often assigned to scout teams that helped determine when people, places, or items had gone down a dark path. Less well liked, the church had its own version called inquisitors.

"A Spotter?" Hans whined. "Do we have to work with one of those stuck up bastards?"

"Nope! You could take the day off of dungeoneering and help me out instead. We could use someone to dig a new latrine, ours is near overflowing." Frank deadpanned with a gimlet stare.

"Oh, look at the time! It is work-with-the-Spotter o'clock," Hans chattered cheerfully as he made his escape from the room.

"Mm-hm," Frank grunted. He waved the rest of them off. "Let me know how it goes–now shoo! The portal Mages will be arriving here in the next few days, and I need to find a suitable location for them to set up. Good call giving that lot to the church, Dale. I hadn't thought about a possible monster breakout."

Dale, feeling a bit down about not dungeon diving this morning, brightened a bit upon hearing these words. Craig noticed his emotional shift and shook his head; sometimes it was easy to forget that Dale was so young. They stepped out of the tent, at a loss for what to do for the next while. Walking around, they played a game of 'notice some random detail', a way to train their perception and attention to detail by looking at all the new people who had arrived. Not all of them were Guild members; quite a few were simple treasure hunters, while others were people interested in joining the Guild.

"Half of these fools will be dead in six months," Craig muttered darkly.

Dale was taken aback by the normally good spirited man's sudden mood shift. "Why would you say that, Craig? They all look decently strong to me. Look at that massive guy. He looks like he could throw me over the mountain!"

"I forgot that you are looking with *just* your eyes all the time. I think you are ready to learn how you use your Essence, at least a bit," Craig decided aloud, ignoring the surprised looks of the men around him. They stopped, and the other men in his group, Hans, the near-silent Josh, and the ranger Steve, now looked upset at Craig's words.

"You think he is ready?" Steve quietly questioned, one of the very few times Dale had heard him speak.

"He's been progressing quickly, much faster than we were able to when we became cultivators. At this pace, if we can get back into that dungeon soon, he'll be breaking into the D-ranks within six months to a year," Craig told the group.

They looked at Dale with surprise, all seeming to simultaneously squint at him to assess him as if for the first time. They nodded unanimous agreement after a moment.

"Looks like it."

"Yup."

"Unfair," pouted Hans.

Dale looked around. "I know that is good. Why are you acting like that is that strange?"

"Normally, it takes quite a few years to get out of the F-rankings, Dale. You got very lucky, a solid group and a good dungeon to train in," Craig informed him. "Listen, it's time for you to learn how to be, well, *actually* useful to us, instead of a liability that just so happens to kill a few rabbits each day."

Dale winced. "Ow, my pride. I thought I was doing better than that."

"You are. I was exaggerating to make a point. So far though, you have been doing everything with just the strength of your body; when you can use your Essence to supplement your weak points, life can only get better for you," Craig explained. "Time to let you in on a poorly guarded secret. You have a Chi spiral, but have you found your meridians?" Dale shook his head, knowing the lesson would progress faster if he didn't pretend to know things he didn't.

"Sit down, and get comfy. Good. Now, feel your center." Dale focused and was soon able to perfectly see his small Chi spiral. "You are looking at the spiral, good. Instead of looking at just your spiral, look around. Look in *any* other direction. Find the 'walls' that are holding your spiral in this place, the boundaries that contain your Essence." Dale was easily able to follow these instructions, easily feeling his limits as they were so small currently.

Craig's voice was soft as he continued directing his protégé, "Find the holes in the wall, the empty spaces that move further into your body, and extend some Essence to these places. Don't be scared when your Essence begins flowing on its own."

The Essence, not used to doing anything but spinning under Dale's control, initially was too slippery for Dale's mind to grasp. He had done a very good job of purifying, and the thread eluded his grip for several long minutes. Finally, of course, he managed to hold it, then was able to extend the Essence to the hole but missed several times, bouncing it off the wall. This was as difficult to him as threading a small needle to sew with.

Slowly, carefully, he poked the thread into the hole, succeeding this time. Thankful that Craig had warned him, Dale was still startled at the rapid pace the Essence unspooled from his center into the meridian.

"Good, now wait a moment before you try anything else. Follow the thread with your thoughts as it moves throughout your body. Also, you may notice this hurt a bit, but it should be nowhere near as painful as the last time we made you do things with Essence." Craig chuckled a bit.

The thread left his center and traveled directly toward his heart. It impacted with the force of a hammer. For a few moments. Dale's eyes boggled as he clutched his chest. The thread looped around his heart in a tight weave until the organ had the thread moving through every part–tissue, artery, and capillary. The purified Essence moved onward, leaving the weave intact as it continued. The pain subsided in its wake, and his heart began to beat regularly again.

Flowing downward, the thread hit his lower intestine with less force and only created a weave in a small area before moving up to his lungs. It split just before them and impacted them both at dangerous speeds, enough so that he coughed up a bit of blood and lost his breath. The weave placed on the heart repeated itself, forming tightly around both lungs, making it hard to breathe until the pattern completed. The split thread moved up his arms until it wrapped around the little finger and began its travel down along a slightly altered path until it found another hole in the walls of his center, rejoining his Chi spiral from an unexpected angle.

Dale opened his eyes and wiped a bit of blood from his mouth. He felt calm and rested, heart beating powerfully while he breathed more deeply than he could ever remember doing. The sense of calm lasted only until he looked up into the expectant eyes of his groupmates, who had looks of relief on their faces.

"What?" Dale nervously stammered.

"That was an interesting choice for the first meridian to open." Craig's eyes were inspecting the weave along Dale's heart and lungs.

Dale was surprised. "I had a choice?"

"Of course. It is good that this is the one you used, though. The heart meridian can be... somewhat dangerous to open once you get older. The initial hit to your heart can kill those that are unprepared or try it without help. Don't worry overmuch. If yours had stopped, we would have restarted it, of course," Craig informed him seriously.

"There are twelve paired meridians, six 'yin' and six 'yang'. Then there are two single sets, the 'governing' and 'conception' sets. Those are what allowed you to formulate Chi in the first place and were forced open when you were younger, usually at birth. You can reinforce them with your Chi, and you should but make sure we are around any time you plan on opening a new meridian."

"Right, so what just happened?" Dale examined the group surrounding his prone form. "I mean, I feel good, but I was bleeding. Did I hurt myself? Did I do it wrong?"

"You just strengthened your heart, lungs, lower intestine, and a few muscles in your arms. In practical terms, this means that your endurance is going to skyrocket, the rate at which you heal will also increase as your body gets used to this transformation," Craig imparted with a smile. "You did the job perfectly."

"As an added bonus, you should be able to see that your Essence seems smaller, but in actuality, it is all still there; some of it is constantly following the unique pattern you have created for it. Before you think that you can just do all of those different meridians in one go, please realize that if you go below a certain amount of Essence in your center, you may die. Just do what you have been doing, and you will be fine; you simply need to build up the amount of Essence you have again before you open a new meridian."

A smile on his face, Craig then directed, "Now, from that meridian, pull a bit of Essence to your eyes, and see what happens."

Dale reached inside himself yet again, pulling Essence upward. His eyes quickly gathered a bit of Essence, and the light in the area became overwhelming. He squinted and was suddenly able to see the flowing Essence in the other men. Their spirals were powerful, howling twisters that spun Essence into smaller twisters that continued deep into their centers.

"Wow!" Dale breathed. He looked at them all, amazed. "You see like this all the time?" Looking around, he could see Essence moving through everything, the colors almost sickeningly bright. The best comparison he could think of was pouring honey on a massive dessert cake with creamed ice on the side, then trying to eat it when you were already full to bursting.

"In the dungeon, yes. Out here, it can be a bit... overwhelming. Practice this on your own, as often as possible," Craig commanded him. "Since it doesn't leave your body, there is no Essence cost associated with this skill. All of it will make its way back to your center when you stop using it. Now, look at the men in this and tell me what I meant when I said they would all be dead in a few months if they planned on delving into the dungeon."

Dale looked at the unknown men, shocked at the thick corruption in their centers. The Essence they had in them was stagnant, simply sullenly sitting there, festering like a disease untreated for too long. "Was this what I looked like to you all before you stripped my Essence?"

"Yes. You were able to see what it looked like inside yourself; this is an outside perspective, which is why it looks a bit different to you. See that giant man over there stuffed full of earth taint?" Craig pointed at the massive man they had discussed a few minutes ago. "For all of his bulging muscles and nasty attitude," the unknown man had just punched someone whom had accidentally bumped him, "within a few months, your arm muscles will be fully reinforced with Essence, and you will easily be able to beat him in an arm-wrestling contest or stop a blow from him as you would a child. Life lesson here, don't forget he will still outweigh you. Don't try to grapple with someone that huge!" Hans laughed at what was obviously an inside joke.

Craig nodded at Hans, also grinning. "This is just the start for you. The more meridians you have cleansed and opened, the more powerful your physical body will become." Craig glanced at Dale, ensuring he had his full attention. "I'm hoping you are beginning to understand the advantage you are gaining over the average person, but remember that in the Guild, we use this power as it is intended to be used; that is, to help our fellow man. Well, those tricky Elves too, I suppose," Craig reluctantly allowed.

"Now," Craig broke into a smile, "I wasn't sure if you noticed when it happened, so have an official welcome to the sixth rank of the F series!"

The others clapped Dale on the back, cheering at his success. Dale grinned, happy that this day had turned out so well. They decided to continue walking around and possibly visit the new priest and see how his preparations to build were going.

They walked to the shining lot, seeing Father Richard praying in the center. They waited a moment until he noticed them and sprang up. "Lovely! Good morrow to you, m'boy!" Father Richard cheerfully called out, walking toward them.

"Good morning, Father," Dale intoned respectfully.

"Beautiful, is it not?" Father Richard gestured towards the lot. "Turns out that giant lot is now solid *quartz*! I thought it was glass but was *so* pleased to be wrong! In an unexpected and fortunate turn, it also seems that this entire sheet collects celestial Essence from the heavens and sunlight. I will be able to build a monastery that will bring people flocking from all corners of the world!" His eyes were burning with fervor, and he was wildly gesticulating.

"Really?" Dale had never heard of objects collecting Essence on their own. He decided to try his new ability, so collected Essence in his eyes and looked at the quartz. The entire clear pane now was filled with solid bars of golden light. "Ah! My eyes!" Dale cried, slapping his hands to his face.

Hans curled his lip and looked at him piteously. "You'll learn, kid."

"Heh. Oh, to be young." Father Richard chuckled. "Anyone know where I can find a good builder Mage? Quarrying enough stone from the area to build this church would take a decade, and the craftsmen I've been talking to are all trying to sell me on sandstone. This place is lousy with granite. Why would I not take advantage of that?"

"We have portal Mages that should be arriving in a few days. If you have the coin, I know a few I can recommend from the Lion Kingdom, for a small finder's fee," Hans stated greedily. They quickly dissolved into discussion while a young boy ran up to Craig, telling him that the Spotter was waiting for them near the stairs of the dungeon.

"About time, those bookworms probably only slithered out of their tent because they were tempted with a new toy," Josh muttered in a voice like gravel. He rolled his thick shoulders, making his armor creak.

They meandered their way back to the dungeon, Hans promising to meet up with Father Richard again soon. An unfamiliar man was waiting for them, his slim frame raising questions as to his status as a Mage in Dale's mind. He focused on the man with his new ability, but the energy inside of what was certainly a Mage was so confusing as to be beyond comprehension, actually making Dale nauseous.

"That's what Mana looks like," Hans muttered to Dale, seeing the odd green tint to his face. "Don't worry about it."

"I hear you have a quandary for me! I cannot wait to begin! Shall we?" The slim man raced down the stairs, bounding down them with no apparent concern for his safety. His words had an odd, slow inflection to them, as if each was savored before he spoke them, clashing with his rapid movements.

"That's what near physical invulnerability looks like," Hans dryly muttered again to Dale. "Really, try not to think about it. They are just... too weird." The team followed at a more measured pace, meeting the Mage as he was staring at the door. They settled in for a wait, which is what they got. The man muttered, gestured, and studied a book he had with him. He peered at the stone touching, sniffing, and even licking it once or twice.

"Freaking weirdo," Hans muttered, earning a glare from the slim man who suddenly shot up the stairs at reckless, astounding speed.

"What? Did I offend him, ya think?" Hans nervously asked as the others looked on in confusion. They glanced up just in time to see the man suddenly jump from the rim of what had once been the simple crevasse opening. A metal object gleamed in his hands as his back arched, swinging downward with a primal scream as he swung a pickaxe. The pickaxe head shattered, exploding in his hands as it impacted the stone, the shaft splintering into sawdust from the inhuman force behind the swing.

The slim man landed lightly, nodding sagely as if he had confirmed a great and profound secret. Lifting the splintered remains of the pick head, he examined it for a few minutes before turning, exposing shredded clothing with untouched flesh underneath.

"Yup! It's cursed earth," he proclaimed cheerfully. "Not getting through *that* too easily!"

He started walking away, humming, when Craig stopped him. "Can you tell us a bit more, please? We have to report to Frank."

"Oh sure, it is stone that has been reinforced with earth corruption with the basic Essence removed!" The man sounded nearly giddy at having a sample to study. "Not easy to do, I tell you what!" He started off again, humming a happy song. Craig was turning red in his effort to remain polite. "Is there a way through, good sir? There are many people awaiting entry to the training grounds below."

The Mage turned, startled, as if he had forgotten they existed. "Hmm? Oh, you can break it if you use enough Mana, but I don't think you will find a willing Mage. Also, it tends to drain all the Essence out of whatever is thrown against is, so I wouldn't recommend trying to break it yourselves."

Hans was a bit more abrupt with the distracted man, "Oi! How do we get in?"

"Well, I imagine you'll just have to wait for it to vanish. After all, if it just randomly appeared, it'll likely vanish the same way." With that unhelpful advice, the Mage skittered up the stairs on all fours and jogged away.

"Frank isn't going to like this," Steve sing-sang fretfully, adjusting his bow and quiver. "I call *not it*!" He shouted the last words.

A chorus of '*not it!*' followed this, except from a confused looking Dale.

"What?" Dale looked around the circle of now-happy faces.

"Thank you for volunteering to be the one to tell Frank." Steve patted Dale on the arm, a grin on his normally stony face.

"Meet us for lunch when you are done!" They walked up the stairs and away, laughing at Dale's misfortune.

No choice but to be the sacrificial victim for them, Dale returned to the Guild tent and waited for an audience with Frank. Roughly twenty minutes passed before he was ushered inside to make his report. When he finished, Frank heaved a sigh and nodded, rubbing his forehead.

"Ah, I see. Don't worry too much, lad. We knew the dungeon was getting more difficult. Think of this as a short vacation before your mornings become far more dangerous. Now, how about you–" Frank looked at Dale for the first time since he had entered and did a double take. "You already have a meridian open? Good for you, Dale! Congratulations."

"Oh. Thank you. I didn't realize it was a big deal until it was over. The guys just walked me through what to do." Dale blushed a bit at the unexpected praise.

"We don't advertise what a meridian can do because it is dangerous to open when you are not ready for it. Imagine someone doing that and having corrupted Essence." Frank shuddered at the thought. Dale did not comprehend the idea until Frank continued, "Think of it like this–suddenly, your heart is surrounded in stone, too heavy to beat, your lungs fill with water, or the blood in your veins turns to fire. Bad, *bad* idea. Better to let people think long life and superhuman strength is a side effect of reaching a higher rank. We don't tell people until they are *ready* for it, got that?""

"Yes, sir." Dale was then shooed out, moving to go get lunch with the others.

The team spent the remainder of the day training, the others taking turns sparring with Dale. Having only a bit over a month of experience fighting rabbits and mushrooms, he did terribly. Realizing the error in their ways, they began with the most basic of basics, teaching him the proper way to hold his morningstar. From that point forward, it was decided; Dale would take turns sparring after lunch with someone so he could become an *actually* good fighter instead of just a subpar stick swinger.

Dale was able to fight for several hours and was amazed that he could continue without getting exhausted as was normal for him. While he did not win a single match, he was able to continue round after round until they called for him to stop. Confused at first, he finally remembered what he had been told about opening his heart meridian. He felt great satisfaction with the already apparent effects. Dale was overjoyed that this huge increase in stamina was the result of opening just *one* meridian. He would ravenously await the chance to see what would happen when the rest were open.

He made good progress in learning to wield his morningstar that day but was nowhere near to mastering even this basic weapon. Understandably, picking up a weapon and suddenly being good with it wasn't realistic; it was a childish and lazy fantasy. Having proper form and being able to maximize your usage of a weapon took an obscene amount of work; it wasn't a magical appearance of talent. Even using a memory stone only taught you how to do something properly. It didn't hone your muscles and reaction times, and it didn't allow you to bypass strength training and endurance building. Dale couldn't imagine how long it would take to learn how to use something as complex as a sword in actual *combat*. Whack your enemy with a spiked ball on a stick? Perfect.

Even learning to use his shield as more than an accessory was harder than he thought it should be. Practicing without the enchanted buckler taught him that you couldn't just accept whatever blow came down; you needed to then angle it away. A heavy blow nearly breaking his arm taught him that you also needed to try to *dodge* at least every once in a while. Getting his legs swept out from under him as he thought of all this, taught the very important lesson of keeping your eyes and mind on your target.

Dozens of these small lessons began building into talent and huge bruises. When he could finally not get up on his own weakly waving his arms in a sad, little attempt to roll over, the men relented and sent him off to take a bath in the cold mountain stream, calling after him to ensure he cleaned his reeking armor.

After dinner, they each sat together and cultivated their respective elements. Dale and Craig sat on a slab of stone while Hans sat in the center of a ring of fire, sweating profusely. Josh was up to his neck in the river, eyes closed and shivering in the snow-fed mountain stream, while Steve danced around to find the strongest breezes. Wind was never in short supply on a mountain, of course.

The next few days followed this pattern for Dale, disappointedly checking the dungeon each morning, getting beat on after lunch, and cultivating heavily in the evening. They woke up on the fourth daybreak to excited people awaiting the Portal Mages' imminent arrival.

"They should be here within the hour!"

"I can't wait to see my kids!"

"A hot bath and a good meal in the capital by next week!"

Dale was a bit nonplussed at these swarming, cheering people. He wondered whether the mountains were really so bad—people really seemed to want to get away from them. A young messenger ran up to him and informed him that his presence was requested by the Guild Master. He followed the boy to the large tent and was quickly shown in. A large map and table had been acquired from some unknown locale; several people were talking in low voices while pointing at the map.

"Oh, good. Dale, looking at this map. Can you tell me where you'd prefer to have the portal set? It is a fairly permanent system once it is built, made of Inscribed stone, metal, and gems. *Very* heavy. Large enough to bring a couple wagons through at a time as well." Frank offhandedly muttered, "Big-ass eyesore too."

Dale joined him in looking at the map, pointing out a good spot. They discussed the pros and cons of the location, but eventually, all agreed that the spot was a good one. Some campers would need to shuffle around, but it was easily defensible and at the top of a small hill, which should keep it in a good location no matter the weather.

"Good choice, now we need to talk about how you can make a profit from this," Frank began seriously.

Dale, thinking of how good the Guild had treated him so far, started by saying, "Well, I was thinking a standard lease would–"

Waving his hands to stop Dale, Frank cried, "No! No, they'd love that far too much! You need to make a *percentage* profit, else you are making coppers on the *gold* here. Please, I'll help you make your argument for the best deal, so when they start making offers, *demand* a hard ten percent. You won't get it, but take no less than five percent profit of the travel cost, or they are robbing you. Remember, this is *your* land, and they *really* want to put a portal here. Nothing like a good training place for a prince or noble to make them grease their coin purse and slo-o-owly pry it open." The evil chuckle at the end made Dale look at Frank a bit oddly.

"I suppose that makes sense." Dale was again confused as to why Frank was helping him make a profit off his own Guild.

"You will *need* that money in order to stand being around them. You'll see," Frank ominously promised at Dale's blank look.

Chapter Sixteen

A caravan of wagons pulled to the outskirts of the still-growing dungeon camp, and officious-looking people stepped out. They looked down on the dirty men that were surrounding them with loopy grins on their faces. With a sniff, one man moved forward to greet Frank, and then they moved into the Guild's tent to discuss logistics. Dale was waiting for them there.

Upon seeing him, one of the new arrivals curled his lip in a sneer.

"What is this *fishy* doing in here?" the man spat.

Dale thought that strange because when other people in the camp had called him fishy, it often seemed affectionate. This man clearly saw him only for his cultivation rank, as such an inferior person that he might as well have been an animal.

"He's here to negotiate the cost of a portal in the area." Frank grimaced, making told-you-so glances in Dale's direction.

"Why?" he scoffed, smoothing away imagined wrinkles from his robes. "How could a *newborn* like him understand the complexities of associated cost in intra-dimensional travel?"

"Mm. More to the point, Dale *owns* the land around here, so I mean more the monetary cost of *you* opening a portal here." Frank managed to get this out with a straight face.

"Oh? The landowner? Him?" He glanced disparagingly at the poor, sweat-stained quality of Dale's clothes. "I suppose we could say, what, ten silver a month? A small fortune to the likes of you as I understand it. Not much around here, is there?" He turned back to Frank like the deal was finished. "Where can I get a proper meal around here?"

"I was thinking more along the lines of fifteen percent profit from all usage of the portal," Dale calmly announced, controlling his anger at this treatment.

"Pah!" The man laughed aloud scathingly as he turned around, pretending he had forgotten Dale's presence. "Where do you find these recruits, Frank? He'd make a better jester than businessman." Coldly turning toward Dale, he added, "I'll give you fifteen silver a month, and you'll be grateful that I bothered to give you anything, damn it."

"Fifteen percent *and* free usage for myself and all goods I care to take with me," Dale countered just as coldly, upping his offer.

"I could incinerate you with a blink of my eye."

"Please don't start a war, James," Frank begged softly.

Thinking he meant figuratively, James sneered at Frank again. "I think we will just place the portal further away then." He turned to leave.

"Best of luck," Dale voiced in a dry tone while Frank chuckled.

"A few hundred feet will not hamper my business any," James claimed, suspiciously looking at them.

"Then we'll say, I don't know," Dale started, pretending to be desperate before laughing and looking him directly in the eye, "fifteen percent and free usage for myself, *friends*, and all goods I care to take with me."

"Brat!" James roared furiously. "I just said I would move *off* the land you own! Surely, the next landowner will be more open to a portal on his land."

"Oh, well, in that case; best of luck," Dale repeated. "Also, please do not call me Shirley. The name is Dale."

James left the tent in a slightly confused but fully angry huff, looking to find someone who owned land in the area. Dale and Frank sat down, shaking their heads. Frank apologized for the behavior James had shown. Then they began eating lunch, talking about training techniques and cultivation. 'Oh, and how did Dale like his team?' 'They were good people!' 'Oh, that's good, any issues?' In a rage, James stormed back in, eyes flashing.

He shoved an accusatory finger at Dale. "You own the *entire mountain?!* That's *bullshit!*"

"It is accurate, though," Frank mildly stated.

Dale responded around a mouthful of sandwich, equally bland, "True, Guild Master."

"One gold a month, which is the best offer I will make!" James puffed up, red in the face.

"He was *quite* rude when he got here, wasn't he?" Dale ignored James, talking to Frank directly. "He isn't getting any politer. We are *eating*, sir."

"*Fine*! We will set up off the mountain! Make people climb for a day, what does it matter to me?!" James yelled.

"Oh, I don't think that's a good idea," Frank grunted.

"I agree, a very bad idea," Dale agreed that it was *indeed* a bad idea.

In a high pitched tone, James screeched, "Stop that! I am your *better*, F-ranked scum. I will not allow you to swindle me!"

Eyes flashing, Dale rose up from his seat. "Just. My. Elder. Good luck getting business, you *elderly asshole.* People trying to climb a mountain that is impassable in winter, which is... a month away? Yup, a month. You know what? No! *I* like it here. *I* have no issue staying, and everyone else can god-damned *walk. I* have no need of a portal. I *refuse* your business! Get off my mountain. I will *not* rent my land to you."

Something very odd happened then. James began protesting, but his arms and legs turned, and he started walking away, screaming in impotent rage all the while. Dale followed, wide-eyed to see what was happening. A group of people gathered to see the man grab a horse in passing and ride off, still cursing and shrieking in frustration.

"What the infernal *abyss*?" Dale breathed.

Frank passed Dale a nonchalant chunk of knowledge, "That would be the effect of being the *magically enforced* landowner of this mountain. Any citizen of this Realm–under the political rank of a Duke–would be forced to leave if you told them to. You cannot force someone to *stay* or to do things for you, but you can obviously make them leave. In a brilliant yet uncomprehending move of forethought, you bought this from *two* Realms, meaning there are *two* Kingdoms of people that would need to obey the command you just gave him."

"Well. Damn." Dale turned to Frank as a realization dawned on him. "Hey! Is that why you have been so helpful to me?"

"Nah, I'm just a polite person. I'm *definitely* this nice to everyone, Heck, I let random people into the Guild all the time." Frank grinned. "Then I let them come to *me*, the Guild leader, any time they have a question."

Dale rolled his eyes. "I get it, I get it!"

A lady from the caravan walked over, eyes flashing. "What was that about? What just happened to James?"

"Ah... He was told to leave the property by the landowner, ma'am. He was *quite* rude and insulted the landowner repeatedly. Trust me when I say that he deserved far worse than being told to 'go away'," Frank explained in an attempt to mollify the slightly glowing woman. "Can I get your name, ma'am?"

"Yes," she warily released the Mana she had been readying, "I am High Magous Amber of the Portal Guild." High

Magous was a title that meant the person was in the upper A-Rankings. "James was *supposed* to be negotiating the terms of a lease for a portal, but as he is otherwise indisposed, would you introduce me to the owner?"

"I would be pleased to!" He turned to Dale, indicating him with a wave of his hand. "This is Guild apprentice Dale, owner of these surrounding lands."

She looked at Dale and nodded, realization dawning on her face as she took in his ranking. "I apologize for the poor attitude of my subordinate Guild member. He forgets that we were *all* at your level at some point. His bias is well-known and documented, and I hope to make reparations as soon as is possible." She bowed slightly toward him.

"I also apologize for sending him off my land. I hope it will not inconvenience you too much. I was... unaware of the ability the contract gave landowners." Dale glanced at Frank as he said this.

Amber grimaced and shook her head. "Please don't worry about it. If he is escorted back to you to ensure his good behavior, may I have your permission to allow him back on your land–with an apology and some form of recompense from him, of course?"

"That would be very acceptable, High Magous," Dale grudgingly allowed as formally as he could manage. Something about her screamed that formality was an absolute necessity.

She seemed to disagree with his assessment. "Please, just call me Amber. How far does your land extend? We will need to get him from the edge, where I assume he is currently pacing and ranting. He will apologize *sincerely* within the hour," she promised while rubbing her head. Obviously, she had a headache coming on.

Dale coughed and blushed a bit. "It may take a *bit* longer to bring him back. I own the whole mountain."

Shock whipped across her face. "Ah, this also explains much." She waved one of her people down and sent him to go collect James with instructions to escort him directly to the main Guild tent. "Now, Dale, if we could discuss the price of a portal set-up? I hope James didn't cost us the chance to get a contract."

"Well, the last discussed price was sixteen percent of the profit and free usage for myself, my friends, and all goods I care to take with me," Dale started, all business as he upped the cost again.

Amber made a small choking sound. "More of James's anger is explained... I don't suppose you'd be willing instead to make a... *standard* lease for the land?" She smiled weakly, knowing he wouldn't go for it.

"I'm sorry, my financial advisors have all demanded that any business in the area must pay percentage profit. As I will be needing to pay taxes to both the Lion and Phoenix Kingdoms, I hope you can see my dilemma," Dale told her very seriously.

Amber smiled, getting ready for one of her favorite pastimes: haggling. "This could take a while. Do you have any refreshments, by chance? It has been at least three days and a few hundred miles since I was able to eat a cooked meal."

They happily returned to their lunch, filling a plate for the Portal Mage. After much haggling and awkward silences, they agreed upon eight percent of the gross profit, free use for him, his goods, and close friends. Happy with the results of the day, Dale then left to train with his group, earning several bruises and putting him in a bad mood from their scolding and his poor performance. He bathed and went to dinner, discussing better tactics and form with Hans, who had proven to be a good friend. As per Frank's orders, Dale returned to the Guild tent after dinner, where he found Amber and Frank talking to a fuming James.

"Of course he makes us wait! Probably stuffing his face with free Guild food while he laughs at making more important people wait on his whims!" James was saying maliciously.

"You really aren't very smart, are you? I really thought better of you, James!" Amber rounded on him, voice cold. "This training ground is a potential *gold mine.* Already the kings of the surrounding Realms plan their visits. Princes and princesses will come here to cultivate, so they can meet on neutral ground while remaining well protected. The *Elves* are a few weeks behind us, for god's sake, planning to build a *city* on this spot, and you *insult* the one person who can just *tell us* to leave?!" She was shouting at him by the end of her spiel.

"He needs us more than we need him! The people here would riot at the thought of losing their chance at portals!" James weakly rebutted, wilting under the powerful gaze of his supervisor.

"Why wouldn't they just wait until the Elves got here? Their portals are just as good as ours, and they care little for our gold!" Amber exclaimed. "We would lose a massive investment because you cannot stop being a prick!"

"You don't need to worry about that too much; I already accepted your offer, Magous Amber. I try to be a man of my word," Dale let the others know he could hear them, striding into the room. He glared at James. "I think that you are not welcome here, Mage James. You have been here a day and already overstayed your welcome. I don't know what it is about me that offended you so, but I will not tolerate insults like you are spewing. Not only is it rude for no reason, it is bad for morale. Due to my daily access to the dungeon, I am actually a higher cultivation rank than the average adventurer around here;

how would these insults be taken by them—your paying *customers*?"

James's face flushed red, indignation within him.

Dale cut James off before he could begin a tirade, "When the portal is set up, please leave. You are free to go *before* then, which is my preference, but I know that may really inconvenience High Magous Amber." She nodded reluctantly as he mentioned this. "Also, if you plan to actually attack me or convince others to harm me, I need to ask you to leave, please."

James, face suddenly pale, had his body whipped around, then started walking away, not in control of his limbs. He visibly calmed himself, taking a deep breath, stopped and turned back to the group watching him. "My actions do not befit my rank. I apologize that I have acted so poorly. Please, allow me to make amends before sending me away."

Dale nodded, amazed at the change in demeanor James was exhibiting. "That is fine, but my decision stands. I *don't* want to make an enemy of you, James, but I cannot allow insults like these. On that note, feel free to talk to me if you can find reasons I should change my mind." James nodded sharply, ashamed, walking out of the tent under his own power for once.

"Well," Frank grumbled, "that was a shit show."

"Yup." Dale, head throbbing, took his leave and moved to find his bed.

The next days followed a simple pattern: early rise, get to know people, train, cultivate. The ground rumbled for several hours each of these days, not making anyone nervous as there was no shaking, only noise. When people were starting to become truly angry that the dungeon was blocked, Frank had to punish a few people for fighting in their restlessness.

Finally, the morning came when the door to the dungeon was open again. Exceedingly cheerful, Dale's team alerted the

Guild. They got into formation and went back to the dungeon's entrance, ready to make some money.

The difference in the room was apparent immediately. Raw iron coated practically every inch of the wall, and the air was as thick with Essence *in the entrance* as it had been only in the Boss's room previously. With only a few violent mushrooms visible to make them cautious, they decided to take their time and absorb the Essence in each room. They knew that would slow them down, but in the end, it would make them stronger. Dale's cultivation speed was so much higher at his new rank, though, that they were able to move forward in a short half hour.

CAL

<I *may* have allowed too much Essence out,> I noted to Dani.

"Nah, that is totally normal. It's a byproduct of increasing your rank then not having anyone pulling the Essence into themselves. It was bound to accumulate, Cal. The huge level of Essence in the air will vanish in a few hours, I'm betting. Especially at the rate this group is cultivating. Don't worry about them. Other people will be in a hurry to make money or get an item or two, so you'll be able to recapture some good Essence," Dani promised.

She was right, as per usual. As my high-powered morning group cleared the second room and sat in the lotus position to cultivate, another group entered and hurried to get ahead of them, likely thinking that the best rewards went to the fastest group. They yelled some derisive comments at the first group as they passed, laughing at their good fortune whilst taking the left branch of the tunnel. They entered a room that had a false back;

after clearing it, they shouted in anger that they had been tricked. Heh. That was even funnier than I had thought it would be. They stomped back, glaring at the still-cultivating group like it was their fault, taking the branch to the right.

"Are they all F-ranked?" Dani wondered, peering at the hustling group through our connection.

<It looks like I'm feeding well today,> I smugly told her. I already was, of course, using my very useful trick of constantly pulling a few strands of refined Essence from the group that was cultivating.

This group cleared the room, joyfully filling bags with the loot they found. Moving on, I was impressed with their ability to take the wrong direction every single time. By the time they limped into the first floor Boss room, they looked tired and sour. Taking out a week's worth of their anger on my poor Bloody Bane, they sat to rest for a bit. I had dropped a holy pendant for them because I was impressed at their tenacity, if not their attitude. I think that I was jaded, being used to professionals at this point.

They got up and were discussing where they should spend their money, so I decided that they needed a boost in the right direction. I dropped a few coppers on top of the stairs, making a loud clattering of falling coins. Of course, they came to investigate and found the tunnel hidden around the bend. Seeing the stairway leading deeper, they became so excited that I almost felt bad for them, but really, does death only come for those who are wicked? Does it spare good people just because they *are* good or excited? *I think not!*

Moving downward, they were on high guard, ready to be the first to explore these new, unknown depths. I directed a squad their way, getting ready to test out my new creations in battle. Seeing my Bashers racing at them from the gloom, two of the humans crouched with shields to block their charge. I had the other Bashers move back as the Smashers raced forward, diving directly into the shields. The poor quality metal bent at the impact from my lovely bunnies, breaking the arms of the men foolish enough to attempt to block them, simultaneously knocking the men to their knees.

The fallen humans screamed in pain for a moment, at least till the Oppressors landed their attack on the heads placed perfectly for assault. The cleave ability came into play, a gust of forceful wind blasted into the humans' screaming mouths, shattering teeth and dislocating jaws moments before their skulls lost the 'whose cranium is harder' challenge.

With two of their five members dead in the first attack, the others tried to run. They did not get far before an Impaler's horn pierced the spine of a fleeing archer. the Smashers caught up to the remaining two, breaking their legs and giving the other Bashers a chance to finish them off. Just like that, I gained enough Essence that I broke directly into D-rank one.

I whooped in joy. <Wow! Those were even more effective than I *thought* they would be!>

"Surprise is a glorious tool, Cal." Dani was nearly as excited as I was for my new rank. Remembering that there were others in the dungeon, I quickly worked to dissolve the corpses and acquire their items. It wouldn't do to have someone becoming alert to their impending doom, after all. I started fantasizing that *just maybe* I would finally get this group that showed up daily? I broke out of my reverie with a start, remembering that the Mobs who helped kill a person would gain a portion of their Essence! I moved the squad that had won their first battle into a hiding place to await lower level groups. As an experiment, I would try to get them to evolve naturally. I needed to keep them separate, so as to ensure I would remember them.

I'd call them Alpha Squad and give them a pleasure warren for when they weren't in combat.

The first group of humans came to the first floor Boss room just as the 'seed' bloomed into a new Monster, so they had to fight him. I wasn't sure if I should be happy... or upset. Having them fight the Boss gave me time to absorb the bodies below, wringing out every last drop of Essence, but now I would need to resurrect the Boss *again*. I vowed that the next time I was going to upgrade my dungeon, I would begin by replacing this useless Boss! Disgusted with my weak Mobs, I dropped the holy symbol I had retaken from the wiped group below, impatiently waiting for them to finish cultivating.

I heard what I had been waiting for. "Look at that!"

"What is it, Dale?" His name is Dale, huh? I'll call them 'Dale's group' from now on.

Dale was as excited as I had hoped he would be. "Stairs leading down!"

"That must be why we didn't pass that group yet. I was getting worried for them." The blond man seemed relieved. Heh.

"Stay worried. A second level means stronger Mobs, and that group was weak to begin with," a harsh voice croaked at them from the cloth wrapped man.

Dale's group went downward, though at the landing paused, looking into the gloom.

"Dale, are you cycling your Essence for enhanced vision?"

"Eh... I am now," Dale sheepishly replied.

"What do you see?"

"Looks like, um, moving Essence. I think earth, air, and... what is that blackish-red?"

"Infernal," a grim voice rang out, slowly drawing a sword...

Dale gave a very unappreciative, "Oh, that's bad I take it."

"What else?" the cloth wrapped man prodded.

"The... earth ahead looks... wrong? Thin, like the top layer of a puddle in winter," Dale notified them.

The man asking questions nodded, though Dale wasn't looking his way. "Good, those are most likely traps. As an earth-affinity cultivator, one of your most important responsibilities will lie in seeing or feeling traps like that. Others *might* see them, but I want you to call out every trap you see. Any you fail to catch in time will mean an *hour* of training with Josh at full speed."

The panic in Dale's eyes made me chuckle. I guess 'Josh' wasn't gentle. Hopefully, poor little Dale wouldn't have to worry for much longer... about anything.

"Those moving Essence blobs are coming at us now!" Dale called out.

"Likely Mobs. Get ready boys!" the blond man holding daggers whooped.

A fresh squad raced at them, moving quickly under my direction for a kill. The huge man in Dale's group moved forward with a tower shield, so I had both of the Smashers ram it. Higher quality than the previous group, the man's shield held under the heavy attack, but the man himself grunted and moved back a few steps.

"Those suckers are heavy. Dodge 'em if possible," he told the others in a strained conversational tone.

I sent an Oppressor to jump to the side of him, pushing off the wall to gain sideways momentum. Thinking he could easily block this smaller Basher, the large man didn't focus as he should have. Therefore, he was knocked off balance as the cleaving wind sliced into both of his legs, opening up shallow cuts where the armor was jointed, even though the Basher itself was stopped short.

The other men rushed in, the cloth-wearing one moving exceedingly fast across the ground. I could feel a bit of Essence interacting with the earth as he moved; this must be a movement skill. He seemed to vanish from his spot and appear behind the Oppressor that had knocked the large man to the side. He punched with perfect form, creating a resounding *crack.*

The perfectly aimed blow snapped my poor bunny's neck; it flopped to the floor, dead. While this impossibly fast man was distracted–I hoped–I sent my Impaler at his back to try for an incapacitating blow. Mid-jump, an arrow landed in its eye! That was odd. I hadn't seen this group having an archer before. I risked quickly looking at their weapons, noticing that the person I had thought was using a staff this whole time was actually carrying a big-ass longbow. The draw weight on that must be *massive* for it to look like a metal-clad staff most of the time!

The remaining Oppressor and two Smashers bounded toward the group of three people standing together, the two heavies flanking the lighter Oppressor. The blond haired man raced right at them, a dagger in each hand. As the Bashers leaped at him, he ignored defense, leaping *higher* than my Bashers and accurately stabbing downward between the armored plates of the leftmost Smasher, severing its spinal column.

When the remaining Bashers landed from their missed attack, a heavy, spiked ball crushed the skull of my unarmored Oppressor. Dale had moved forward without my noticing, the little brat! I may have been too focused on the jumping man while Dale landed his attack. The man with the... bow? staff? stepped forward and slammed the metal-shod end on to the last

Smasher, dazing it long enough for the dagger wielder to finish it off. Just like that, the battle was over. For now.

<Whew! That was intense. What do you think, Dani?>

"A good test of their abilities. I can already think of a few improvements we should try for the next batch." Dani quickly reminded me, "Give them some good loot!"

<Fair enough.> I had a few silver and copper coins rain down as well as a few healing potions I had gotten from a well-funded but underpowered group recently. I threw in a holy symbol for good measure.

"Well, I think *that* was worth it!" Dale gasped, excited at seeing silver glinting in the treasure.

"Hmm. We have not even gotten to a room on this floor, and already the Mobs were stronger than the Boss on the previous level. Should we continue or go warn the Guild?" the wise, unarmored person polled the group.

"Hard to warn against that which we don't know." The dagger user was placing the bodies of my Bashers into a bag he had, which I felt was *far* too small to hold them all. I wanted a closer look, but his aura forced me to remain frustrated.

"I suppose that's true. We continue."

<Yes! They're still coming, I get another chance!> I delightedly told Dani.

"Yay, you!" she cheered.

Dale's group moved further in, Dale calling out the traps placed throughout the tunnel. He missed one, and I was really looking forward to them boiling in acid when the cloth covered human ruined my fun by stopping the group, pointing at the ceiling and telling Dale he had an appointment with Josh when they were done. The big one, who I now assumed was Josh, was gleefully rubbing his hands together and dancing around *just* outside of the range of my trap.

Twice, I tried to ambush them with squads while they were distracted with the low powered, original Bashers. Sadly, each time they were defeated, though I was able to form a dent in Josh's gigantic tower shield. He grumbled like a thunderstorm when it happened, whining till the one they called Craig reminded him the dent could instead have been in his legs. As much as I wanted to eat them and their equipment, I was still very impressed by their teamwork, perception, and coordinated efforts.

They moved on, clearing room after room, cultivating in each. After a bit, I noticed something odd about their behavior. They never took a wrong turn! I was confused as to how they found their way until I heard Dale ask the same question.

"Well, here is a fork in the tunnel. Which way do you think we should go?" Craig looked at Dale, though it was obvious that Craig somehow knew the answer.

"I'm not sure. I've never been here," Dale responded, a bit frustrated.

"Neither have I, but I know we need to go to the right! Look at the quantity of Essence swirling in the air. The more Essence a path has, the more likely that it is the correct way to the Boss room," Hans glibly informed him, throwing around precious information.

"Oh, that makes sense." Dale accepted this answer easily, and they started down the right-hand path.

<*Really?* Dani, is there a way for me to get around that? I didn't realize they could just follow the stupid *air*!> I demanded crossly. What a ridiculous thing for me to not notice.

"We'll have to think about it. Maybe we could open small tunnels like air vents to more evenly distribute it around the cave?" Dani responded evenly.

<I could do that,> I decided slowly, thinking about it. <Actually, I'll do it tonight for sure, and I'll make a viewing hole in one of the really nasty traps that looks into the Boss room, just to taunt people. Heh-heh-heh,> I chuckled darkly. <Oh look, there's the final room! Oh no! *Squish!*>

The group was in the last room before the Boss battle, and I planned on making it a spectacular fight. A few more groups of adventurers were at different stages of the dungeon by this point; one was even approaching the stairs down to the second level. Worst case scenario, even if this didn't go as I wanted, I had another few chances to gain some Essence.

Dale's group entered the room, noting the Silverwood tree and looking for the Boss. It was rather dark in there, and the Boss with all of his granite armor was well camouflaged with earth Essence, making him look like part of the wall unless moving.

Instead of relaxing as I had hoped, the human snacks grouped closer together for defense. Dang. One of them tossed out a flask that broke on the floor, which started putting off a lot of light. Well, I'd be absorbing *that* pattern when we were done, thank you very much!

Now illuminated, it was obvious that that giant mobile boulder was actually a Mob, so he wasted no more time, charging directly at them. I was nearly screaming with excitement as the battle was joined! I had direct control of my Boss, my mind merged with Raile's simplistic thoughts, so I was able to better control how this battle would progress. Josh boldly moved to block the charge at first, but a yell from Craig forced him to dodge at the last second.

Now, I had a lot of momentum. Raile was a big ol' boy, so when I missed, I couldn't exactly turn him on a copper. Crashing into the wall with the grinding of stone, I quickly redirected my Boss to spring back to the attack. For a several-hundred-pound, stone-covered rabbit, I still moved pretty quickly. Instead of sprinting this time, I ran at them and leaped, gaining momentum and covering distance as only a rabbit could do. Plunging down like a meteorite intent on the extermination of all life, a shockwave shook the ground, knocking the armored members of the team off balance. The lightly armored men sprang into action to distract me whilst their comrades regained their footing.

Hans ran at my Boss, trying to wedge his daggers into the joints of my armor, but with a satisfying shattering of metal, the wedged daggers broke off as Raile moved, shaking off the weak attack easily. Ignoring the lone fighter, I began racing toward the off-balanced team members; Josh had no choice but to attempt blocking with his massive shield. He plunged the arrowhead-shaped base into the ground, leaned into it, and braced himself with a roar of challenge!

Raile pounded the shield with a mighty blow, and it *almost* held. Sparking with released Essence, the obviously enchanted shield was able to redirect some of the force back at Raile, slowing his charge and doing a bit of damage, before the previously dented area gave way. A flash of lightning-like Essence joined into the cacophony of sound when the metal plate shattered, Josh being thrown backward as his defenses were annihilated.

Raile was effectively stopped for a heartbeat. With his momentary halt, the others took the chance to rain blows on him. The blunt staff and spiked morningstar were whooshing through the air and dealing some damage, cracking the granite armor and transmitting force to the flesh beneath. The single dagger Hans retained simply glanced off the armor, as was intended–a useless tool in a fight like this. I laughed when Craig punched bare-knuckled at Raile, sure he would break his fist. My laughter was rudely cut off as the punch shattered the armor in a fist-sized area, and he struck Raile's shoulder, breaking that too.

<That guy is strong!> I exclaimed in wonder. <Why the crap is he here?!>

Raile started moving again, limping a bit but still *very* dangerous. Charging Dale, I was able to land a glancing blow to his oversized armor as he danced out of the way. Even this light hit made him fly to the ground; I heard a crunch from his ribs. The others ran at Raile, attempting to keep his attention as Dale recovered, but I. Sensed. Blood! I turned and got Dale in my sights and started charging. A few feet away, Raile slowed drastically. I could no longer see out of his left eye.

Raile crashed to the ground, twitching. I was confused, still trying to order him to attack. Though he tried as hard as he could, he could not follow my command. Raile soon stopped moving entirely. I changed my view to get a better picture of things, no longer looking from his eyes, noticing feathers where Raile's eye had been. Ah. An arrow had somehow made an impossible shot, piercing Raile's eye and brain. With a furious mutter, I dropped some loot. It had been a good, enlightening fight. I'd get them eventually.

I rained quite a bit of silver, the steel dagger I had been working on with the Honing Inscription, and a steel helmet with an Inscription that boosted the protection granted against physical attacks. Also, as I absorbed Raile's pattern for the first time, I learned that the ability he had was called 'Avenger'. I was a bit disappointed that I could not understand what it did, but it apparently held some requirement in order to be used.

"Dibs," Hans called, pointing at the dagger. Steve collected the silver, while Josh tried on the new helmet. Dale was sitting against the wall, wheezing a bit, but breathing easier than I felt he should be with broken ribs. Grr. He wasn't even coughing up blood or *anything*!

"Let's take a look at you, shall we?" Craig pulled off Dale's armor. I really wished I had a Mob in here for a sneak attack. No, no. I had to be a good sport about these sorts of things—they beat me fair and square; I didn't want to be a sore loser. Craig pushed on the bones that were broken, aligning them with his Essence while Dale gasped in pain at the movement.

"Drink this." Craig put a recently acquired healing potion to Dale's lips, and within a few moments after drinking, Dale was breathing easier. "That is higher quality than I thought it would be," Craig muttered. Of course it was! I had pride in what I produced, after all. I'm not some snake-oil peddling herbologist! The original potion had indeed been barely potent, but I was able to make a much purer version when I had the pattern. While they were otherwise distracted, I ate the broken tower shield, then the remnants of the light potion. I had a chuckle at the strangled cry Josh made when he realized the halves of his old shield were gone.

"Damn it! I was still paying that off!" Josh raged, pounding the rock where his shield had been laying the last time he saw it.

They cultivated for a while, a cloud of swearing constantly flowing from Josh, then decided to head back. Another group was in the second tunnel of this floor, and my attention was now mostly on them. Surprising me, they had managed to take out a few squads without sustaining too much injury. They broke the leg of a Smasher, so instead of letting them finish him off, I had it jump into an acid trap on the wall, killing it but also releasing a flood of acid that drenched all but one of the small group.

Screaming as their flesh boiled, melting in their armor, the remaining squad quickly ended them. Since he was distracted by the horror he was witnessing, a horn found the soft flesh of the one who had managed to avoid the spray. By the time Dale's group reached that point in the tunnel, all that remained was a series of acid scarring on the rock below, which I would soon fix. Dale's group never even noticed the recent demise, too focused on warning the other groups they found along their way, which I growled at.

<I don't like them warning other people that are already in here! Gah! Dani, these guys are so frustrating,> I pouted, angry that they were always one step ahead of me.

Dani suggested an easy solution, "How about we make an exit to the surface from the Boss room? Easier for them to leave and better for us to get them out of here so they can't tell people about new obstacles."

<You think we can do that?> I questioned. Because of the concentration of people above, the mass of auras made it really hard for me to extend upward at all, to the point where we had decided it was a futile effort.

"If we make it below ground and just push it upward... somewhere there isn't really a strong concentration of people, it should be doable? I'll go look for a suitable place tonight, okay?" Dani promised me as I calmed down and thought about it.

I slowly agreed, not really wanting her to go anywhere dangerous. <If you promise to be careful. Some really gigantic auras have been showing up recently, even stronger than the first group that cleared the dungeon.>

Returning my attention to the people moving in my dungeon, I started picking off groups with my well-placed traps. None of the groups that came down into the second level were above F-rank, so were easy pickings for my squads of mid-F-ranked Bashers. Beyond Dale's group, only one other returned without casualties, even then only because they left after the first fight they had with a squad. The other, cocky, F-ranked groups provided me with enough Essence in one day for me to move into the second rank of the D-series.

CHAPTER SEVENTEEN

Dale and his group retraced their steps out of the dungeon, whooping in relief when the sun was again shining on them. The battles today had been hard, even when most of them were in the C-ranks! They stopped at the accounting tent near the top of the stairs to log the money and treasure they had found. After paying the twenty-five percent Guild tax, they were given a large bonus for handing over the bodies of the newly slain Mobs.

"These are interesting!" the clerk cooed. "The Spotters will be happy to have something new to look at. We'll have a list of their extra vulnerable points ready for you tomorrow. Anything else to report?"

"Yes." Craig cleared his throat, knowing he was about to become very unpopular. He reached into his belt pouch, retrieving his Guild badge which marked him as having quite a bit of authority under Frank. "I'm declaring the second floor a D-ranked minimum. While these are mid-F-ranked Mobs, the squads they move in easily push them into the danger level of the D series."

The clerk nodded and quickly set out a document for him to sign. As a magically bound document, this would forcibly ensure that members of the Guild below D-rank could not enter the second floor, forcing them to have a C-or-higher-ranked person with them who would have to give them special permission to enter. Since all members had sworn to follow the Guild's rules, this may cause grumblings but would be followed until a higher ranked member revoked his decision.

Unfortunately for a lot of the people trying to enter the dungeon, they were not Guild members. This meant that they didn't need to follow Guild rules, and they would push themselves to attempt the second level; especially since the rain of silver Dale's group had declared had made their eyes bulge with greed while drool formed on their chins.

"And the new Boss? Any information on it?" the clerk continued inquiring, writing everything down as a report bound for the Guild leader.

"A several-hundred-pound, stone armor covered bunny," Craig announced in a harsh tone.

The serious way he said 'bunny' made a few people snort and chuckle; even the stoic Josh had a smile playing about his lips. Craig blushed a bit but grimaced and said nothing to stop them.

"Heh... Ahem... Okay, danger level?" The clerk tried to hide a chuckle.

"*Mid* D-ranking. Actual cultivation at F nine, but its speed, armor, and weight make it very hard to damage. Blunt weapons are suggested. Few easy weak points, the eyes have armor surrounding them, and though the mouth is unarmored, stone hangs over from its nose–another possible weak point–to cover the mouth unless it opens. Which it did only once when it was in pain from a broken shoulder," Craig succinctly stated.

Dale was very impressed at the detail Craig provided. He hadn't seen the mouth open at all. Really, he hadn't thought about the possible points he should have been hitting. Mainly, he had swung for the head, trying to concuss it with the heavy, spiked end of his weapon. His ribs still twanged a bit, and he felt that may have been avoided if he had been paying better attention. Lesson learned.

"Loot dropped?"

Craig continued his report, "After the first floor Boss, roaming squads of improved Bashers," he pointed at the bodies on the table, "dropped mid-quality of low-level healing potions, rarely a holy pendant which we will most likely bring to Father Richard for his inspection, and a mixture of several copper and a few silver."

"And the Boss?"

Craig spoke in a low tone to try and prevent others from overhearing, "Dropped a small amount of silver coinage and two *possibly* Inscribed items, a helmet and a dagger. We will be getting them both checked for quality and safety before activating them." Craig didn't speak quietly enough and caused an explosion of noise, especially from the groups that were now forbidden to enter the second level. Rune inscribed items were worth up to several hundred gold—even a poor quality one might be worth fifty.

"Make sure we get a copy of the Spotter determination and value and remember that if you sell them, twenty-five percent goes to the Guild. You are allowed to use anything you earn or give it as a gift, but if it is sold, you will be compelled to pay the fee, so be sure you know that the person you give it to won't screw you over. If stolen, your debt is absolved unless it is recovered. Anything else?" the dry, bored tone continued as the now uninterested clerk looked at his notes.

Craig nodded and spoke loudly, obviously for the benefit of the people listening in, "Just one thing, the traps in the lower level are *far more advanced* than the upper level. We did not set any off, but we came upon one that had been set off by another group. The floor and walls were scarred by some force, and there was no sign that the unknown group survived. Stay safe, friends."

The crowd which was on the verge of fury calmed a bit. They all knew this most likely meant that group was dead, as there wasn't ever a body to recover if a team fell in a dungeon.

Maybe it *was* for the best that they stayed out of the lower level, and Craig was not just trying to hoard all of the good loot.

"Ah, by the way," Hans turned toward the attentive crowd, "in the first room right there," he pointed at the entrance below them, "there is a *massive* iron vein along the wall. Good way to earn some cash while you cultivate!" An explosion of motion followed as those too weak to reach the second floor raced to buy picks from an overjoyed entrepreneur who had set up a small kiosk nearby. His inflated prices suddenly not an issue, he quickly made enough to later find Dale and ask for some land to set up shop. Dale agreed and assigned him a plot of land–for a percentage and a discount of course.

DALE

While the masses were distracted, Dale's group went to have lunch. After a meal that was barely better than the dirt it was grown in, they cultivated in consideration of Dale's sore ribs, promising him they would spar after dinner. Dale readily agreed; today showed just how poor his combat readiness was. In comfortable silence, each settled in to cultivate again. Pretending that it was not because he was bored of cultivating, having spent nearly five hours passively and actively cultivating in the Essence rich area underground, Craig determined that Dale had enough Essence built up to open another meridian.

"Now, the only reason you are ready right now is that you opened the first of the *paired set*. You opened the yin heart meridian, so the yang lower intestine meridian will be much easier to open. You don't have the Essence to open one in a new set, so make sure to listen to my direction," Craig directed in a serious manner.

Dale nodded, preparing himself. As before, he sank into his center and pulled a thin stream of Essence from the spinning Chi. Moving it along the 'wall', he searched for the small holes he now knew existed. Craig stopped him a few times until he apparently approached the correct one. It was nowhere near the first and didn't seem to go to the lower intestine. His brow furrowed in confusion, but Dale still did as he was told. Craig hadn't been wrong yet, after all.

Dale fed the Essence into the hole, and it was again sucked from his control. The Essence left his center, somehow splitting and moving directly into his little finger on each arm. On both, it crossed the wrist and ran upwards along the opposite side of the forearm as the heart meridian did until it reached the back of Dale's shoulder where it ended at the uppermost part of the back or the bottom of his neck.

At this position, after creating weavings along its route, it traveled along the skin across his neck and cheek until it reached the outer corner of his eye, finally ending in his ear before somehow reconnecting into his center and joining the spiral from another small hole. Everything sounded a bit fuzzy, so he opened his eyes and blinked away tears. Wiping them from his check, he saw that it was actually blood dripping from his eyes.

Wiping at his ears, the fuzziness vanished as drops of blood were wiped away there as well. Surprised blood wasn't coming out of his skin at this point, he asked why he was bleeding. Had he been hit while he was so focused? What he should expect now?

Craig waved at him to try and calm him down and slow the flow of questions. "As your meridians are opened, they are also cleaned. The impurities in your system that are forced away have to go somewhere, after all. That blood is helping the filth to be washed out, that is all. You aren't damaged. Actually, you are now far healthier."

"I see," Dale murmured, thinking out loud about the incredibly foul poop he had taken after his heart meridian had opened. Now it made sense why it had connected to his intestines; it was depositing impurities.

"I bet you do!" Hans called, interrupting Dale's reminiscence. "Your vision should clear up. Any issues you had before are gonna be gone. Oh by the way... HA!" Dale gasped as Hans shouted next to his head, his hands clapping to his ears with a wet smack of blood.

"Yup, looks like your hearing is improving as well!" Hans laughed, grinning maliciously.

"*Mean*!" Dale gasped. 'Heh' was the only apology he got.

"Get ready for a few sleepless nights, kiddo," Steve rumbled fondly. "You are going to wake up to a herder on the next mountain farting tonight." The men laughed uproariously at this.

"I know the one! He's been eating too much roughage if you ask me! He needs to add some fruit to his diet!" Josh sounded off. The laughter only increased at this comment.

They calmed down after a bit, spirits much lightened. Craig continued the lesson, "As they say, eyesight and hearing will be better for you and should stay that way. It is called the lower intestine meridian because as food enters your intestines, your body will now purify the food you eat much more efficiently, and you will even be using it for Essence gathering, as some of the... extra... will have the Essence drawn out of it."

"Oh, that's handy, I guess." Dale was far more excited about the improved senses, though.

"Your farts are gonna smell like death because of it!" Hans chimed in.

"You're lucky ya have your own tent!" Steve crowed.

Craig sighed with a smile. "No manners, any of you. Alright, since we seem to have a surplus of energy, how about you start your punishment training with Josh, Dale. You did miss that trap." Josh jumped to his feet, face lighting up—he had forgotten that he got to beat up Dale by himself for an hour!

By evening, Dale was exhausted. With the intense day that he had, sleep was only seconds away when he finally got to bed. Enhanced senses or no, that night, he slept like the dead.

Chapter Eighteen

The last group of people had finally left, making it far easier to alter myself. Those human auras inside of me had a nasty habit of making it difficult for me to directly affect things. I added openings from each cave to another and let them level out the Essence in the air. It was slow, but I figured by morning you couldn't cheat my empty rooms anymore. Not the way they had been, anyway. Just to be safe, I reconfigured the tunnels so that people couldn't just retrace their steps.

Next, Dani flew out and looked around for a while. She came back with very interesting news. There was a giant sheet of quartz above us, not quite *directly* up, but nearly so from the Boss room. With her directing me, I moved the rooms above me out of the way, creating a cylinder of empty space up to the sheet while holding the integrity of the dungeon intact. Quite a lot of work but far easier at my new ranking.

From my gem, I had perfect vision in line of sight but had mostly only seen the hole I was in and so used my influence to see. The downside was that I could only 'see' as far as that influence extended. Now, for the first time in my life, I looked up and saw the stars.

<Wow. That is so beautiful! I cannot believe people can go up and see them every night,> I articulated with a hint of jealousy, peering beyond the Silverwood tree above me and out into the stars.

"Most people don't bother," Dani quietly voiced, also enjoying the view. The sheet of quartz above us acted as a giant telescope, letting us see further and more clearly than usual. It was especially beautiful when the moon came into view; it seemed *huge*.

<Why is that?> I asked quizzically, disturbed that people actually ignored this beautiful scenery.

She seemed to match my disappointment in others. "Most people tend to only look at or think about things that have value to them at that moment. They look so hard at what they want that they drown out the beautiful things that would give them hope or allow them to look beyond their small lives.

They lose sight of living, trying to get to the *next* goal, the *next* important thing. They forget that everything is important, that the little moments of happiness added up overwhelm the greatness of the few large moments. Like making a friend smile or making it to the two hundred and eighteenth page of a book. Sometimes, it isn't about finishing your objective, it is about enjoying yourself on the way there." She focused on me. "That's why I have so much fun here, Cal. You put detail into the little things, and even when you are beaten, you reward those who did well. You care more about being amazing than you do winning."

<Thank you, Dani,> I choked out, feeling overwhelmed with joy at having such a good friend. <Really, you mean a lot to me as well. If there is ever anything I can do for you, anything you really need, I hope you know that I will do it for you.>

"Well, I suppose the first thing you could do is build an exit!" she shouted, breaking the sober mood and startling me badly. We both laughed at how shocked I was.

<That I can do!> Together, we designed a gazebo-like structure made of thick granite. For the rest of the night, I carved a series of large Runes into the stone, about an inch under the surface. All of them linked together so that I could use a single power source to activate them. When I finished it, dawn was only an hour away. I created a spiral staircase under the gazebo, building all of this in a small area just off of my Boss room.

I opened the ground up to the surface as far as I could reach, about three feet below the surface and raised the gazebo on the stairs I was creating underneath of it. As it rose, it spun with the creation of the spiral under it. When it finally reached the edge of my influence, the top of my first building punched through the loosely packed dirt at the top. I could see the gazebo break into the surface through the clear quartz nearly one hundred feet above.

When it shuddered to a stop, I connected its corruption stone to the inscribed Runes and felt the gazebo become even harder. The energy sluggishly filled it, glowing with a harsh, purple-brown color. I was pleased to feel that the runes were perfect. The door out could only be opened from the inside. Anyone attempting to re-enter would be crushed like a bug or find themselves in a stairwell that had no exit at the bottom when I dropped a wall in the way and let them slowly suffocate. Good times. Well. For me.

Catching my attention as I was looking up, I realized the Silverwood tree had seemed to enjoy the new light coming in. A few leaves had unfurled over the night as the moonlight bathed us. What was that? There was a person, wait, two people directly above me! I was suddenly worried looking at the quartz above us. That could be broken, couldn't it? It was at the edge of my influence, but if I strained, pushing *really* hard, I was still able to make molecule thin patterns in the sheet with acid, slowly widening them until they were useful Runes. Since quartz was just stone, I planned on hooking it to a corruption stone.

My plan failed in the most wondrous way. When I finished the Inscription, a bright, golden light flashed through the Runes. I looked at it carefully, the whole thing had been filled with celestial energy! On closer inspection, Dani informed me that the entire three-foot-thick quartz was just... *stuffed* full of celestial energy.

"Somehow, someone made this into celestial glass," she gibbered, awed at the beautiful light we could see when we focused. There were no visible markings on it, even though the Runes I had placed were obviously active. Odd. I couldn't focus on that right then, though I truly wanted to solve this mystery. You see, dawn had come, another first for me. For the first time in my life, I was able to watch the sunrise. Even better, I got to do so with my best friend, the only being I loved as much as myself.

DALE

A soft, grinding noise slowly roused Dale, his newly enhanced ears throbbing at the new and unusual sound. Rubbing sleep from his eyes, he walked out of his tent and meandered around as he looked for the source. It seemed to be coming from the lot the church would be built on, Dale wondered if some earth Mages had arrived build it. He wandered over, planning to see how it was done, and noticed a gazebo.

"Earth Mages? Father Richard?" Dale called. When no one responded, he went over to inspect their work. It was a single piece of granite that had no seams as far as he could tell. They must not have put the door in. He decided to look at it with his Essence sight ability, which was *much* easier to use now that the new meridian was open in the corner of his eye.

Inspecting the work, he could only see its natural Essence and was impressed by the control the Mage who made this had used. Normally, there was overflow which had a 'flavor' to it known as the 'Mage's signature'. The smaller the 'signature', the better control the Mage had and the more the work was worth because it would interfere less with Runes added on later. Looking closer, he saw beautiful Runescripted patterns cut *inside* the stone itself.

"That is so cool! I need to get this guy to teach me!" he thought, very excited to meet this master Mage when he returned. About to turn away, he saw what almost looked like earth Essence starting to follow the loops and whirls of the internal pattern. Entranced, he watched as the slow-moving substance filled the pattern.

When it reached the last open spot, the stone suddenly pulsed, seeming to tighten and grow darker. Some loose sand shook off, and he was showered with dirt. The rock was suddenly opaque to him, the beautiful pattern no longer visible. It looked exactly like the slab of stone over the entrance had, as a matter of fact.

Now nervous, Dale turned to run and tell someone about this when Father Richard walked up with a, "Morning, lad!"

"Would you look at that?!" He whistled. "Is this whole piece a single slab of granite?"

"Father, this is, if I am correct, cursed earth," Dale released in a rush.

"Hmm, I think you are indeed correct." Richard frowned a bit. "It looks a lot like that blockage did over the entrance to the dungeon. Come look at the quartz with me over here. It came awfully close to it. I hope it didn't do any damage." The look of nervousness on his face convinced Dale to help before informing the Guild.

They moved to check for any damage to the quartz, Father Richard frowned as he saw scratches along the bottom of the slab with the sparse, pre-dawn light. Just before the sun crested the ridge to signal the start of a new day, the entire slab shone brilliantly, as if *it*—and not the sun—was the herald of the morning.

"Ahh!" both of them yelled, clutching at their eyes. Blinking rapidly in an attempt to clear the spots dancing in their vision, they stumbled about in pain, Father Richard swearing in a very non-priestly way.

Silence followed by a gasp escaped Father Richard. Dale looked over with swimming vision to see him looking down with wonder in his expression. True sunrise had arrived, and Dale looked directly down to see the Boss room he had fought in yesterday as if it were only a few feet below.

"What?!" Dale joined in the gasping.

"That's the Silverwood tree?" Father Richard pointed.

"Looks like it. But how can we see this? It has to be so far underground!" Dale exclaimed.

Father Richard didn't answer, instead looking at the quartz again, looking for the scratches that had been there. After a few moments, he flopped down into a kneeling position.

"It's a miracle," he murmured, touching the smooth surface.

"Father?"

"Dale, the entire... the whole thing. It's been enchanted. No, those are Runes—it's been inscribed!" Tears of joy sprang to Father Richard's eyes as he read the Inscription that Dale could not even see.

"It's the church's best Essence level Rune! Protection, increased celestial energy, and dissolving of infernal bonds." He was freely weeping now. "It's a miracle."

"I can't see the Rune. The Essence in the way is too thick," Dale ashamedly mentioned, disappointed in his ability. A flash of insight crossed his mind. "Father, is it the same

Inscription as... this?" He pulled out the pendant he was wearing which was filled with Essence of no particular elemental affiliation.

The Father's eyes locked on to it and his expression changed to almost anger. "Where did you get this?"

"It was a drop in the dungeon, from the Boss of the first floor and the Mobs beyond," Dale informed him nervously.

"Ah, sorry, I didn't mean to worry you. This is indeed the same Rune, but as I said, it is one of the most powerful Essence level Inscriptions we have. I was just surprised to see it out of the hands of a cleric. Would you let me see it?" Richard politely asked.

"Of course, Father." Dale handed it over, glad he wasn't in trouble with this powerful man.

"Yes, it is the same," Richard spoke, almost to himself. "Useless, though."

"Useless?" Dale was rather disappointed to hear that. Several people around the area had them for good luck.

"Yes, though filled with Essence, only celestial type is able to activate the full Inscription. Other types *may* be able to use the other parts, like this physical protection... I haven't looked into it," Father Richard muttered, tracing the pattern. He looked at it again, frowning. "Can I try something on this?"

"Sure." Dale shrugged. It was useless anyway.

Father Richard smiled, held the pendant and started saying a short prayer. The first words had barely left his mouth when the pendant glowed with light, obviously activating.

"Wondrous!" Richard exclaimed, eyes shining. "You say this is a drop that is fairly common in the dungeon?"

"Yes, the first Boss sometimes drops it, but we got three yesterday on the second level," Dale bragged.

"I can activate them! Look," Father Richard held up the pendant, "the Essence it contained has taken on celestial affinity!"

"Great!" Dale was enthusiastic yet still somewhat confused.

"Here, lad. Would you like me to bind this to you? You are its rightful owner, after all," Father Richard offered.

"I'm sorry, I don't know what you mean, Father," Dale stalled, nervous for an unknown reason.

"Oh, it isn't dangerous. If you place a small thread of Essence to a certain place on your items Rune, it will only activate for you if you are the first to do so. Many don't because then the resale value drops quite a bit, and you can still activate the Rune like normal. But someone else could get ahold of it and bind it, rendering it useless to you," Father Richard explained.

"Well, it wouldn't hurt to learn how, right?" Dale grinned. He loved learning new things.

"Right," Father Richard assured.

"Okay, let's do it!" Dale affirmed, excited for the new knowledge.

"Since you still use Essence, your power does not extend far past your physical body. Basically, you need to have contact with the place you want to put Essence into. Your armor, since it is enchanted, has the power deposit placement on the inside against your skin, and your weapon has it on the grip. You can see it if you just look." Dale didn't inform him that he didn't know how to activate his gear; he now planned to practice, though.

Continuing his lecture, "Look here, every place you input energy is the same glyph or a variant of it. That is the standard activation site. Here," he pointed to another spot, "is the binding glyph of the Rune. Again, it looks similar across all the Runes I have ever seen. Try to put a tiny, *tiny* amount of Essence into it."

Taking the pendant back, Dale concentrated on pulling Essence to his fingertip. Having done this for his eyes often now, it was easy to do only on his little finger, close to the meridian. Getting a mirthful look from Father Richard when he poked the glyph with his pinky, he felt a tiny tug from the pendant, and it glowed softly for a moment.

"Good job, you did it on your first try!" Father Richard praised. "You are the first non-cleric I know to have this particular active protection. Now, can you feel where it is?" He took and moved the pendant back and forth, and Dale felt as though he was being pulled in the same direction. "You'll always be able to find it if it doesn't break."

"*Very* cool," Dale enthused, eyes shining.

"Remember to activate it when you need it. Just having it does nothing!" Father Richard professed. "By the way, I'll be letting people know that I'll pay fifty silver for each of those, so pass it on."

"Aren't Runed items worth gold usually?" Dale looked at the cheap priest.

"Only if they are able to be activated!" Father Richard responded with a cheeky wink.

"Sneaky old man," Dale *very* quietly muttered.

"What was that?" Father Richard growled.

"Nothing!"

As Father Richard watched Dale walk away, he thought about the now enchanted quartz and the Runed pendants.

"Maybe this post... *wasn't* a punishment?" He dared to hope.

Chapter Nineteen

Dale moved away to meet up with his comrades. Following his nose, he quickly found them eating breakfast. Trying to tell his story, he was shouted down by the group, banished until he was fully armored since he was under strict orders to wear his gear at all times. They would hear no argument, yelling over his voice every time he tried to explain himself. Exceedingly frustrated, Dale went back to his tent to get geared up and found a masked man rummaging through his things!

"Hey!" Dale shouted in surprise. "What the abyss are you doing?"

The startled man looked up, eyes narrowing. His information had *specifically* said that Dale would be in the dungeon by now. Ah, well. He was probably going to have to kill him later anyway. The masked man pulled out a long knife and lunged at Dale.

His reactions trained from months of battle, Dale jumped to the side, barely avoiding a slash at his throat. His mind whirled with options, but he was without weapons or armor so he froze up, earning a brutal kick to his knee. Knocking Dale to the ground, the masked man raised his dagger to deliver a coup de grâce, ending his existence. Panicking, Dale screamed the first thing that came to mind.

"*Get off my mountain*!" Dale ordered with a frantic squeal. Mid-swing, the man turned and started jerkily walking away, his dagger flying from his hand at the unexpected and unwanted movement.

Dale, relieved, shouted after the angry and confused man, "To anyone who sent you, anyone who was sent by the same person, and anyone who knows what you were doing, leave! And never come back!" Dale had no idea if that would work, but he figured it was a good idea to at least *try* to get rid of other potential problems. There was now nothing he could do than just to watch the would-be assassin make his escape, so he stood up, shaking with reaction. Dale glared as he watched the man go. He was sprinting away now, obviously trying to outrun anyone Dale might send to find him.

Dale rushed to put on his armor, not feeling safe until he had every piece properly equipped. He then moved to find his group and tell them the events of his morning. At his rushed words about the assassin, they pulled him along to the Guild Master, making him repeat his story.

Frank tried to be sympathetic, but it was obvious he was preoccupied and not actually worried. "Dale, he was probably a thief that panicked when you showed up. It sounds like he didn't try *too* hard to kill you if he just... ran off."

"No, I ordered him off the mountain right before he could kill me!" Dale stated passionately. "He had me dead to rights. It was the only thing I could think of! I was about to *die*, Frank!"

"That was smart. Good work thinking on your toes, kid," Hans soothingly stated, slapping Dale comfortingly on the back.

Frank shook his head and sighed in exasperation as he looked over another requisition form. "Still, while I *am* sorry it happened, there really isn't much to be done! He obviously wasn't in the Guild if he tried to attack you, so I have no legal right to hunt him down. Actually," Frank paused and mused a moment, "banishing him was a solid punishment. After all, he is now several hundred miles from any real civilization with no food, water, or equipment."

Dale was taken aback. He hadn't really thought making people leave would have such deadly consequences for them. Living off the land was easy around here, wasn't it? His family had done so for generations... Calming down a bit, Dale recited the rest of his story, "Some other things happened this morning as well." He relayed his conversation with Father Richard, telling them of the cursed earth gazebo and the massive Runescript that had appeared on the quartz–Runescript being the proper term for many Runes that interlocked together to form a larger Rune, of course.

"Amazing!" Dale cynically thought it a bit ironic that Frank was interested in this story and not the one where his life was in danger.

"That one chunk of quartz would be worth the yearly economic output of a *city*! That was *before* it was inscribed! To think, all of these amazing events happened up here, in the middle of nowhere! And, well, the cursed earth is concerning of course, but we will have to study it before making any decisions." He shooed the group off when they had nothing else to report, telling them he would be busy for a few days, looking into these matters.

"Well, that was certainly interesting." Craig looked at Dale, whose face still drawn from the stress and sudden events. Taking pity on him, Craig continued, ""Let's go kill some Mobs, shall we? That'll calm your nerves a bit." He punched Dale on the arm, getting a weak smile back for his camaraderie.

"Anything you say, Craig. It has been one heck of a morning, you know?" Dale sounded exhausted already.

A cheerful Hans came to the rescue. "These things happen, and the longer you live, the worse you'll see. That's why we're training you up, so you can take care of yourself when we all move on. Ya can't stay here forever, right?"

Dale's face clouded. "I hadn't really thought about it. I've never been off these mountains and I... You know what? Yeah, let's go kill something."

"That's the spirit!" Hans shouted. "To battle!" Taking off at a run for the dungeon, the others had to hurry to catch up. They couldn't let him have all the kills, after all.

Cal

<They are later than normal,> I conversed with Dani optimistically. <Think they're getting complacent?>

"More likely they were looking at the new building and the giant window you made into here," Dani muttered reproachfully, making me look up at the growing crowd of people above us. They sure did seem excited to see my room. Hard to blame them for looking at my beautiful work, after all. I was preening under all of the attention I was getting.

"Voyeurs," Dani muttered, hostility coming off her in waves. "I gotta stay invisible all the *time* now."

<Well that is the price we pay for this glorious sunshine,> I teased her, projecting the image of a lazy person stretching.

She huffed at me. "Fine. You'll miss my pretty colors soon enough. How is Dale's group doing? I assume... I mean, it *is* them again, right?"

<It is. Apparently, I didn't do a lick of permanent damage to them yesterday. Dale must have healed really fast for him to be dancing around like that.> I was watching the energetic lad bouncing around with his stick.

<At least they seem to be having trouble finding the right path today. Looks like that system worked out.> Indeed, they were even now moving toward a dead end. On the first floor,

though, so they quickly were able to bypass the trap and move back to the correct path. I decided to listen in on their conversation.

"Did I just pick the wrong path?" Dale was asking, "I thought I could just watch the Essence. Were you guys just testing me?" He looked around at the stony faces. "I swear I am using the technique!" He finished desperately when no one talked.

"It's not that, kid, chill," Hans waved him down, speaking in a perplexed tone. "I thought that was the right way as well. What do you think Craig?"

"No idea," Craig's tense voice muttered. "It's all different today."

Steve chimed in softly, "This may be dangerous, boys. If we can't tell where to go, we may walk directly into traps. Be extra careful today."

"Vigilance!" roared Josh, badly startling everyone. A couple of them even had to force themselves to stop attacking on reflex.

With a withering glance, Steve rounded on Josh. "Yes, thank you for your input. Very helpful."

I chuckled at that. <Dani, looks like there is some infighting going on here. I didn't think this would be enough to make them panic like they are.>

"Losing your way can be scary!" Dani shuddered.

<Pff, I don't get it. It's not a big deal.>

"You can't get lost! You don't go anywhere!" Dani gasped at my nonchalant dismissal.

I quickly directed her attention away. <Oh look, they are fighting the Boss.>

They had made their way through the admittedly easy first-floor maze, quickly ending the useless Boss, which made me explode with frustration again.

<Damn it! Stupid thing always dies!> I judgmentally thought of the weak, plant-based monster.

"Why not put more Mobs in there? Or a squad and call 'em the Boss." Dani seemed perplexed at my dislike of the current Boss.

<Is that a good idea? Then they know what to expect on the next floor.>

"I think they already know. The squad system is too strong already for most of the groups, even though they are common Mobs on the second floor. I do agree that the first floor is too easy. A squad will be a good challenge at least."

<What would I do with the Bloody Bane? I know it is stupid, but I made it, and I don't want to just toss it away...>

She was ruthless, probably sick of me complaining about it all the time. "It's weaker than your *common* Mobs. How about put it near acid traps and pitfalls? Pull people into them instead of hoping they fall on their own, or use it as a sacrifice to set traps off. That worked really well with that injured basher, right? Plus, the first floor is so weak now that Dale's group is just waltzing on through. *Dale* could clear it by himself now! Heck, when is the last time someone even got badly *injured* there?" Dani stopped my interjection with a harsh truth, "You need to devote some of your Essence to upkeep and upgrades, not just constant expansion."

<Bah. What's wrong with hoarding?> I grumbled, unhappily acknowledging that she had good points. <I am going to need a week or so to get that level of Essence to spare unless a few people die off today. Let's try and get Dale again. Seeing him run for his life always cheers me up.>

Ooh, taking them down today may come to pass! They were moving into a tunnel on the second floor that would drop a stone door behind them, flooding a small space with acid. I could hardly *wait* to taste that C-ranked Essence from the main group. I caught my 'breath' as they walked in, and with a joyful yell, I *slammed* the door down behind them. Their shouts of fear made my excitement rise to a fever pitch as I made preparations for large inputs of Essence.

"Calm down! There has to be a way out if we aren't dead yet!" The ever calm Craig took control, looking around. His eyes widened as he saw the acid beginning to pour in, his mouth forming a grim line.

"Look around for a lever, an opening, a button—anything out of place!" Hans directed, the sound of pouring liquid and hissing acid nearly drowning him out. The air was starting to become toxic as the stone melted, releasing fumes. Craig was moving his hands in complex patterns, light remaining where his nimble fingers moved.

As Dale looked around wildly, his Essence-infused eyes caught upon a lighter patch on the wall a foot above his head on the other side of the tunnel. "There!" he shouted, pointing at the spot. Acid had pooled between them and the button, so Steve pulled out an arrow and notched it to his bow.

"No! You may break it!" Hans shouted, pushing the bow aside.

"Josh!" Craig snapped, hands still fluttering. "Boot!"

The benefit of working as a team for a long period of time was that complete sentences were rarely needed in dire circumstances. Josh moved over and held his armored leg up, the boot next to the glowing pattern in the air. Craig moved his hand again, and what was obviously an enchantment flowed into being on the bottom of the proffered boot.

"Go!" Josh ran at the acid flowing across the ground, not stopping as he flung himself at the bubbling fluid. I watched and waited for his foot to start melting when it became submerged in the hissing acid. Sadly, the Rune on his boot flared to life, making the acid recede just enough to leave a dry spot on the floor where he landed. I was horrified as the area around him cleared of all liquid, though it was nearly a half inch deep just outside that zone. The others were on higher ground, but he should have been *ooze* by now! He sprinted, nearly flying across the now clear ground and leaped to meet the button on the wall.

With only a minor complaint, I saw the acid stop flowing and quickly drain away, leaving only scarred stone to show it had ever been there. Boo. These guys were resourceful. The door slowly raised behind them as the last dregs of fluid vanished; I was nothing if not fair.

"That was amazing!" Dale shouted, pumping his fist into the air and giving Hans a wild hug. "I never knew enchanting was so fast!"

"It normally isn't." Steve glanced at Craig with admiration. "Fast enchantments are dangerous. I *highly* doubt Craig would have done that if we weren't in deep shit there."

Craig gravely nodded. "Agreed. Let's avoid that in the future."

"What? That was cool! When will you teach me to enchant?" Dale excitedly bubbled.

"I may not. It depends on what you want to do when you learn all the other options. Enchanting isn't popular because you permanently lose a bit of your cultivation base for each enchantment and have to re-refine the Chi. Rebuilding your cultivation base is hard, as you know. When you use your Essence for other, *normal* things, it will flow back into your center over time," Craig tiredly lectured. "With enchanting, it is just... gone."

"Oh." Dale was less eager now. "You said what you did was dangerous?"

"If I did it wrong, it might have exploded or maybe just dissipated. If I made a correct Rune but not the one I was going for, it might have had... unintended effects," Craig hedged.

"Like if you made the inverse," Hans spoke out in a low tone, eliciting a shudder from the others.

"What?" Dale hesitantly probed.

Josh took over, "The inverse of a Rune reverses its effects. Simple right? In this case, instead of repelling the acid, it would have attracted all of it in range."

Dale joined in the shuddering, thinking about what would have happened if the acid had completely covered poor Josh. It would have been like he never existed.

"But he made it. Wouldn't he know if it were the inverse?" Dale prodded.

"When he made it, yeah. But what if he applied it upside down in his hurry before activating it?" Hans explained.

"Oh." Dale was quiet for a moment. "I'm glad it worked out."

"I think we all are. Let's go kill a Boss," Josh rumbled. "I need some fresh air."

They moved away from the dead end, systematically searching each area, skillfully avoiding traps until they finally found my Boss room. They were concerned at the bright light coming from the room until they saw the source, at which point they were excited by the new, bright fighting arena. I say arena because we certainly had an audience today. People had been crowding along the area above until this group finally showed, at which point they started cheering and placing bets. Somehow, the sound came in clearly from above, yet I am fairly certain they could not hear what happened down here.

My priorities had shifted a bit. While I did indeed still want some tasty Essence, I *really* wanted that fluid repulsion enchantment. So when my Boss barreled out to the fight, amid cheering which filtered down from above, he charged directly at the large man, Josh. This must have surprised them; I think they expected me to go for Dale as per usual.

Raile crashed into the defiantly held tower shield, easily bending it. This was a weak, shoddy substitute for the one he had lost in here previously. Josh shouted in pain as the metal crumpled around his arm, forced away a few feet before he tripped and sprawled flat on his back. Raile bounced forward as blows began raining on to him, his massive weight landing on the sundered shield held up for protection. The tortured metal began caving in as Raile furiously attacked the only exposed area, Josh's feet.

Clamping down, Raile shook his head like a dog tearing into steak, but he was knocked away with a powerful blow from Craig. Trying to preserve Josh, the blow had sent Raile away from Josh's head, actually helping me pull the boot off. Thanks, Craig! With an audible *snap,* Raile broke Josh's leg as he was launched away, the boot flying into the distance.

I devoured the boot and the enchantment it held with a moan of pleasure, filing the information away for later use. Wow, does Craig make tasty enchantments! So much Essence! Raile returned to the battle, attempting to maul the man on the ground but was being body blocked by the others. Dale pulled Josh on to his good foot as Raile bounced high and started descending like an avalanche toward the place Josh had lain. Unable to dodge fully out of the way, both Dale and Josh went flying.

Josh's head slammed into the wall, where he slumped to the ground unconscious.

This was going far better than expected! Now *two* tasty people were on the ground for me to squash, while Raile had taken almost no damage yet! I bounded in, ready to finish them. I jumped, my temporary body angling to flatten Dale when an arrow slammed into the armor of the head I was inhabiting. The force didn't penetrate, but it did knock my–Raile's–skull forward, creating an awkward landing that pushed my head into the wall *next* to Dale.

He stared into Raile's eyes as I struggled to regain control. Luckily his stick wasn't small enough for him to swing and do damage in this confined space. Thinking I had the upper hand, I was shocked when Dale reached into a pocket and withdrew a gleaming dagger that he slammed into the eye next to him! That bastard! He had never had a dagger before! Vindictively, I angled Raile in his death throes so he would land on Dale, hopefully crushing the life out of him. As Raile's corpse landed, I could hear the breath explode from Dale's body alongside a meaty *crunch* which made me rather cheerful. Maybe this battle wasn't a waste!

The others worked quickly to lever Raile's body off of Dale, showing a non-breathing adventurer. Hans jumped over and pushed on Dale's chest a few times while furiously screaming. I am fairly certain the screaming did the trick, forcing Dale to take a breath in subliminal fear. While he coughed explosively, I sadly watched all of that Essence get away. Drat. They moved to Josh, who moaned as they removed his helmet.

"You okay, big man?" Hans probed, patting Josh on the arm.

"Yah," Josh groaned, slowly getting up. "Powerful protection Rune on that helmet. Shoulda squashed me like a bug." He spat out a bit of blood, gesturing at the giant Basher. He looked over at Dale and frowned. "How'd you kill it, lad?"

Dale was still trying to get his mind off of nearly being killed. "I, uh... I had a dagger on me. I was able to stick him before he got back up."

"I didn't teach you to use a dagger! Is it new? Do you have a new teacher you like better?" Hans feigned hurt at the thought of another man teaching him how to use a knife.

"No! Ha... Just nearly got stabbed this morning and decided to take a trophy," Dale wheezed. He handed the dagger over so Hans could see it.

Craig looked up from the dead Basher. "Dale, you didn't penetrate its brain. How did you kill it?"

"Craig." Hans had a serious tone in his voice, which made everyone look at him. A serious Hans made everyone nervous. "This is a Demonologist blade."

"Are you certain?" Craig inspected the blade as well. "I see no infernal Essence on it...?"

Hans shook his head. "Infernal Essence doesn't hold well in Inscriptions. It pulls its energy from its victims to power itself. I am... unsure what this Rune does, but we should get it to a Spotter *immediately*."

Hans turned toward Dale. "The life Essence in that Boss Mob was *ripped* out. Good job with those reflexes, but you should never use an unknown weapon, especially one with an obvious Inscription like this." He held up the dagger. It was plain to me that the twisted pattern nearly *screamed* its hatred for life.

"I didn't even think about it." A downcast Dale kicked at a loose rock. "I was so caught up in today..."

I was watching that dagger. A new Inscription was something I dearly wanted to eat. Especially if I wouldn't have a chance later, them giving it away and all. I had planned on giving them just standard loot, but I wanted a distraction. I generated a shower of silver coins to catch their attention and dropped a massive, metal tower shield behind them when they looked toward the money.

The resulting *boom, clatter* was enough for them to jump, badly startled. Jumpy, aren't they? At the same time as the noise, a Glitterflit I had been directing smacked into the hand Hans was holding the dagger in, sending it flying. The distractions provided me with a brand new dagger and Inscription which I would be sure to study. Only Hans saw a flash of gold as the Glitterflit sped into hiding again.

"Son of a–" Hans began shouting.

"What happened?" Steve whirled around as a joyful *whoop* sounded from Josh.

"It's *beautiful*!" Josh stated, voice somewhere between a whisper and a scream. "Look at this pattern! These Runes are *immaculate*! I can't wait to use it!" He was holding the inscribed, massive shield with his non-mangled arm, the other bent at odd angles which he ignored. "So *pretty!*"

"Something took the dagger!" Hans tried to warn the group.

"Can I keep it?" Josh was asking, looking around at the others wildly. "Please?"

"None of us could use it, Josh." Craig moved toward him, speaking softly, "It is all yours, okay? How about we head back now?"

"So I can keep it?" Josh again begged.

"Of course you can," Craig promised soothingly, looking into Josh's eyes. "I think you have a concussion, my friend."

"No, it's a shield," Josh assured him, holding it a little higher.

"I know it is. How about you look at it for a while?" Craig turned toward the group. "We need to go. An injury to the brain is one I do not feel... ready... to heal."

"A moment please." Steve gathered the fallen coin, looking for any other dropped things. What a greedy adventurer! I had no intention of giving them anything else. After all, I had not regained any of Raile's lost Essence thanks to my new knife. "Let's be off." Hans nodded as he finished his search.

They turned to go, so I dropped a rock near the hidden stairwell. They turned, weapons drawn, to look at the disturbance. Hans flew forward, hoping to catch whatever it was off guard and so was the one to find the stairs.

"Over here! A stairwell!" He waved them over to this unknown obstacle.

They looked at the stairs and almost ignored them, nearly leaving for the known route when the lolling head of Josh convinced them to move upward. After the first few steps, the door behind them swung closed, the only light in the area being the Essence in the stone around them.

They reached the top after a few minutes of huffing and puffing–three hundred eighty steps wears anyone down, I'm told. I wouldn't know. No legs. As they touched the wall, it swung outward, revealing a cheering crowd who was describing the battle they had just witnessed. The cheering got louder as the raucous crowd noticed the famous fighters had suddenly joined them.

A cleric ran over, healing light flowing from his hands as he reached for Josh. A few less interested people tried to force their way into the stone gazebo I was closing. *I* didn't try to stop them. A few made it in, cheering at their good luck. Those few ran down toward the Boss room while the door closed behind them. Little did they know it wouldn't reopen. I guess this battle wasn't an entire waste for me today! I was sure their constant crying would be annoying for a few hours, but I was also sure it wouldn't last *too* long. Not much air in the stairwell, after all.

I turned my mind to the knowledge I had gained that day, thinking over the concepts and ideas that were flowing through me. The Inscriptions were very interesting, but I was very curious as to what I could do with inverted runes. It reversed the effect of the Rune, Craig said, hmm? I drew an inverted Rune on the ground in a small room and powered it with a tiny burst of Essence. This was the Rune that would increase the strength of armor when applied normally, so I was unsure of what would happen when it was inverted.

I dropped a boot on it and watched it glow, though seemingly nothing was happening. After a few seconds, the boot sagged and fell apart, the leather falling into scraps! Already joyfully thinking of the applications, I tried again, this time with a metal helmet. I carefully watched it as apparent stress fractures made their way along the metal. Anywhere it connected to another piece of the metal, it quickly corroded until it finally clattered apart. What remained on the Rune for a while longer fell apart further until only oxidized, rusty metal scraps remained.

"Holy cow!" Dani breathed. "It looks like what you do to anything that doesn't have an aura when you absorb it! This could be a way for you to get patterns for armor even when you don't take down the person wearing it!"

<I agree! This could be fun, let's test other inverted Runes too! Also...>

"Yeah?"

<What's a cow?>

CHAPTER TWENTY

Dale walked out of the gazebo and was so stunned by the sudden noise and crowd that he couldn't stop the people who pushed past him into the waiting tunnel.

"That's a terrible idea!" he shouted as they rushed downward, the door seamlessly grinding closed behind them.

Craig just shook his head and waited for the cleric to be finished with Josh, who had focus returning to his eyes as the celestial energy flowed around his brain, clearing the built-up blood and reducing swelling. Josh blinked a few times as the cleric moved back a step, then thanked him.

"Ow!" Josh suddenly shouted. "Ahh! My arm!" The *very* bent arm by his side was apparent to all. A few weak stomached people were noisily sick as they noticed the ruined flesh. More were sick as they watched the arm get pulled on by the others to straighten it as Josh screamed in pain.

"Pull it straight, you heartless bastards!" Josh was shrieking. "Do it! Ahhh!" The flow of celestial energy appeared again, quickly soothing and strengthening the proffered arm.

"You missed a kink there," the nameless cleric noticed, pointing to a knot on Josh's ankle. Hans looked at the spot, and before Josh could tense up, he quickly twisted the foot, the grinding of bone audible only until the retching sounds drowned it out. A burst of Essence set him right, the ankle healed again if tender.

"Well, that was unpleasant." Josh panted in an attempt to seem nonchalant. His face pale with tears streaming showed that he was not immune to the pain. "Luckily, it won't happen again." He held up the new shield, flaunting it for the onlookers, then reached out and bound it to himself with a burst of Essence. "Just in case." He winked at Dale.

Turning to the cleric, Josh motioned him close. "Thank you for your timely assistance, brother. Please, accept this, a token of my thanks." He handed the man several silver coins, his portion of the day's dungeon dive.

The dumbfounded cleric stammered his thanks as his team pulled him away to begin their day in the dungeon.

"Why would you give him so much money?" Dale scoffed quietly at Josh, who was looking fondly after the retreating cleric. "That is enough to live comfortably for a month!"

"A good healer is a man you curry favor with! You see, lad, there is a very important lesson to be learned here. When you are able to be generous, do so! There will always come a time when you cannot afford what you need. People will be far more likely to help you when you fall on hard times if you are free with money in the good times." Josh smiled a bit painfully at Dale.

"Go out of your way to be respectful to the one who brings you your food, holds your money, and most importantly, those who work to heal you. That cleric expected nothing for his service and now goes into danger with less power because of me. How could I do less for him?"

Dale hung his head a bit. "I had not considered things that way. Sorry, Josh. I wasn't trying to sound like he didn't deserve it. I think I've just had a bad day, and my manners have gone to trash."

"I know, lad." Josh had never looked so uncomfortable, including his recent bone-shattering. "You're a good man, just... Remember that you have had some very lucky breaks, and life is still pretty hard for other people. Try to give back. People will appreciate it if they know the person they depend upon is good-hearted."

"I'll try. I'm going to go catch a nap before lunch, I think."

Hans scoffed. "Smelling like a sweaty rabbit turd? How about you go bathe instead?! Nap he says! Nap indeed!"

"I need to go give my report to the Guild and get some guards and a scribe over to this new exit," Craig announced, already walking away from them. "The Guild needs its taxes."

DALE

Roughly a month passed, and the team settled into its routines. Dale had just returned from bathing one night after dinner when a shout rang out.

"They are going to open the portal!" Anyone not engaged in a serious task started excitedly moving toward two stone obelisks standing proudly on the small hill. Dale decided it might be fun to join, as he had never even seen a portal before. The anger James had for him had kept him away from the site they were building on.

A sonorous chant was swelling, and energy like static was flashing along the paired standing stone obelisks. Dale moved into his Essence enhanced sight, trying to understand what was happening. Mana was thick in the air, though it was normally invisible to the naked eye. With the activation of his analysis ability, it was readily apparent. He had thought that all Mana would look alike–like Essence did–and with a group working together like this, he had expected a harmonious linking of energy as they meshed their sympathetic energy toward a single purpose. In his mind, Mana was going to be beautiful.

The reality was almost... disgusting. It was a clash of primary colors and a visionary cacophony. As one man directed his words, his chant, Dale saw it as a polka-dotted scroll that unraveled and wrapped around the stone. One woman, singing, seemed to have inky bubbles roiling from her mouth which burst in a sequence of light, filling precious gems with power. Amber had the most terrifying Mana moving away from her, the oily coloration roiling in light and impressions, unrefined chaos that the mind interposed its own images on.

Dale shuddered, looking past the Mana, instead trying to look at what they were putting Mana *into.* The twin obelisks stood, one exactly the same as the other, though in reverse, as if they were mirror images of the other. Slowly, brightening Runescript flowed up and around each in so many varied and opulent ways that it was nigh impossible to find where each began and the surrounding Runes stopped. Each Inscription was filled with gold that had been poured in a single sitting, leaving not a single break, weld, or splatter along the glowing lines.

Exactly the same amount of power went into each stone, and they began to hum to their own song, dulling each time the Mana reached a new gem set into the patterns. At precisely the same time on each standing stone, the gem would grow nearly too bright to look at, then darken as the Mana continued up the flowing, golden pattern. The crowd was silent, completely awestruck as enough energy was accumulated into this one spot to begin to punch through the dimensional boundaries. The power became audible, snapping and hissing, the sound of a star detonating and being reborn as a furious and colossal terror of the void.

The opening expanded, and a hole of pure darkness was pulled torturously to the artificial terminus represented by pure, glowing energy. The edge of the hole in the universe extended, straining to this glowing end, finally hooking like a fish taking bait—that is, furiously and with dark intent of escape. The chanting increased, and the impossibly black interior shuddered before finally relinquishing to the Mages' control, shimmering into a vision of another locale in the world.

Silence reigned for but a moment as the crowd tried to comprehend what they had just witnessed—some hardened men shaking in terror—before a roar of approval tore from the throat of an astonished onlooker. Then cheering, shouting, the men praised the makers of this wondrous relic. The exhausted Mages beamed as a festival air took hold, people rushing to enlist the services of these esteemed experts.

"I want to get to the capital of–"

"I have important–"

"Please! I haven't seen my–"

"Get out of the way! I'm–"

The rush of noise, and soon violence, was shocking to Dale. This entire event reminded him that there was more to life than training and fighting but also the spectacular end goal you could achieve when you had been training. It was a paradox that made him freeze up, torn between rushing back to the dungeon or just joining the melee that was rapidly spiraling out of control, just to feel alive.

"*Enough*!" a familiar voice sounded, laced with absolute authority. The sound reverberated through his entire being, insisting upon *instant* obedience. Sixty percent of the fighting men and women stopped, their bodies no longer their own to control, while the others looked like they were moving through thick tar, their motion slowly coming to an absolute halt. Some of the weaker people passed out, their lungs unable to pull in air. All then collapsed to the ground, breathing restored to the gasping group.

"Are you animals? Are you no better than the creatures you come here to fight?!" Frank was walking toward the new portal. "I am *ashamed*! Ashamed of my own people! Any Guild members who started a fight, go to the clerks and pay the fee for fighting with your brothers-in-arms. Any who protected another, go collect a bonus from them."

"Any *non-Guild* members, if you ever want a chance at joining the Guild, go and make amends, *now*. It is standard that if you have attacked a Guild member outside of self-defense, you may not join the Guild! We will pardon you this *one* time as the majority were from *my Guild*!" Frank roared furiously, face an unhealthy maroon color. "I will *not tolerate this*! If any do something so foolish again, their Guild fee will be raised to fifty percent of all valuables gained for a year! A third time and they are out of the Guild and *blacklisted*!"

He stared around at the quaking people and snorted in disgust. "Why are you still here?! You have your orders! Get moving!"

People scrambled in all directions; some would have been trampled if the threat of Guild expulsion were not hanging in the air. Hans walked over to Dale, standing by as they watched the ocean of motion.

"Well, that was fun." Hans chuckled glibly.

"What did he do to them, Hans? This has been so... messed up." Dale shuddered. "I just want to go to bed."

"Never seen ol' Frankie in action, eh? Not too surprising. Not too much around here calls for the workings of an A-ranked Mage." Hans stretched a bit as he began walking to the portal.

"He's a Magous?" Dale's eyes widened in shock. He had been rude to Frank on several occasions...

"Ohhh yes. You don't get to be in charge of things if you are weak, my boy! Those Mages can get pretty scary. How their power manifests is... mind numbing," Hans expressed in a low, dark tone.

Dale agreed with him, "I saw. What was all of that? Essence seems to look pretty much the same, doesn't it? Why is Mana so different?"

"Mana is... unique to the person who uses it. It is the true name and power of *something* that influences reality in the way they want it to. From what I understand, when you first say a word in that... 'language'–for lack of a better word–your Essence becomes a concept of reality that you have uttered."

Dale was more confused than he had been at the start of the conversation. "How then do they do different things? Don't they have control of just *one* thing?"

Hans shook his head. "Something you will have to learn is that all of reality is really one single event. Though the concept they interpret is different for everyone, it can affect most things equally. Dangerously. It is a terrifying power to wield. I cannot even imagine what spiritual energy looks like–never ran into an S-ranked before," Hans nearly whispered, giving a small shudder.

"What did Frank actually do, though?" Dale insisted on understanding at least *one* piece of this talk.

"From what he told me of the Word he uses, it seems to be the basis for movement. *Really* hard to explain," Hans apologetically informed him. "Think of it like this, when you move your arm, first your muscles bunch, then leap toward your target, right?"

Dale nodded affirmatively.

Hans smiled. "Right, so all of that *potential* movement, which builds up when your muscles are getting ready to move, is the concept that Frank's words embody. He took everyone's *potential* movement away."

"Holy..." Dale was stunned at this. "Didn't some stop instantly, though?"

"Yeah, all the Guild members he outranks. So every Guild member that was in the area." Hans glanced at Dale. "You do understand that entering the Guild, signing that document, ensures that everyone *has* to follow lawful orders, correct? That is what he enforced just now."

"Wow." Dale shook his head. "That is just the next level up from Essence? I... cannot understand what the higher rankings would be like."

"Guess we're just going to have to wait and see," Hans happily chattered, clapping Dale on the shoulder. "Feel like getting a hot meal halfway across the world? If I recall correctly, you get free access for yourself and friends!" He finished with a broad wink.

"Why not? You'll show me around, right? I've never been off the mountains." Dale suddenly contemplated what he would be able to see soon.

"You know it! Get your money. I know *just* the place to bring you." Hans grinned, a worrisome glint coming into his eyes.

They went and prepared themselves, then regrouped and joined the rather long queue that was slowly moving into the portal. Dale spotted Father Richard ahead, nearly bouncing as he waited his turn. Dale had to laugh at the man's antics.

"Think he is going to go find some stonemasons?" Dale casually looked over at Hans, pointing at the powerful priest.

"Who?" Hans peered about.

"Father Richard, over there."

"Oh. Most likely, I guess. Ah, Dale, about Father Richard, I've heard some–"

A bellowing voice reached them abruptly, "Dale! Dale wait, please!"

They turned toward this voice to see James, the portal maker, running toward them. He stopped, panting, face flush and eyes wild.

"Oh. Hello, James," Dale spoke coolly. "How can I help you?" Dale was still rather displeased with James, the Mage's insults still fresh in his mind.

"Dale, please, I want to apologize. I wronged you and acted like a buffoon, holding prejudices for no reason other than to have them. Please don't make me leave," James begged. "This place… I've never seen anything like it!"

"Oh, now we get to the crux of it," Hans interjected snidely. "Realized how profitable this area is going to be? How the dungeon has been churning out Runed items like a merchant churns out turds?"

Dale looked at Hans, startled at this unforeseen attitude. Hans, mistaking the look, gave an explanation, "They churn turds out frequently. Because they eat so much. Dale? You okay?"

Dale's face was beet red. Abruptly, he erupted into laughter. Hans looked a bit confused until he also started laughing. James looked shocked, then affronted, assuming they were calling him names, laughing at him for some reason.

"You don't have to be cruel about it. I'll go. The enchantment is already pulling me toward the portal. I may as well just…" James decreed sharply. He turned and started to pace away.

"W-wait!" Dale snorted around his laughter. "You're fine, James. You don't have to go. Just try not to be an ass to everyone. It isn't too fun when someone has so much power, and you can't do anything to stop it, right?"

"No. It. Is. Not," James enunciated bitingly.

"Well, that's what you were trying to do when we met. I hope you can see the parallels in the situation. Bullying me and being pushy, with no regard for my opinion, simply due to your overwhelming strength." Dale smiled to soften the insult. "Let's meet up and talk sometime. I'd love to hear about portal making. Plus, I really would rather have you as a friend than an enemy."

They left James standing there with a shocked look still on his face as they walked over to the open portal, which they stepped through after a brief talk with the attendant, who marked something in a ledger book.

Chapter Twenty-One

Dale dropped to the ground heaving.

"Ah, the best and worst feeling in the world," Hans chattered, glancing fondly at the portal.

"The... worst... ye-blargh." Dale didn't puke, the long distant breakfast being the only reason. The dry heaving wasn't fun, though.

"Oi! Move it, you're about to be trampled!" the attendant on this side of the portal shouted.

"Oops. Forgot to tell you to close your eyes when you came through." Hans grasped Dale, moving him forward as more people appeared in the spot they had been. Luckily, the design of the portal made it like walking through a door, not creating matter in the same area, else portal magic would have quickly gone out of style–with the exploding people and whatnot.

Dale looked around, quickly forgetting his nausea. This was a beautiful area, and the trees and flowers gave off a heady fragrance. A tang of salt was in the air as well, reminding Dale that the Lion Kingdom capital was adjacent to the ocean. The whitewashed stone of the surrounding buildings gave off a glare where the sun struck them, making him quickly avert his eyes. His clothing, thick wool under the armor he wore constantly, was already beginning to accumulate sweat as his body registered the heat and humidity of the region.

"This is..." Dale breathed.

"Hot, beautiful, and filthy," Hans supplied cynically.

Dale looked at him askance. "Filthy?

"Under all that paint and rosy perfume, this is still a city. Last year, the shit piled so high in the streets that the King finally noticed, since his daughter's horse slipped in it, and she got a bit... messy." Hans quieted near the end of his tale. "Don't go telling that story too loudly. They're still a bit, hmm, sensitive about it here. Anyway, the Kingdom paid off the Guild and hired water Mages to flood the worst of the streets. This allowed careful flushing of everything foul off and away. Even the homeless that lived in the streets."

"That's... good? Getting rid of the poop, at least... Seems a bit temporary, though," Dale ventured. "They just washed people away?"

"Right, good head on those shoulders, boy-o. Well, he also bought most of the earth Mages in the city, their services at least, and they've been building an elaborate sewage system under the city. Have been for the better part of a year." Hans grimaced with finality. "And yes, they don't particularly care about people who refuse to work for a living. To be homeless in the city, you need a license from the Beggars' Guild, which is not a Guild approved by the Realm."

Dale decided he didn't really want to get into a political discussion, so he returned to the sewer system, "Why does building it take so long? Seems like it wouldn't be too hard to make a tunnel with Mana..."

"Ah, now you come to the crux of the matter. Stonework is hard and expensive, but when it is done right, it stays in place pretty much forever. Stone Mages convince the stone that *this* is the shape they've always wanted; it would take intense destructive power to convince them otherwise," Hans sagely imparted wisdom. "The King *does* care about his working citizens, though, which is the only reason this project is being successful. Since the cost is so high, short term planners don't really see the worth of the idea, as the common citizens are the main beneficiaries of it."

"Oh, well, I guess I don't really see why it's such a big deal if they can just cheaply wash it away every once in a while," Dale suggested.

"There is the argument of the uneducated, my friend. Filth in the streets like that causes unrest, disease, and is a strong blow to morale. Not to mention, who likes shit on their feet?" Hans intently made eye contact. "The sewers will make the place healthier, wealthier, and happier for *everyone*. More so for cultivators like us, who may live here a *very* long time."

Dale was quiet, considering Hans's words. "Hans, why do you know these things? I mean, I know you've been around for a longer time than me but..."

Hans was quiet a short while, a considering look passing along on his face. Finally, he began softly, "Dale, I... don't want you to think poorly of me, but I'll tell you a bit about myself if you'd like."

Dale nodded, eager to learn about any of his tight-lipped squad mates.

"Alright, well, I grew up here," Hans started as they walked along a palm tree-lined street. "I was the lowest of the low, basically an orphan for how much I saw my father, and my mother died before I ever knew her. Undisciplined, wild, and hungry, I joined the street gangs that roam the streets. Kids my age, governed by usually just one adult, someone who survived in the gang long enough to be called an adult at least. The guards are not... kind... to thieves if they are caught."

Dale gazed on in surprise; he had never expected these revelations. He remained quiet, knowing an interruption might stop the flow of information.

"I... distinguished myself a little *too* much. I was careless and boasted of my success. A thief, a *real* thief, from one of the hidden Guilds, approached me and offered training. It is not an offer you say no to—not if you plan to live. Soon after, I was being taught everything you would expect—stealth, legerdemain, better ways to pickpocket." Hans glanced at Dale to see if he had his attention.

"Anyway. Then I was suddenly learning things I *didn't* expect. Numbers, letters, politics, current events, etiquette. They had a plan for me to make a big haul. I ended up in the Guildhall, of all places, at a fancy dinner for the sons and daughters of nobility. We talked, danced, and ate fine food. No one suspected a thing, but many of them walked away with less jewelry or fewer coins," Hans reminisced fondly. "Such easy marks."

"But my real target was a cache of memory stones locked in the same rooms, the cultivation techniques of the great houses of nobility." Hans caught the surprised look on Dale's face and grimaced. "Not all cultivation techniques are equal. The royal family draws Essence in as a raging river compared to the trickle of most commoners' slow drippings. If someone had access to this outside of the royals, it would allow for even cultivation all around the Kingdom."

"Why isn't that the case then? Do they just like to subjugate their populations?" Dale spoke with heat in his voice.

"What? No!" Hans yelped, surprised. "The lifespan of Mages and above is measured in centuries. The entire time, they are capable of siring children. Can you imagine what would happen to us if we had hundreds of millions capable of living for that long? They keep their abilities so they can rule wisely and justly, as well as being the last line of defense for their Kingdom. Their minds don't wander; their bodies are strong."

Dale was confused. All he had ever heard was that royals and nobility took and took and never gave aught back. Hans was saying that it was actually because they were trying to preserve their reliant citizens.

"Dale, everyone *can* cultivate, but as you know, it takes time and effort. Also, lots, and *lots* of pain. People still go off to adventure, but a large portion of them die quickly. What if *everyone* was a full-time cultivator? No other professions would flourish, and civilization would stagnate. We need everyone, from the lowliest cleaner to the mightiest warrior. Without all of what we are, we would *all* likely die off."

Dale finally nodded in acknowledgment. "I see. So if we had no farmers because they were more interested in becoming fighters, people would starve for their neglect. No clothing makers, no chefs, no cleaners."

"Exactly! In fact, that happens when war breaks out. Other jobs get forgotten, and the entire Realm suffers for it. It is a sad fact of life as a human," Hans told Dale, clapping him on the arm with a happy smile. "Now, back to my story. I had opened the drawer with the memory stones and was taking my leave of the party when a flesh Mage showed up."

At Dale's incomprehension, Hans informed him, "A flesh Mage is a water Mage who specializes in changing, distorting, and all around altering of bodies. Usually human 'flesh', you see? They can find anyone, anywhere, if they have even a drop of their blood. They can also follow people from the imprints they leave on the world. Since I had opened the cabinet last, they somehow followed my trail back to the Thieves' Guild."

"They sound horrible." Dale thought about what kind of a person you would need to be to willingly work on living people.

"They are actually rather popular. They are very good healers and can make people look however they want, given time. Women go to them to remove blemishes or supposed disfigurements or just to enhance their natural beauty. Men go to them for similar reasons. In my case, though, they were coming for revenge," Hans explained, looking a bit despondent.

"When they found it was a den of thieves, they carelessly massacred everyone there, but finding all the memory stones intact, they stopped caring about me and left–the only reason I am alive today. Instead of blaming them for the deaths of my 'friends', I was impressed by their ability to do whatever they wanted. I joined the Guild as soon as they would take me, years later."

"When did that all happen?" Dale queried.

"Oh, forty-ish years ago, maybe forty-five? Who remembers? Besides, we are here!" Hans exclaimed, pointing up.

Dale looked away from his friend and saw they were standing outside a garishly colored building with suggestive yet refined paintings on the walls. His face got red as he made the assumption as to what kind of establishment this was.

"Hans–" was all he got out before he was pushed inside by his grinning friend.

Several hours later, they emerged.

"Okay, Hans, you were right," Dale groaned as he exhaustedly waved a hand at his friend. "I never knew this could be so... amazing."

"I told you this was the place to be," Hans purred.

Dale moaned, "I will never not come back here. It could never be better."

"What if you were married. Would you tell your wife that?" Hans teased.

"Yes, she would have to accept it. Or I could bring her here, and she could try it for herself." Dale sighed contentedly.

"I don't know. She may like it too much, and that could get expensive." Hans winked at him. Just then, a busty lady walked over to them.

"Hello, I hope everything was as pleasurable as possible for you today," she softly addressed them in a husky voice.

"Madame, everything was as wonderful as it could have been," Hans heaped praise on her. "There is no better place to have a meal than at the *Pleasure House*. I don't know how your cooks do it, but it is worth every copper."

"I will send your compliments to the chef." She laughed with a smile. "It has been too long, dear Hans. Visit again soon. I'd love to get to know your friend better." She looked at Dale, considering. "Actually, I have a granddaughter about your age, and if I know Hans, you would be a good match for her."

Dale was blushing as hard as Hans was laughing. "Ha! You always know how to tickle my sense of humor! No, Madame, he is a cultivator and has no time for relationships. Maybe in thirty years."

"Mm. A cultivator? So young! And already nearly into the D-rankings. Quite a catch indeed," she murmured, glancing at him solicitously.

Dale was still too tongue-tied to babble anything, so Hans again took over, "Such a gracious host! Maybe the next time we visit we can meet this lass?"

"When might that be?" she challenged archly, expecting him to say something fancy and disappear for years again.

"Ah, when the wind blows us back to this fair city." She *humphed* and started walking away when Hans surprised her. "Luckily, that may be soon, as a portal just opened to this young man's home."

"A new portal? So you are training at the new dungeon. Is it true that it is... unaffiliated? The Essence? Anyone can absorb it?" She seemed suddenly nearly desperate, which she tried and failed to hide.

"Yes!" Dale finally loosened his tongue and responded too loudly. He coughed. "Uh, yes, it is. So far."

"Do you know any way that I could send my granddaughter there to train as a cultivator?" Madame demanded.

"Uhh." Dale looked at Hans for help.

"Also, I could not send her there alone. I would need to establish a restaurant there myself. I am sure you all needed to work out land management there. Have you met the owner? I hear he is allowing businesses to set up for a beastly amount of money, but I would still go."

"Where did you hear that from?" Dale thought he was being fair to people.

"Members of the Mages' Guild eat here regularly. Some of them were the first through the portal, and they came here with their gossip," she proudly announced. "I hear that the landowner is even making the church pay a tithe to *him*. Then he refused the services of the portal Guild until they gave in to his outrageous demands. Bet you didn't know *that*, did you?" she finished a bit smugly.

"No. No, I didn't," Dale dejectedly replied.

"I've met him, and I think he was being more than reasonable, Madame. The Mages tried to browbeat him into submission, and the Church offered up a small percentage of its profits for prime realty," Hans admonished her. "In the end, they both got fair deals based on what they could pay."

"Oh! So you actually *do* know him then? Do you think he would welcome the idea of a *Pleasure House* in the area," Madame inquired, not seeming to notice Dale's introspective look, "or a team that would allow a young lady to train with them?"

"He'd go for the restaurant if you fed him and offered a fair deal," Dale muttered hollowly. "I don't know any teams but my own so..."

Hans cut in darkly, "Madame, you know that to get on a Guild team you need to be in the Guild. I wouldn't trust another team with the proper care of a lady in a place where there are ways to make a body disappear, without worry, in a way no one will question."

"You are right, of course. I'll start with the dining house then. Who is in charge there right now? Jeffrey?" Madame seemed to understand that these two wanted to be left alone and so tried to hurry the conversation along.

"Frank," Dale droned monotonously, all happy thoughts of food long past.

"Well, that'll make this easy then." She laughed. "He can't resist me at all, and the landowner will assuredly want good food available for his tenants."

"I'm sure he will," Dale mumbled, earning an elbow to the ribs and a glare from Hans.

As Madame walked away, Hans turned curiously to the usually cheerful young man. "Dale, what is the matter with you?"

"Does everyone think so poorly of me?" Dale blatantly questioned him.

Hans eyed him, finally deciding not to lie. "Only those who don't know the facts or you," he admitted reluctantly.

Dale looked at the ceiling and exhaled noisily. "So... everyone."

"Lad, most people don't know you are the landowner but are *still* jealous that you make it into the dungeon every day when they get in maybe once a week. Others see your fine armor, not the man inside it, and covet that. People are always unhappy with those that have better fortune than them. You'll be fine, just give it time. The portal being open will let everyone get around much easier. That should relieve tensions quite a bit. After all, people can show up on their scheduled day to train, not just sit around on their thumbs feeling sorry for themselves," Hans lectured, trying to force Dale out of his funk.

"Now, pay this tab. All that advice isn't free, after all."

Dale nearly choked as he noticed the amount on the bill. "You're outta your mind! Abyss no!"

Cal

"Okay, Cal, that was amazing. I didn't think the inverse of the Rune would be *that* effective." Dani was looking at the bubbling, hissing crater that was all that remained to show a group had been standing there recently.

I was still basking in the glorious flood of Essence that had filled me. <Hmm?> I thought at her languorously, sipping delicately at the Essence storming around me. Her words clicked after a second. <Well, you should have! Have I ever given you a reason to doubt my amazingness?> For some reason, there had been a short period of time where no one was entering my influence. It had coincided with what sounded like a thunderstorm overhead, though the sky was clear from what I could see. In that short window of opportunity, I was able to make some hasty changes, including a new trap.

"Well, I wouldn't have thought of it. That was a really ingenious trap," Dani praised me, playing to my ego.

<Thanks! It made sense to me. Most people will try to avoid boiling acid, you know?> I chuckled with her.

The trap was a bridge in the tunnel system that had to be crossed. On the bridge was a series of Runes across it that pushed the acid away and held the acid suspended to the sides of the bridge. If someone stepped directly on one specific pressure-sensitive pattern at the midpoint between the acid 'walls', the stone the runes were on would flip, and the corrupted core would then pass its energy to the inverted Rune. I was rather happy to have found a use for my water corruption cores.

When the inverted Rune was powered, the suspended acid sloshed across the entire structure, flooding it instantly. The Runes were nearly indestructible when filled with corruption, as far as I could tell, and so I was able to easily regrow the bridge around those Runes when it was destroyed, as I did now. Sadly, the fallen group of adventurers had only standard gear compared to what I had been seeing–nothing magical and nothing fancy. Just plain, boring metal and leather. Woe is me that those I slay cannot be more financially stable.

These ones had health potions, though, which was surprising given that most of the people who take serious injuries here die. Someone was making a *fortune* on people who would never get a chance to drink the potions. Hmm. Really, that is a good point... Was I getting too dangerous? Almost everyone who got hurt died nowadays... I felt that this was a good way to get overpowered people in here fast. I needed to start throwing the lower level guys a handout, or they would stop coming. How best to do this? I turned to my best source of ideas: Dani.

<Dani, should we give out some more freebies?> I was proud that I was using this word for the first time; it was fun to 'say'. Freebies. Ha! <I feel like the weak groups are grumbling a lot.>

"What about the iron mining? That seems to calm them down a bit," she querulously put forward. It was a literal sore spot; the chipping away of iron *constantly* gave me the equivalent of a headache.

<I'd rather not make more of those mining areas. How about potions? I can make them really easily. How about I make a cistern that has health potions flowing in them? Maybe that light potion I got too,> I offered a few concepts floating around in my mind.

She considered for a moment. “Not a bad idea, but then the apothecary up there will go out of business, leave, and there will be at least one less person you get a chance to eat. Oh, how about adding some gemstones to the iron every once in a while?”

I ventured a solution, <I can add those. I have so many different kinds from jewelry people wear in. Hmm. What if I made a few of these cisterns but poisoned them randomly? Then no one would feel safe using them without going to him first, he would get work, and I wouldn't have his half-rate potions to throw away.>

“That sounds good.” She pondered thoughtfully. “Might even get a few people to willingly drink poison.”

<Ha. I like it. Let's put the health one on the first floor right before the Boss room and the light one in a dead-end on the second floor. That may convince people that it is the way to get into the Boss room with all the light it'll give off.>

“Diabolic! That is a spectacular idea!” She was so excited that she was merrily glowing, and neither of us saw the look of greed cross the face of the man stealthily watching from above. No one in the area had seen her before now.

<Hey! Someone is past the last trap down here! Ready for a fight?>

“You know it, Cal!” Dani joyously bubbled. She returned to invisibility, getting ready for the show. A five-man group hesitantly walked in, surprising me with their low levels. Only *one* was out of the F-ranking, and he was a low D-rank. For the first group to get here, outside of Dale's, to be so low ranked astonished me. Well, free food and all that I supposed. Beggars and choosers and whatnot. I took direct control of Raile, wasting no time charging at them as quietly as possible.

"There it is!" a panicking voice shrieked.

"Why is it so *big*?" yelled another. "It didn't look *nearly* this big from above!"

"Just get ready!"

Another yell from above alerted me that people had noticed a fight starting and were scrambling to make bets. Cheering filtering down gave the group determination as they dived to get out of the way of my charging Boss. One dived a second too late, and Raile's armored paw, as large as a small bear's, crushed the bones between himself and the floor, grinding the now shattered leg into the granite. The man's scream resounded in the enclosed space, and the cheering abruptly cut off. They must have realized they were about to see someone die, a first for the Boss room. The show became a whole new event, as people prepared themselves to witness death firsthand.

The other group members sprang to their fallen friend's aid, valiantly and pointlessly charging. I ignored the downed man; he had no ranged weapons that I could see. His screams would do more damage to the group than his death would. Making directly for the rest of the group, Raile sprang upward and came to the earth with a thunderous clap of stone striking flesh. One of the men had shoved the other out of the way, taking the entire weight of Raile's body himself and dying silently. Raile nearly slipped as he regained his footing, blood and gore oozing from the underside of his armor as he turned to attack again.

The furious men now got as close as they could, beating on Raile with flanged maces and armor-shattering warhammers. They had certainly brought the correct tools for fighting Raile; even so, the damage they did was surprising, especially for such a small, weak group. I thought for a moment, realizing they were attacking in fury, their pulped friend driving them to become enraged. As Raile moved to jump again, a lucky swing from a warhammer hit the joint of his knee *just* before he pounced. The jump interrupted, Raile flopped down, knee cap broken. Still dangerous but far less limber, he squealed and ran at another man, clipping him with his charge.

Oof! was all I heard over the crash of armor and the wet tearing of skin as bone became visible from the inside of my victim's chest. He spun mostly out of the way of the attack, falling to his knees as he wheezed for breath with broken ribs.

Another mace crashed down, taking out the mobility of Raile's *back* legs this time. Raile pulled himself along as the teammates, those able to do so, cheered. Cockily, one walked around to the front of a *very* slow moving Raile and raised his mace to start trying to break through his armor. After a few hard hits, Raile flopped down, stunned, as the granite chipped and cracked. The attack broke off for a moment as the man caught his breath. He wiped his brow, smiling and laughing, obscuring his vision just long enough for a golden streak to reach Raile and *boop* him on the nose.

A scream too high pitched for the humans to hear went through Raile as his legs twisted, mending his bones. His head stopped ringing, his torn muscles healed, and he leaped at the man in front of him, bearing him to the ground. There was not much power to the attack, as he had not had time to build momentum, but that mattered little as the man's body caved in under Raile. The man weakly tried to strike him, failing as the rush of Essence flowing to me signaled the man had been killed. Triumphant, I turned Raile's head to look for more adversaries as the pointed end of a warhammer smashed down on to the cracked armor on Raile's head, crushing through it and into his brain.

<Ah!> I shrieked silently. Luckily, the mind-speak that I used wasn't audible, else I'd have given myself away. <I did not see that coming! It came out of nowhere! Whoa!>

Dani silently comforted me as the men rolled Raile away from their fallen comrade. Very respectfully, the ambulatory members laid him against the wall and moved to collect their other fallen comrade. They walked to where he had been obliterated, but I had finished absorbing him by then. They looked confused, then horrified as they turned to rush back to the man they had placed by the wall.

<Too late.> I silently burped.

The men were entirely destroyed as a group. The ones not openly weeping were staring stony-faced at the somber spectators above them. Their audience had a few intermixed who were swapping silver, and the adventurers below quickly grew furious.

"They made this fight look so easy! Not once were they seriously hurt!" one was raging. "I'm gonna make sure everyone knows this fight is ridiculous! No one will ever bother coming down here again!"

<Well, we can't have that,> I thought. Time to distribute some loot. I figured since these guys were low ranked, it would be fair to give them a *way* bigger reward than Dale's group earned. I bet that would stop the cries of anger!

A rain of items fell around Raile, catching the men off guard and making them startle badly. Heh. Gotta have fun somehow, right? I dropped a massive warhammer with an Inscription at each end, both powered by Essence they would have to provide at the hilt. The Rune near the hilt allowed the hammer to be near weightless, while the one at the top made the force of the swing be multiplied many times over. If they could use that in a fight correctly, it could shatter Raile's armor like glass. In a sneaky move, I had also placed the 'binding' site directly under the activation; whoever used it would be the *only* one who could until that owner died at least.

I dropped one boot, which had a perfect liquid repulsion Rune. I bet that one would become *very* popular when people found out about the acid trap. The Rune was large enough to have an area of effect that surrounded the person wearing it; they could jump in a lake without getting damp. On a whim, I also gave them a sword with the sharpening augmentation. Inside of it, I placed a low-powered Beast Core that would be able to hold a charge from the activator, allowing them to use it freely in combat if they charged it beforehand.

That oughtta do it. They looked at the loot uncomprehendingly, so I dropped three extra large pieces of gold. *That* shook 'em out of their reverie, and looks of joy replaced the bitter anger on their faces. They were still grieving but could sell these items for enough to live in comfort for the rest of their lives if they stopped being cultivators. The man who had killed Raile picked up the warhammer and, in a decidedly stupid act, activated the Rune. The oversized hammer suddenly light in his hands, he nearly stumbled.

He took a few swings, one-handed, to the amazement of all onlookers. Then grinning darkly, he swung as hard as he could at the corpse of Raile, which shattered into hundreds of shards. One of those shards flew into the head of his teammate on the ground with the broken leg, killing him near instantly.

<Oh, *yeah*!> That had worked out so well! The energy joined my spiral, pushing me over the edge into the third rank of the D series. I had not been paying attention to how close I was, so the sudden expansion of my power surprised me.

"Oh, *no*! *No*! *NO*!" The warhammer-wielding man cried as he dropped to his knees next to his impaled friend, openly weeping. The last remaining man gathered the loot, and slowly, the two ascended the stairs together, taking strength in their friendship and survival despite the horrible cost. They opened the door at the top to condolences and cheers. I turned in contemplation toward Dani.

<So. Where should we put the cisterns for those potions? Or should we make fountains instead?>

DALE

A lazy day in the capital was just what Dale had needed. A vacation from the dungeon, no matter how short, had greatly relaxed him. He and Hans had gone to a bathhouse and soaked in the steaming water for hours, relaxing their muscles as professional cleaners washed their armor and clothes. Then as twilight threatened, they returned to the portal area and paid an exorbitant ten silver for a return trip, a sobering reminder that they only got to *leave* their home for free.

"Ow. My wallet," Hans whined as they made their way through the portal.

Dale dropped to the ground, dry heaving again but not as violently as the first time. "Ow. My body," he whined, making Hans laugh as Dale made fun of him.

"You forgot to close your eyes again, I see." Hans pulled Dale to his feet and looked up at the camp swarming with unfamiliar faces and sounds. One area seemed far more energetic than the rest, so they moved to take a look at what was going on. Hans got closer, then they saw a duo of men being escorted to the portal by none other than Guild Master Frank. One of the men, maybe in his mid-twenties, was holding a gigantic warhammer; both were being followed by two men carrying small but heavy chests.

"What's going on do you think?" Dale murmured to Hans.

Hans shrugged, and they followed the men to the portal, where they vanished after a brief talk with the portal attendant. He waved down Frank as he walked back and wondered aloud about what was going on.

"Oh. You haven't heard then?" Frank raised his eyebrow in surprise. "You must have just gotten back."

"Heard what? We took the evening off and went to the *Pleasure House* for dinner," Hans prodded him.

Frank looked shocked. "Without me? Fine, see if you get a bonus this year. What you just saw was the first group to complete the dungeon, besides yours of course."

Dale was perplexed. "Just the two of them?"

"Well. Those were the survivors. They were non-Guild and ignored the recommendation that it was a D-ranked minimum," Frank told him a bit sadly.

Hans winced. "Five-man team to start?" Frank nodded, and Hans shook his head empathetically.

"Why are they leaving? Did they just give up after their friends died?" Dale inferred.

"Well, one of them did. The hammer man is coming back if he can find anyone to team up with anyway. Activated that warhammer when it was dropped by the Boss and took a swing in petty revenge. That rock covered rabbit shattered, and a shard killed one of his wounded teammates. Most people don't see it as an accident but as an idiot with a stupidly powerful weapon." Frank shook his head at the foolishness.

"Oh wow," Dale commiserated with the poor man.

Hans mind went on a different route. "Is he thinking of selling that hammer off?" Greed was lighting his eyes.

Frank grimaced at the typical behavior. "No, it bound to him when he activated it. The Spotters say the binding and the activation are in the same spot. That hammer is his till he dies. They did get two other inscribed items and some loose gold, which will make you very happy, Dale."

"Why? What?" Dale looked at him confusedly. "Three people died. I'm not happy! I'm not a bad guy. Why does everyone seem to think I am an asshole?"

"Um. I'm thinking there is something going on that I don't know about..." Frank seemed a bit confused himself. "Not what I was talking about, though. Remember how you make a portion of everything that is made? Even the three percent you made off just those two items paid off more than half the debt for your armor. Combine that with the open portal and your personal dungeon dives, I'm betting you will be paid off in a month, less if more people complete the dungeon," Frank stated cheerfully.

What! They must have been worth thousands of gold then!" Dale was flabbergasted.

"They certainly were! One of them was a boot that repelled all liquids, and with the new acid traps, it sold at auction for nearly fifteen hundred gold," Frank cheerfully told him.

"Was it...? Was it Josh's boot that Raile, the Boss Mob, took off?" Hans's eyes bulged as he tried to hold back a deep laugh.

"Hah! It was! The size is different, though!" Frank crowed, slapping his knee as he laughed. "He's gonna be so pissed!"

Dale wanted to know what the other item was, so Frank told him about the unique sword that had been found, while Hans's jaw dropped lower and lower.

"It holds a charge?!" Hans finally exploded. "Why would you not wait for me to get back here before you sold it?!"

"You know how these things go–sell it for the best price or put it up for extended auction. They heard a good price and chose to sell." Frank's grin told Dale he was happy to have had less competition.

"*You* bought it! I knew it!" Hans was furious. "You have to give me a chance to buy it!"

"Nah," Frank allowed, very blasé about the situation. He spun on his heel and ran.

"Whaddaya mean, 'nah'?" Hans roared, running off after him.

Dale looked at the portal, thinking of the loss that group must be feeling. He hoped the gold they had earned would help them through. Now, it was time to get some rest; he had a long day of monster hunting tomorrow. Maybe he could get some new items?

DALE

Dale's group was just walking into the dungeon. The first thing they did each day was clear the first room completely to make sure there was no issue for the miners who came in to collect iron each day. Dale was still in constant wonder that no matter how much iron they tore out each day, the walls were unblemished in the morning, promising a good, easy mining operation.

"How was the city?" Steve casually questioned, kicking a Shroomish as it tried to chomp his foot. It disintegrated in a puff of spores from the casual blow.

"It was amazing! Did you know they have Mages building a sewer system there? I wonder if we could do something like that here," Dale wonderingly put forward. The others stopped and looked at him strangely. He wasn't sure why Hans was laughing at him so hard he couldn't breathe. "Are they not building it? Hans, what the abyss?"

"All the wonders of the capital and you are most excited about the... sewers. Nothing else caught your attention?" Steve interrogated him levelly. "You need to go places without Hans. His politics will ruin your day."

"We had fun! We did other things too! He brought me to a pleasure house," Dale chattered indignantly.

"He did *what*?!" Craig gasped, turning and glaring at the man.

"Not like that–" Hans tried to explain, glares directed at him.

Dale continued talking over them, "I met a Madame. She gave us a discount because we went to her together, and she thinks her granddaughter would like to come train here."

"Hans, you disgusting pervert," Josh coldly stated. "How could you do that to the lad? You went together? At the *same time*? With a *grandmother?*"

"Well, how else do you do it? Who wants to do that alone?" Dale sounded a bit exasperated at the questions.

Hans was literally on the floor crying with laughter as he tried to hold up his hands in surrender. "N-n-n-no, guys! Guys! Hahaha! W-we went to *the* Pleasure House! The one Madame owns! He, he doesn't know what this sounds like! The restaurant!" He could say nothing else as he gasped for air around his laughter.

The others started chuckling, then laughing almost as hard as Hans. The look of confusion on Dale's face made them laugh even harder.

"What? What's going on?!" Dale demanded. "I've never been off these mountains, come on! What's the joke?!"

They regained their feet and started walking, ignoring his angry questions and laughing as they went further in, some patting their naive companion on the back and shoulders as they walked. Working quickly, they cleared several rooms, constantly making their way toward the Boss room. A splashing sound garnered their interest, but before they were able to discern the location of the bubbling liquid, the new Boss Squad was attacking them.

CHAPTER TWENTY-TWO

<I made some improvements to that Boss room,> I informed Dani.

"Oh yeah? Added some traps or something?" Dani managed to tear her gaze away from the impending battle.

<Uh. That would have been better, wouldn't it? No, but watch this!> The Boss Squad was in full attack mode, but the Impaler ran straight at the wall—which opened enough to allow him into a small tunnel that ran along the room. It had loops in it that would grant a full speed sprint into the main room, hopefully taking people by surprise from an unexpected direction.

One of the two small, rock-covered Smashers went directly for Josh, who braced himself with a grin and held out his shiny, new tower shield. At the last moment, he thrust it forward! *Clang, sn-nap.* The Smasher's neck broke with an organic tearing sound, his spine protruding from just below the base of his skull.

"Yes! It's so much better than my last one!" Josh roared in celebration.

<What does that one do again?> I worriedly queried Dani.

She answered pensively, "It returns part of the momentum of the attack back on the attacker, doesn't it? That heavy charge had a *lot* of power in it, I think."

The infernally enhanced Impaler chose that moment to erupt from a tunnel opening behind Steve just then, landing a successful sneak attack. His sharpened horn burst through the thick leather armor just below Steve's kidney, the angle of the horn opening his spleen as it punched through his front. A pained gasp is all the sound the man could muster as he fell to his knees.

The Impaler lived up to his name well. Setting its paws on Steve's back, it pushed backward, adding more damage to the ravaged body it was standing on. Not yet out of the fight, Steve whipped around and crushed the skull of the offending Impaler with his bare hands. He then pulled the last bit of horn from his body with a soft grunt before casually sitting down. Dale shot forward and caught an Oppressor with a swing, snapping its spine. Craig moved in a blur of motion, killing the two remaining Mobs as Hans ran to help Steve.

"You're gonna be alright. Don't you worry 'bout a thing." Hans held his hands against the gushing wound. "We're ten minutes from the most powerful healer you'll ever need." He scooped Steve up easily, keeping pressure on the wound with his arm as he lifted from the ground.

"Well, I didn't open all those meridians so I could dance," Steve sputtered blood mid-sentence. "I'll be fine! I've had worse when I was caught with that noble girl, remember?" He gurgled a bloody chuckle.

"Well, that's for the best because I have to tell ya, you got two left feet," Hans quipped, starting for the exit. "Plus, you are too good for a backwater noble family anyway."

Dale caught their attention, "Wait! Look! This is pouring out a health potion!"

I focused on Dani for a second. <Did we poison that one?>

"No," she crushed my hopes, "we wanted to get people used to the idea of a healing fountain in here."

<Dang it! Of all the frikkin people who could have needed it first...>

Dale pulled out a flask and dunked it into the churning cistern, which had a fountain flowing into it. I had decided on that design. I wanted both function and form. I'm a sucker for pampering myself. Dale moved over to his friend who was bleeding out, helping him drink as much as he could.

Craig then instructed Dale to pour the potion directly on to the wound. Then they watched anxiously as it swiftly closed. The hanging scraps of meat pulled together into working tissue, the blood vessels flowed back together, and the ruined nerves returned to a working system.

The potion was high quality, as was everything I gave out. The potion did more than the eye could see, stimulating bone marrow to produce blood cells and fluids, mimicking proteins for growth, but still, a scar would remain. The healing process took a lot of energy, usually provided by the person doing the healing. Since a potion didn't bring in much extra energy, I was certain Steve would be *very* hungry soon. He would have to eat to replenish his system. Hopefully, he would starve soon enough that he would become distracted—and *I* could eat *him*.

Crisis averted, they sat to cultivate as Dani informed me that the first of the gems had been found, so I took a look. Yup, people were going nuts over the small chunks of emeralds they found. I would keep it interesting; there were also ruby, rapis, and—really rarely—diamonds! Each of these was in a little hollow between layers of iron and stone that people would naturally come upon while mining if they worked hard enough. In these hollows, there was also....

"Augh! It's a– *gack*," The mining man's voice cut off as an uncovered Bane fired a poisonous thorn into his shouting mouth, the lucky shot going through the roof of his mouth into his brain.

<Yes!> I just got my first pickaxe! I had really been wanting one of these! <Dani, the 'trap Mobs' in the wall actually worked!> A rush of Essence made its way to me, filling me with a sense of well-being. <Ahh, that's the stuff.> A thought occurred to me then—maybe I hadn't had it before because I was a lower ranking, but at D-rank three... Perhaps I was more empathetic?

<Dani?> I felt oddly detached. <When a person dies in here... do I eat their soul?> The thought of even *passive* Necromancy like that was disturbing to me.

"What? No!" Dani was shocked, making me feel instant gratitude that she understood my concern. "Souls are *terrifyingly* powerful, especially when freshly dead. When a being dies, they release a burst of energy which separates their bodies and souls. *That* is the rush of Essence you get access to."

<Oh, thank goodness. Sorry, I never thought of it before. Wait, I was a human, wasn't I? How was I captured then?> I realized she may just be trying to calm me.

"Honestly, I have no idea. It must have been a specially prepared stone made by someone so powerful I cannot even comprehend it. It would need to be an S-ranked Necromancer, at least. I have never heard of a Necromancer becoming that powerful though," Dani mused. "They are always killed. Well..."

<Well what?> I growled. I *needed* to know anything she did.

"Well, Necromantic cultivation isn't actually... illegal. It just has a really bad reputation. The main way they get more powerful is by absorbing the burst of Necromantic energy that results from something dying, similar to what you do..." She trailed off.

<And this is important because...?>

"Ahem, well, Necromancers get killed because they obtain more energy when strong emotions are passing through the person at the time of death. So, most quickly delve into torture and murder and other illegal things," she whispered. "If they didn't get caught doing that, though, they wouldn't even be in trouble... Though demon summoning, a branch of Necromancy, *is* illegal everywhere," she finished in a rush as if that tidbit would appease me.

I sighed, a neat trick without lungs. <Okay, so maybe I am too hasty in my judgment. Maybe I just hate murderous, evil Necromancers?>

"That's the spirit!" she enthused. "Ah... hah."

<Bad. Shame on you for that terrible pun,> I admonished her, though I was smiling on the inside. <Then what is the deal with Necromancy? What do those cultivators do besides kill people?>

"The most common thing is to raise the dead. That isn't, well, the act *itself* isn't illegal, but some places will really dislike it for obvious reasons."

<Walking dead guys? Yeah, I can see that,> I quipped.

"Pretty much. People really don't like desecration of their loved ones. Now, while the reanimated creature has to do what the summoner wants, the summoned creature is always, *always* insane." She shuddered and cuddled up to me.

<Why is that?> I was really curious now.

"The only souls that are able to be summoned are those that have run from the Creator's judgment. They fear the void, the nothingness that awaits them, or the abyss, which is terrible for other reasons. They wander the earth and can never stop moving. They can never sleep, never taste, never feel. By the time they feel a summoning, they are jealous of the living and will do anything to kill them, to absorb the energy of their death." She sounded close to weeping.

<That sounds like a horrible existence. Is that what makes them so dangerous?> I was morbidly curious.

"No, the average undead isn't that smart. They will take the most direct route for anything. They have no forethought anymore. They aren't used to having a corporeal form. The really dangerous ones are actually the demons," she fearfully let me know. "They are *confused* for undead because they need to inhabit a corpse in order to have a corporeal form, but they are actually incredibly intelligent and horrifically cunning. There is a rumor that they hate the one who summons them and, if given a chance, would kill their master. *Wrong*. They *cheerfully* obey their summoner, doing everything they can to keep them alive and happy. You see, if their master dies, the demons are *yanked* back into the abyss."

"If a Necromancer were a good person, they would be nearly the best at almost any profession. Working with dead things is the domain of those with the infernal affinity. Since humans and other sentient things are made of all the different essences, as they get stronger they discover that they can use their lesser affinities to augment themselves," she told me in a puzzling manner.

Seeing my confusion, she continued, "Take Dale, for instance." She made me look at the cultivating group. "He has a major earth affinity. In the C-rankings, he may find that he has a minor affinity with fire Essence as well, making him a magma cultivator. Fire and water? Steam cultivator. Each distinct affinity he is able to use and cultivate from will give him better options and make him more likely to ascend into the B-rankings."

<So humans can use all of the affinities? Why does he only cultivate from earth then?> I had been wondering why most of them only pulled from one source at a time.

"The best affinity they have will allow them to get the purest Essence as fast as possible. The older ones who know the truth–that they could pull from all sources if they found a way to unblock themselves–hide this fact because it can lead to *really* corrupted Essence in a hurry," she informed me with a small smile.

<Well, that makes sense, I suppose. Back up a bit, though. Why would a Necromancer be good at most professions?> I had realized she had glossed over that.

"Oh, well, think of it like this. A blacksmith who imbues Essence into his work to make it better is a magma cultivator, usually the case anyway. If he had infernal and earth as his affinities, he or she would not even need a flame to shape the *dead* earth into the form they wanted. Also, they would instinctively know the best way to make a weapon to produce the deadliest version that it could become." I got a chill as I thought of the implications and possible uses.

<Does that hold true for all of the combinations?> I wondered aloud.

"Not always. It will rely on personal skill, but typically, Necromantic cultivators can reverse the knowledge of how to destroy things into a foundation to making things better. If they are smart, they could be some of the best in the world, but killing is so much easier than the slow route they would need to take. They can't cultivate like other humans, with meditation and pulling from elements, but neither can celestial Mages, so their growth is very slow usually." She ended her tale as Dale's group began to move again.

This was my chance to get them, so I decided to take time to ponder Dani's words as the day continued. Dale now led the way, calling out stress points and possible traps with far more accuracy than he had started with a few weeks ago. With a start,

I realized that those stress points were like irritants to me. When the group was further along the tunnel, I would smooth those points, which felt really good, like a muscle relaxant must to a human. I should listen to their conversations more often, I chided myself.

I tried so hard to trick them into dying, but they avoided all of my ambushes so skillfully I felt they were playing with me. I had a bit of luck when they were crossing the bridge; some acid got on to the cloth surrounding Craig's hand. He lost a little skin but had the cloth off himself very quickly. It splashed into the acid pool with a hiss, and the information it contained came to me. I realized that it was *very* interesting stuff, but I would need to work through it slowly. I had never seen such a small item so intricately Inscribed with Runes.

They kept coming, falling for the light fountain room, going well out of their way. They walked in and looked confused until Steve recognized what the shimmering liquid was, convincing everyone to use any open flask to contain some of the potion. Having filled most of their flasks earlier with the healing potion, only a few were available for this shining fluid. Somehow, the light in the room must have distracted them from the Runescript on the ground around the shining cistern. To their dismay, as they walked away all of their shoes, boots, and foot wraps degenerated into piles of scraps. Heh. Barefoot adventurers.

They corrected their mistaken route, making it into the Boss room. I was looking for the best route of attack when I heard the big one, Josh, mention something rather concerning.

"Did you hear about the new quest? Apparently, there is a Mob in here we haven't seen before, a gold colored one that healed the Boss yesterday. Huge reward for the first one caught, double if it is alive. Also something about a Wisp, but I haven't seen anything like that here."

"Oh? Well, let's find it. Daddy needs a new pair of shoes." Hans earned himself some booing from the group of barefoot individuals.

They were in for a surprise today! The crowd above was cheering again, placing bets and preparing for the battle. Well, let's see if I can't make them lose some money. I had made a tunnel around the room that opened up several feet above head level, and only the thundering of stone and the cries of surprise from above made the small group look up as Raile dropped toward them from on high.

They scattered in time–blast it–but were now isolated and off balance. Raile nudged Hans as he charged Josh, sending the first spinning and catching a barely prepared Josh's shield. The Rune worked overtime, small chunks of Raile's armor crumbled into powder and cracked. My curiosity was satisfied as Josh still went flying. During the distraction provided by the flying man, Raile charged the weak link, Dale.

"Come on, you overgrown rabbit! I've been practicing!" Dale turned and ran.

<What the...? He's running!>

Dani softly chuckled into my head. "Maybe he's been practicing his cardio?"

<Huh?>

"His running ability." She uttered something condescending under her breath about my lack of vocabulary.

<No matter. Raile has him now.> I watched proudly as Dale reached the wall just before Raile did. Raile pounced at him from a charge, ready to do maximum damage as Dale dropped to his back and slid into the wall, pushing off at an odd angle to maintain momentum. Raile smashed into the wall full

speed, stunning himself and dropping to the ground where Dale no longer was; pushing off the wall had moved him just enough.

<You know, this kid is really starting to frustrate me.> I grunted as the group's blunt weapons broke through the armor over Raile's head and killed him.

"I think you are starting to like him. You've always liked a challenge." Dani laughed at my long-suffering moan.

<Well, I won't fall for that again. I'm going to give them weird loot, too. I've been working on these.> I dropped a pair of boots for each of them. They cheered until they saw they were all left-footed. Heh. I dropped a pickaxe and a right-footed, armored boot with the same force enhancing Rune as the warhammer I had dropped yesterday and a dagger with the inverted form of the Rune that had been on the Demonologist dagger Dale had killed Raile with. I had studied it; turned out that the original dagger would pull the Essence out of its victims until it had enough to summon a powerful demon under the wielder's control.

The effect of the dagger they had now... I was unsure of. Maybe it would summon an angel? I'm sure I would find out eventually. After a brief discussion, they agreed to sell the pickaxe and share the profits, though they cast lots for the inscribed boot. I'm fairly certain Hans cheated, while Dale *fairly* won the dagger but decided to get it checked by a Spotter before he decided to use it or sell it. Hans had no such compunctions, putting on his ill-gained boot and strutting around in mismatched footwear. With a look of glee on his face, he jumped and stomped down, activating the Rune.

WHAM. A shockwave knocked Hans to the shattered floor, laughing all the while.

"Woo! Look at that! Left a footprint an inch deep in solid granite! I have *so* many plans for this!" Hans whooped as he prepared to stomp again.

"Maybe you do that in an open area next time?" Steve called sourly, holding ringing ears and wiping rock dust off himself. The others nodded their assent.

"What?" Hans replied, pawing at his ears.

"Exactly," Steve loudly stated. "Let's go. I still want to see a healer for my back. And my ears now. Then lunch, I'm *starving*."

They climbed the staircase, allowing not very bright people to again push past them at the top. The newcomers had decided to ignore the warnings, it seemed. Yum. There was no other group close to the second floor Boss room, though the first Boss room had been cleared while I wasn't focused. I fixed my floor; really, smashing up my floor wasn't the way to entice me to give good items again.

<Oh, by the way, Dani, I am quickly going to look at the hand wrapping that fell off of Craig. It was stuffed full of Inscriptions and was *really* full of Essence. Let me know if anyone comes in,> I nearly whispered, my mind going over the patterns and layouts that had originally seemed to be a simple hand wrapping.

"What? Oh, fine. I'll let you know if anyone makes it in here," Dani grumbled. "Now I'm a watchdog."

Meanwhile, I was astounded. These were definitely Runes, but they were so strong! Only one of them I felt confident I could use without destroying something, and none of these were Runes I would give out for defeating the relatively weak Mobs in my dungeon. This was coming from me, the one who happily gave out an enchantment on a hammer that could be used to blast open a mountain pass.

I focused in on the one Rune I would feel safe using; it looked exactly like a smaller version of the fractal of energy surrounding my Chi spiral. I compared the two in my mind. The Inscription had a slightly different curve in a few places that was odd to me, as it forced the pattern to be non-symmetrical. Was this a Rune for absorbing Essence?

I had to find out. In a dead end room on my second floor as far away from my Core as possible was where I experimented with unknown Runes. I lovingly thought of it as the 'horrible failure with a few successes room'. Long name, amazing results. Over time, if I had been unable to repair the stone in there, there would only be a smoking, simmering room full of molten rock and odd noises. It seemed that poorly made Runes tended to explode. Who knew, right? That was one of the... nicer effects.

The Runes that I used corruption with that also turned out to be badly made Runes had more... interesting effects. An air Rune I had drawn on a rock allowed it to scream, which it did *constantly*. Luckily, a Rune exploding underneath it had interrupted the flow of energy to the screaming rock, making it go silent again. Of course, now I wondered if rocks were alive. Dani told me I was being ridiculous, but... Screaming rocks didn't seem to worry her much. As a rock-like being, I felt for the poor little guy.

A multi-Essence Rune that I tried to make had convinced me not to try combining corruption again until I knew what I was doing. It had created a rift, which used all of the Essence so fast that I was angry at first. The rift snapped shut after only the blink of an eye, but the rotten, clawed hand that had made it through in that timespan was a testament to the continuation of working *freaking carefully*. Definitely had opened a rift into the abyss there. I *really* didn't want to be responsible for allowing unbound demons on to our plane of existence. It did teach me to give the Runes very little power when I first activated them, at least until I was sure of their capabilities.

I digress–I wanted to see if this new Rune was used to accumulate Essence. I *very* carefully recreated the Rune to the molecular level, double and triple checking it to ensure that it was exactly the same as the one I had taken from Craig. I prepared myself to activate it but was interrupted when Dani informed me that people had entered the Boss room.

<Now? Dang, I was just about to activate that new Rune. How long was I working on that?> I dazedly looked at Dani.

"You were focused for about three hours; this is the sixth group that has come down to the second level. All the other ones got injured or turned around for some other reason," reported General Dani.

<Yes, ma'am!> I tried to match an accent I had heard. <Preparations are complete, ready for battle!>

"Why did I have to be bonded with a weirdo?" Dani muttered.

<I'm hurt!>

"Quiet down. Here they come."

<They can't hear *me* if I don't want them to,> I bragged. <Not *my* fault you have to make sounds to be heard.>

A head poked around the corner of the tunnel. "Hey! We made it!"

"Told you we would! Quiet down now, I want to have surprise on our side," a deep voice admonished.

Fat chance of that happening.

"You have the net? Remember not to kill the Boss *too* fast." Oh boy, this group was cocky. I would soon show them the error of their ways.

"It's always wandering around, so group up and make sure to stay light on your feet. We know that one group in the morning plays up how hard it is to kill that beast. If that F-ranked group made it, we should have no trouble. Watch out for the giant *bunny,* boys. It might still actually be able to do some real damage," Mr. Deep Voice sneeringly preached. "Get ready... Go, go, go!"

The five-person group ran in, weapons ready but stopped and looked around confusedly when there was no apparent enemy to fight. Oh. They must have been in the dungeon when I revealed the overhead ambush it could use now. Screams were coming down from the gathered crowd, but they ignored them, thinking it was the cheering that usually happened. I took the opportunity to look at them all carefully. They were all in the low D-ranks, the highest being Mr. Deep Voice at D-rank two, several ranks higher than my F-rank nine Raile.

The sounds above rising to a crescendo suddenly, the deep-voiced man looked up and, with a startled yell, dove to the side in time to miss dying but not fast enough to get away from the wave of blood that washed over him and the *remaining* members. Most of them took some damage, even if it was just from human teeth pinging off exposed flesh.

"Where did it come from?"

"Bobby! No!"

Their party in disarray. I expected a quick finish to the fight, but the leader rallied them; they fell into position with the speed of much practice. Shock turning to anger, they charged Raile as a unit, a first for me I was pretty sure. I tried to leap at them, but two shield bearers bashed Raile simultaneously, hard enough to make his movement falter as the remaining two attacked the weak points in his armor, the joints on his legs. A few repeated blows were enough to force the joint into facing the wrong direction. Raile keened as both legs on his right side were broken.

"Move back!" came the order, followed by the group smoothly retreating from the prone body in front of them. I was shocked. I knew that teamwork was effective, which is why I had made the squads, but this was at a level I had not been expecting. Even Dale's group had more trouble than this. Now I could see that it was because they were forcing Dale to fight and get experience, else they could have likely walked through here without issue.

"Get ready. It happens when he is hurt like this."

I was confused for a second until I saw a Glitterflit sprinting toward the downed Raile.

<Oh no!> I gasped, though only Dani heard.

The speed of the Glitterflit allowed him to avoid the hastily swung weapons, but it had to slow down to heal Raile. The healing energy dissipated into Raile as a net collapsed around the squirming, golden bunny.

"Got it!" a voice laughed. "Piece of cake!" He poked the gold rabbit with a sword he was holding, which, as it turned out, was a *very* serious mistake.

The now-healed Raile had just gotten to his feet when the soft cry of pain from the Glitterflit drew his attention. Raile's pupils dilated as his long-dormant ability awoke for the first time. The armor fell off of his body everywhere but his head, which shoved obsidian-sharp fragments of granite upward to create a deadly crown. The ability 'Avenger' flashed in my mind as I analyzed this unexpected change. I was finally going to see it in action!

The previously ponderous yet deadly Raile moved faster than I had thought was possible. His armored head impacted the chest of the man holding the net with the force of a battering ram constructed by giants. The spikes tore the poor man's armor apart like it did not exist, leaving a gaping hole in his abdomen.

The force of the charge carried the man under Raile's power into the wall, where he slowly slid down to the floor, quickly decomposing into goo, under *my* influence now.

The Glitterflit was still caught in the net, but it had been dropped on the ground. The D-rank two man barreled toward Raile, his sword easily piercing Raile's unarmored flesh with a soft sound, like a tomato being chopped. Raile fell quickly, still savaging what little remained of the dead man until he too succumbed to death's embrace. The completely shaken men gathered the net, Glitterflit, and the loot that I dropped, including a ring with a weak inverted Rune of liquid repulsion, then made their way to the surface.

Chapter Twenty-Three

Dale was excited as they waited outside the Spotters den. He would have called it their tent, but he had gotten a look inside at the filthy, cluttered area and could only consider it an animal's living space.

"What do you think it does?" he asked excitedly, shifting from one foot to the other. "Maybe it lets you stab things as far away as an arrow can fly!"

"Ehh..." Hans replied, stepping harder than he needed to make the earth bounce around them. "Looked a lot like that demonologist dagger we lost in there."

"That Rune looked completely different!" Dale proclaimed. "I get to keep this one."

Hans scratched under his armpit, sniffing at the result before answering, "Nah, looked like the same Rune, just backward. Prolly the inversed Rune."

"Correct! You know your Runescript! Are you looking to become a Spotter when you grow up?" a cheerful voice assailed them. The Spotter had poked his head out and was offering the dagger back to Dale.

"*Abyss* no," Hans blithely stated.

Exasperation on his face, the Spotter wisely started to ignore Hans, "Well, this is a surprise for us, just so you know." His face brightened as he talked to Dale. "Normally, we charge a few gold per service, but the fee is waived as we had never seen this Inscription before! So, since we get two Runes out of it for our books, we will also give you one more on credit!"

"Thanks! What does it do?" Dale happily wondered.

"*Well*," the Spotter started excitedly, making Hans groan, "the original Rune was used to summon demons with the energy it would gain by killing people or creatures, which it would store in an attached Beast core until released. *This* one will allow you to *banish* infernal creatures by stabbing them!"

"Oh, that's... good?" Dale uncertainly stammered.

"It's *wonderful*!" the Spotter erupted. "Necromancers and their darker subset of demon summoners *hoard* their knowledge! We almost never get a chance to study them. Every piece of the puzzle gets us closer to stopping them if another war breaks out!"

"Oh. I guess I just haven't really seen any undead, in, um... ever, I guess," Dale confessed as Hans started giggling softly at the Spotters bulging eyes.

"Just think! Instead of blasting them with enough Mana to rip a hole back into their dimension to banish them, you can just poke a demon with this and *its own energy* will be used to send it away! With the added benefit of weakening it! This new Rune may be the key to every future war!"

"Hmm," Hans jumped in, "seems like that Rune should be worth more to you than just 'one on credit' to me."

"Standard terms and conditions apply. Thank you for choosing the Mages' Guild." The Spotter disappeared back into his tent.

"Hey!" Hans shouted in shock.

Dale laughed. "It's fine, Hans. I'd rather this Rune be out there if someone else needs it. It won't do *us* much good, though. Shall we go see what we can sell it for?"

"I suppose that is the best we can do." Hans glared darkly at the silent tent. He accompanied Dale to the Guild tent to list the item for auction. They were talking to the clerk when Father Richard and Guild Master Frank walked in, heatedly discussing the church's lot.

"I don't care that people are using it for an arena! I am building the church there, and that is final! They want to see fighting, they can listen to a sermon at the same time!" Richard was saying hotly.

"At least charge admission! You could triple your earnings in a single move!" Frank was obviously exasperated.

"Not everything is about profit! There are things worth more than money! I would never put a rule in place that might make people not have access to a place of worship!" Father Richard was aghast at the notion.

"Well, but, if you build a church around it, no one will be able to see into the Boss room! The light will be blocked!" Frank decided triumphantly.

"I'll make the ceiling clear! If I can do it to three feet of solid stone and dirt, I think glass might be manageable!" Father Richard boomed with finality. He turned and noticed Dale. "Oh! Well, hello, how is your training going, young Master Dale?"

"Ah, hello, Dale, Hans." Frank coughed. "Aherm, what are you two doing here?"

"Doing well, Father! We found a uniquely Runed item in the dungeon. We are here to start an auction for it," Dale answered them each in turn.

"Really? More inscribed items so soon! This place is a treasure trove!" Frank happily cheered, earning an 'I-knew-it' look from Father Richard. "What does it do?"

"We just came from the Spotters. Turns out we found an item they had never seen before." Hans was trying to drive up the price to the bored Guild clerk. "It has a Demonologists Rune in it."

"*What*? Really?" Father Richard was now fully interested, startling Hans into silence. "Those are jealously guarded. What does it do?"

"Oh, right, your order is comprised of demon hunters." Dale realized why the interest had suddenly grown. "It is an inverted demon summoning Rune. They promised that if a demon were stabbed with it even a little, the Rune would turn their own power against them and banish them back to the abyss."

With a groan and sagging shoulders, Father Richard turned distrustful eyes on Frank. "That isn't funny, Dale. Alright. Who set this up? That kind of Rune doesn't exist. We would have found it before now. That kind of thing doesn't just... fall into your lap."

"It almost went into my throat a while back. The same day you made that huge celestial glass area, someone tried to rob me; when they failed, they dropped a dagger accidentally. We lost it in the dungeon, but the inverted version showed up today," Dale explained quickly. Frank nodded in agreement when Father Richard looked his way for confirmation.

"Dale," Father Richard slowly announced, "if this is true, I *need* to have that dagger. Are you splitting the profits of that?"

"No, but we are on a different item. I *won* this one," Dale cautiously stated. He hadn't liked the way Father Richard had said 'need'.

"What is the asking price on it right now?" Father Richard probed with shining eyes.

"A little over three thousand gold, though likely worth more with that information," the clerk loudly interrupted, also eying the dagger. She worked based on commission.

Father Richard looked crestfallen for a moment before looking up, his face setting in resolution. "Dale, I don't have that kind of money. Everything I have is going toward building the church. Earth Mages aren't cheap right now. I can offer you two hundred gold and another... offer."

Three thousand gold was exceedingly tempting, but Father Richard's mysterious manner was also intriguing. Dale decided to hear him out. "What might that offer be, Father?"

"If you give me the dagger, I'll pull you into the D-ranks *tomorrow*," Father Richard pledged grimly.

"What? No!" Frank shouted. "Absolutely not!"

Hans audibly gasped. "Do it. Screw money. Do it, Dale. Damn it, *do it*."

"He hasn't even mastered all of his meridians! He can't use his own affinity yet!" Frank continued shouting, face becoming red.

"It will be just as easy to teach him those things at the next ranks and will take twenty years off of his breakthrough." Father Richard's eyes never left Dale.

Dale was just confused. "What do you mean you'll *pull* me into the D-ranks? Isn't that impossible? I can't cultivate that fast, no one can!"

"It isn't discussed, but it is possible. It doesn't happen often because of what can... go wrong," Father Richard hedged. "I can do it, but it requires you to trust me absolutely and me to trust you in turn. I won't lie, there are risks, but this is all I can offer."

Dale stopped for a moment, thinking carefully. He enjoyed his life right now, but several months of constant training had only given him a moderate boost to his ranking. He had put on muscle but nowhere near what most other adventurers accumulated over the years of hard living and fighting. He didn't want to spend twenty years getting to the next stage in his life. This was the very first time a shortcut had been revealed to him.

What was gold to someone who might be able to live for hundreds of years? "Also pay seventy-five silver on all future amulets you buy from me, and it is a deal," Dale agreed to Frank's chagrin and Hans's and Father Richard's enthusiasm.

"Can I come?" Hans begged. "I've never seen this before, but I hear it is horrif– I mean amazing to see!" he quickly finished with only a quick flash of guilt.

"He can bring anyone he wants to. Those he trusts only, I would suggest." Father Richard turned to Dale. "May I have the dagger for safekeeping? I *swear* on my Mana I will honor our agreement."

"Of course, here." Dale offered up the dagger.

Father Richard took it with a nod. "Thank you, I would recommend you take the rest of the night off as well as all day tomorrow. This process can be... taxing." He turned to Frank. "Please authorize a payment to him from my account."

Frank shook his head. "Fine. I will *also* be there, just so you know. You better not let anything happen to him."

As they parted ways, Hans devolved into excited laughter and slapped Dale on the back. "Good on you, lad! Not even twenty-two, and you are going to make it into the D-ranks! Also, this means you are out of debt to the Guild, even with the interest!"

"Wait, there was interest on buying my armor?" Dale's voice was shocked.

Laughter was his only answer.

Cal

<The last group just left. Can I go back to that Rune now?> I whined petulantly. Dani had been resolute that I focus on the attackers, claiming that they made it through the traps and monsters too easily when I was distracted.

"Sure, sure. Go back to your little hobby," she dismissively replied. "I'll be over here, bored and alone."

<Perfect, thank you.> I turned my attention away, ignoring her squawk of anger. She had said it was fine, right? Plus, I had been waiting all day to activate this Rune! Fully cognizant only of the small area it encompassed, I fed a small stream of Essence into the activation pattern and watched as Essence flowed through the whorls and swoops of the Rune. At full activation, nothing happened.

<Huh, it isn't doing anything, Dani.> I looked around, not seeing her anywhere. <Dani?> She must have left the dungeon if I couldn't sense her. Well, it would be good for her to get some exercise. She had been sighing a lot lately. I returned to the puzzle represented by this Rune. It was active, I could tell, but it didn't seem to be doing anything. The Essence level in it was staying constant, which showed that it was neither gaining nor losing Essence.

What was I missing? I pictured the Rune as it originally had been but saw nothing different from what I was doing. The Rune had been active when I took it, so Craig knew something I did not. I puzzled over the idea for a bit while keeping an eye on the Rune, just in case it did something. Near midnight, Dani flew back in.

<There you are!> I called with no small relief. <Did you have fun?>

"I did." She surprised me by apologizing, "I'm sorry I left in such a huff. Sometimes I forget that you don't have the same social norms as flesh and blood creatures. You literally *need* to focus on yourself, and I was jealous because I've been kinda bored."

<Bored? Why?> I was genuinely curious.

"I don't have anything to do! I give you advice like, I dunno, once a month?" Dani spoke sadly. "You don't really need me. I just take up your time and energy."

<I don't think that's true!> I proclaimed indignantly. <You are my only companion! What can I do for you, Dani?>

"I don't know." She dramatically sighed. "I can't affect anything in here without your help, and I can't go too far away without dying of starvation."

<Would you like to travel?> I was puzzled. <I think we could make that happen.>

"No, it's impossible. I can't store Essence, and I'm made of energy so I am only as strong as the amount you can loan me." She seemed a bit blue.

<Awww, you're changing colors,> I noticed sadly. <Maybe we can figure out how to connect you to a Beast Core? I have lots of those, all full of energy.>

"No, it's too dangerous to try to alter me like that."

<Well, let's try on this.> I created a 'seed' with the pattern I had gained from her when we first bonded, creating an exact replica of her body.

"*Ahhh*! That's horrible! Did you just make me into a *Mob*?" she shrieked, horrified.

<Well, errm... Technically?> I stammered. The new Wisp floated around mindlessly, each motion watched by Dani.

"It... it's not intelligent?" she stammered.

<It only has the same instincts as a rabbit,> I carefully informed her. <I didn't give it very much Essence at all.>

Reversing her admonishment abruptly, she said, "I look so pretty! Okay, Cal, let's try to hook her up to a Beast core..."

It turned out to be a very good idea that we tried on mindless Wisps. The first one collapsed into the Beast Core faster than a rock sinks under water. Dani looked sick when it happened, and I felt terrible, of course. We continued trying until late in the night, and Dani kept looking sicker the whole time.

<Are you okay, Dani?> I gently prodded.

She shook a bit. "Not really. I've just seen myself die hundreds of times, Cal. Can we... move on to something else for a while? I'm sorry I was so hard on you earlier."

<Of course! I didn't realize how bad that would, you know, affect you.> I cringed, feeling like a jerk for not considering her mental well-being. This is what got me into trouble the first time, throwing myself single-mindedly into a task without asking her thoughts on the matter. Which reminded me...

<Would you help me figure out what is wrong with the Rune I was working on? I activated it, but nothing seems to happen.>

She shivered. "Bleh. Anything to get away from this for a while! Let's take a look." She zipped over to the room it was in, though she could have seen it through my mind instead. I guess she wanted actual physical distance from where hundreds of Wisps had just died.

"It looks fine." She studied the Rune. "Nothing has been happening? It's been active for a while?" With my affirmative answer, she continued, "So it is stable, just having no effect. That's odd." She moved closer to inspect it, landing at the outer edge.

She suddenly moved, following the lines and movements of the Rune, screaming the whole time. "Ahhh! It's got me, Cal!"

Indeed, her whole body was being pulled along the lines, condensing down from her previous size until she reached the output pattern near the center and stopped, nearly half her original size but glowing intensely. As she remained in the center, stunned, her body once again began growing, and her fear stopped, shock taking its place.

"Cal! The Rune freaking *refined* me. Like I was loose Essence! Now it's dumping Essence into me like *I'm* a Chi spiral!" Her amazed sounding voice broke my panic.

<Oh! So something has to be in the center of the Rune for it to collect Essence into! That makes sense! That Craig guy prolly had the Essence go into his meridians, and it flowed to his center from there!> I exclaimed in a burst of inspiration.

"Mmm... most likely," She groaned happily. "This feels soooo good."

<Isn't it dangerous for you to take in so much Essence? Won't you pop?> I questioned her, worried again.

"Nah, Wisps just get larger. The ambient Essence in this room is already draining out, though. Now I'm barely getting a trickle. Ah well," she murmured contentedly. "I bet you could charge Cores like this, though. Just put one in here."

<Good plan, lady.> I thought a moment. <Hey, what would happen if I made this Rune really big? Like, *really* big?> I questioned casually, an idea sprouting.

"I think it would just pull Essence from a larger area," she thoughtfully replied, "but it wouldn't refine as well. I suppose a big Rune like that could help increase the Essence in the air but..."

<I want to try something. Get away from the Rune real quick.> I waited for her to comply, then made a larger version of the same Rune, placing the *input* activation sequence of a second Rune at the *output* of the first. I then created a Beast Core at the final output and activated only the first large Rune. I watched the Essence flow along its pattern; then reaching the second Rune, the Essence automatically activated that, too!

With no Essence to draw beyond that given to it from the first Rune, the second Rune refined the Essence into fine threads which poured into the Beast core! Success! I had so many plans for this now. I could use it to speed my passive cultivation, create areas that would be powered by Essence without me sacrificing my cultivation, and maybe I could even find a way to use this method to create my Mobs more efficiently.

"My only concern for this is that larger runes take more Essence to activate, so if you make a really large one, there is a chance you would not be able to or you would die trying when it drained you," Dani interrupted my beautiful daydream.

<That may be a problem. Suppose I save a portion of Essence in a Beast core every day? Then I could use those if I needed them.>

"I think it will depend on how big you want the Rune to be," Dani stated, looking at me in a way that made me feel slightly guilty.

<I want it to be *really* big.> My daydream was back.

CHAPTER TWENTY-FOUR

Dale woke up just before dawn, as per usual. He got up and started putting on his armor before he remembered that he had the morning off. Not knowing what to do with himself, he started inspecting his armor. He knew it was enchanted but was unsure what those enchantments did. He thought for a moment, remembering that enchantments were effects that were always on when activated until they ran out of the stockpile of Essence they were originally imbued with. He found the activation sequences but decided to check with his group before activating them for the first time. It may last for years, but an enchantment was temporary, unlike an inscribed Rune.

He equipped all of his armor, putting his morningstar into the loop on his belt bandolier and went for a walk. No real destination in mind, he just enjoyed the pre-dawn morning, the quiet that was never present during the day. He sat down on a boulder and watched the sunrise over the Phantom Mountain Range and felt that today would be a good day. A soft sound made him turn, where he found a few people standing near him.

His initial reaction was to scream, but as he gasped, they held out their hands in a peaceful gesture. He blew out the breath, not really reassured as he had seen unarmed people release enough energy to kill a city; not holding a weapon meant nothing to him anymore. Weapons weren't the dangerous portion of someone with the intent to kill; the person doing the killing can find oh-so-many creative ways to make sure you die.

"Good morning," one of the robed figures carefully articulated with an unknown, androgynous accent. "We apologize for startling you, but we needed to speak."

"Ah... what, ah, what can I do for you?" Dale's eyes were darting around for an escape route. People always thought that just because someone didn't kill you instantly, they weren't going to. Faulty logic, really. People may want information or services, then want to silence you as well.

"We are a delegation from the Elven city of *Tal en' Ohta*, of the *Huine* nation. We were told that you are the human landowner of this area, and that if we did not want to start a war, we would need to deal with you for access to the Silverwood tree. My name," she–the androgynous form turned out to be a she–pronounced, "is IL-Anwa Essa."

"Welcome, ill anna ess," Dale butchered the name. "Can I please call you Anna so that I don't continue to incorrectly destroy your name?"

"That will be just fine, though, I'd prefer if you called me Brianna. My name translates better into that.'" Brianna breathed a small sigh of relief. "I take it you prefer plain words over standing on ceremony then?"

"Yes! Please! I am not a cultured man. I have lived in these mountains my entire life thus far, and the small amount of schooling I have is thanks to my mother pressuring me to better my life. Etiquette was never among those lessons." Dale looked a bit desperate.

"This works well for me, Dale." Brianna had a hint of a smile touching her lips. "I am an ambassador for our queen and have been given the right to arbitrate an agreement between us, which will allow us access to the Silverwood tree with a favorable compensation to you."

"I see, and what would this entail?" Dale cautiously inquired, his warm, gold hoarding inner weasel coming to life.

As Brianna nodded, one of her companions stepped forward with a small chest which he opened to show gleaming gems nearly the size of Dale's fist.

"Are those diamonds?" Dale gasped, astonished at the size of the gems.

A look of annoyance crossed Brianna's face for a moment. "No, far more valuable. These memory stones contain knowledge of fighting skills and Essence-based techniques for fighting. You use earth Essence, yes? If you were to master these techniques, you could shatter mountains with a wave of your hand, make the earth tremble with a punch, redirect the banks of rivers with a command, and topple walls of a city you intend to conquer!"

She took a breath, eyes shining as she breathed a bit heavily. "There is also a cultivation technique in here that is similar to the one our nation gifted the King of the Lion Realm hundreds of years ago when his Kingdom was but a small town. Now he uses it to amass power and rule."

"What do you take from this deal? That is a lot of wealth just to see a small tree," Dale suspiciously and insightfully inquired.

"It will not be small for too long," she promised mysteriously. "What I am asking for is the right of *our* nation to have care of the tree. Allow us to protect it and build a city around it to house a part of our population. We will allow others to cultivate near it, but the final say of decisions regarding the tree will be ours."

"I don't understand. Why are you asking for this? What is the big deal, and why are you emphasizing 'our nation' like that?" Dale challenged hotly, beginning to feel a bad headache building. Brianna held up her hand angrily and waved to the side. Dale was confused until an Elf stepped away from his back, a dagger vanishing into his sleeve.

"Oh for shit's sake!" Dale stood up furiously, getting into a defensive position.

"My most sincere apology," she began earnestly. "I am royalty. They are not too fond of heated words, but that is *not*," she directed at those with her, "how I deal with people. *I am not my mother*." The others looked away from her at that, embarrassed by this light treason.

"Allow me to explain, Sir Dale." Brianna sat on the rock with him, motioning for him to re-take his seat. "Please understand that this is information that is somewhat sensitive to our kind. You do know that whenever a Silverwood tree is found, Elven-kind attempt to claim the area and build fortifications?" Frank had mentioned this to Dale, so he nodded.

"Well," she continued, "humans think that we do so for the benefit it affords in cultivating. This is only a small side bonus for us. The real reason for our interest is that the pollen from a Silverwood tree allows my race to become fertile, able to bear children."

Dale was shocked. This was not the direction he had foreseen this conversation taking. Brianna laughed at his stricken look. "Oh, don't get me wrong, sometimes we get lucky, and a child is born without it—maybe one in five hundred couples is so lucky. But a Silverwood tree allows *all* of those couples given access to become fertile, which is why they are so well-protected when found. Without it, we would become extinct."

"Ahem." Dale tried to keep his voice from cracking. "I see. So if I allow you to build a city, what is the downside to this deal?"

"What do you mean?" she pleaded with wide-eyed innocence.

He eyed her critically, a dangerous life had afforded him a keen nose for danger, and she reeked of it. "I would happily give you access, but you want to build walls to keep others out. Who?" he demanded. One of the guards took a menacing step toward him, only to be waved off again with a glare.

"Fair question, young one. I was not expecting any resistance." She released a small chuckle. "Oh, fine. Our nation is in decline. We have no Silverwood trees of our own, and the cost of the pollen has tripled in the last few decades as other nations have swollen. We have earned a bad reputation since then, becoming mercenaries and killers in order to gain the pollen we need."

"So..." Dale gulped as he looked at the Elves surrounding him, "you would be..."

"Dark Elves, yes," Brianna despondently muttered with an air of finality.

There was a long, very awkward silence.

"Does this mean you will reject our offer?" Brianna begged despairingly.

Dale paused a moment, thinking. "No, but there are details we need to work out." He looked up to see Brianna waving furiously at the guards.

"You! Go sit down on your hands! What part of 'this is a peaceful talk' didn't you understand?" she fumed angrily. "Sorry, Dale, he is really dagger-happy today."

"Um. Ohhh-kay. Those details. Right, you can have access to the tree, but any shops will cede a portion of their profit as a tax to me. I will need to pay taxes to both the Lion and the Phoenix Kingdoms. That is not cheap. You can work to build the city, but you need to work with me and the Adventurers' Guild to determine the best way to complete those fortifications," Dale determinedly decided.

"Also, none of your people are to start fights, harm, or kill humans without being provoked. I don't want a race war here. I am sorry to say people will likely be afraid when they find the Dark Elves have come." Dale brought up, "As you say, you have a bad reputation. Also, your people must honor my claim as owner of this land, deferring to my wishes for the area. Is this agreeable?"

"So long as we have exclusive rights to the tree itself and all products of it–not including the Essence refined by others of course. Also, you have a council, correct? A group of people who make decisions for the area?" Brianna questioned knowingly. "I want a place on that council, a vote on any politics for the area."

"Sure. I do have a council but have never seen them in action. Either they have never met, or I just wasn't invited," Dale easily obliged. "So long as you accept that my word will be the final one on the matter, council or no."

"The deal is struck then. Our people will arrive soon, and we will begin construction of a shining city," Brianna solemnly stated. She stood, bowed, and with a word, she and her people vanished.

"...I need to stop going for walks alone," Dale muttered unhappily. This was the second early morning walk he had almost been stabbed on. "Hey! They took those techniques with them! Assholes!"

He began walking back to the camp, hungry and more than a bit grumpy. This was his first morning off in months! Everyone wanted something, dang it. He trudged into the mess hall and angrily spooned the bland porridge into his mouth. Hans noticed him and joined his table.

"Wide awake already! It's almost like someone taught you good habits by soaking you with a bucket of ice water," Hans glibly mentioned, deftly swiping Dale's toast.

"Humph," Dale grumped.

Hans shook his head. "The plight of the young! Morning is such a horrible time to be awake! Are you not pleased that you are going to be cheating your way into the next ranking series?" He seemed serious suddenly. "I know that three thousand gold is a lot to give up. I'm sure you could change your mind."

"That's right, that's today!" Dale's mood brightened considerably. "It will take me four ranks higher than I currently am, and my spiral will look like the design you all have, correct?"

"It is called a 'fractal' and is something you would have learned how to do over several months to avoid hurting yourself," Hans consideringly mentioned. "I'm actually wondering how he plans to get around that. Just knowing how to do it isn't enough."

"We'll find out soon enough, I'm sure." Craig appeared behind them. "I don't suppose you would reconsider this, Dale? I have heard that this process is at least as painful as getting your Essence stripped."

Dale looked stricken for a moment. "Of course it is," he breathed. "Now they tell me." He shook his head; this day was going downhill so fast. He stood up and decided to go... somewhere. Really, he had no hobbies or job anymore. Every day was an amalgamation of fighting or training to fight. What was the endgame?

Dale sat back down with a sigh as he tried to relax. Hans looked at his depressed friend and took pity on him. "Dale, what's the matter, my friend?"

"I don't know. Everything I used to do seems so simplistic now. I fight and fight, but for what?" Dale replied, not really expecting an answer.

"Well, that makes sense. You are smarter than you used to be. Quite a bit smarter, too, I would assume," Hans told him with enthusiasm. "You rarely see smart people happy to live a humble life."

"What? All I do is fight all day! Sure I know more about fighting, but that doesn't really make me smarter..." He trailed off as Hans shook his head.

"Mph nhpo yokrk eddsenve is–" Hans started, blasting crumbs out of his mouth.

Dale made a disgusted face, "Not with your mouth full, please. That's nasty."

"Ha." Hans quickly swallowed. "It's because your Essence is able to purify your body. No longer fighting against blocked channels, your body gets stronger, faster, and your brain is a part of that. A healthy mind makes more connections, allowing you to experience the world on a deeper level than you could before. You will see how things link together and be able to see how one action affects another. There are people who do that as a profession, you know."

"Really?" Dale was exceedingly interested.

"Yup," Hans disclosed, eating more toast. "Sstpotters," he finished around the mouthful, spitting several crumbs out.

"Spotters? That sounds about right." Dale laughed at Hans's disdain for the group.

"Well, really, everyone does. Other professions just use those connections in a *practical* way. Like a fire Mage knowing that melted sand makes glass and that some sand is better for it than others," Hans extrapolated. "The more connections that you understand, the faster your power will grow, which is why being a Spotter is so appealing to many."

"What will *I* be able to do, though?" Dale insisted earnestly.

Hans shrugged. "Whatever you like. First, you need to see where your talents lie within the earth. Everyone has different strengths and weaknesses, and the uses for Essence are endless."

Dale deflated again, "So it comes down to waiting again." He grumped sourly.

Hans laughed a dark laugh. "Welcome to life, kiddo! Where you need to work for everything worth having, and anyone trying to give you a handout is just waiting to use you until you are useful to them."

Craig spoke up then, "That's a dark outlook, Hans. No matter how true it may be. Dale, when you reach the D-rankings, you will be able to exert control over your element. I will teach you then, as we had always planned to do. It seems it will be years sooner than we thought it would be, though. Gaining control of your element is the best part of being a cultivator, in my opinion."

A familiar face in the crowd of people grabbed Dale's attention as he was thanking Craig for his consideration. "Hey! Hans, is that... Madame? What is she doing here?"

"Yup, that is her alright. Annnnd, wel-l-l, she's prolly looking for us so she can yell at me." Hans was barely understandable around the hemming and hawing.

Dale rounded on him dangerously. "...Why?"

"Remember how when we were there, at her restaurant, she was talking about starting one here? She would most likely have set up a deal with you right then," Hans reminded him, "Well, she *really* hates not knowing what's going on. Since we didn't tell her who you were, she's likely pissed at you."

"Why yes, she *is* pissed at you," a deceptively soft, decidedly female voice hissed next to their ears. They had only taken their eyes off Madame for a moment, then she was behind them. Her hands clamped down on their shoulders. "Let's talk about this outside, shall we?"

Dale and a stammering Hans were unceremoniously dragged outside while Craig carefully focused on his food, avoiding Hans's and Dale's pleading looks.

"Did you not like my food? Was my service subpar?" she interrogated them, a dangerous glint in her eye. "Why was it that you made me wait days to find out that the young adventurer that dined in my business was the *owner* of the land I so badly wanted to create a fine dining area upon?"

"Madame, your food was fit for a king! We had just–" Hans promised.

With a glare, Madame ended his babbling. "Not you. *Him.*" She nodded at Dale.

Honestly? It was because I felt really bad, insulted that you had such a low opinion of me without even meeting me," Dale boldly began. "You had no idea who I was, but you spouted mean gossip and cruel rumors."

Hans gaped at him, mouth working silently as he shook his head. Madame turned red, eyes bulging out a bit.

Whoo, Dale thought, thinking she was reminiscent of an owl when she did that.

Madame took a deep breath, and Dale prepared himself to be lashed brutally by her words. "*That* is... fair, I suppose." She sighed in embarrassment, rubbing at her temples. "I haven't left the city in years. I forget that not everyone enjoys gossip as the city folk do. Please know that I didn't try to upset you. I was only trying to make conversation."

A bit stunned by this turnaround, Dale stammered, "Uh. Don't worry about it." All the heat and argumentation he had been building up to rushed away.

"If I didn't ruin my chances, I would still like to create a *Pleasure House* in the area. My granddaughter will be joining the dungeon dives as a cultivator, and I want to stay busy while I keep an eye on her," Madame humbly requested.

Dale sighed, now rubbing at his forehead. "It's fine, Madame. We'll work out the details, but is ten percent too much to ask from you as a tax? You'll also need to build your own restaurant, but we'll pick out the location later. I have an appointment to get to."

"That will be just fine. Please, Madame is my title. My friends call me by name, and I would greatly enjoy being your friend," the short lady proclaimed.

"Of course, Madame. I need all the friends I can get." Dale was greatly cheered by this statement.

"My name is Chandra; it is a pleasure to do business with you. We will talk later then." With a smile and a wave, she walked away.

Shh-ann-drah," Dale repeated. "Man, am I bad at names." He turned toward Hans. "You think she will have trouble with making the building?"

Hans snorted. "Doubtful. She'll likely grow it in a day. She's an A-rank *nine* plant Mage. She's the closest thing to a Saint I have ever seen. Heck, she trained *Frank* for nearly a decade."

Dale's mouth dropped open. He hadn't even thought to look at her cultivation. A bad habit he would need to break; even regular-seeming people could be horrifyingly dangerous if he didn't even bother to *notice* them. He needed to keep his eyes and ears open and get used to all of the overwhelming input. It may save his life someday. He activated the Essence flow to his eyes, watching the overlay appear, colors becoming brighter, the flows of the heavens and earth visible to him once again.

"You feeling okay, Dale?" Hans enquired worriedly.

"Yeah. I'm just working through some stuff. Hey," Dale realized he hadn't mentioned his earlier encounter, "I met an Elven ambassador this morning."

"Really? Today already?" Hans seemed surprised by the sudden conversation topic. "It is, what, eight o' clock? Did they shake you out of bed?"

"Naw, I had gone for a walk around dawn. They found me on the outskirts of the camp," Dale nonchalantly stated. "They wanted to make a deal for access to the Silverwood tree."

"Were they surprised when you told them it was in the dungeon?" Hans demanded gleefully.

Dale was stunned for a moment. "Uh, I may have failed to, um, mention that."

Hans thought this was a hysterical riot of course. "Wait, they made a deal to see it, and they didn't even ask questions? Typical High Elves, never really thinking of the details. They're all about the 'big picture'." He chuckled at the thought of the dainty Elves trying to ward off Raile. "It should make for a fun afternoon if we watch 'em, though."

"High Elves?" Dale was confused. "What are High Elves? Or is that just what they call themselves?"

"Oh boy, you could get in some real trouble. I'll find someone to tell you the whole history, but basically, there are High Elves of the nation *Luminaria.* These guys are the largest nation and spend most of their time as merchants, artists, or thinkers. Rich beyond any need to actually work, their King is an S-Ranked expert, and their cities shine with light and wealth.

They like to think of themselves as 'above' other Elves, thus 'High' Elves," Hans explained with a shake of his head at the thought.

"Next, there are Wood Elves, shorter than the High Elves and a bit more reclusive. They live in the *forests*! Surprise!" Hans dictated. "Seriously, though, they are not a fan of the High Elves. They think they are too hedonistic or something. They live more simply but have a greater connection to the earth and the elements. They are ruled by a council of S-ranked elders and rarely leave their woods. Though seen less often, they have great power. They grow and collect food and animal products for themselves and other Elven nations."

"There are the Sea Elves, who live on boats their entire lives. They facilitate trade between all the races of Elves and man, trying not to take sides in conflicts. They work for themselves and are considered rather mysterious."

"The fourth type are known as 'Wild Elves'. They are the outcasts of their societies. Basically feral, they scorn society, civilization, and the rules of others. They have the worst reputation of any of the races of Elves, practicing dark arts and infernal summoning. They have no homeland, living only where they can get away with their dark deeds."

"The fifth and final are the Drow or Dark Elves. No one knows where they live, only where they can go to get in contact with them. Dark Elves also have a dark reputation as assassins and mercenaries for the other races. The worst of their lot are 'Moon Elves', the best-known assassins of any race." He pondered for a moment. "Anyway, Dark Elves work for the highest bidder and will change their allegiance mid-fight if offered enough. Never work with them unless they sign a Mana-contract, else you could quickly end up dead," Hans finished, a bit out of breath.

Dale listened raptly to these descriptions. He had never much considered the outside world and was constantly amazed by how intricate it really was. Someday, he promised himself, he would travel and see everything the world had to offer. He would live long enough to see it all if he became strong enough.

"Well, I might be in trouble." Dale gave a weak chuckle. "I didn't make a deal with the High Elves, it–"

Father Richard walked up to them at that point, forcing Dale to abruptly stop talking, so he made motions to Hans that they would talk at a later date.

CHAPTER TWENTY-FIVE

"Oh, there you are!" Father Richard exclaimed cheerfully. "Listen, I didn't think about it, but making you wait until noon seemed like torture. Are you ready now, or do you have other things on your plate?"

"Well, no, but I just ate and–" Dale began frantically.

Father Richard cut him off with a wave. "No problem, my child, you'll likely vomit either way. Might as well get it over with!"

Hans chimed in, "You aren't trying to avoid Frank being there, are you? I can go get–"

A slightly panicked look crossed Father Richard's face. "No, no." He hastily stated, "No time for that if you want to join us! I have the area prepared. We need to get to it!"

Dale's wrist was grasped firmly, and he was all but dragged along behind Father Richard. They were moving toward the celestial infused lot, which made Dale gasp when he saw it. A white granite, coliseum-style arena had appeared around the entirety of the area, perfectly framing the quartz. Beyond that, a massive chapel was glowing in the morning sun. Father Richard was also using this as an opportunity to showcase his purchase, it seemed.

"If you look over there, there is a healing ward that connects directly to the exit from the dungeon. That way, people can be checked in and healed as soon as they leave their fight. Next to that is the vault, which I personally blessed and enchanted, to hold valuables as we begin our function as a bank. Sermons will be given next to the quartz. The roof is perfectly clear glass, so we will function in all seasons. The doors are granite reinforced with steel and Essence to protect the worshippers within," Father Richard babbled happily.

"Over there is the dormitory. We can have up to thirty people living there comfortably or near one hundred uncomfortably. Kitchen, library, garden." Father Richard turned toward Dale. "So? What do you think?"

"I'm amazed. This was built overnight?" Dale gaped at the gleaming building.

"Of course not," was the scoffed reply. "We started after lunch yesterday. I could only hire that team of Mages for twelve hours or so."

"How did I not see this when I went to breakfast?" Hans squinted at him suspiciously.

Father Richard smoothly countered, "Must have been dark."

"I think there is more to it than that." Hans narrowed his eyes further. "No rumors, no one noticed the work, why? What were you hiding?"

Father Richard looked at Hans furiously, then Dale and admitted, "Well, the church was a bit... bigger than I had planned at first."

"How much bigger?" Dale questioned him, features hardening.

"It's only... three lots," Richard mumbled.

Dale looked at him oddly; the way he said those words was so quiet yet perfectly clear. "Three lots?" Dale barked incredulously. "What the heck?! I didn't approve that!"

Father Richard rubbed his forehead. "We couldn't dig. That was the issue. Everything had to be on one level because if we went down, we would affect the dungeon. So the place became more... ranch style than monastery style."

He turned his head to Dale. "I'm sorry we didn't ask first, but we will happily pay the difference in price that those lots would cover."

Dale was undecided on his feelings in this matter but concluded that being angry at the man who was about to alter his innards was not a good plan. "It's fine, Father. Please just ask permission next time. There are a lot of people that want to live here."

"Thank you, and sorry again. Maybe you would like to have one of the rooms for a while? I have no acolytes here yet, and I'm sure a bed would be preferable to the cot you have been sleeping on."

"Throw in a room for each of my team, then we'll call it good," Dale grunted after catching Hans's pleading look. Sometimes it was easy to forget Hans was in his sixties. The cot would have been murder on his back without the reinforcement that cultivating provided.

"Done!" Richard beamed. "At least until I have students who need them."

Dale nodded. "That's fair. They are who the rooms were intended for anyway. Where are we going?"

As they continued at a brisk pace through the winding corridor, Father Richard told them, "The practice room. It was made *especially* thick and enchanted to hold in spells and block outside influences. It blocks sound and holds in heat to a set temperature. Also, it has a very strong lock. We won't be disturbed there, which is of the utmost importance. Once this process starts, if we end early, you may die."

"This is sounding more and more fun," Dale deadpanned.

The three men arrived at a glowing, stone door. "Here we go," beamed Father Richard. "After you!" He swept the door open, showing a circular room roughly twenty feet in diameter.

They all walked to the center where Father Richard and Dale sat while Hans flopped on to the ground in a prone position.

"Are you ready to begin?" Father Richard intoned in a ritualistic manner.

Dale nodded, too nervous to respond.

"Good. Now, go into your center. Sink into it as deeply as possible," Father Richard commanded, waiting as Dale followed the order. "Excellent. Now, this is going to be hard to do. I want you to listen to my voice, very carefully following all of my directions. Take my hands. Now, feel the meridians along your hands, and extend your Essence outward, allowing it to flow into me."

"This will feel like you are giving up Essence. You are. This will allow me access to your center, following through to your own source of power. If I were an unscrupulous person, I would be able to take your entire cultivation base and keep it as my own," Father Richard told him, making Dale rather nervous.

Dale followed the command; with a feeling like an artery being severed, Essence began to pour out of him like blood from a mortal wound. In seconds, he had been reduced a rank, dropping to F-rank five–which terrified him.

Father Richard's calm voice sounded, "Prepare your mind, Dale. I am going to speak a True Name, the name that allowed me to gain my status as a Mage. Linked as we are, you will understand it. If your mind is weak or unprepared, it may break you."

He leaned toward Dale and spoke a word. Hans heard it as *sonder*, while Dale's eyes went wide, then blank. Blood began to erupt from the ear that had been spoken into, though the flow quickly stopped. Dale's mouth worked, but no sound came out and goosebumps rippled across his skin.

In Dale's mind, the effect was far more intense. He was suddenly able to understand a basic truth of life that he had never really considered before. He found that each person was unique. Every being in existence was living a life as vivid and complex as his own in its own way. They had their own ambitions, friends, enemies, hopes and dreams. The life of each individual was an amazing, epic storyline that continues–grandly and invisibly–to interact with everything else that lives.

There were tens of millions of these interactions that shaped the universe, millions of lives that he had never before considered, which suddenly sang to him, bombarding him with information and ideas that threatened to strip his individuality. One voice stood out among the rest, guiding him to return to his own mind, filling him with power and control.

"There we go, Dale. Good lad. Welcome back, now," Father Richard was saying. "Good, now you have access to my Mana, yet I can still shape your center. Focus inward, and watch what I am doing."

Dale, still stunned by the outpouring of others, found it hard to focus on himself. He finally managed and watched incredulously as his Chi spiral became more dense and brighter without his input. It was a mesmerizing effect, truly hypnotic. The Essence he contained was exceedingly pure; the Essence pouring into him from Father Richard matched his exactly.

"This may hurt, Dale," Father Richard murmured. "Shattering your Chi and Essence spiral is a process that takes between days and weeks naturally. I can easily handle the amount of Essence you have, so I am going to do it all at once. Look closely. You are now at the peak of the F-series; this is currently what your Chi spiral looks like. Your center is full of energy, which is too dense for you to *really* contain anymore."

"This," Father Richard was now straining, sweating profusely, "is D-series zero, where your spiral becomes.... a... *fractal*." He *pushed* with his mind, forcing Dale's Essence to shatter into billions of shards. Father Richard had certainly been correct earlier; Dale vomited directly on to Father Richard's body and face.

Father Richard tried not to gag as he continued his work. "Please turn your head to the side if that happens again," he managed to say through gritted teeth.

Dale nodded and blushed, returning his attention to his center. He was weaker at this moment than he had ever been in his life; only the energy moving through him kept him upright, his muscles locked in place as though lightning had struck him.

Father Richard kept muttering, directing Dale's energy as he wanted. He smoothed the shards into place, a nucleus of power forming in the direct center. That nucleus formed into an infinitesimally small spiral, directing the resulting power throughout Dale's body into his life-force. Other spirals began to form, draining their Essence downward to be further refined by the next spiral in the series. The process continued for an immeasurable time, for them anyway, as they watched the progression as closely as possible.

As the danger of dying from lack of Essence began to wane, the process picked up speed. The spirals grew, moving further and further away from the origin, soon straining the boundary of his center. Father Richard gleefully exhaled as he released a final burst of Essence, affixing an enchantment he had prepared to the terminus of the spiral. This enchantment would keep Dale's Essence in this fractal formation until Dale was able to hold the pattern for himself.

"Finished," Father Richard happily stated. "Listen, Dale, the Chi threads are rough right now, broken beyond my power to repair. As you cultivate more energy, they will smooth and fix themselves. All the tiny breaks will be mended. Time and effort on your part are the only things you need to become whole again. When the threads are fixed, you will be able to feel the *real* power and cultivation speed this rank affords you."

"Thank *god*." Hans's outburst caught Father Richard completely off guard, making him flinch. "You trapped me in this room with you and a pile of vomit for *two days*. The least you could have done was show me how to open the stinkin' door!"

Dale stood shakily, his body adjusting to the flow of energy within him. He didn't feel stronger, but that may simply be due to his near starvation as he waited for the process to complete. The others watched him carefully, making sure he didn't abruptly die or explode.

"Well," Dale was looking down at his soiled clothes, "I don't suppose you have baths in here?"

Father Richard nearly slapped his forehead. "How could I forget bathrooms?" he rhetorically muttered in horror.

"No matter. Let's... go get cleaned up, then find food. I'm... I'm not sure if I am okay." Dale was wobbling while standing, trying to remember something... something that had happened when Father Richard breathed a word, but it slipped away as does a dream, leaving only the word 'sonder' in his mind with no context to it. He felt like he had forgotten a profound truth; all he could remember was the process he had undergone afterward.

Father Richard opened the door, and the small group slowly moved to find a spot to bathe along the river, sore from the lack of movement over the last few days. Father Richard happily scrubbed the dried vomit off of himself, shuddering even as he did so. Dale reached into himself, trying to follow the complex path his center had become. He was nervous that he would need to hold this pattern himself soon, though Father Richard assured him it would become as easy as breathing.

Clean but still damp, the three started walking toward the mess hall when a voice reached them, "Try the *Pleasure House* for lunch today! Forget the watered-down gruel the Guild offers. Fill up with a real meal!" A young teen boy was shouting, trying to find customers for the new business.

"It's already running?" Dale was surprised and a bit upset by this development. "Where did she build it?" They walked over to the herald, asking for the location of the restaurant. The boy sneered at them as if they were insane.

"There are two permanent buildings in twenty miles, and you can't find 'em?" The boy pointed it out to them rudely, "'S'over there." He pointed in a direction, and they gladly left the unpleasant young man alone. They walked toward the area he had pointed and whistled as the building came into view. Whereas the church had sprawled, this restaurant went straight upward. At least four stories tall, the building was made out of gleaming walnut trees which were growing and interweaving into an interesting design even as they watched.

Dale snapped his fingers. "That's what it is! It looks like a really tall copy of the one in the capital."

The others nodded, and Hans piped up, "Yup. She is all about brand recognition. When it is done growing to how she wants it, she'll carve it herself. All of her places look the same, so everyone knows where the best food is." They joined the queue moving toward the door; in a few minutes, they were in a small waiting room as a host took their names and started to put them on a list. When she made the connection of Dale's name and something she had been told, she blanched and ran from the room.

"Dale!" Hans's voice was mockingly horrified. "What did you *do* to the poor girl to make her run off like that?"

The other people in the room rounded on him with dangerous looks, starting to become rather rowdy, when the girl and Madame Chandra walked back in.

"Dale! There you are! You caused quite a stir, vanishing like that. Come in, come in! We'll be using the *private* dining area," she told the host in passing. Chandra personally walked them up several flights of stairs, stopping them at the very top. "Do you know how my businesses work?"

Dale shook his head. She smiled knowingly and explained, "The floors are based on price and quality of food. The higher you go, the better it will be–though more expensive. Don't get me wrong, all of our food is *sumptuous,* but as any true gourmand will assure you, high-quality meals of varying ingredients are still very different. A quality salad will not match the flavor complexity of a quality steak dinner, for example."

Chandra threw open the door, allowing a wave of tantalizing aromas to flood out as the group filed in. There was a kitchen attached to the dining area; she explained that each floor had its own kitchen and wait staff. No sooner had they been seated than a thin soup arrived for them to sip whilst they awaited their meal. The decor in the room was stunning, and the soup vastly superior to anything Dale had eaten in this area previously.

Several servers emerged from the kitchen as the last person finished their appetizer. Each of the servers laid out a massive steak covered in finely diced herbs and a spicy sauce Dale had no name for. They ate with gusto; each time they felt full, their stomachs would demand more. After the deprivation of the last few days, they ate like wolves, stuffing themselves as full as possible. Chandra watched them, shocked at their poor manners until she took a good look at Dale.

"Who did that to you?" She gasped in horror, one hand going to her throat while the other clenched into a fist. "Dale, how did you reach the D-rankings in two days?"

Father Richard waved his hand. "I did. We made a deal for it."

Chandra was *not* pleased. "And you thought this was a good deal? There is, what, a thirty percent survival rate? *Maybe*?"

Dale was shocked at this tidbit of information. "That low?" He looked incredulously at Father Richard. "You gambled a *seventy percent* chance that I would die for a *dagger*?"

"I knew you could do it!" Richard waved at them nonchalantly. "I put myself at risk too, you know."

Chandra glowered at him. "If it were up to me, I'd kick you off this mountain right now." She looked meaningfully at Dale.

"Oh come on!" Richard looked up nervously, eyes darting between them before settling on Dale. "It turned out fine! He didn't lose his mind or die or bleed out or..." He trailed off as he saw his words were having the opposite effect he intended. "Ahem! Anyway, it turned out for the best! Look at him! Already in the D-ranks and only twenty-one years old!"

"Hmm." Dale looked at him. "If this weren't so freaking tasty, I'd be mad at you." He took another considering bite, just to make sure he still wasn't mad. "What is this, Madame? It's so flavorful!"

"This is seared Raile steak. Freshly butchered this morning, of course," she boasted, still glaring at Father Richard.

Dale looked at the meat oddly. “As in the Boss Mob? Is this safe to eat?”

“Of course it is!” She turned the conversation to another topic suspiciously quickly. “About my granddaughter coming here to train, I was wondering if you might be willing to put her on your team.”

“Isn’t five people the maximum?” Dale got out around a mouth full of rabbit steak. “I’ve never seen more than five go in at once.”

“What?” she said, surprise evident in her voice. “You already have a full team? You made D-Zero today, I thought?”

“What? What does that have to do with anything?” Dale looked at Hans for assurances, but he wouldn’t meet his eye. “Hans? Did... did I get kicked off the team?”

Hans shook his head a bit sadly. “Not quite as bad as that. At the start of the D-ranks, Guild rules state that you need to form a team of your own. You can have one person in the C-ranks join you for guidance, but the rest need to also be in the D or high F-rankings. The team is still here to train you and show you how to use your Essence and whatnot, but Guild law stands, even in your case.”

Dale considered this for a moment. The dungeon would be far more dangerous from now on, but he thought he had a good handle on the correct way of doing things after half a year of constant fighting. If the other parties that had completed the dungeon were any indication, the rewards for a lower leveled team were drastically higher than what they had been earning.

Taking a deep breath to calm his tumultuous thoughts, Dale made a request, “Hans, if Craig will still train me either way, would you join my team? You are fun to work with, and I think that you would help me pick a good group.”

A bit choked up, Hans replied in the affirmative. He was truly happy that Dale thought so well of him. Through his bawdy jokes and teasing, he had really come to think of Dale as a friend, and it was good to see that feeling reciprocated.

Dale cleared his throat. "Your grand-daughter?" he prompted Madame Chandra.

"Yes! Of course!" Chandra started, almost flinching a bit. "Rose! Get in here!" Her manner was nervous, and she was casting pleading looks at Hans. A tall lady walked in from the attached kitchen, fluidly moving across the walnut wood of the floor. She stood nearly six feet tall, had grey eyes, flowing black hair, and a slim, willowy figure. Dale was impressed by her graceful movement, but growing up in the mountains had him looking at her a bit critically.

In his mind, she was too tall and thin to do the work required of the highlanders. His people were of average height with packed muscles and stout frames. He understood better why Chandra was looking for a team for this girl; she didn't look like she could survive an unescorted night in the city, let alone a dungeon in the mountains. His vision flipped to his Essence enhanced vision, and he looked at her center, roughly at the same time as Hans.

Father Richard gasped in anger. "You *just* shouted at me for pulling Dale ahead in the rankings, yet you *clearly* did the same for her! Look at her center! It's barely even healed from the trauma, *just like Dale*, and you try to foist her off on them!"

Rose looked a bit stricken. Embarrassed by the sudden judgment of her, she opened her mouth to speak. Chandra cut her off unintentionally, "You don't get to yell at me in my place of business, Richard!" The tree they were in suddenly swayed ominously. "Look at her! Tell me *why* I did it! I know *your* reasons. You wanted to get away with not having to pay the worth of something and so handed out power like a treat!"

Father Richard was taken aback and looked at the girl again. His eyes widened fractionally. "Oh. Oh, you poor girl, I am so sorry. Please forgive my assumptions."

Dale, of course, had no idea what was transpiring. "Oh, spit it out. What?! What's wrong with her?"

Rose's face was becoming the color of her namesake. "Excuse me, I am *right here*," she seethed, turning toward Dale, "and nothing is *wrong* with me, you ass."

Her voice was cultured and delicate for the harsh words. Dale was instantly mad at her. "I'm not going into danger with someone who can't even be around people without them feeling sorry for her unknown weakness," he announced harshly.

"Dale!" Chandra was aghast. "Where is this coming from?"

Dale looked at her coldly, the cold steel of a man who has had to force others to show him respect every time their opinions differed. "This is coming from a *highlander*. I *worked* for what I have. I paid fairly for my increase in rank, if not in time then in goods. What gives her the right to come in here and start attacking me for asking a simple question? I'm guessing as well that you simply pulled her to the higher ranks for free. The look in his eyes and tone of voice," he pointed at Father Richard, "tells me other people's charity and pity falling on her is not an uncommon occurrence. Her reaction," a gesture at Rose, "shows that she has a chip on her shoulder that will get us killed if we take her. Either she will not be able to pull her weight, or she will try to overcompensate and do something stupid. I need people that will work to keep me alive as I do the same for them, so find another team or explain why it benefits *my* team to take her with us."

The others in the room were stunned into silence. They had not seen this side of Dale, and now they were realizing that—just maybe—they should be a bit warier of making decisions for him without his knowing consent. Hans broke into a proud grin when he realized that Dale had made a well-reasoned argument, while Father Richard started to sweat a bit over the future expansion plans he had for his church.

"Dale," Chandra started uncomfortably, "Rose is—as I've mentioned—my granddaughter. My son, before he was murdered, eloped with a High Elf and eventually blessed us with Rose. She has been ostracized in society for being a half-breed." her eyes darted to Rose to see if she was offending her, but Rose's eyes were flint hard as she tried to stare Dale down. "That by itself is not too much of an issue. The real problem is her Essence."

Dale looked at Rose's core again. It had the same reconstructed, shattered look that his did. "What? It looks really pure, so, yay you. Beyond that, I see no other issue."

"What do you know about Essence affinities?" Chandra probed patiently.

Dale looked at her. "Not too much, I suppose. I know we all have them and they get stronger over time as we affect them."

"Well," Chandra smacked Rose's arm when she rolled her eyes, "you see, we all are able to eventually use other elements to pull Essence from. As you grow, so does your capability to use other affinities. Your main one will always be your strongest, though. Rose is... well, special."

Rose rolled her eyes at this, obviously hearing it for the thousandth time. Chandra charged on, "She began life with a dual affinity. That means she has two main affinity channels and *has* to train them both at the same time. Usually, this is not an issue. If she had fire and earth, she could cultivate near lava, glassblowers, or some such. This is not the case, as she has the opposing affinities for celestial and infernal."

Hans's eyes were wide; he breathed in amazement, "A *chaos* cultivator. Alive?"

"Just so." Chandra nodded reluctantly. "As such, Rose has *never* been able to cultivate. She would have died if I did not pull her up into the D-ranking as a child. The scars in her cultivation have been there for nearly twenty years. She cannot *use* Essence for fear that the lack will kill her, as she cannot replace what she uses."

The news he was given disturbed Dale; the others also seemed uncomfortable at Rose's plight. "Well," Dale hemmed, "I may have been hasty in my snap judgment, but the fact of the matter is that this does not change things. If she cannot fight, it would be too dangerous for all involved to take her with us." He clandestinely ate another bite of the rabbit steak that was beginning to cool.

Rose broke into the conversation hotly, "I am the best archer you will ever meet, *and* I do it all without using Essence! Once I *am* able to cultivate, I can only improve."

"Can you work as a team? Can you follow orders? Will you duck when I say duck? Have you ever been in combat or just shot at stationary targets?" Dale was brutal in his questioning. "These are the same questions I needed to face when I first became a cultivator. The others knew the answer and took the time to train me for *months.* You know the first job I had in the team? I quote: 'Don't die, that is your only job until you become useful.' My team will not be experienced and strong like theirs was, so I *can't* protect you like they could me. So I ask you again. Why should I risk my team's life and my own for you?"

Rose's face was burning, and Dale knew his questions had hit their target. Like arrows. Ha, because she was an archer.

Anyway. "I can be a good teammate," Rose quietly promised. "I am a fast learner and know the stakes. Just give me a chance to prove myself! No one... no one else will even *look* at me without that stupid *look* on their face!" She pointed at an affronted Father Richard.

"Okay then. We'll see," Dale made his decision with finality. "I'm going back into the dungeon tomorrow morning. Meet me at the mess hall at dawn, and we will make a *temporary* place on the team for you. If you can't handle the dungeon, I will take no blame for the outcome." He looked at Madame Chandra when he mentioned this; she nodded gravely.

Rose's face cleared, and she soberly nodded, not trusting herself to speak. She was teetering between jubilation and fury with this man who talked to her like a child. She left the room without another word.

"Thank you, Dale?" Chandra halfway questioned, thinking that maybe things had gone well.

Dale shook his head. "That was how Craig taught me. That and letting Josh beat me on the sparring grounds for hours at a time. This life is not for the faint of heart, which I am sure you know. I'm nervous about this whole situation. Not only about going in with an untested team, but her attitude really worries me. I know that I could have handled that better, but I needed to know if she would react professionally. Make no mistake, I intend for my team to be *exceedingly* professional."

"I was worried about her reaction because I feel like people have either only treated her one of two ways–giving her what she wanted and not spoken harshly to her out of pity or given her nothing and despised her for shortcomings that are not her fault. If she could not control herself here when it was only harsh words, how could I trust that she would care what I had to say mid-battle? Her lack of experience with other people and teamwork could seriously hurt us."

"Still. Thank you, Dale. Is there anything I can do to repay you?" Chandra motioned to the food still on the table.

Dale was quiet for a moment. "Yes. I hate to admit it, but I am ignorant of the world. I may have made a very bad business deal recently because of it." He thought of the Dark Elves. "I can read the trade language, I can do my figures well enough to count small amounts of money, but I have no other administration skills. I just found out that my purchase of armor had interest on it and have no idea how to calculate that or even look for it on future deals. If Frank had wanted to ruin me, all he would have had to do was give me a document ceding my rights to the land and told me that it was a Guild application form."

Dale looked at Chandra. "I've been flying by the seat of my pants, going with the flow and listening to others. My council makes major decisions without me, and I have no idea if those are ideas that I would agree with. I need to find a way to take a stand and really *know* what I am doing. Can you find me some teachers? If I am going to live as long as they say, run my own team, and build this camp into a city, I need to do better in nearly every aspect of management."

Chandra was impressed by his forethought. "I can think of a few people. I'll make some arrangements, but it won't be a cheap or fast process. We could speed your understanding of words and numbers with the use of memory stones, but the cost is even more astronomical."

Dale perked up. "I hadn't thought of that! How much does it cost?"

Chandra laughed at his shift back into the young man she thought she had known. "The spoken and written languages are always sold apart from each other–fifty gold each. The finest counting system is provided by the Dwarven Underkingdom and is roughly one hundred gold."

Dale's mind boggled at that cost. Who could afford that kind of expense?! Then he remembered that he could, given enough time. He supposed that it was normally reserved for nobles or other wealthy people. "Why is that number system so expensive by itself?"

Chandra nodded at his question; it was a good one. "The number system is very complex. It consists of more than simple concepts like the others–adding, subtracting, and dividing. What sets this system apart is their advancement into higher mathematics, which gives answers to questions such as: how many loads of gravel do I need for a road? What angle does this building need to be built at for the road to have the correct size? What is the compound interest rate of loans from multiple banks? How much weight can a support of this size hold if it is placed horizontally? Believe me when I say it is worth the cost."

Dale nodded slowly. If he wanted to be trusted to make large decisions, he needed to make the sacrifices *now* to learn what he needed. "How about other things? I'll need to know history, how to argue, and trading skills."

"I'll see what I can do. Might I make a suggestion?" Chandra raised a hand to slow him down. Dale nodded, surprised by her subdued question. "Work to open the pericardium meridian. It is known as the guardian of the heart and will allow you to function normally with half the amount of sleep you normally will get. If you want to learn quickly, you will need to devote a substantial amount of time to your studies. Opening that meridian will allow you to do so without interrupting your current work schedule."

"Thank you." Dale warmly smiled. "How about a teacher to explain the meridians as well?"

With a laugh, they turned back to their meal and discussion.

Chapter Twenty-six

<Well, what do you think we should do next?> I questioned Dani, thinking I had all my preparations complete.

She thought for a moment, looking around the room. "I don't know, Cal; it looks like it is ready. Should you just activate it?" The once smooth floor of the Boss room was now intricately patterned, the Runescript of hundreds of matching Runes deeply scoring the floor.

I had planned this out well, the pattern of each Rune interlocking seamlessly to the next. I had adjusted my walls to allow enough space for the large pattern to end perfectly at the entryway of the room, to maximize the amount of Essence pulled in. I had not yet explained to Dani the steps I *really* wanted to take.

<Here's the thing, I told you I wanted the Rune to be *big*, right?> I started nervously.

She answered brightly, "Well yeah! Look at them! That is the most beautiful, largest Runescript I have ever seen! You should be proud! I know I am."

I 'blushed', <Aww, thanks, hun. But... I'm not done.>

"What do you mean?" Her voice took on a tone of exasperation.

<I want it to be *BIG*, Dani.>

She snorted. "That's what every male says."

<...Huh?>

"Nothing. Explain."

<I want to adjust my floors so that the floors themselves are massive Runes.>

If she had a jaw, it would have dropped. "*Cal!* I don't know if you will be able to activate *this* Rune. How would you possibly activate one so large?"

I quickly laid my plan out to slow her tirade. <I know, I know. It might be the work of years to save that amount of power, but I figure I will make small adjustments to my dungeon every night until I finally get the configuration I want. Until then, activating it won't matter anyway, right?>

"I... guess," she doubtfully allowed. "Seriously, though, you should try activating just *this* one soon. We don't want you too weak to join in fights when people get here if it fails."

I braced myself and followed her advice. I reached out and touched the activation sequence, beginning to funnel Essence into it. Faster than a chubby kid eating cake, the energy began to flow out of me. Faster and faster it poured, and soon, the loss began straining my reserves. This was the way of Runes; if you activate one, it will try to take every drop of needed Essence out of the person activating it. If you did not have the necessary Essence, it would drain you–to death. Quickly, I reached out for the Cores I had filled to the brim with Essence, draining them dry as I channeled the potent power though myself.

Too quickly they ran out, shattering as I took even the Essence binding them together. One after another, the cores around me fell to pieces, making me hope I would not soon be among them. As the last one broke and my internal light began to dim, the Rune flared to life! With a rush like wind in a thunderstorm, loose Essence in the dungeon began flowing into the Boss chamber. The huge Rune that began at the door of the room began to glow! Slowly at first but then with increasing light and speed. As the shining power became too bright for the human eye to see, like a blacksmith's welding tool, the Rune found an outlet for its stored power.

The next Rune in the link activated under the power of the first and pulled Essence of the heavens and earth to itself. The first Rune had now absorbed all of the loose Essence in the room and was still pulling from the hallway. I felt parched, as though I had a throat and had not had a sip of water in decades. I held the Essence in myself as closely as I could, shepherding it in its pattern as even *it* reacted to the potent Runescript.

One after another, the linked Runes activated. The light of their combined patterns formed fully around the room—a spiral around me. When the light suddenly stopped, an imperfect Rune in the sequence suddenly exploded into an unintentional activation! I watched in horror to see what would happen when it became fully active. The Essence was still pouring into the Rune from those before it, the failed Rune taking in a terrifying amount of power as it began to activate.

<Um. Dani?> I squeaked, fear pouring off of me in waves. I quickly formed a large amount of acid on the Rune in an attempt to destroy it. The acid began its work, but it was too late.

The room shuddered, and a black disc grew upward from the broken Rune. A powerful leg stepped through a newborn hole in reality almost... tentatively. The black, fur covered paw extended claws which dug deep into the floor; the unknown creature began to pull itself into the room. The disk didn't get larger, but the form was able to slink through the opening.

The paw alone was nearly twenty inches wide, the claws lengthened that by seven inches when fully extended. The leg revealed that it was connected to a large, cat-like form. The powerful body was half again as large as a tiger and pitch black.

A tail twitched back and forth in anticipation, the creature obviously excited by this new hunting ground. Along its back, four tentacles extended from each of its leg joints; each of them had its own mouth and was tipped with a sharp, claw-like stinger which dripped venom.

Its head was very similar to a mountain lion but had no mouth. Instead, it had an extra eye in the center of its forehead, the only bright spot on its body. It moved around the room, sniffing at the new scents and enjoying the scenery. A hiss of acid made it flinch, whipping its tentacles with their gaping maws into an attack position. The Rune was finally destroyed, and the black disk vanished silently. The Essence slowed its travel through my dungeon as the other Runes slowed their collection with nowhere to deposit what was already gathered. Dani was huddling in my puddle near me, both of us terrified as to what we had unleashed into the heart of my being.

It padded toward us sniffing the air like there was a great delicacy nearby. It looked right at the area under the Silverwood tree where we were quietly hiding. From the tentacles, tongues flicked out, licking their sorry excuse for lips. It crouched, silently stalking us and getting closer an inch at a time. A thundering noise made it halt as Raile exploded on to the scene. Raile ran directly at the creature while shadows filled the room, collecting heavily within a ten-foot perimeter of the Cat.

Lucky for Raile, I knew where everything in my dungeon was at any given time. He charged unerringly at the Cat, who lightly leaped over Raile, casually whipping him with one of its tentacles as it spiraled in the air. Raile was slammed to the wall with enough force to shatter several feet of it from that light strike but doggedly returned to his feet. He charged again, this time following my attack pattern, jumping as the Cat jumped. It seemed surprised as they both flew at the wall but recovered fast enough to wriggle itself around Raile's body. It pushed off his back to double the force of Raile's jump, slamming him into the wall hard enough to fully shatter his armor.

The Cat attacked, two limbs pinning Raile to the wall as he whimpered for a moment. Obviously savoring Raile's helplessness, the pointed stingers on the great Cat's tentacles pierced my Boss's body repeatedly, perforating him five times *each* in two seconds. Effectively pincushioned, Raile died, still held against the wall as the Cat disemboweled him. The Cat ate a bit of meat, then dropped the body in disinterest, turning back toward Dani and me.

It hissed at us, ignoring the chance for a massive meal. I realized this was a creature that killed for sport. Obviously hating all other creatures, it didn't even bother to eat its kills beyond what it wanted at any given point. It stalked back to our position and started to slither a tentacle down to where we cowered. For some reason, it had completely ignored the Silverwood tree, a poor judgment call. As its tentacle brushed a root, a line of fire raced out from the long-dormant enchantment the Elf had placed on the tree many months ago. The fire sliced the tentacle clean off, making the Cat yowl and sprint away, vanishing into the tunnels of my dungeon.

"C-c-c-cal," Dani stammered, fear invoking a physical reaction. "I-i-is it still moving? Away, I mean?"

I didn't answer her right away; I was far too focused on a dark mass. The sliced off tentacle was still writhing toward us, intent on finishing us before it perished. Luckily for us both, before it could perform its dark deed, I felt a small burst of Essence as it expired. Information on the animal flooded my mind with its death.

<It's okay, Dani,> I soothed her as best I was able. <It's gone for now.> I was tracking the Cat as it moved along my

dungeon, slaying Bashers and leaving their corpses to rot, though I quickly reabsorbed them. Actually, I was glad to regain some Essence; I was far closer to empty than I was comfortable with.

"What was that?! What just happened?!" she cried out hysterically.

I thought of everything I now knew about the animal. <That was a Beast. It is called a 'Distortion Cat'. I didn't get the information I need to replicate it because it seems the tentacles are a different creature. They are a parasite that forms a symbiotic relationship with the Distortion Cat. Becoming bonded with the tentacle parasites causes it agony every second until they are fully dependent on each other, making the Cat's mind descend into hatred for others.>

I kept up my flood of information to give her something to focus on, <It is an *amazing* hunter. When it feels threatened, it thickens the darkness in the area to hide. If it is too bright, it *distorts* the light—bending it around itself, effectively becoming invisible while an illusion forms a few feet away. Then it attacks with its tentacles, the illusion and real thing hit the same spot to lend credence to the illusion being the *real* Beast.>

"Stop telling me how *cool it is!*" she demanded. "Where is it now? Is it going to come back in here?"

<It's already on the first floor. It's, uh, killing. Killing everything it finds. Well, I mean, it's leaving the plants alone. Oops. Spoke too soon. It ate the mint plants.> I directed every Basher to hide as best as it could. I watched the Cat move closer to the entrance where even at *this* hour, a few intrepid souls were mining. It was a few hours till dawn right now. Watching the inattentive miners, I actually felt a little bad for increasing the quality of ore they could collect after dark. It had seemed like a good way to keep people in here. Ah well.

The miners shouted in anger and confusion as the room became pitch black, running for where they thought the entrance was. Not *one* of them made it out. The Cat was crouched next to the exit, and as each approached, the tentacles would flash out slashing throats, piercing eyes, even wrapping around a neck and killing one man by suffocation. These men were all in the F-rankings; they had no chance to defend themselves from this killer. After its gory fun, the Cat poked its head out of the doorway through the 'bubble' in place which increased the Essence density, its face meeting fresh air. If I didn't know better, I'd swear it chuckled as it scented all of the prey above.

It ran up the steps and was lost to my senses. <It's gone, Dani. It went outside.> I was digesting the Essence that had made its way to me from the slain miners. Turns out this wasn't really a bad deal for me after all. A little fear, a *lot* of Essence. Dani shook, unspeaking, simply trying to take comfort in my presence. I turned my attention to the runes that had failed in the room. The large ones were still working correctly, but the one that had created a minor portal was burned off the ground and may have damaged the others.

I traced the remaining Runes, looking for flaws but found none. This worried me. I had not found any flaws the *first* time things went bad, after all. I smoothed the stone in the damaged area and began again, slowly cutting into the stone and creating the pattern I needed for the Inscription. Though somewhat recovered thanks to the miners' deaths, I still had far less Essence than I felt I needed. I was sitting around two percent capacity, so working at all was exhausting. I went slowly, double checking every bit of the pattern, looking for any flaw. I found none, so I finished with the activation Inscription, watching as the pent up Essence from the large Runes filled this new one.

I held my 'breath' as the slightly smaller Rune activated and 'sighed' with relief as it worked as I had expected it to. Each Rune, in turn, activated, the spiraling activations coming closer and closer to me with each revolution. The last Rune activated, I braced myself to fill with the Essence which was *howling* through my tunnels to power this massive series of Runescript. Nothing happened.

<What the...?> It had worked for Dani! Why wasn't I gaining any Essence?! I checked my work furiously, looking for anything that may explain why this was not working correctly. The Runes were glowing brightly; the Essence was there for the taking! Wait. The Runes were glowing... They were containing the Essence. Right, Dani had been able to cultivate only while in the *output* area of the Rune. It didn't just release the Essence into the air; it held it in place. I could be moved over to the Rune, but that would put me in an awkward position, not to mention I was *super* low on Essence.

I cast about for a solution to my problem but only frustrated myself. Dani picked up on my agitation and quizzed me, "What is the matter? Is the Cat coming back?"

<No, it isn't coming back, sweets. I'm upset because I can't reach the Essence from those Runes.> The discouragement in my voice pulled her out of her fear, and she bent her mind to helping me. What a good being to be bonded to for life! We went through several options, but nothing seemed to fit my needs. Then Dani verbalized something that made just... just *perfect* sense.

"Well, why not use the inverse Rune? If these normal Inscriptions collect Essence, the inverted Rune should release it, right?" Dani shyly contributed.

<If I had lips, I would kiss you, you beautiful, shining orb!> I fervently exclaimed.

Dani blushed. "Oh, stop, you big ol' flirt."

I bent my will to the task, creating one last Rune in the set. It looked wrong, like a scar on the floor next to the perfectly formed non-inverse Runes surrounding it. Luckily, it was *really* small. We're talking about an inch in diameter. The first Rune in the doorway had a *radius* of nearly six feet. The thick, condensed, pearlescent Essence that had been contained by the final Rune cascaded into the activation sequence of the inverted Rune.

Essence dripped out–*literally* dripped. The Essence had been collected in such a large quantity and forced into such a heavily purified and condensed state that it was in liquid form. Each drop was a shining gem and moved with a viscous swaying as it was pushed forward by the droplets forming behind it.

<Look at *that*, Dani.> My mental voice was a whisper as I watched the area slowly fill with flowing Essence. After a few seconds in the open air, the liquid seemed to steam and slowly moved back into a thick, mist-like state before dissipating into the air like humidity. Even with the Runescript then grabbing it and returning it to the center, the room was soon again dense with Essence. The air was easily two to three times as thick as it had been since the Essence couldn't escape and just continued to become more potent.

"Cal, can you quickly make a drain? Let it sink down into a reservoir under us and the tree, so as it evaporates, it comes up through the hole where we are," Dani directed me quickly. Her words pulled me from my stupor, my utter excitement had been holding me still. I formed the drain as she had requested, lining it with the tungsten I had found in my first attempt at making a tunnel. I wanted nothing breaking *this* reservoir, no sir! The condensed Essence slipped into the opening, flowing in a manner more befitting molasses, yet draining all the same. A tiny droplet was made every few seconds, but each one was purified Essence and therefore *exceedingly* potent.

The reservoir I made filled very slowly. In an hour, it had only collected about an eighth of an inch of Essence. Once in the open space of the reservoir, it again evaporated into the air of the small area. Soon, the air pressure made it try to go back up the drain. I opened a miniscule hole under me, allowing the Essence to flow up into where I made my existence.

<Bubbles!> I shouted joyfully. The pressurized Essence had agitated my puddle, resulting in—you guessed it—bubbles! Not only that, but I greedily cultivated the flowing Essence, quickly regaining my lost strength. I gained roughly half a percent of my capacity an hour, a huge amount. To put it in perspective, the seven F-ranked miners that had died had only given me roughly the same amount, half of a percent *each* that is. This means that if the rate continued, I would gain the equivalent Essence of a *life per hour*!

The amount I was able to take in was not *nearly* the amount the reservoir was allowing into the room at large as the released Essence gently blew past me, but I wasn't worried. I'd get it all eventually! I was basking in the healing feeling of happiness when I felt a hole appear in my glee. Oh no.

<Dani,> I urged her to stop eating and pay attention.

"Hmm? What? This is nice," Came her languid response.

<The Cat. It is back in the dungeon.> Instantly losing her cheerful attitude, the hunted feeling appeared in Dani's manner again.

<It's injured, though. It is bleeding heavily and limping. Still able to—> I winced as it wiped out the Boss Squad on the first floor in moments. <Still able to fight, it seems,> I finished. I watched as it went to the healing potion contained in the cistern and sniffed it. It shook its head and narrowed its eyes, then

continued back down toward us. Dang, it knew I had poisoned that potion. Ah, well. That would have been helpful.

The Cat quickly wound its way through the second floor, wearily returning to my room. As it crossed the threshold it stopped, nostrils flaring as its eyes—all three of them—widened. It cautiously stepped further into the room, then rushed to where the most concentrated Essence was condensing. It stared at the liquid Essence like someone that had just been handed a baby, a bit uncomfortable and unsure of what to do—would moving it break it?

One of its three remaining tentacles gently moved down to hover over the few drops that hadn't gone into the drain and flicked a tongue out, sucking in the concentrated Essence. The tentacle spasmed, flailing back and forth in pseudo-pain—like a human taking a bite from a lemon. The drop of Essence sped down its throat, moving into the stomach of the Cat's main body. The Cat dropped to the floor, gasping through its nose as it struggled to absorb the potent energy. Successful after a few minutes, it got to its feet and reached for another drop. This continued, lick, swallow, spasm, repeat, for nearly half an hour.

Finally seeming to have enough, it lay down, contented. As if finally noticing my attention, its eyes flicked to where we were. *Hiss.* Well, I guess it still wasn't friendly. It fell asleep facing the door, tentacles moving and keeping watch of their own volition.

<I don't think it is going to go away,> I mentioned to Dani.

Exasperated, she looked at me. "Ya think? You just *had* to feed a wild animal."

CHAPTER TWENTY-SEVEN

Dale awoke to a ruckus in the camp. Having slept behind the stone walls of the chapel on a soft bed, he could hardly make himself become concerned about what *might* be going on. He yawned, walking over to where Hans was sleeping.

"You know wha– *Yawn*, what's going on out there? Festival?" Dale tried to rub the grit from his eyes.

"Nah," Hans grunted uncaringly. "Might as well get up now, though. We still need to find some more party members."

They started getting ready for the day, putting on armor and sharpening weapons. That reminded Dale to ask about the enchantments on this armor and weapon. Hans told him it was a standard protection and feather enchantment on his armor, meaning that it weighed next to nothing when it was equipped. For the morningstar, there was a stability enchantment on it that would push the ball and spike away from the shaft, increasing the range on the weapon by about a foot and making it very hard to block the attack.

Dale activated the enchantment on his weapon for the first time. "So it just... floats there?" He doubted the effectiveness in a nonplussed tone.

Hans waved his hand over the area between the ball and the hilt showing that there was no resistance. "Try and stop that with a sword and see what happens. The sword hits nothing, you hit their head. You can adjust the distance too and make it a surprise attack. Suddenly, you have range! In battle, surprise kills, yeah?"

Dale nodded. It actually seemed a much more interesting weapon now. They moved out of the chapel to see a roaring mob of people. Guild Master Frank was shouting them down, trying to restore order. A few people were crying as healers moved among them. Hans and Dale looked at each other, nervous only for a few seconds before they moved in to see what was happening.

"Listen!" Frank was bellowing. "We have no information right now! We believe it was a breakout, monsters escaping the dungeon. We don't have any knowledge beyond the fact that a few F-ranked people were slain and several people were injured before a Mage blasted an area it was believed to be in. No, we don't know what it was–it was too dark! Please, we have not seen anything in the dungeon that a proper group cannot handle! Go about your business. We will give you any information we can find."

Hans tapped Dale on the arm. "We better hurry and find a group if we want to get in there. They might close it off while they look into this." Dale was pulled over to the mess tent where they found Rose waiting for them. She was in leather armor that was obviously heavily enchanted from the glow coming off of her. Inscribed armor and weapons rarely glowed and only then if they were breaking down, allowing Essence to escape. Enchantments on armor were made of layered Essence and would, therefore, shine as it was consumed in order to power the Rune. In short, glowing enchantment? Necessary! Glowing inscribed Rune? *Really* bad.

"You made it through the night. Good," Rose deadpanned. "Where are the others?"

Hans leered at her. "Well, my Rose, we have been unable to find anyone else worthy to travel in your company. Sadly, we must now scavenge the bottom of the barrel in our search."

"I am not *your* Rose. What positions do we have filled? What are your specialties?" Rose looked back and forth between them.

Hans gave an elaborate bow. "Oh, how my heart aches to hear you say such words! I, ma'am, am a humble knife wielder. I specialize in ending threats before they become aware of me or my comrades' presence."

"An assassin. Just great." Rose grunted in a very unladylike noise. "Swell company you keep, Dale. What do you do?" Hans looked a bit affronted.

Dale was unsure. "I'm, uh. I fight with a mace and buckler?"

Rose nodded. "A fighter. Good, hopefully, you'll specialize soon. What are your talents in the earth domain?"

Hans intercepted the question smoothly, "He has not found the path he will walk yet. He has been focused too hard on getting to this level, I am afraid."

"Fine, so we have an assassin, a fighter, and a ranger." She drew her bow to explain her term. "That's a good mix to start, but we need to fill our party out with some other people."

Hans nodded. "Good thinking! Smart *and* beautiful!" He graced her with a wink as she rolled her eyes.

"I'm not into old men," Rose denied him coolly. Hans pantomimed, clutching his heart as a massive form walked up to the conversing group.

"Did I hear thou art looking for someone to enter into the dungeon with thou and thine?" a gravelly voice boomed, the words giving off a feeling of near archaic speech.

Hans looked over, eyes flaring at the interruption. "Mmhmm, we are. I'm sorry though, lad, F-ranked aren't allowed to the second level anymore," Hans dismissed offhandedly, returning to his determined flirtation.

The voice corrected him, "Not if they are *members* of the Guild. I am not. Also, I have already proven my worth in combat, finishing the second floor with my previous compatriots." The dawn broke at that moment, allowing light to begin flooding over the horizon. The young man came into view, an odd type of armor on him. Metal plates were interspersed with furs, leaving a large amount of flesh showing. That flesh was rippling with dense muscle, drawing their eyes up to an arm casually holding an oversized warhammer single-handedly. The man's eyes were green, his long hair a deep red.

"Barbarian," Rose breathed, eyes shining. Was her breath coming a little faster?

Hans smile genially. "Now the problem is that you can't join a Guild group, can you?"

The man's eyes darkened, his face stony as he set his jaw, nodded, and turned silently away. He paused as Dale called after him.

"Hold!" Dale commanded. "What is your name?"

The warhammer came to rest on the ground. "My name? I bear the name of my father and my father's father, for generations uncountable. We are the mighty hunters of the frozen north, giants among the men of humanity. I *am* what you call a 'barbarian'," He lifted his chin disdainfully. "I am the warrior known as Tom."

"Tom," Hans sputtered. "Your name is Tom. All that build up and your name is Tom."

Tom squinted at him meaningfully, "Is this an issue?"

"No, not at all... Tom," Hans cheerfully denied.

Dale snapped his fingers. "You were the one who killed a teammate." He remembered.

Tom's face fell. He nodded. "To my great shame, it is true. Now, no others will allow me to join them in battle, as they fear I would turn on them as would a rabid dog." He looked up, setting his features. "I swear to you, it was an accident, a moment of battle rage instilled in me over the loss of my comrades. I took out the fury of their deaths on the giant creature, Raile, with an untested weapon. His armor shattered, the shards impacting and killing my dear friend."

Dale nodded. "That is what I had heard. Hans is correct, though. You cannot join us without joining the Guild. Would you be opposed to that?"

Tom looked at him, as confused as if Dale had sprouted a breast on his forehead. "If they would have me. I know of none who would willingly turn down that chance."

Dale glanced at Hans. "It is customary that a man is tested before joining, yes? Can we call this dungeon run a test and deal with the paperwork tonight? His Essence is very pure."

Hans groaned. "Fiiiine. Ugh." He looked at Rose. "Wait, *you* are in the Guild, right?"

"Yes," was her verbose response.

"Can I join you as well?" a small voice piped up. "I know you are good people, to believe in Tom and his innocence as I do. I can help." A robed figure stepped into their midst. Dale looked at him, recognizing him as if from a long forgotten dream.

"You!" Dale exclaimed excitedly. "You're the cleric who healed Josh when Raile crushed him!"

The cleric brightened. "You remember me?" he inquired hopefully.

"How could I not? You are in the Guild and," Dale squinted for a second, "a D-rank four?"

"Five," he responded proudly. "My name is Adam."

Hans was less pleased. "Oh, sure, let's just bring anyone who wants to go! We don't need to test people, nahhh. Let's just grab a few randos and charge on in!" he grumbled, moving off toward the dungeon entrance. "Thought I was going to be part of choosing the team, but noooo."

"Works for me. Just remember that right now this is on a temporary basis, okay everyone? We don't know you yet." Dale shrugged. "Let's go then! Unless anyone needs some time to prepare?" The shaking of heads announced their readiness. They moved as an excited group to begin their incursion to the dark and desolate depths of the dreary dungeon. They climbed down the unguarded stairs, ignoring the crowds of people milling around, no one seemed to mind that they were moving down anyway. Just before they entered, Hans pointed out that blood had poured out of the entrance. Beyond the drying blood was a perfectly straight line on the floor, after which the ground was perfectly clean.

"This is the line where the dungeon *really* begins." They stepped across and began their descent.

Just after they entered, Guild Master Frank made an announcement to the gathered people, "We are going to build a wall around this entrance today. The entrance and exits to it will be guarded at all times to prevent this sort of tragedy in the future. Until then, the dungeon is closed! We will send a team to check on it after the wall is built, but until then no one goes in! The Guild will be providing food to anyone who wants it free of charge until this event is concluded."

While that didn't get any reaction, his next announcement that freshly imported beer and ale would also be free for the event *certainly* got a loud cheer.

DALE

"This is weird!" Dale shouted, smashing his morningstar into a Basher. "They have never been so aggressive before!" The Bashers were absolutely *throwing* themselves at the group, heedless of their losses or injuries. Tom swung his hammer back and forth, crushing several with each swing. If the Rune on it had not allowed for it to be light enough to swing around like a small branch, he would have been overwhelmed already.

"Stop whining and kill *faster*!" Rose shouted back. Arrows were leaving her bow at a prodigious rate, so many in a short time that Dale was wondering how she hadn't run out.

"Anything for you, my sweet Rose!" Hans chimed in, suddenly vanishing from sight. Unleashing his true ability for the first time Dale had ever seen, nearly a dozen Bashers suddenly fountained blood and dropped to the ground.

The fight unexpectedly over, each of them sank to the ground to catch their breath. All except Hans who was watching Rose, hoping for a hint of approval. They were only in the *second* of the four main rooms and already nearly exhausted. The Bashers were far more numerous than they ever had been, a veritable swarm of life that tried to crush others beneath an onslaught of flesh and bone.

"What is going on here?" Adam panted as he held his knees.

Dale shook his head. "No idea, but we can afford to go slowly. I say we take our time, get to know each other, and cultivate. Then we come up with a plan to deal with all of this."

Rose got a very uncomfortable look on her face. Dale noticed and tried to guess at the reason behind it. "Rose, try to cultivate in here. I need to as well. The sooner my Essence is fixed from that shattering, the better. I think it would benefit you as well."

All except Hans–who was on lookout duty–sat in the lotus position and began to draw in the power of the heavens and the earth. A shocked look passed Rose's face as if she had thought this chance would be too good to be true. Essence filled her, being drawn in twice as fast as anyone else, as Dale watched in shock.

"Do you have a really good cultivation technique?" He smiled at her. "That is amazing!"

Rose shook her head, her voice coming out dreamily as her main focus remained on her cultivation. "It's because I have a dual affinity. I have two open paths for Essence to flow along, but they both have to be used in parallel; else it sticks in my meridians, and I cannot get the Essence to my center."

Dale realized his own focus had faded, so he quickly began drawing in more of the Essence. All of the people in the D-rankings drew in massive amounts of Essence, yet still, Tom's center was filling faster than all of them. He bragged for a moment to tease them, then realized that it simply meant he could hold much less Essence in his center than them. He *was* only in the F-rankings, after all.

"Is the Essence... *fading* in here?" Rose curiously examined the surroundings, unused to the effects cultivating might have on the dungeon.

Dale nodded. "It usually takes, I don't know, half an hour? This was ten minutes, at best!" He looked at Hans for confirmation.

"Look at this! The Essence in here is... moving?" Hans questioned, his eyes bright enough that Dale knew he was using Essence enhanced vision.

"It is going deeper inward!" Adam exclaimed in amazement.

Hans nodded gravely. "That's what she said."

"Rose did not utter a word," Tom corrected him, confused by this turn of the conversation. "Where is the Essence going?"

"I guess we are going to have to find out!" Hans jauntily began strutting deeper into the deadly dungeon. They all stood up and resumed their journey, moving into the tunnel that connected the rooms. Dale had to pull Rose out of the path of traps several times.

"I don't suppose you have any open meridians?" He was a bit exasperated as he pulled her away from *another* rock fall she had almost triggered. "Can you cycle Essence to your eyes?"

"I know how..." Rose flushed. "I've never done it, though. I've just never had a way to replenish my Essence if I used it."

Dale nodded. "We'll explain it when we clear the next room." They stepped around the corner and went very still. Row upon row of Bashers blocked their way across the room.

"This should be interesting," Hans noted, slowly drawing his daggers. As if that was a signal, the swarm bounded toward them with deadly intent.

Chapter Twenty-Eight

I watched the Cat until it finally awoke. Stretching powerfully as all cats seem to do, it exposed a regrown tentacle that the enchantments on the Silverwood tree had sliced off. It glanced at the tentacle and purred, pleased by what it saw. The tentacle reached down and pet the Cat, reminding me that they were separate creatures. The huge Cat glanced up at the celestial glass above and hissed. Apparently, it did *not* like the brightness of the room. A few people had gathered and were looking down, commenting on the unexpected sight of the Cat. It gazed around the room, all three eyes again locking on the space where Dani and I cowered under the Silverwood tree.

It padded over and peered down at where we were. The night before had taught me caution, however, and I had reduced the size of the opening as well as lined the space with poison and spikes. No one would put their hand in *this* jar without losing a chunk of it. I could feel the malevolent gaze of the Cat as it tried to determine if hunting me was worth the trouble. In the disconcerting way of all cats, it seemed to lose all interest and instead walked away and resumed basking in the thick Essence, occasionally lapping up a small droplet of the super-concentrated Essence.

I was also getting stronger and was back to near thirteen percent capacity. To achieve my next rank, I needed to strain against the bounds of my current capacity until they weakened enough for me to achieve a breakthrough. If I had a week or so, I could easily move into D-rank four, possible even D-five if I had uninterrupted time to cultivate. The sun had risen, though, and soon, I felt the steps of a group coming to try their luck. I turned my attention to them, as the Cat didn't seem to be threatening me anymore.

I no longer felt the need to hold back. With this influx of Essence, I had enough to fully devote my creatures to attacking and could restore them to full strength without the worry of running too low to defend myself. Right now, it was far more important to me to get every drop of Essence I could in an attempt to force a breakthrough. If that meant cannibalizing my troops, so be it! I'd rather use them to take out the humans, though. I called every Basher out of their hidden warrens, forcing their minds to the breaking point as I ordered all of them to fight to the death. The heavy pressure of combat that I was going to apply was now just beginning in the second room of the first floor.

Dale's group had new people in it. I recognized a few of them from their time in my dungeon, but the female was entirely new to my depths. I caught their names as they talked and prepared to give them the fight of their lives–a real battle. As they wasted their time cultivating, I arranged all of the remaining Bashers of the first floor into ranks in the next room. When they attacked, they would move as a wave, the first rank jumping, then the second directly after. The third rank would start *charging* as soon as the first hit and jump to attack when the second wave landed their attacks. Then they would reform in their lines to do it again, over and over until the humans were pulp.

The lazy adventurers made their painfully slow way to the third main room of the first floor, stopping in shock at the arrayed forces. They reached for the weapons they had foolishly put away... which was when I gave my command to attack. The waves of Bashers charged forward, flying recklessly toward the uncomprehending adventurers. With a sound reminiscent of a drumline being played, the smooth horn of each of the Bashers found a home somewhere. Some were dodged and hit the tunnel wall, many hit the front line adventurers. A few hit those in the rear, Rose and Adam, who cried out in pain louder than those standing on the front line. Those cries drove my Bashers into a frenzy.

My lines of Bashers kept up a constant battering of the adventurers, even as they began to counterattack. A warhammer I had gifted Tom some time ago came into play, the enchantment releasing a shockwave of force with each successful hit that was enough to burst the eardrums of the nearest Bashers if not kill them directly. The Bashers *actually* hit would vanish in a spray of viscera, the force of the strike quintupled by the potent enchantment. The roaring barbarian was soon covered in gore and began laughing as the blows seemed to not affect him. He charged forward into the room, leaving his companions behind as he sought a glorious death in battle. I was more than happy to oblige him.

He spun his whole body in a spiral, killing a half dozen Bashers in midair. Their coats now sanguine where they were once white, the Bashers howled like dogs as they threw themselves at this lone target. Several were able to impact his knees from behind, driving him to the ground with an *oomph*. Racing toward his head from all sides, many were rebuffed as arrows slew them. A dagger attached to a swiftly moving Hans *snicked* into the battle, killing as many in near a second as Tom had managed the entire fight. Still, several Bashers landed their attack but were knocked away at the last second by a glowing barrier. The cleric had formed a wall of solid Essence around his kneeling comrade's head, though the cost of driving his Essence so far from himself was making him shake and sweat.

Dale had also joined the melee, swinging his morningstar to deadly effect. The spikes on the ball, if they did not kill the Bashers directly, opened massive gashes that bled out the small bodies in seconds. Powering through arrows, Rose never stopped moving as she weaved amongst the attacks, firing at a speed which numbed the mind. If a Basher got too close, the hardened shaft of the bow would swing at them, most often crushing their spines. As many Bashers as there were, they still were simply no match for such a well-equipped team. I needed to increase my ability. This purge of creatures may actually be just what I needed to start filling the lair with more dangerous Mobs.

The party stood in the room—until they fell to the ground that is. Adam fell first, the strain of holding the barrier draining him to a paler color than was his norm. He hit the floor with a small *splash* as he fell into the lake of blood and bodily fluids. The others followed suit, except Hans who eyed the floor with distaste. Despite a few splatters on him from the wildly swinging warhammer, his clothing was still immaculate. The blood soon vanished, except in the areas where the human auras were too close. Small puddles of blood were soon the only remnants, but even those vanished as the party moved away from them.

They sat down and began cultivating in an attempt to recoup the expenditure of Essence they had used. Adam especially was working hard to swiftly condense the cultivated Essence, and color began returning to his face. The expended Essence had returned to him quickly. Well, technically the Essence had actually looped out from him, formed a barrier around Tom's head, then returned to Adam's center when the barrier was dropped. Still tiring, I assumed.

Dani asked me to explain what was happening, so I connected with her to allow her to see as I did. We closely inspected the group. The lanky, rangy form of the blond Hans was our first; we watched his blue and roving eyes inspect his surroundings for any threat.

Dani murmured to me, trying not to get the attention of the Cat, “You think he is about average for a human? I heard Rose call him an assassin under her breath, and I remember someone saying assassins tend to blend in.”

<I don’t know; he has a... well, practically a noble bearing, don’t you think?> I serenely murmured.

Dani whipped her attention to me. “Are you feeling okay?”

<Mmmm soooo much Essence from that. I’m having trouble absorbing all of it in one go.>

“Well, turn some of it into loot drops then!” she demanded. Oops. I had forgotten. I dumped a bunch of potions, poisons, and a few trinkets. Coins clattered to the floor, drawing their attention.

<Oh, that did help a lot.> I sighed in relief. <Good call.> We then returned to our inspection of the people as they took the bribe–I mean, collected loot. Rose was tall, raven-haired, and dusky, looking like she could blend easily into the shadows before ending her prey, a true hunter if I ever saw one. Adam was also tall but was very pale and had little musculature. Since his cheekbones were prominent, he had a noble, aristocratic look to him as well. Tom, the barbarian, stood over six and a half feet tall and was all hardened muscle and hair. His freckled face spoke of a life outdoors, and his wild, red hair was as long in its braid as was Rose’s. His chest hair was as long as the short hair on Adam’s head. I bet he could braid it if he wanted.

This brings us to Dale. Good ol’ Dale. He was a husky young man and had the look of someone who had transformed fat into muscle through hard work. While his muscles were not as well defined as Tom’s, I knew for a fact that he could land a hit with the best of them. He had the common look of the area, brown hair with a well-trimmed beard and mustache and common brown eyes. I was *very* familiar with Dale and looked forward to absorbing him. During our scrutiny of them, they had finished cultivating and began to move to the next room, planning their attack on the first floor Boss.

DALE

"That-*pant*-was-*pant*-insane," Adam managed. The Essence he had forced out of his body was slow in returning, and cultivation had only been able to restore it to a certain point. "What the heck is going on?!"

Hans looked troubled, which had the effect of making Dale very nervous. To see Hans without a sarcastic grin felt like a true portent of doom. He had even stopped flirting. Hans looked startled when Dale lightly punched him to get his attention.

"What's on your mind, big guy?" Dale prodded, giving Hans a look that conveyed his worry.

Hans shook his head. "This is making me remember a tale I heard a while back. I didn't think it was true. According to legend, sometimes it seems that a dungeon is suddenly filled with danger, far more than is typical. There is always an event of some kind that sets it off, and the dungeon seems to be filled with raging creatures and sudden maliciousness." He nodded at Dale. "We've had a taste of that when we came here to find the cursed earth blocking the entry. I think... I think we should leave."

The others, especially Tom, cried out in surprise and negation. Hans, the strongest killer in the group, wanted them to leave? They argued with him furiously for a few minutes, though he eventually won the argument with a simple reminder.

"Tom, as a Guild hopeful, cannot enter the lower level without a C-ranked cultivator to grant him permission, and I will *not* grant it. He could enter if he were to forever leave behind his chances of joining the Guild. The rest of you I outrank, and I order you to stay out of the lower level," Hans calmly stated with steel in his voice. He began walking back to the entrance. Tom was the first to follow, face as red as his hair as his anger threatened to engulf him.

"Well, dammit," Rose muttered harshly as she joined them. Dale and Adam fell into the line. They continued picking their way back to the entrance with Dale pointing out each trap to Rose so she could familiarize herself with the features of them. Soon, her sharp eyes were allowing her to point them out before even Dale saw them, making him swell with pride at his teaching skills.

The normally Essence-filled air had very little in it currently, making Dale nervous. Something was very wrong in the dungeon, and they were running away from finding the source. The dungeon was everything to him, a source of wealth and power that he was only just beginning to taste. His rumination was interrupted as he walked into Adam, who had abruptly come to a stop in front of him. Startled for a second, Dale started to glare until he saw what had caught the group's attention.

A wall of light stretched the span of the doorway, shimmering and seeming to whisper secrets that begged for the attention of the listener. It was... seductive. Dale found himself drawn toward it, his mind lost in the pulsating glory he beheld. He was jerked off of his feet–to his great protest–and placed facing away from the entrance along with the other members of the group. His mind was filled with rage at the treatment, soon washed away by confusion.

"Wh–" Dale paused and cleared his throat. He was so thirsty suddenly. "What just happened?"

Hans was the only one looking back the other way. "Barrier spell," he answered shortly. "Touch it, get fried by Mana. We may be screwed."

"Someone trapped us in here?" Adam whispered, eyes getting round.

Hans shook his head. "No, someone locked everyone *out.* I think we must have missed something important. Frank wouldn't just lock this place down without good reason. Something must have spooked him beyond a minor breakout of Bashers. Dammit! Why didn't we wait for more information?!" he shouted abruptly, startling the group.

"Screw information, why did we skip breakfast?" Tom groaned, his stomach realizing it had been forgotten. His reminder made everyone realize they had not planned well for this dungeon dive. Stomachs rumbling all around, tempers started to flare. A few minutes of arguing got them no closer to a solution, forcing them to make decisions.

"Hans," Rose started, "how long until this barrier is removed?"

Hans shrugged, knowing where this would lead the conversation. "Likely, they are building defenses around the stairwell. Normally, this would take a day, maybe two, but the earth Mages that would do that quickly are all tied up building a sewer system at the capital. It could be a week before the door is open again."

"Well, then our path is clear," Dale announced. "Hans, there is no way but onward. We need to clear the dungeon and leave through the Boss room."

Hans began to worriedly fret. "Listen, if there is something that spooked Frank enough that he would close the place instead of fighting it right away, I don't think it would be wise to charge in blindly. It is *very* possible this will end with all of our deaths. Are you okay with that?"

"Of course not, Hans! We need to *try*, though. We won't last a week in here without aid. I'm betting no one brought more than a few sips of water, for one. Next, we have no food and no shelter. We can either face whatever the problem is now, as healthy as we are going to get or wait until we are weak from hunger and thirst. What say you?" Dale challenged him.

"I *say* it is still a bad idea. Sadly, it is the best we've got unless." He looked around to see if anyone else had ideas. "No? Onward then, I suppose." They shrugged and turned toward the deep dungeon, retracing their steps until they stood outside of the Boss room on the first floor. They shared their knowledge of the normal tactics, getting into formation as best they were able. Moving cautiously into the room, they prepared to fight.

Cal

Only the normal number of Mobs stood in the room, the five members of the Boss Squad. I had cycled out the normal squad with the Alpha Squad that I used specifically for ambushes I *knew* would succeed. The Alpha Squad had grown and were easily the oldest Mobs in the dungeon at this point–the only group that had not died. Intelligence shone in their eyes, showing me that if they had a Beast Core, they would be sentient by now.

The Essence that they absorbed from each kill had increased the potency of their attacks, adding their affinity as elemental damage. Their bodies were now striped in the colors of their Essence as well. This would be a win-win battle for me—either I rid myself of these persistent interlopers or I reclaim the upgraded patterns of the Alpha Squad. In both situations, I could only get stronger. Dale's group entered the room, ready for battle.

I was actually taken by surprise. Before I could send the attack signal to my squad, an arrow accurately flew across the room and sliced the jugular of one of the two Oppressors, effectively reducing the number of my multi-attack Bashers to one. With a cry of rage, the remaining squad left their bleeding, twitching brother to his fate. The Alpha Squad was well used to working together at this point, which showed in their movements and tactics. Utilizing its ability to its fullest, the remaining Oppressor leaped off the earthen affinity Smasher and unleashed his attack from a distance. A blast of air as sharp as a blade raced away from him in a horizontal line, aimed downward from a high point of the jump to slash at an angle.

The blast hit the ground in front of Dale's group, blasting shards of stone into the party—who lost sight of the charging Mobs in the resultant dust cloud. The impact of the Smasher's feet on the ground allowed for the humans to successfully dodge when the massive Bashers tried to ram Hans and Adam during their momentary blindness. The infernal Impaler slipped into a hidden tunnel and began to circle behind the group. A warhammer landed on a Smasher, shattering its armor downward, literally shredding the animal's insides with what had previously been its greatest protection.

A bow, acting as Rose's staff, slammed into the other Smasher, but its hard armor made the attack ineffectual. The Smasher turned and battered Rose to the ground with a heavy attack; she cried out as she fell. Tom's hammer descended like the judgment of god on to her aggressor, blasting the dying Basher into a mess of flying gore with the power of his attack. Hans was attacking the final Oppressor, dodging its rapid attacks while barely seeming to touch the ground. Soon, his flashing blades overwhelmed the poor creature, allowing it to join its brethren in death's release.

No other assailants visible, the group tried to catch their breath and began to sit down. I watched a flash of fear cross Dale's face as a memory impacted him. Eyes flashing silvery-brown, he glanced around the room. Raising his morningstar, he ran at Adam, who was working to heal Rose, her leg shattered. With a primal yell, Dale swung at the cleric, the morningstar on a crash course with his midsection. I watched in glee, having no idea what was making Dale attack his friend but glad to see it happening.

Mid-swing–just as Adam's eyes began to widen with the realization that he was under attack–the top of the morningstar released from the shaft of the weapon, traveling out in the same, smooth arc the weapon's hilt was traveling in. The spiked ball missed Adam by a foot, yet buried itself in the skull of the Impaler just as it left the hidden tunnel, horn blazing with infernal fire. Skull shattered on the first hit, the hellfire then raced along the Impaler's body, consuming it absolutely.

CHAPTER TWENTY-NINE

The head of the morningstar came back to the hilt, resuming its place with a *click*. Adam returned to healing Rose but had to ask how Dale had known what was about to happen. Dale was exceedingly relieved that he had made the correct call.

"A while back, a guy in my old group, Steve, was standing in that spot and got skewered by a smaller version of that thing. I didn't see it except right when we came through the door, so I knew it was trying the same trick," Dale tried to say nonchalantly, still shaking from battle reaction.

Hans came and clapped him on the back. "Nice work! You've been practicing with that weapon then? Worked out the enchantment? I'm impressed by your control there. If you hadn't known *exactly* what you were doing, you would have crushed Adam's ribs! When did you start working out the kinks of it?" he babbled excitedly.

"Erm," Dale sheepishly looked around, "I, ah, that's actually the first time I've *really* used it..."

Hans looked on in shock as the others laughed a bit bleakly. "He's mad. I'm stuck in the dungeon with a madman." Hans was near inaudible as he passed judgment on Dale.

"Hey!" Dale yelled as the others laughed harder. "Better than skewered!" The group ignored him as they settled in to cultivate. Thanks to Adam, Rose was already healed from the fight.

"You do good work, Adam," Rose praised him, "Thank you for fixing me up."

Adam blushed furiously; he was very unused to female attention, regardless of his aristocratic looks. Perhaps because of them really. No commoner wanted to worry that their child would be slaughtered on suspicion of being a Royal bastard. "Um, anytime. Really. Sorry I'm not more... useful... in a fight."

"A fight is not over until you are fighting the next one!" Tom declared what was obviously ancient barbarian wisdom. "Healing is as much a part of this battle as was my turning of those bunnies into flying orbs of goo!"

"Thanks? I think?" Adam muttered, trying to parse what Tom had declared. Tom looked very pleased with himself for some reason.

The Essence in this room was still fairly dense, so the group was able to recuperate much of their lost energy. Even Hans joined this time, needing a bit of a pick-me-up. A few minutes into this, Rose suddenly cried out and clutched at her chest.

"What? Rose, what's wrong?" Adam shouted, by her side in an instant, preparing to heal her.

"My Chi!" Rose gasped, tears in her eyes. "It's healing! Get back, I need to cultivate!" The others took a step back as she drank in Essence as a sponge takes in water. Switching to his enhanced sight, Dale watched as the trillions of shards and imperfections in her spiral began to smooth, the natural flow being restored. Tears were pouring down her face as she smiled a *real* smile for the first time since Dale had met her; he watched as her center became whole.

As the last of the broken Chi threads fixed themselves, the Essence around her increased the speed of refinement, howling into her center as her body took in the Essence it had been denied for over twenty years. In only a few minutes, the loose Essence in the air was depleted to the point that she could not pull another drop, though her entire being cried out for more. Her center being restoring had an interesting effect on the rest of the group. Her smile had increased morale, and the relaxation in her stance told of her release from decades of pain. Determination solidified, the group resumed their dungeon dive, descending into the second floor.

Dale led the way, determined to clear the sub-level and heal his own center. The difference in speed between Rose's cultivation before and after healing proved that his increased speed was but a fraction of what was possible. He threw himself at the first roaming squad of upgraded Bashers they found, killing two in as many strokes. His sudden violence and initiative shocked the others, and they became caught up in competition.

Arrows—missing teammates by fractions of an inch—thudded into weak points in the Bashers. A warhammer moving faster than it had any right to transformed bounding bodies into jelly, splattering the barbarian with gore. Dale's morningstar cracked bones and rock armor, and a well-placed dagger from Hans severed the thread keeping their enemies tenuously attached to life. Adam watched the laughing, blood-crazed team he was a now part of and began nervously praying.

Soon, they were standing in the first room breathing deeply as they attempted to calm themselves and replenish their stamina. The gore from the groups of Bashers in the room still dripped gently from the ceiling, intermittently splattering them with viscera. They dropped to their meditative poses and began cultivating, Dale working as hard as he could without sacrificing purity or density. Easily outstripping even Adam, Rose cultivated with the force of a tornado, drinking in Essence through two open channels of affinity.

They relaxed a bit as the room drained of Essence, flowing unnaturally fast out of the room and deeper into the dungeon. They stood, preparing their cooling muscles for more fighting and entered the tunnel. Only one other time had the path to the final room been so clear, though this time the

Essence was rushing toward the Boss room, not away. Rage abated, they moved with more caution, skirting around traps carefully instead of recklessly. The enemies Dale's group fought against had *tactics* used against them instead of just force and anger. Soon, they stood in the third main room, looking at the odd loot they had just found.

"Is this arrow type even usable?" Dale handed the items in question to Rose. The metal shaft was weighted at the tip, round and heavy.

Rose inspected it, held it to her ear, and shook it. "It has some kind of liquid in it?" she whispered wonderingly. "I... *could* use it, but I have no idea what would happen. What about those daggers, Hans?""

Hans had an odd look on his face, a nearly sickly grimace. "Yeah, these are usable. They are the weapon of a killer, not a fighter. I'm... not sure I want them. Look at this." He held up the daggers, pointing at the tiny Inscription on the hilt directly opposite the point.

"If I am not mistaken, that is the inverted liquid Rune we've seen previously. If I do this," here he twisted the dagger hilt, opening a small, hollow compartment, "and fill it with poison," which he did, a vial of poison having recently dropped as it had in every room thus far, "when I activate the Rune, the poison will be *injected* into whoever gets stabbed, depositing it deep inside their body. That will make it spread very quickly." Hans actually shuddered. "I think something is going on here."

Dale looked at him sharply. He had learned to trust Hans's instincts. "What do you mean?"

"It is almost like the dungeon now *wants* us to succeed, which makes me nervous. Earlier, it threw everything it had at us in an attempt to stop or kill us. Now, it is outfitting us with poison and odd weaponry. I think... I think we should make sure to use this stuff." Hans fiddled with the new assassin's blades.

Even Adam had found a weapon he could use, an oaken staff banded in tungsten. It had the Inscription to become light as a feather on it as well as a spiked end at the base that could be used for walking or stabbing. The top held a fist-sized topaz stone, which would allow him to focus his celestial Essence away from his body better than even a diamond would. With the staff being so light, he could weave it through the air like a baton, and the heavy weapon would still hit as hard as normal.

Dale looked at a glass vial he had found at his feet, trying to determine what it could possibly be used for. The shape of it was fanciful–an odd rounded shape on one end, while flat with a small convex part at the base. The vial would never stand on a shelf, the cylindrical shape and odd ends would make it roll around. Plus, there was no discernible way to open it, making him assume it was intended to be thrown or smashed. The conundrum made him scratch his head, the blood drying there was making him itch. He glanced at his weapon, and a thought occurred to him.

He activated the enchantment to allow the head of the weapon to move away from the hilt and placed the vial there. The odd, flat-then-grooved pattern of the bottom fit on to the hilt, and the head came back to rest on the curved top. It was now obvious that if he hit something, the vial would shatter, coating whatever he struck with the liquid contained within. He pointed this out to his group, and they decided to try and use it after he promised he would dodge the liquid.

Tom got nothing else that was obviously for him. They supposed the warhammer was enough as it was. Feeling left out, he coated his hammer in poison, grumbling about not having a new toy. Feeling as prepared as possible, they made their way through the oddly empty tunnel, entering the Boss room to a strange, frightening sight.

Cal

"Cal," the whispered voice of Dani pulled my attention away from Dale's group. I had just dropped them the gear I felt would help them kill the Distortion Cat prowling in my Boss room.

<What?> I refocused my attention on her, then upward, to where the Distortion Cat was staring directly at us. <Ahh!> I shrieked in surprise! When had that thing gotten so close? I had thought I knew its every motion. It narrowed all three of its eyes and began threading a tentacle down the shaft, carefully weaving it among the hundreds of roots between us. The tentacle seemed to stretch, growing thinner and allowing it to skirt around the spikes I had placed around the perimeter.

"Oh crap, oh crap, oh crap, oh crap," Dani whispered as the tentacle drew ever nearer.

The end was drawing close, so I tried to comfort her as best as possible, <It is going to be alright, Dani. I'm... I'm so sorry I couldn't protect you.>

The tentacle drew nearer, the maw opening and a tongue flicking hungrily around, forked like a snake. The gaping maw reached for Dani, wanting no more than her death.

"Well, that is new. Looks like it's stuck. Hit it quick!" a voice directed softly, but in the silence of our impending death, they may as well have been shouting. The tentacle quickly began retreating, trying to escape while not touching the roots. It sliced poorly along a spike, opening a shallow wound as the Cat hissed.

I turned my attention out of my immediate surroundings, watching the unfolding battle. Dani softly cried in relief.

DALE

The heavy hitters of their group were charging, and an arrow was already in the air. The Cat hissed again, and shadows began billowing out of it, darkening the room as the front line slid to a stop, unsure of this new ability. The arrow missed the Cat as it dodged, but the modified tip shattered at its feet, making a puddle of brilliantly shining light that the Cat accidentally dropped a back paw in. Now free of the shaft under the Silverwood tree, the Cat started to move–oblivious to the light shining with each step it took.

The room was now fully darkened, the light from above stopping against a wall of umbra only a foot below the celestial quartz. The furious Cat sprinted silently to the edge of the room, then charged at the group from their left, trying to catch them off guard. The shining paw was the only reason Tom noticed the pouncing animal. With a great shout of intermingled fear and adrenaline, he swung his mighty warhammer to intercept the Cat's path. The Cat spun in midair, a tentacle snapping out and impacting the ground, throwing it out of the way but interrupting its own assault.

It faded back into the darkened room as the group moved to form a defensive half circle. Hans, Dale, and Tom stood with their backs to Adam and Rose, who, in turn, stood against a wall. Dale began calling out orders, telling everyone to begin using their Essence viewing abilities. Unfortunately, the darkness in the room was created by Essence so this vision could not penetrate the inky darkness. Rose pulled an arrow halfway back, squinting into the shadows and preparing herself. Adam looked around, trying to find any way to help. He looked to the heavens as he prayed, and an idea wriggled into his brain.

The Cat decided to end this farce of a battle and used a potent ability, a powerful sonic wail. The maw on each tentacle opened wide and shattered the still air with a pandemonium of noise. The roar was quadra-tonal, each maw having a slight variation of sound. Laced with infernal energy–the source of darkness itself–the noise hit the group as a physical blow, stunning them and paralyzing their muscles as the Cat charged in for the kill. Dale could feel the death of his new friends approaching but could not struggle away from the bonds the sonic wail had imposed on his mind and body.

Dale's mind went into overdrive; the word 'bonds' had triggered a memory. The Cat appeared out of the darkness, now sauntering toward his helpless victims. Dale forced himself to reach out to the pendant he was wearing, infusing it with Essence. A ripple of golden light whooshed out of the pendant, destroying the infernal bonds placed on him. Dale leaped at the startled Cat, swinging his morningstar at its head. A tentacle blurred, moving in to catch the blow, shattering the glass vial and dumping the contents on to the massive Cat.

As the liquid poured across the front of the Distortion Cat's body, light began to glimmer on it, increasing to a brilliant shine. At the same time, the liquid that had made its way on to the fur and skin of the Beast began melting anything it touched. The Cat howled and bounded back into the darkness, though its shining form and loud hissing gave its position away. The effect of the sonic wail ended; the rest of the group was able to spring into action. Rose began firing arrows as fast as she could line up the shots, Tom, Dale, and Hans charged the shining Beast, and Adam started an incantation.

Incantations were the verbal form of releasing Essence or Mana. Using an incantation tended to be frowned upon if a Rune was available because it permanently used up a person's Essence for an instant, single use effect on the world. This allowed cultivators to shape their Essence or Mana–aided by hand gestures or movement–into the form they needed at that moment.

Incantations were especially powerful because they used all of the Essence provided in a single, massive burst. The Mages who had opened the portal recently had used incantations to quickly and evenly distribute power to the Runes inscribed on the portal obelisks, for instance. Heedless of the battle continuing, Adam carefully added his Essence to the spell forming from his words and actions.

The Cat was too agile to hit easily, each blow of Dale's morningstar or Tom's warhammer easily dodged while the tentacles smacked arrows out of the air. Hans stopped moving, concentrated for a second, and seemed to vanish into the darkness as he took a single step backward. He moved as quickly as the wind, hovering over the floor by a quarter inch. He suddenly shot high into the air and dove down, timing his attack for when the Cat was dodging a series of blows from the other fighters. The Cat moved too quickly, and while he was unable to land a killing blow, he did manage to stab his daggers into the Cat's flanks and activate the Inscriptions, injecting poison deep into the wounds.

The Cat whipped around and focused entirely on Hans for a moment. Three tentacles slammed into his torso while the other dropped to the ground and provided stability for the attack. Hans braced himself as best he was able, crossing his arms in front of his face as the attack landed. Now flying through the air for an entirely different reason, he felt both of his arms break at odd angles and something inside him ruptured as his torso was impacted. He collided heavily with the wall and fell on his face awkwardly, unable to arrest his fall with his unresponsive limbs.

Tom landed his attack for the first time in the battle, crushing the tentacle that was providing stability to the massive Beast. The tentacle vanished in a gout of black blood, being ripped by the roots from the body of the Cat. Screaming, the Cat turned on him lashing out with its paws. The only thing that saved Tom from having the arteries of his neck severed was the acid which had destroyed two of the malice filled eyes and reduced its depth perception. The sharp claws tore open Tom's chest, spraying the area with red blood over the black. Tom fought on, doing his best to ignore the potentially fatal wound.

Several arrows had found their mark, and a second tentacle now hung limp, connected to the body only by a scrap of flesh. Dale swung at the main body of the Cat, dealing some small damage but not enough to seriously hurt the Cat. The spikes only penetrated half an inch; its thick fur and tough, leathery hide underneath protected the Cat from real harm. The glow on the Cat was beginning to lessen, so it took an opportunity to vanish back into the shadows, a now-soft glow the only indication of its position. It charged at the wounded Tom when Adam finally finished his incantation.

Adam held up his staff, celestial Essence pouring from the topaz in the top like a sieve as his face grew *far* too pale. A beam of light shot upward, entering the celestial quartz far overhead. With this sudden influx of Essence, the Quartz above glowed stronger, flooding the Inscriptions with Essence which rebounded the energy downward, greatly extending the power and range of the Runescript placed upon it. The Runes, similar to the pendant Dale wore, tore through the veil of darkness below, dissipating it all at once. The Cat–which had leaped at Tom–was smashed to the floor by the massive pressure of the celestial Essence, while the others took a deep breath with feelings of hope filling them.

Tom did not waste the moment and swung down at the prone Distortion Cat, landing a blow even as it twisted away. The massive force behind the hammer shattered the spine of the Beast just beyond its back legs, rendering them useless. It roared and used the remaining tentacles as legs, dragging itself into the brilliant light–vanishing entirely. It appeared again a few feet away, running this time at Adam who had collapsed to the ground in exhaustion. Rose stepped in front of his fallen form, firing arrows wildly at the Beast charging her, but every attack seemed to either miss it or move right through its body without causing damage.

Rose screamed in frustration and terror as a tentacle raced toward her, tossing her aside with bone shattering force. It mauled Adam, vengefully tearing open his legs with vicious attacks. Dale and Tom reached the Cat, simultaneously swinging at it. Both missed, though the warhammer continued on and clipped the *real* form of the Cat, launching it away with a yowl. A lightly glowing silhouette was visible, though the illusion in front of them didn't move. Tom took another step after the Cat but stumbled and fell to the floor, too weak from blood loss to continue. His hammer clattered to the floor as he fell unconscious.

Dale grabbed the warhammer and nearly fell over trying to lift it. "Right," he thought, "it is bound to Tom." Dropping the hammer, he raced after the Cat, viciously swinging his weapon into its acid eaten torso. With contemptuous ease, the Cat sent him flying in the same manner as it had Hans before.

CHAPTER THIRTY

"Cal, we have to do something!" Dani frantically demanded, "If they die, we are screwed! It'll come back here and... and..." She was unable to finish the thought.

<But what can I do?> I demanded. <Almost everything in here is dead–all of the creatures, Raile, and...> A thought hit me like a thunderbolt from on high. <I've got it, Dani.>

DALE

The Cat half-limped, half -dragged itself toward Dale, its single working eye fixed on the heart beating in Dale's chest. Dale tried to struggle into a defensive position, but his limbs were broken, each small movement causing excruciating pain. He gasped for breath as a tentacle raised up above his body, plunging down directly into his heart. Although Dale's heart had been reinforced by opening a meridian, the sharp point of the tentacle went directly through, leaving a perfectly round hole in his body. The hole began at the skin of his chest and exited his back where the talon had driven deep into the stone below him. The tentacle slowly receded, twisting as it did so as to inflict maximum pain to the dying man.

The Cat lowered its ruined face to his and hissed evilly, watching for the last bit of life to drain away from Dale. Dale stared into its eye, even as his own vision went dim. The bleeding hole of the Cat's neck poured black blood on to him. Wait, what?

The huge body flopped over on to its side, head torn clean off. Tom stepped into Dale's view, chest seemingly fully healed; only shiny scar tissue was present to show that he had been mortally wounded.

"Adam! Get thyself over here, 'tis bad!" Tom boomed, dropping his warhammer to the ground as he cradled Dale's still form. Dale's vision darkened entirely as his body was filled with celestial light.

"It's too late," Adam whispered, tears streaming down his face. "I fixed the damage to his heart, but it is just... too late."

"No!" Hans ran to his fallen friend. "I refuse to believe this! Work *harder*!" His voice broke on the last word.

"I have nothing left to give." Adam sobbed. "I'm drained to near death myself." He shook, his body wracked with sobs.

"Here!" Rose ran over to them, vials in her hands. "Pour this down his mouth!" She held out a healing potion.

"Rose, he is gone... It won't help," Adam informed her morosely.

SLAP. Her hand rocked Adam to the side; he looked at her startled and astonished out of his depression. "You *will* do what I say! *Now*!" she screamed in his face.

He took the vial, handing it to Hans, who poured the potent healing potion down his fallen friend's throat. No effect was visible, no miracles appeared.

"Now *you* drink this!" Rose directed, handing Adam another vial that blazed with concentrated Essence. She gave another to Hans, directing him to administer it to Dale. Reluctantly obeying her, Adam drank the contents of the vial. It never reached his stomach, the potent Essence being absorbed directly into his center, lighting it up like a dawn forcing away the hold of night. The Essence rushed through him, filling him to his maximum potential and then continuing, the overflow of Essence beginning to burn out his meridians.

Quickly—full of panic—Adam returned to Dale and attempted to revive him. The Essence in Dale from the vial was now sitting in his center like a lump, unmoving. No matter what technique Adam tried, it refused to move, to connect to Dale's life-force. His ministrations restarted Dale's heart, but the man refused to regain consciousness.

"I've done... all I can." Adam slumped. "He *is* alive, but... I think not really. Let's get him out of here so we can at least give him a proper burial." The stunned, sickened members of the team gathered his body and prepared to leave.

Cal

"He isn't all the way dead, though!" Dani gasped. "You won't get his Essence anymore!"

<I got all the stuff in his center, but you are correct; I didn't get his life-energy. They must have revived him somehow.> I looked at them wonderingly. I couldn't absorb him since he was alive, so the others had placed him near the exit as they moved to take a trophy of the great Beast they had slain. With the human auras no longer blocking him from my sight, I was able to inspect Dale carefully. Since he was dead—but not really—I was able to learn everything about his body near instantly, as I had with Dani. I was quickly able to determine what the issue was and corrected it in his body, as I would a stone in my walls.

This did not bring him back; the Essence in him was no longer funneling into his quickly dimming life force. Even the liquid Essence in him began to sputter and make its way out of his body. There was still more Essence in him than there had been; truth be told, the overdose they poured into him would have made his chest explode if his body were alive to contain it. Now, it was just dissipating into the air.

<Dani, if he gets out of here before he dies, I don't get that rush of energy. If I fixed his Essence, do you think that would wake him up? I want another chance at his death Essence,> I explained, looking at the residual Essence in Dale's body. <I think I could do it.>

"Will it cost you too much Essence?" she reminded me, to which I responded with a negative. She kept asking questions, the primary being, "What will happen if it doesn't work?"

<It may kill him, which isn't really an issue I suppose. It doesn't feel sporting to just kill him, though. He did just do us a huge favor, even if he doesn't know it. Plus, well, I want to see if I *can* fix him. If I don't do this, I may never get another chance to know if I could do it. You know me, I have pride in my work. If I try this, I want to do it right.> I bent my will to the task at hand despite her protests. I extended Essence into him, trying to reestablish normal flows to his life-force. I tried dozens of different things, but the thick Essence in him refused to stay in a cohesive pattern. It seemed that it wouldn't unless he were to apply his *own* will to the task. I *could* make it stay–if I were to always have him in my dungeon–but the group was already preparing to leave. He showed no signs of waking up nor of being damaged enough to die properly.

I was getting frustrated. <Dani, nothing is working! The Essence is just... floating out of his body! It won't stay where he needs it! Too fast to be good for him and too slow to kill him before they leave! What can I do?>

Dani had no idea either, obviously. "You know his pattern better than I do, Cal. If you don't know what can help him, there is nothing I could do."

<His pattern? His pattern! That's it!> I compared his pattern with the things I was able to create and found a *single match.* Me. One of the first things I had ever really understood was the body that I resided in. A soul gem, not just a Beast Core. Dani had told me that this was as large as I would ever become. From here on out, the Essence would be poured into me like a dimensional pocket, always able to be filled but never being full.

I shifted Dale's intestines around a tiny bit; creating a perfect soul gem around his center, just below his heart and *almost* against his spine. The Essence which had been escaping him was quickly drawn back into what had been his center, now a highly refined Beast core—a Masterwork soul gem. Now, the issue was that no Essence was able to leave the gem and all the Essence contained in him was being slowly drawn into it. Working quickly but carefully, I surrounded the gem with a perfect layer of Runescripted diamond.

Diamond, I had found through exhaustive testing, allowed for all Essence types to move through it well. It was a spectacular conductor for *all* of it. Each type had a gem that allowed for perfect flows but needed to be purely that type of Essence. For instance, the topaz head on Adam's staff allowed celestial Essence to flow perfectly but would greatly impede all other types.

Where his cultivation had drawn in the Essence of the heavens and the earth, I made a Rune—which would activate by cultivating—to draw in that power to his center and now core. At each place around his meridians where energy would flow out into his body, I placed that same Rune but inverted it in order to send energy *out.* At each corner of the new soul gem, I placed tiny yet powerful Beast Cores which would absorb only the corruption his cultivation produced. With luck, I would be able to use that for something in the future.

I had done all I was able for his body; his mind would need to heal on its own. Luckily, everything I had created was small, therefore quick and easy to make. His organs were repaired, and drawing in Essence should be really easy for him now. The only question I had was, would this work or kill him when everything became active? I was really excited to find out! I kick-started the fractal pattern of the Essence and forcefully activated every Rune within him. Then I moved my mind back to enjoy the show.

DALE

Hans turned back to his fallen friend and began walking toward him. From the dead Cat, they had gathered each tentacle, the last good eye, all of its teeth and claws, and a few other samples of strange organs. The Cat weighed nearly half a ton; they certainly couldn't carry everything. Hans's eyes were shining with the light of Essence, which he used to find the important bits of the Distortion Cat. He definitely wasn't using it to hold back tears. He glanced over at his fallen friend and saw Essence streaming around Dale in an incredibly advanced, incomprehensible pattern. With a shout of rage, he started to run to Dale's rescue but pulled up short as his eyes followed the trail of Essence to its source.

It appeared to be coming from the... Silverwood tree? Hans knew that Silverwood trees were powerful and mysterious, but what was it doing? He stood away from Dale, motioning the others back when they tried to move to Dale in panic. Hans watched the barely breathing body as closely as he could, but the thick Essence dancing around Dale prevented him from seeing what the pattern was creating. Several minutes later, the light finally stopped flowing, though Dale's form remained unmoving.

They walked over to his body, realizing that even the mysterious forces of the dungeon's Silverwood tree could do nothing. They tried to inspect Dale for recovery but could detect no Essence whatsoever in his center. With a sob, Hans realized his comrade, his student... his friend... was truly dead.

Chapter Thirty-one

Adam reached over to close Dale's eyes but stopped as they shone a brilliant, molten silver. With a gasp, he tried to move back, falling awkwardly on to his butt. Dale started convulsing, his entire body shaking in the sudden onslaught of muscle spasms.

"Hold his head!" Adam immediately took control of the situation and shifted his thoughts back into a healing mindset. "We need to keep him from damaging himself! He's alive!"

Hans was by Dale's side in a flash, keeping his head from bouncing around on the hard rock. "What is happening?!" Hans shouted at Adam, who was trying to recover from his position on the floor.

"Besides Dale having a seizure? No idea," Adam stated grimly, lying perpendicular across Dale in an attempt to hold him against the floor. "All I know is his heart is beating, and he is breathing again."

The group piled on to Dale, holding him in different places. Adam, being so light, was nearly thrown as one spectacular shake tore through Dale's body, tearing muscles and popping blood vessels. Hans was watching everything closely and suddenly cried out.

"Look! Look at that! His Essence is... *pouring* through his body!" Hans was flabbergasted. "It's going through his meridians... He hadn't opened those ones yet!"

"What?!" Adam looked with Essence enhanced sight, worried that this was Dale's death throes. "Is the Essence escaping his body?"

"No. No!" Hans shouted, realizing what effect the Essence was about to have on Dale's body. "Everyone, get off of him!

Now! Trust me!" Listening to his order, the others reluctantly let go while only Hans remained to hold Dale's head. A rancid, waxy discharge started finding ways out of Dale. Through the pores in his skin, his eyes, ears, mouth, and less... pleasant... orifices came this loathsome fluid. It drained out of these exits as fast as liquid removed itself from the vicinity of a liquid repulsion Rune. Dale's body seemed to deflate as the seemingly endless torrent continued. After what felt like hours, it did eventually stop, and Dale finally stopped shaking. Now in what seemed to be a natural slumber brought on by exhaustion, the group tried to get close enough to help carry him away. Unfortunately, the smell made all but Hans retreat as far away as possible.

Dale opened his eyes, blinking in the bright light of the room.

"Buddy?" Hans cajoled in a broken voice. "You there? Are you... Can you tell me your name?"

"Hans?" Dale looked up into Hans's beaming face. "Wha...?"

Hans looked at him with sad eyes, smile vanishing. "Oh, no. Dale... Hans is *my* name."

"Oh. My. *God*. Be serious for once, you shit!" Rose shouted at him, braving the reeking odor to smack him on the head.

Hans's smile returned as he looked down at Dale. "You all there, buddy?"

Dale nodded as best he was able. "What happened? And who," he grimaced and spat out some foul fluid, "who let that Cat shit in my mouth?"

All but Dale started laughing as the tension of the past few hours caught up with them. Eventually, Dale tired of scowling and joined in. A few moments later, wiping a tear from his eye, Dale sobered a bit. "So seriously, though, what happened?"

"You died!" Hans replied cheekily. The others glared at him, making Hans mutter, "What? He got better."

"Before that, please." Dale released a strange chuckle/sigh at his incorrigible friend.

Tom took over, "When I fell, and you charged the Cat in a suicide run, I was losing blood faster than I could regain my will to fight. I tried so hard to join you, but could not muster the strength to continue." His face was downcast and ashamed. "Seemingly, my prayer to die in battle was rejected this day, and I was flooded with the berserker energy of my forefathers. This energy healed my wounds and allowed me the chance to finish our foe. I beg of you, forgive my weakness." He bowed towards Dale's prone form.

Rose pushed Tom aside, shaking her head. "Not what happened? Not even close. When you charged the Cat and held its attention, those golden rabbits snuck out of hidden tunnels and infused us with healing energy. There were *dozens*, Dale. All of our wounds righted themselves nearly instantly before they ran off, but I think we will carry these scars forever." She nodded at the slashes across Tom's chest and Adam's legs, which, by rights, should *never* have had the chance to heal.

"Wow." Dale's head flopped back, and he looked enviously at the huge slashes of scar tissue on Tom's chest. "The ladies are going to love those scars."

Hans laughed deeply and evilly. "Finally! My teachings are starting to take root! No worries, Dale, you have some very impressive scars yourself." Dale glanced down at the raised circle of scar tissue directly over his heart.

"Well, that can't look good on the inside," Dale muttered anxiously.

Hans shook his head, still somehow amused. "I don't think it will be an issue, m'boy! I *do* think you need a long bath. Maybe... two. Or three." He sniffed and shuddered.

"Yeah, what is this stuff? It seems to be coming from me, and I can't seem to stop... smelling it." Dale's attention was now back on the clinging fluid, bringing the horrid smell to the forefront of his senses. "Seriously, normally you acclimate to horrible stenches, yeah?"

"Unless I am mistaken, it seems that all of your meridians were opened *simultaneously*. If you were awake for that process, it likely would have shattered your mind with the pain. Obviously, this must have taken a huge amount of Essence. While you had some in you, it wasn't nearly enough to account for everything that happened," Hans informed him. "It seems the Silverwood tree is what supplied the Essence and–I think–it revived you as well."

<Oh good, they don't realize it was me.> Dale shook his head at the unexpected sound. A strange, flat, tonal voice had sounded in his head.

"What?" Dale was looking around.

The Silverwood tree–" Hans started, concern showing on his face.

"No, I heard that. What was that other voice?" Dale interrupted him with a wave of his hand.

<Dani, did he hear me?> the voice rang in Dale's head again. <Is that possible? I am not projecting to him!>

Hans was looking at him, very concerned now. "Another voice? No one else talked, Dale. Let's get you a nap, huh buddy?"

<Good idea, Dani. They always seem to forget things when they have new toys.> Dale whipped his head around, trying to find the person speaking. A sudden clatter of metal

sounded in the room as loot dropped around them, closer than to his body Dale had ever seen appear. Normally, loot seemed to fall in an area well away from people.

"Holy crap! Look at these!" Rose shouted, peering at the pendant she had just picked up off the ground. "This is a Runed item! Anyone recognize it?" They all looked at the pendant but did not recognize its Inscription. There was one for each of them, but they were loath to use them without it being inspected.

<Oh, come on, Dani. If they use those *outside* of here, I'll at least be able to get more Essence if they die *in* here. Plus, I want to see if it works. All they should have to do is have it pressed against their skin near a meridian.> Dale was sure there was an invisible person standing behind him and whipped his demolished weapon around. He glanced at the remains of his morningstar. It had been mostly destroyed by the acid and shattered by the Beast they had fought.

<Fine, fine! I have a better version for him anyway.> Dale was starting to panic. A *thunk* at his feet made him jump and yelp. A shining, pristine morningstar lay underneath him. There were a few differences from the original. For one, the head of the weapon seemed to be crystal with electrum filled Runes forming a powerful Runescript on it. Electrum was a mix of gold and silver—both soft metals—so Dale was unsure of its usefulness in combat. Next, the hilt was also covered in Runescript, but this time in a way he somewhat recognized. The Rune was the same he had on his—it would send the head of the weapon out a few feet from the shaft, giving him range in combat.

The most noticeable difference, though, was the *ridiculous* size of the thing. Where his hand would go was normal sized and long enough that he could use both hands to swing it if he gave up his shield. From that point upward, the shaft was *three times* larger than he was used to, looking like a large sapling or small tree. The crystal head of the weapon was twice the width of his head if you included the spikes. Dale picked the weapon up. More accurately, he *tried* to. Still weak from freaking *dying*, he could barely shift the weapon. He looked at the hilt and saw the same Rune there as Tom had, which would make the weapon feather light.

Dale reached for his Essence which was instantly available to him. The ease with which it moved at his command was startling in itself. Maybe it had to do with all of his meridians being opened? With a small burst of Essence, he activated the Rune, unknowingly also binding the morningstar to himself. Now easily lifting the massive weapon of war, he gave it a few practice swings. He remembered that he should test the range of the activation that moved the head away, so he pointed it away from his friends. He aimed at the wall roughly ten feet away and activated the Rune.

The shards of stone flying through the air and the thundering of rock being shattered made the entire group dive for cover. Shock covered Dale's face as blood from a new cut across his cheek dripped down into his mouth. He deactivated the Rune, and the head of the weapon returned to him, affixing itself on to his hilt.

"I feel rather tired of unknown weapons killing my friends in here," Tom calmly stated, brushing rock dust off of his arms. "Very interesting, though."

"I think we should do our cultivating and leave." Rose directed in a deceivingly calm manner. Locks of her hair had been sheared off by the razor-sharp stone, and it was obvious she was working hard not to attack Dale. Face pale, Dale nodded, and they all sat in a meditative pose in the center of the massive Runescript on the floor, near where Essence was appearing in liquid form. They each agreed not to drink it after hearing

Adam's account of its use. Though it would fill them with Essence, Adam warned that it would make their Chi spiral unstable, possibly burning them, making their centers explode, or damaging their meridians beyond repair. The only reason Adam had survived its use was that he had been almost entirely out of Essence, and even then he had had to use most of it as fast as possible.

The highly purified Essence in the air still allowed them to cultivate for far longer and with greater gains than they ever had been able to before, stretching the bounds of what they could hold at any given time. Dale had another shock as he began. As he opened himself to the heavens and the earth, Essence flooded into him in a titanic wave of energy. He gasped and tried to understand what was happening.

In a flash, he realized what was different. He had only ever pulled in Essence along the most open channel, his earthen affinity. After waking up, *all* of his affinity channels were open. He was pulling Essence in from every possible source simultaneously. The wave of energy blasted along his spirals, refining deeper and stronger Chi threads.

The fractal pattern in his center, which had become even rougher and more splintered after dying, smoothed itself, repairing every flaw along the millions of spirals. When this process finished, his cultivation speed became even *faster*. In a short time, he had broken into D-rank one, shattering his previous boundary to advancement at a speed that *should* have been impossible. By the time they were finished cultivating for the day, he was halfway into D-rank two. Dale decided to keep the information to himself as they began their ascent into the world above.

Cal

"What a day!" Dani said, sagging with relief. The tension in her voice was finally receding.

<No kidding! You would not believe what I got out of that Distortion Cat. First of all, I reached D-rank *five*!> I bragged while shining in pleasure as she happily chattered at me. <Also, I have enough information to make that Distortion Cat if I want. Well,> I coughed as she looked at me in horror, <a young version of it anyway. A D-Rank three at best, but with this Essence well,> I directed her attention to the liquid Essence, <I think they can rank up quickly. No tentacles–those were what made it insane. Without that parasite, though, it'll have a mouth and could be altered with corruption like the Bashers were!>

"Maybe... Maybe we wait a few days? Before trying new things again?" Dani pleaded. "Let's just relax some? Maybe a month or two?"

<Anything for you, Dani. Um. There is one little issue.>

"Oh lord. What did you do now, Cal?"

I thought hard on my answer. <So, you know how I can feel all of my creatures, experience what they do, and influence them? If they were created by me, they are always Mobs...>

Dani looked extremely nervous. "Yes...?"

<And when I use my Essence to give them life or whatever they also come under my influence, they become dungeon born? Though if they are smart or strong enough, I can't directly control them, but they can hear my commands and experience what they do?>

"Spit it out, Cal."

<I think... mind you I am not certain, but I *think*... I may have made Dale, um, dungeon born.>

"... Damn it, Cal..."

EPILOGUE

Far to the south, a stinking hole of a swamp denoted the boundary between the Lion and Phoenix Kingdoms. Each spring, the snow melts of the Phantom Mountains would wash through here, thickening the sludge with fertile silt. This always caused a population boom for the insects, as they found places to lay their eggs and fed well off drowned animals. Deep in the swamp on a plot of land only accessible by the brave or the knowledgeable, stood an ancient fortress.

There was nothing about the fortress that seemed out of place; it was a mold covered ruin beneath the notice of any well-groomed noble, and no commoner would willingly come into this swamp. If someone did manage to stumble upon this place, they may remark on the grotesque statues and carved work on the walls. They may see the shrunken skulls on spikes every few feet along the battlements with burning eyes that seemed to follow them as they walked. The same people *may* feel compelled to mention the odd lights, the chanting, and screams of pain and horror that intermittently escaped this place. The only issue was, those people never seemed to survive long enough to warn others.

"Finally," a dark voice pulsed, sounding raspy from lack of fresh water. "I want a drink, a bath, a woman, and a hot meal. I don't care what order." The man who had months ago attacked Dale–followed by being forced off Dale's mountain–squelched the remaining distance through the clinging mud to the entryway of this lost fortress. He looked into the burning eyes of a skull and sneered. "Oh, hurry up and open the door. You know who I am."

The skeletal grin mocked him and chattered a few times, its jaw chittering as the trapped spirit attempted to attack him. With no body to extend its reach, it finally sent a mental command to the undead manning the gates, and the drawbridge started opening. The rusted, screaming hinges slowly pried themselves outward. The man groaned as he thought about what was coming, then walked into the courtyard. Undead of every type bustled around, completing the tasks assigned to them. Workers and warriors all, each fervently awaited the moment their commands would allow them to feast on the flesh and Essence of the living beings of the castle or outside world.

A sibilant voice caressed his soul as much as the man's ear, speaking to him and his deeper self, "Welcome home, little *morsel*, the Master has been waiting for you. I do hope you have good news for him. He has been ever so... agitated, recently."

The man looked up in disgust at the demon looking down over the courtyard, expertly enforcing his will on the undead below. A 'taskmaster', the demon excelled at creating perfect order. The decade-long restoration of this fortress would not have gone nearly as smooth without its expert direction.

"Stay out of my head, and don't speak unless I tell you too. Bad enough that I have to smell you and be on the same plane as you. Hearing you is just too much filth for my mind to bear." The man then arrogantly turned his face away, stopping with a startled yelp as he found that the demon was now directly in front of him. It grinned, satisfied by its small victory, mockingly bowing out of his way. Speed increasing, the now apprehensive man rushed to the inner sanctum to make his report. The demon had never before done anything like that.

He hurriedly knocked at the door, trying to get his breathing and mind under control. He had no opportunity to clean or rest; the Master had demanded his report as soon as possible. The demon would never have interrupted his Master otherwise. The door swung open into a perfectly silent room. As he stepped across the threshold, all outside noise died. Even the light that dared enter here seemed muted, the color leached out of it. Passing through shades of grey and black, his pulse accelerated, roaring thunderously in his veins, the sound of it threatening to burst his eardrums.

He stopped a dozen yards from the Master in front of him. The Master was sitting in a lotus style meditation pose. Not out of reverence or respect did the man stop his forward movement. No, it was the dense Necrotic energy thick in the air which forced him to remain where he was.

"Master," he murmured, being as meticulous as possible in his presentation of manners as he genuflected. "I have come with news of the newly formed dungeon. As you predicted, it is *already* becoming a place thick with life and treasure. The acolytes sent there with the soul gem you created some time ago did not completely fail, it seems. Their sacrifice created the dungeon, though they were unable to nurture it as they had been ordered. More than that... a Silverwood tree has bloomed within it!" He remained as he was, head pressed to the ground long enough that he began to wonder if he had been heard. Perhaps the Master was resting? He began to sweat harder.

"You did well, my child," a modulated, honey-sweet, deep voice responded. "For too long now the light has been burned into the world, forcing it to give more and more to the greedy children of the sun. It is time to return the soothing darkness to the land and allow it to rest. The creation of the gem took but a moment. We need not concern ourselves with a small dungeon on the edge of the world."

The prone man nodded as best he was able, unable to speak with the power of the Master's voice ringing in his body.

The explosive power contained in that voice knocked dirt from his clothes and shook dust from the ceiling. The deep shadows, swirling with tortured faces, wailed soundlessly as the Master stood. It had been five years since he had moved from the spot he was sitting. The floor below now crumbled to dust, reduced from once beautiful marble.

“Gather the acolytes,” the Master commanded. “Meet me by the tar pits. We have slaves to... awaken.” He faded away like the morning mist as he began to complete his goals. “Also, bring me someone with a soul suitable for becoming an infernal dungeon. It is time to build an arsenal.”

The bowing man tried not to cry out as the infernal aura surrounding his Master brushed past him, scalding his arm from this distance although it was his *own affinity*. He stood and rushed off to obey, not a complaint–nor any thought except instant obedience–crossing his terrified mind.

AFTERWORD

Thank you for reading! I hope you enjoyed Dungeon Born! Since reviews are the lifeblood of indie publishing, I'd love it if you could leave a positive review on Amazon! Please use this link to go to the Divine Dungeon: Dungeon Born Amazon product page to leave your review: geni.us/DungeonBorn.

As always, thank you for your support! You are the reason I'm able to bring these stories to life.

THE DIVINE DUNGEON UNIVERSE

THE DIVINE DUNGEON

Dungeon Born (Book 1)

Dungeon Madness (Book 2)

Dungeon Calamity (Book 3)

Dungeon Desolation (Book 4)

Dungeon Eternium (Book 5)

THE COMPLETIONIST CHRONICLES

Ritualist (Book 1)

Regicide (Book 2)

Rexus (Book 2.5)

Raze (Book 3)

About Dakota Krout

I live in a 'pretty much Canada' Minnesota city with my wife and daughter. I started writing The Divine Dungeon series because I enjoy reading and wanted to create a world all my own. To my surprise and great pleasure, I found like-minded people who enjoy the contents of my mind. Publishing my stories has been an incredible blessing thus far, and I hope to keep you entertained for years to come!

Connect with Dakota:
Patreon.com/DakotaKrout
Facebook.com/TheDivineDungeon
Twitter.com/DakotaKrout

About Mountaindale Press

Dakota and Danielle Krout, a husband and wife team, strive to create as well as publish excellent fantasy and science fiction novels. Self-publishing *The Divine Dungeon: Dungeon Born* in 2016 transformed their careers from Dakota's military and programming background and Danielle's Ph.D. in pharmacology to President and CEO, respectively, of a small press. Their goal is to share their success with other authors and provide captivating fiction to readers with the purpose of solidifying Mountaindale Press as the place 'Where Fantasy Transforms Reality'.

Connect with Mountaindale Press:
MountaindalePress.com
Facebook.com/MountaindalePress
Twitter.com/_Mountaindale
Instagram.com/MountaindalePress
Krout@MountaindalePress.com

Mountaindale Press Titles

GameLit and LitRPG

The Completionist Chronicles Series
By: Dakota Krout

A Touch of Power Series
By: Jay Boyce

Red Mage: Advent
By: Xander Boyce

Ether Collapse: Equalize
By: Ryan DeBruyn

Axe Druid Series
By: Christopher Johns

Skeleton in Space: Histaff
By: Andries Louws

Pixel Dust: Party Hard
By: David Petrie

Appendix

Adam – A mid-D-ranked cleric who joined Dale's group.

Adventurers' Guild – A group from every non-hostile race that actively seeks treasure and cultivates to become stronger. They act as a mercenary group for Kingdoms that come under attack from monsters and other non-kingdom forces.

Affinity – A person's affinity denotes what element they need to cultivate Essence from. If they have multiple affinities, they need to cultivate all of those elements at the same time.

Affinity Channel – The pathway along the meridians that Essence flows through. Having multiple major affinities will open more pathways, allowing more Essence to flow in at one time.

Amber – The Mage in charge of the portal-making group near the dungeon. She is in the upper A-rankings, which allows her to tap vast amounts of Mana.

Assassin – A stealthy killer who tries to make kills without being detected by his victim.

Aura – The flows of Essence generated by living creatures, which surround them and hold their pattern.

Bane – An F-ranked Boss Mob that is a giant mushroom. It can fire thorns and pull victims toward him with vines made of moss.

Basher – An evolved rabbit that attacks by head-butting enemies. Each has a small horn on its head that it can use to "bash" enemies.

Beast Core – A small gem that contains the Essence of Beasts.

Brianna – A Dark Elf princess who intends to build a city around the dungeon.

Cal – The heart of the Dungeon, Cal was a human murdered by Necromancers. After being forced into a soul gem, his identity was stripped as time passed. Now accompanied by Dani, he works to become stronger without attracting too much attention to himself.

Celestial – The Essence of Heaven, the embodiment of life and considered the ultimate good.

Center – The very center of a person's soul. This is the area where Essence accumulates before it binds to the life force.

Chandra – Owner of an extremely well-appointed restaurant, this A-ranked Mage is the grandmother of Rose. She also spent a decade training the current Guild Master, Frank.

Chi spiral – A person's Chi spiral is a vast amount of intricately knotted Essence. The more complex and complete the pattern woven into it, the more Essence it can hold and the finer the Essence can be refined.

Cleric – A cultivator of celestial Essence, a cleric tends to be support for a group, rarely fighting directly. Their main purpose in the lower rankings is to heal and comfort others.

Corruption – Corruption is the remnant of the matter pure Essence was formed into. It taints Essence but allows beings to absorb it through open affinity channels.

Craig – A powerful C-ranked monk, Craig has dedicated his life to finding the secrets of Essence and passing on knowledge.

Cultivate – Cultivating is the process of refining Essence by removing corruption, then cycling the purified Essence into the center of the soul.

Cultivator – A cultivator is one who cultivates. See above. Seriously, it is the entry right before this one. I'm being all alphabetical here.

Dale – Owner of the mountain the dungeon was found on, Dale is now a cultivator who attempts to not die on a regular basis.

Dani – A pink Dungeon Wisp—Is that important?—Dani is the soul-bound companion of Dale and acts as his moral compass and helper.

Dire – A prefix to a title that means "Way stronger than a normal version of this monster." Roughly. Kind of paraphrasing.

Distortion Cat – An upper C-ranked monster that can bend light and create artificial darkness. In its home territory, it is attacked and bound by tentacle-like parasites that form a symbiotic relationship with it.

Dungeon Born – Being dungeon born means that the dungeon did not create the creature but gave it life. This gives the creature the ability to function autonomously, without fear that the dungeon will be able to take direct control of its mind. The dungeon can "ride along" in a dungeon born creature's mind from any distance and may be able to influence the creature if it remains of a lower cultivation rank than the dungeon.

Dwarves – Stocky humanoids that did not appear in this book.

Elves – A race of willowy humanoids with pointy ears. Unlike the stubborn Dwarves, the Elves deigned to allow themselves into this book.

Enchantment – A temporary pattern made of Essence that creates an effect on the universe. Try not to get the pattern wrong, as it could have... unintended consequences.

Essence – Essence is the fundamental energy of the universe, the pure power of Heavens and Earth that is used by the basic elements to become all forms of matter.

Father Richard – An A-ranked cleric who has made his living hunting demons and heretics. Tends to play fast and loose with rules and money.

Fighter – A generic archetype of a being who uses melee weapons to fight.

Frank – Leader of the Adventurers' Guild.

Glitterflit – A Basher upgraded with celestial Essence, it has the ability to mend almost any nonfatal wound.

Hans – A cheeky assassin who has been with Dale since he began cultivating. He was a thief in his youth but changed lifestyles after his street guild was wiped out. He is deadly with a knife and is Dale's best friend.

Incantation – Essentially a spell, an incantation is created from words and gestures. It releases all of the power of an enchantment in a single burst.

Infernal – The Essence of death and demonic beings, considered to be always evil.

Inscription – A permanent pattern made of Essence that creates an effect on the universe. Try not to get the pattern wrong, as it could have... unintended consequences. This is another name for an incomplete or unknown Rune.

James – An uppity Portal Mage who may have learned the error of his ways. We shall see.

Josh – A massive shield-wielding human, Josh is very strong and sturdy. He is always there to protect his friends as best he is able.

Mages' Guild – A secretive subset of the Adventurers' Guild, one only Mage-level cultivators are allowed to join.

Mana – A higher stage of Essence only able to be cultivated by those who have broken into at least the B-rankings and found the true name of something in the universe.

Meridians – Meridians are energy channels that transport life energy (Chi/Essence) throughout the body.

Mob – A shortened version of "dungeon monster".

Necromancer – An infernal Essence cultivator who can raise and control the dead and demons.

Oppressor – A Basher upgraded with wind Essence, it has the ability to compress air and send it forward in an arc that slices unprotected flesh like a blade.

Pattern – A pattern is the intricate design that underlies everything in the universe. An inanimate object has a far-less-complex pattern that a living being.

Raile – A massive, granite-covered Boss Basher that attacks by ramming and attempting to squish its opponents.

Ranger – Typically an adventurer archetype that is able to attack from long range, usually with a bow.

Ranking System – The ranking system is a way to classify how powerful a creature has become through fighting and cultivation.

> G-rank – This lowest ranking is mostly nonorganic matter, such as rocks and ash. Mid-G contains small

plants such as moss and mushrooms, while the upper ranks form most of the other flora in the world.

F-rank – The F-ranks are where beings are becoming actually sentient, able to gather their own food, and make short-term plans. The mid-F ranks are where most humans reach, before adulthood, without cultivating. This is known as the fishy or failure rank.

E-rank – Unexplained in this book

D-rank – This is the rank where a cultivator starts to become actually dangerous. A D-ranked individual can usually fight off ten F-ranked beings without issue. They are characterized by a "fractal" in their Chi spiral.

C-rank – The highest ranked Essence cultivators, those in the C-rank usually have opened all of their meridians. A C-ranked cultivator can usually fight off ten D-ranked and one hundred F-ranked beings without being overwhelmed.

B-rank – This is the first rank of Mana cultivators, known as Mages. They convert Essence into Mana through a nuanced refining process and release it through a true name of the universe.

A-rank – Usually several hundred years are needed to attain this rank, known as High Mage or High Magous. They are the most powerful rank of Mages.

S-rank – Very mysterious Spiritual Essence cultivators. Not much is known about the requirements for this rank or those above it.

SS-rank – Not much is known about the requirements for this rank or those above it.

SSS-rank – Not much is known about the requirements for this rank or those above it.

Heavenly-rank – Not much is known about the requirements for this rank or those above it.

Godly-rank – Not much is known about the requirements for this rank or those above it.

Rose – A half-Elf ranger who joined Dale's team. She has opposing affinities for celestial and infernal Essence.

Rune – A permanent pattern made of Essence that creates an effect on the universe. Try not to get the pattern wrong, as it could have... unintended consequences. This is another name for a completed Inscription.

Impaler – A Basher upgraded with infernal Essence, it has a sharpened horn on its head. At higher rankings, it gains the ability to coat that horn with Hellfire.

Shroomish – A mushroom that has been evolved into a barely dangerous Mob. Really, only being completely unaware of them would pose danger to a person.

Silverwood Tree – A mysterious tree that has silver wood and leaves. Some say that it helps cultivators move into the B-rankings.

Smasher – A Basher upgraded with earth Essence, it has no special abilities but is coated with thick armor made from stone. While the armor slows it, it also makes the Smasher a deadly battering ram.

Soul Gem – A highly refined Beast Core that is capable of containing a human soul.

Steve – A ranger who uses his bow as either a staff or a ranged weapon. Rather quiet chap.

Tank – An adventurer archetype that is built to defend his team from the worst of the attacks that come their way. Heavily armored and usually carrying a large shield, these powerful people are needed if a group plans on surviving more than one attack.

Tom – A huge, red-haired barbarian from the northern wastes, he wields a powerful warhammer and has joined Dale's team.

Made in the USA
Monee, IL
03 October 2021

79294035R00236